"I
SEE GREATNESS..."

... Gundrig said. "I see something special for you, Lionors, a life unlike that of anyone else.

"You will be privileged to scale the heights, but you will also feel the terrors of the depths. You will know extremes of happiness and sorrow. You will live to be a great age.

"You will be a queen, but you will die uncrowned and unknown."

She paused.

"That is all; the stones say no more ..."

⊁⟡⊁⟡⊁⟡⊁⟡⊁

Lionors

Barbara Ferry Johnson

AVON
PUBLISHERS OF BARD, CAMELOT AND DISCUS BOOKS

LIONORS is an original publication of Avon Books.

AVON BOOKS
A division of
The Hearst Corporation
959 Eighth Avenue
New York, New York 10019

Copyright © 1975 by Barbara F. Johnson.
Published by arrangement with the author.
ISBN: 0-380-00408-9

First Avon Printing, August, 1975.
Fifth Printing

AVON TRADEMARK REG. U.S. PAT. OFF. AND
FOREIGN COUNTRIES, REGISTERED TRADEMARK—
MARCA REGISTRADA, HECHO EN CHICAGO, U.S.A.

Printed in the U.S.A.

For David,
who has given me constant encouragement
and has never been jealous
of my literary love affair
with King Arthur.

⊠ *Prologue* ⊠

It was nearly midnight, and still I could not sleep. I stood alone in the courtyard, while beneath my feet the rain-bathed cobblestones glistened in the pearl-gray light of a new moon. Cool air, washed clean of impurities, flowed over and around me. In the western sky a falling star arched across the heavens and slipped below the horizon.

For three days the land had suffered under a malignant storm. On the first day, a violent wind roared in from the north. It tore fragile nests from branches, uprooted strong young saplings, devastated fields of unharvested grain, and created havoc even among the stabled animals. The sky had thundered in rage; spears of lightning rent the black clouds and blasted great oaks with fiery scars. On the second day came the pounding rain that flooded the burrows of the small, earth dwelling creatures and sent people scurrying for shelter, whipping cloaks off shoulders and stabbing at unprotected faces and hands with pinpoint blades. The deluge poured down chimneys with a force that put out fires, leaving behind wet, sputtering coals. The hardest hit cottages, their roofs torn off and their sides stove in, looked as though a giant fist had crushed them.

On the third day, as suddenly as it had appeared, the wind died down, and the storm ceased. From the west came a blinding flash of light, the brilliant rays of the setting sun piercing the clouds. Although heralding the end of day, the sun went down in a colorful burst of glory, as if proclaiming that it was not dying, but would rise again at dawn.

Nature's mood was now calm, but I knew it was but a brief respite, a time to catch our breath, for dark, heavy clouds in the east augured the coming of another storm.

Nerves taut, every sense alert, I was waiting, as I had waited throughout the past week, for the message I had been warned to expect.

From the gate I watched the road that curved around the meadow, skirted the edge of the forest, and then disappeared amid the tangled undergrowth. Everything looked peaceful, but something was amiss. I concentrated, listening to the night noises, trying to distinguish between the various sounds as I had been taught, while still a girl, by a shy, slender youth, not quite a man. Yes. Among the familiar, muted sounds of the night, I detected bird calls and animal cries that were not those of nocturnal creatures. Something had awakened them.

Gradually, I perceived the first faint, barely audible rumblings of a cart, its well-oiled wheels rolling steadily over matted leaf mold and the rhythmic, muffled *clop, clop* of hoof beats on the spongy ground, the hoofs heavily padded to deaden the footfalls.

The cart was moving at a fairly rapid rate. The driver knew his way through the dense forest. The speed of the wagon increased when it moved out onto the open road, and I was waiting at the gate when it slowed to a halt.

The driver, shrouded in a heavy woolen cloak, leaned down to speak to me. The hood of the cloak fell forward, almost obscuring the white beard and gentle eyes, but a brief glance was enough for me to recognize a face both notorious and well loved.

"It has happened at last," I whispered, "just as you prophesied."

"Yes, Lionors, and now I need your help. There is no one else I dare ask." The driver turned his head, and now I, too, looked down at the floorboard of the cart and saw the burden it held. A rough, gray, slightly frayed blanket was draped over the body of a man. I did not need to remove the pall to know who lay there.

"It is he, isn't it?" When I put my fears into words, my heart turned to stone.

"Yes," the old man sighed. "He was felled in the great battle this morning, a battle that had raged for three days. In the confusion of the skirmish I was able to carry him from the field before anyone was aware he had fallen. It is imperative that neither his enemies nor his people know he is dead. It must appear that he has simply vanished for the present and will return at any time. It is the only way we can keep all that he labored for from being destroyed. You are the one person I trust to keep the secret. We must bury him where his body will never be found. He once mentioned an island where the two of you often went."

I nodded. "Let me call Will, my steward. He is trustworthy, and we will need his help."

"All right, but hurry. He will be missed as soon as the flanks retire to regroup."

With Will taking the reins, the old man and I set out on our sorrowful journey. I sat on the floor of the wagon, holding the precious body close in my arms.

"Stay next to the wall here, Will," I cautioned, "and then we can go through the next gate and across the pasture to the break in the wall close to the river. There is a skiff hidden in the reeds."

Our river crossing went smoothly, and once on land, I led the way to a clearing in the center of the island that was protected by a barrier of trees. Beneath the sheltering boughs of a majestic oak, we dug the grave. Just before lowering our heavy burden, I lifted the blanket and kissed for the last time the face that had been my life and my love for as long as I could remember. Our prayers were silent ones, and in silence we returned to the manor.

With only an embrace for a farewell, I bid the old man good-by. From the door I watched him walk slowly but with unfaltering steps across the courtyard. Old but ageless, stooped but still strong, he was vanishing into obscurity after performing his final act of love and devotion for the one person who for so many years had given meaning to both our lives. My heart ached for this gentle man. Many people feared him; many called him charlatan and necromancer, but I knew him as a dear, devoted friend. Bent as much with sorrow as with years, he took up the reins of the cart and was soon enveloped by the dark night. I knew I would never see him again.

Before he left me, Will spoke once in a hushed tone. "It was he."

"Yes, Will, it was he, and never forget, nor ever tell, what we did tonight."

Distraught with grief and loneliness, I thought about the many times over the years I had walked across the meadow to the river and rowed to the island. A "magic island" a little boy once called it, because it had been the setting for only happy times: of picnics, of learning to swim, of falling in love. Until tonight, when Merlin and I bore Arthur, king of Britain, to his final rest at Avalon.

"So in the meanwhile there came a damosel that was an earl's daughter; his name was Sanam, and her name was Lionors, a passing fair damosel; and so she came thither for to do homage, as other lords did after the great battle. And King Arthur set his love greatly upon her, and so did she upon him, and the king had ado with her, and gat on her a child. . . ."

Sir Thomas Malory

Le Morte D'Arthur

⊠ Chapter One ⊠

The day matched my mood: gray and sullen. Less than twenty-four hours earlier my father had promised I could saddle my mare and ride the first few miles with the hunting party. They were going to fly two new gyrfalcons that Matt, our falconer, had been training. The day of the promise had been a clear, brilliant blue day, faintly tinged with the memory of summer yet with just enough of a chill to stir the blood and make one long for a brisk canter across the meadow, chasing rabbits or watching the wheeling, soaring falcons as they sought and captured their prey.

But the morning of the hunt dawned with ominous black clouds, and I awoke to rain so heavy that it almost hid from sight the branches of the pear tree outside my window, its shadowy, leafless arms soughing in rhythm under the onslaught of the gale. The orchard and the river were enveloped in a hollow mist, and the world floated in space with no visible horizon.

To add to my misery, I felt the first twinges of a cold: the sore, scratchy throat, the irritating tickle in my nose. Then at breakfast I began to sneeze.

"No hunt for you, young lady," scolded Marta, our housekeeper and my nursemaid, and she went off to inform my father that this was no day for her charge to be out riding.

I was miserable. A promise was a promise, and to a ten-year-old, nothing, not even a storm, was reason enough to have one broken. Right after breakfast Marta took me straight back to bed, placing flat, heated

1

stones wrapped in flannel around my chest and making me drink herb tea into which she had put a spoonful of honey to cut the bitter taste. I was feeling wretched, feverish and cold at the same time, until the hot stones and Marta's pungent brew lulled me to sleep. I awoke only momentarily when I heard the clatter of horses leaving the stable yard and the voices of men calling to one another. Sleepily I snuggled farther down into the bed, content and warm between coarse linen sheets and a coverlet of lamb's wool.

Sometime later Marta returned with hot soup for lunch.

"I think you're feeling better, dearie. Drink this, and then you can come to the kitchen and sit by the fire."

The soup was hot, but I drank it as fast as I could. Wrapping my blue woolen robe around me, I went down the broad stairs, through the main hall and larder, to the large, low outbuilding where Marta presided over a bevy of cooks and scullery maids. It was a cheerful scene that greeted me in spite of the wind and rain still howling outside. Jelly was being made from the last of the season's tiny, tart crab apples.

"There you are, lamb," Marta said. "Sit here, and I'll bring you a little something."

The huge kitchen was smoky from the separate fires burning in the great stone fireplaces; each fireplace was large enough to roast a cow whole or to hold several cauldrons on long, black iron arms extended over hot coals. Many pots hung over the fires now, some with the bubbling crimson juice of the crab apples and others holding melted beeswax or tallow for sealing the casks that stood empty and ready. It took dozens of casks to provide sweet jelly for our household throughout the year. At one of the long tables scullery maids were preparing the fruit; others were measuring and stirring, or ladling the rich liquid into casks. Near me, one maid was carefully skimming the surface of a cauldron with a long wooden spoon, taking from the top the sugary pink foam that would keep the jelly from being crystal clear if it were allowed to get into the casks.

2

Marta came back to me with a large chunk of fresh bread and a dish of the pink foam to dip it in.

"Here, eat this and stay right by the fire. It won't hurt you to sit up a bit."

I concentrated on my feast of sweet jelly and bread, and it was some time before I was taken with a strange feeling that I was being watched. I looked up. A wizened old woman huddled on a bench before another of the fires. She held a piece of bread and a dish of jelly, as I did, and as I looked at her, she stopped the slow gnawing of her toothless gums and stared at me with unblinking eyes that possessed a magnetic force. I remembered the first time that I had seen this old woman, some years earlier. Frightened, I had clung to Marta, who was big and warm, with a generous lap and soft bosom, just right for comforting frightened or unhappy little girls.

"Marta," I had whispered at the time, "who is that old woman sitting over there? She scares me."

"Why," said Marta in her gentle, reassuring voice, "you've seen her before. She lives in a hut just inside the forest and comes here to warm her old bones or get a bit to eat when she's been out walking."

I had snuggled closer. "I don't like the way she's looking at me. I'm scared."

"There's nothing to be scared of. She's just an old woman."

Old she was, and to my young eyes, ancient and ageless.

"Well," I said, "she looks like a witch."

"I doubt that Gundrig is a witch," Marta said, "but there are those who say she follows the old religion, worshiping the pagan gods. She is descended from one of those ruthless marauders who came years ago from across the cold sea, out of the northlands."

Gradually, through the years, I ceased to be afraid of old Gundrig and began to look forward to seeing her in the kitchen. If I passed her in the fields, she always wished me good morning or good evening, and from her it seemed more like a benediction than a mere greeting.

3

Now, having finished her bread and jelly, Gundrig tottered across the room on her feeble legs and sat on the bench beside my stool. How old she was, no one knew, but her long, thin hair was white and fell around her face and over her shoulders like a shadowy water-fall. Her rheumy eyes were almost hidden under gray-white brows edging her rough, protruding forehead. Gundrig was so thin that her chin and cheekbones seemed in danger of piercing through her parchment skin.

For a few minutes she said nothing; then she reached down into her rags and brought out some oddly shaped, flat stones, holding them easily in her palms so that I could see them.

"Do you know what these are, Lionors?" She spoke in a husky whisper.

"No, ma'am."

"These are rune stones, and with them I can see into the future. Would you like me to tell your fortune?"

"I—I don't know." I was as curious as any child about what the future had in store, but for some reason even my ten-year-old mind sensed that she did not mean tomorrow or next week when she said "the future." I looked around to hear what Marta would say, but she was busy on the other side of the kitchen.

"Can you really tell me?" I asked.

In answer, Gundrig rose from the bench. Squatting on the balls of her feet, she swayed back and forth to the rhythm of a barely audible chant, then tossed the stones lightly on the brick hearth. For several seconds she studied them intently, almost as though she had forgotten I was there. Her eyes narrowed; her brow wrinkled as she examined the position of each stone in relation to the others and to the cabalistic design in-scribed on it. Once or twice she looked at me and then back at the stones. Quietly, in a voice that seemed to come less from her than from some far distant place, she spoke.

"I see greatness," Gundrig said. "I see something special for you, Lionors, a life unlike that of anyone else. You will be privileged to scale the heights, but

4

you will also feel the terrors of the depths. You will know extremes of happiness and sorrow. You will live to a great age. You will be a queen, but you will die uncrowned and unknown." She paused. "That is all; the stones say no more."

What she said did not make sense to me then. Such general statements of happiness and sorrow mean little to a child, but the word *queen* carried meaning, and I smiled to think of that. Someday I would sit on a throne. More importantly, if I were queen, nothing, not even a storm, could keep me from going out to ride if I so desired. I could see myself in long, velvet robes, waited on, sitting on my throne smiling at everyone, wearing a golden crown. Then I remembered the word *uncrowned,* and I turned to her again.

"What did you mean 'uncrowned'? How can a queen be 'uncrowned'?"

"Do not ask; I can tell you no more. There is a great cloud. It conceals its secret from me. The cloud will pass with the wind, but whence comes that wind, only the wind knows. That is all the stones said, but someday you will know what they mean."

"But what about tomorrow," I insisted. "Will I go riding tomorrow?"

Gundrig cackled and looked out the window. "Yes, you'll go riding tomorrow, but the sky tells me that, not the stones. It will be fair. I can tell you only what the stones say at any one time. But I will tell your fortune again for you sometime, I promise."

The next day did dawn bright and clear, and I did go riding out with the hunt. At ten years old one soon forgets the words of previous days, and seldom did I think of the rune stones or the future they had predicted for me. To my mind there could be no such thing as an uncrowned queen, or one that no one had ever heard of, so if I thought of that morning at all, it was to laugh at the silly words of a babbling old woman.

But I was fond of old Gundrig, and during the next few years I went seeking the dilapidated charcoal burner's hut in the forest in which she lived her simple existence. Her hesitant, shuffling movements had forged a narrow trail through the undergrowth, turning this way and that to avoid a large tree here, a stagnant pool there. The path ended at the edge of a circular clearing, and the weather-beaten hut in the center looked as though it, like the trees, had grown from beneath the ground. The clearing had been created naturally by the charcoal burner as he cut bushes and trees to feed his fires, but supersition had it that the clearing was a magic circle formed during the ritual worship of the old gods. Gundrig was safe from human predators because the people in our area said the place was still haunted by the spirits of these old gods. To disturb them was to bring down their curse in the form of withered limbs or dead livestock.

Gundrig kept a pot of hot herb tea constantly steeping on the hearth. When she heard me coming, she tucked an apple and a few buttery scones among the ashes, to be plucked out juicy and hot after I joined her on the one bench in the room. Sometimes we sat together saying nothing, enjoying the warm fire and tasty fruit and bread. If the day were a pleasant one, we took closely woven reed baskets and went into the woods to gather the medicinal plants from which Gundrig would later make salves, powders, and tisanes. From one tree she would strip a narrow bit of bark, from another a few of the leaves, never taking enough to harm the tree. One bush would yield up a cluster of berries; a second, a bit of misshapen root; another, more tiny leaves. Close to the ground, often at the edge of a bubbling spring or a meandering stream, we picked pungent herbs and tiny many-colored flowers. Once we had our baskets filled, we returned to the hut and carefully sorted our harvest into separate piles. When the weather was too cold or rainy to venture out of doors for long, Gundrig allowed me to assist her in the preparation of the collection for storage or for more immediate use. Following her directions, I carefully tied branches of leaves and berries into small bunches that would hang from the ceiling, drying in the ever-present smoke rising from her peat fire. When she pulverized those that had been hanging long enough to become brittle, I

6

gathered up the small piles and put them into linen bags. While we worked, she told me what each was for, the amounts to use, detailing which to pick in each season and which were deadly unless purified by a chilling frost, those that were dangerous if not measured carefully and those that simply added a distinctive flavor to food or drink.

I began the habit of returning to my room and writing down what I learned during each visit. There were receipts for brews to relax the nerves or put one to sleep, cures for headache, stomachache, female cramps, and a variety of fevers. There were special herbs for salves to reduce the itch of a rash and poultices to draw out infection. Through the years I collected enough receipts to bind them together in a large book.

Some three years later, the rune stones spoke again to another mystified listener.

⊠ Chapter Two ⊠

My father was Earl of Sanam, both the title and the estate descending to him from the time of the Roman occupation of Britain. They had been bestowed on our Celtic ancestor in recognition of his devotion and courage in helping to repel a marauding tribe of Picts from the North.

My father was content to wear the diadem of an earl rather than the crown of a king, feigning a humility he neither felt nor followed. Unlike many nobles in Britain, including some with higher rank than he, my father owed allegiance to no man, save Uther Pendragon, king of Britain. Although our lands could be crossed, traveling at moderate speed in a single day, their location made them some of the most valuable in all the southwestern section of the country. Many another lord, passing through or coming to pay allegiance, looked with covetous eyes on the gently sloping, low-lying hills, so peaceful yet so perfect for lookouts or ambush in times of danger. The level land between the river and the hills was rich and fertile, producing twice the harvest of most other estates. The fiefs on our land were happy to have my father as their lord, for their cupboards were always full, and my father's strength kept petty wars away from our boundaries.

Perhaps because we were located near important routes of trade and travel between both the southern and western coasts and London, my father was able to maintain a much-needed oasis of neutrality among the often warring neighbors around us. From the time of our early ancestor, the Earl of Sanam had assumed the role of mediator in border disputes, and the tradition was carried on through each generation, the rival factions in various skirmishes seeking an audience with the earl to help settle claims.

Because of the many years of peaceful coexistence with our neighbors, our home was a manor house rather than a fortified castle. It stood on the foundations of the original Roman-style villa occupied by the first Earl of Sanam. A *U*-shaped building, the three sides of the manor house enclosed a vast courtyard paved with stones, while a shoulder-high wall and double gate on the fourth side kept out unwanted intruders. A high-ceilinged main hall occupied the entire center section, with a number of smaller rooms in each of the arms. My favorite of these was the shelved library in which my father kept the Greek and Latin manuscripts and scrolls collected by the first earl, a learned scholar as well as a strong fighter. The appreciation of scholarship, as well as the manuscripts, had been inherited by my father, and many were the hours we spent in the library, seated comfortably before a small fire, while my father first read to me and then taught me the scholarly languages.

Another room was maintained as father's office. It held the records and account books, which detailed the annual harvests and the births of lambs and colts along with other business matters concerning the manor and village. There were storerooms of various sizes, the largest of which was the armory, filled to capacity with battle axes, hatchets, swords—long, short, and broad—pikes, shields and bucklers, knives, daggers, lances, spears, maces, bows and arrows, and morning stars, the last a deadly spiked iron ball attached by a short chain to a stout handle. All were kept in battle-ready condition, honed and polished by the armorer. Cupboards contained chain mail, helmets, and the pennants bearing the Sanam crest, a white lion rampant on a blue field, which flew from standards during battle or at tournaments.

Next to my father's library was the room he was

9

proudest of, a bath that contained several wooden tubs that were filled by hand from kettles of boiling water. Although the tubs had replaced the original large sunken bath, the room was a restored version of the bath in the original Roman-style villa, and there were still traces of the early mosaic tiles in the floor and on the walls. Not many guests took advantage of this aspect of our hospitality, thinking my father somewhat dimwitted for being concerned about cleanliness and for putting himself in mortal danger of catching a chill. But he continued to bathe at ease, ignoring the bawdy jeers of his friends, while the hot water soaked away the dirt and aches of the day. In turn, I had my own wooden tub, which Marta would place in front of the fire in my bedroom. As a child I fussed and sputtered at having to undress and be scrubbed by her, insisting that my skin was being rubbed raw by the rough huck towels she used to dry me. But in time I, too, looked forward at the end of a long, hard day to soaking in hot water fragrant with the aroma of mint or thyme that Marta put in the bath.

At one end of the main hall a broad stairway ascended to the second floor. Here were the family bedrooms and guestrooms more elaborate than the communal sleeping quarters below. Although my father did not maintain a retinue of knights, there were sleeping accommodations for at least twenty.

Above the main hall was a large solarium, a general sewing room, which contained spinning wheels, looms, and tapestry frames. All the women of the household, including myself, took their turn at spinning, weaving, and embroidering the linens and materials needed to furnish the manor. Ours was a busy household, with many people to care for. As a child I learned to work the simpler tapestry stitches, and when I was old enough to handle them, I learned to work the looms and spinning wheel. The sewing room was usually a gay place, the walls echoing to light hearted chatter and songs accompanied by the thrump of the loom and the whirring of the wheels. I seldom minded spending my customary two or three hours a day there except when

10

the weather was especially beautiful and I yearned to be outside.

The manor house was surrounded by outbuildings: the stables, the mews, the kitchen, granaries, workshops, and sleeping quarters for the servants. Among and beyond these were the kitchen gardens and orchards that produced a variety of fresh vegetables and fruits. Less than half a mile away, down the road toward London, was the village in which lived the fiefs who worked our land as well as such freemen as the blacksmith and the innkeeper. Nestled in the center was the village church. In the opposite direction a narrow but navigable river formed the western boundary of our land and ran down to the southern coast.

We were not too many miles from the coast and upriver from a particularly good landing site, a small bay sheltered from winds and rough water and protected from sudden attack by high, rocky cliffs. As a result, we frequently had travelers crossing our land, seeking shelter in our buildings or the hospitality of our well-laden boards. In addition, much of our land was covered with a fine forest, abundant with deer and boar of such quality that my father's frequent invitations to join him at hunting were well received. The broad meadows and fine roads welcomed others who often came long distances to go out with my father, falcons and hawks on their wrists, to try for smaller game. As a result, I learned early to be at ease with strangers and with those older than myself. My mother having died when I was eight. I often took my place as hostess for my father at dinner, sitting down in the main hall with twenty or thirty guests, most of whom were men.

On a sparkling September day, three years after old Gundrig had read the rune stones, my father was entertaining at his annual autumn hunt. The assembled lords and their entourages were too many even for our spacious manor, so on the day of their arrival the meadows just beyond the courtyard took on the aspect of a village fair. There were tents almost as far as the eye could see, ranging in size from those large enough to contain the tables, chairs, and beds brought by many

11

of the nobles to others so small that they would hold only one or two servants ranking high enough not to have to wrap themselves in their cloaks and sleep under the sky. There were cooking fires in front of most, fires bright enough to rival the sun and turn midnight into noon. During the day the eyes were dazzled by the colors and designs of the tents, brilliant reds and blues, bright yellows and greens. From the top of each flew a pennant with the colors and insignia that proclaimed the name and rank of the occupant. Although the hunt was an annual occasion, never before had I seen such a large number attend, due no doubt to a lull in fighting now that Uther Pendragon had united much of Britain.

On the second day of the hunt I chose to stay at home, having wearied of the confusion engendered by the multitude of people, horses, and birds. By midmorning, though, I was bored with my self-imposed seclusion, and I thought about saddling my mare and riding out along the river. Then I decided I would rather walk. It was a pleasant day, and I could pick some of the late-blooming wild flowers to bring back to my room. I walked through the kitchen garden and out the side gate. From there it was about three hundred yards to the river, and though I stopped now and then to gather flowers, I was hot and tired when I arrived at the water's edge. Sitting on the bank, I took off my shoes and was dangling my feet in the water when I was startled by a voice coming from somewhere above my head.

"Hello."

I looked up to see a boy—although I suppose he thought of himself as a young man—sprawled out on a branch of the tree under which I sat.

"Hello, yourself," I answered.

He climbed down from the tree. He was not wearing the rough garb of a servant, so I decided he was probably a page who had slipped away to avoid being ordered about by those left in charge of the tents. As he was brushing the leaves off his tunic, I asked him who he belonged to.

12

"Belong to?" He looked startled. "Oh, you mean who am I with?"

"Yes, if you want to put it that way."

"I am with Sir Ector. Who are you with?"

"I am not *with* anyone," I answered haughtily. "I am Lionors, daughter of the Earl of Sanam, your lord's host."

"How do you do." His bow was more mocking than conciliatory. "And Sir Ector is not exactly my lord. I am his son."

From the sensation spreading over me I knew I was blushing with shame and getting more and more embarrassed at the whole situation: being startled by a voice from the tree, being caught barefoot with my feet in the water and my skirt above my knees, and now being almost rude to the son of one of our guests.

"I'm sorry," I said, "but I assumed all of the guests were on the hunt."

"I would have been, but my horse went lame. I wasn't too disappointed, though. Too many people. More clutter than hunting. Confuses the birds."

"I felt the same way. Would you like to walk along the river with me?" I asked. "I am on my way to my favorite place, an island no one else ever goes to."

"I would like that," he said. "If I go back, someone is sure to find something for me to do. By the way, my name is Arthur."

While we talked, I had a chance to observe him closely. Although not much taller than I—Marta was always complaining that I grew straight up like a young sapling and out of my clothes faster than she could make them—he was older than I first thought, at least two years older than I. I was abashed at the thought that he might consider me a child and was merely being polite to his host's daughter. Slim, almost skinny, he was still in what Marta called "the gawky stage." His youthful, fine-featured face was highlighted by clear, deep green eyes and blond hair that sparked with red glints when the sun touched it. (I realize as I look back over these words I am writing that I am describing Arthur not with the eyes of a young girl but as

13

I remember him now after the passage of many years. It is memory that sees the open, ingenuous face, the inquisitive eyes exploring the minute details of new surroundings, and the sensitive nature that forbears hurting anyone because it is so easily hurt.)

We walked silently and in single file along the narrow, barely discernible path between the river on one side and the tall, furry grasses on the other. In a few places the edge of the bank had collapsed into the river, and we had to proceed warily, for weeds covering these cave-ins misled one into thinking he was stepping on solid ground. As we walked, the river had been getting wider, and soon we came to a place where it divided into two arms, encircling a small, heavily wooded island. Going to the water's edge, I pulled back some rushes, revealing a shallow skiff I kept hidden there. I had found it one day, drifted up onto the shore, and seeing that it was watertight, I had made my first excursion to the island that had caught my imagination. It had lured me since the first time I saw it. Now, since finding the boat, I was able to go to the island whenever I wanted.

Arthur was doubtful that the skiff, lying as it did so low in the water, would hold the two of us, but assuring him we could always swim if it sank, I gave him one paddle while I took the other. He had looked somewhat askance when I mentioned swimming, but one of my father's unorthodox ideas on education included teaching me to swim because of our close proximity to the river, into which he was convinced I would fall or jump any day.

With two in the skiff, its thwarts dangerously close to the water, we made slow, silent progress, concentrating our energies in favor of getting the most distance out of each paddle stroke instead of conversation.

Once on the island we beached the boat, securing its bow line to a convenient willow branch. Then we found the path my previous excursions had worn through the grass, and we followed its winding contours between clumps of aspen and willows until we came to a clearing under a magnificent oak tree right in the middle of the island. Its huge limbs roofed a carpet of short grasses and clover on which lay a number of large, flat stones upholstered in moss. Here and there fairy circles of toadstools rose above the smooth sward. Sequestered from the outside world by bushes, tangled vines, and tall trees, the small area was very green and quiet and cool. I indicated a boulder for Arthur to sit on; my favorite, it was especially large, hollowed out and curved so that it resembled a seat. I thought of it as a throne in comparison to the smaller, less imposing rocks. I sat on the grass and leaned back against a tree.

"How do you like my secret place?" I asked.

"I like it. It's peaceful here." Arthur stretched out his legs, moving around until he found the most comfortable position.

"I named the island Ave Lion. I think I had just learned that *Ave* in Latin means 'hail,' and the island always seemed to be calling to me to come over. I first used my whole name—Ave Lionors—but that was too much of a mouthful. I think 'Ave Lion' has a haunting, musical sound to it."

"I don't have an island," Arthur said, "but I have a favorite room, almost a secret place because I have never seen anyone go there. It's at the top of one of the towers of Sir Ector's castle, right under a pointed roof that slopes down to its floor, so while I can stand up only in the middle, I can lie on the floor and look out the narrow slits in all four directions. I can see for miles, over the fields to the forests and hills beyond."

My curiosity prompted me to interrupt him. "You call your father Sir Ector? That seems rather formal."

"He's my foster father. I have lived with him since I was a baby. Kay—he's two years older than I—is his real son."

"Oh, I see." I said. "Well, go on. I didn't mean to interrupt."

Arthur continued his story, telling me about how, looking out from the tower, he imagined himself a great commander leading his men, positioning them in strategic places so they could swoop down and wipe out the enemy coming over the hill.

"But that's just daydreaming," he muttered. "I will never lead an attack."

"Why not?"

"I will never even be a knight, just Kay's squire after he has been knighted. I don't get upset about it often, only when Kay and I have been tilting at the quintain and I best him at it. No, most of the time when I am in the tower I imagine myself as a bird, a hawk, maybe, flying over the land, wheeling and soaring above the vast forests and broad lands. I try to think as Merlin taught me the birds think."

"Merlin?"

"He is our tutor, Kay's and mine, but while Kay is busy training to be a knight, Merlin takes me off for special lessons. Sometimes we go to the mews, and he introduces me to the falcons and hawks and peregrines—he has names for them all. He explains the peculiarities of each: how they like to be treated, the conditions under which they fly best, and so on. He says they are a lot like people. That is what I meant about thinking like a bird."

"I often go to the mews with my father," I responded. "I love to nestle the baby kestrels in my hands and watch them through the weeks as they grow into full-fledged falcons. But I never had any idea of thinking like a bird."

"There is so much you can learn from the habits of the wild animals. I have learned how to stay so still by a burrow that the rabbits will come out and eat from my hand. We like to lie flat on our stomachs and watch the moles and badgers tunnel out homes under hillocks and roots. Wait a minute, I'll show you what I mean. See that spider web?"

"Yes." I looked at the fragile web suspended between two slender twigs, barely visible behind the leaves.

"Did you know she spins it from her own body excrescence?"

"Of course I know that," I flared. "Who doesn't?"

16

"But did you know that her fine filament—so fine that if she attaches it to just the right spot, her prey can't see it—is one of the strongest materials on earth? Fairies unwind the web and use the thread to make their clothes."

"Oh, come now," I scoffed, "you don't believe that!"

"Careful, don't mock the little people. You never know when they are listening. Merlin believes in them, but he also showed me there is more magic and wonder in the natural world than in the supernatural."

"So—" I tried to appease him —"what do you learn from a spider web?"

"It's not the spider web itself; it's what it stands for." He began to speak slowly, like one explaining something to a child, and I was certain he was quoting his tutor word for word. "Merlin says that often the greatest strength is invisible, the strength of faith. It cannot be seen, but we have it in ourselves, ready to use if we need it in the face of enemies or problems. It can also be the strength to know that you are right and others are wrong."

He paused a moment, then continued. "Take that ant over there, for example. He can carry several times his weight in food, more of nature's magic. But man, too, can carry more than he realizes if he puts his mind to it. About the time you are sure you can't do something or carry a burden, say of responsibility or choice, think of the ant. Merlin says you can actually feel the strength surge through you, and then the problem becomes easy."

"Does Merlin see everything in nature as a lesson for man?" I asked.

"Just about," Arthur answered. "We talked the other day about the process of birth. Every animal, including man, must reach a certain stage of development before being born, but each takes a different length of time. No more, no less. Merlin wanted me to understand that most things in life cannot be rushed; they have their own time in which to develop and their own moment at which to appear. We must wait patiently until the proper moment—but no longer. We must be both patient and ready."

I found myself fascinated by the kinds of lessons Arthur was learning and hoped that someday I would meet Merlin.

"Do you always understand what he is trying to tell you?"

"Not always," Arthur said. "But Merlin assures me I will when I need to. Sometimes I know what he means. For instance, one day when I was raging about being me instead of Kay, Merlin suggested I put myself in Kay's shoes. Pretend I was him for a whole day. When I did, I knew that no matter how much I wanted to be a knight, I wanted to be me, not someone else. So Merlin told me to remember this whenever I was jealous of someone, that to do what he does, or have what he has, I would have to be that person."

"Do you get jealous often?"

"Only when I see Kay preparing for knighthood. I know I could be a good knight. I may be smaller than Kay, but I am smarter and faster than he is. Aren't you ever jealous of anyone?"

"Sometimes," I sighed, "I wish I were a boy."

"But then you would have to go off and fight."

"That sounds like more fun than counting linens and overseeing the kitchen as a lady of the manor."

"Do you think you could kill someone?" Arthur asked.

"I—I hadn't thought of that. But I could go along, take care of the weapons and bind up the wounds."

"That is squire's work. That is what I will do for Kay. You would like to be a squire; I would like to be a knight, but we have to accept the fact that we can't."

"Maybe not for real," I said, "but we could pretend."

"It's not the same thing at all."

"It's make believe," I urged, "like the little people. You can't see them, but you believe in them. No one else will know you're a knight, but you and I will."

"We don't have a sword or spurs," he argued.

I was not going to let him get out of it that easily.

"We have branches and leaves. This is make believe, remember?"

"There's no oil for annointing."

"I'll think of something," I said confidently.

As Arthur knelt before me, I tapped him on the shoulder with a long stick, then tied leaves around his shoes. Without his seeing, I had picked a few wild strawberries still clinging to the vines, and squeezing them on his head, I said, "I dub thee Knight of the Strawberries."

Arthur jumped up, furious, strawberry juice running down his face and the back of his neck.

"That is not fair," he screamed, but I was rolling on the ground, laughing too hard to hear.

In a minute Arthur saw the humor of what I had done. While sitting on the ground trying to wipe off the pink juice, he began laughing, too.

"Strawberry knight is right," he hooted. "Slightly red in the face but very tasty, and at your service, ma'am."

"You're going to have to wash it off. Those leaves don't do much but smear it around."

"A swim, that's the answer," he said. "Now I'll show you how to catch fish with your hands."

"I've never caught any in any way."

"You've never been fishing!" He looked at me in mock horror. "Come on, and I'll show you how to do it without a line. Wait a minute. Do you have something on under that dress you can wear in the water?"

"Certainly. When I come to the island, I'm always ready to swim."

I stepped behind a bush to slip out of my dress, under which I had a short shift, while Arthur did the same with his doublet and hose. Stripped of cares as well as clothes, we raced each other to the water.

I had known how to swim as long as I could remember, and it was as natural as breathing, but catching fish with my bare hands was something else. I knew enough to stand absolutely still, but each time a fish swam by and I put out my hands to catch him, he would give a saucy flip of his tail and swim off free.

I tried to copy Arthur's technique. First he pursed

19

his lips and blew gently on the surface, just hard enough to ripple the water in tiny waves that moved across the surface in concentric circles. Instead of scaring the fish away, it seemed to attract them. As they slowed down, concentrating on the center of the circles, as though expecting to snap up whatever had disturbed the water, Arthur, with almost no motion at all, slipped his hands under the fish and in one quick movement had the prey in his grasp.

However, when I tried it, the fish just lay back and laughed while I either got a face full of waves or made no impression at all. And all the while Arthur was tossing fish after fish up on the bank. He crowned his success by diving under the water, swimming a few yards upstream and then back again.

"Well," he boasted, "if you can't catch fish, do you think you could learn to breathe under water?"

"Probably not. You just want something else to lord over me."

"No, this is easier," Arthur assured me. "Break off one of these hollow reeds, then snap it off so it is just long enough to stand up out of the water while you're holding the other end in your mouth under water."

We had to search and test carefully to find just the right reeds. They could not be too slim, or they would not stand up straight. Any that were too dry crumbled when we broke them. When we had two perfect ones, Arthur showed me what to do.

"Now lie back like this, or sit down if it's shallow, and put your head back slightly. Hold your lips snugly, but not too tight or your mouth will get tired. Remember, though, do not forget and breathe through your nose or you'll either drown or come up spluttering. Once you get the knack, you can stay under water indefinitely."

I practiced until I could do all my breathing through my mouth.

"Now," Arthur said, "we'll try a new version of hide-and-seek. Close your eyes and count to fifty. I'll go hide among the reeds and you see if you can find me."

As I turned around and began to count, I heard Arthur splashing through the water. Then silence. At fifty I opened my eyes, confident I could spot his reed immediately. But if it was there, it looked exactly like all the rest, swaying in the slight breeze. There were no ripples, nothing to give Arthur's position away. There were several clumps of rushes, so I carefully swam up to and around each one. Still no Arthur. Then it dawned on me. He was tricking me. He was not lying among the reeds at all. He had swum back to the island and was probably standing on the shore laughing at me right now. Catching fish by hand! Breathing through reeds! The whole idea was to make a fool of me, and he was succeeding only too well.

There was one way to get back at him, swim to the boat and return to the mainland. See how he liked being left on the island! He would have to swim across with all his clothes.

Just then a head emerged above the surface, and there was Arthur in the middle of the clump of reeds right next to me.

"Did I scare you?" he grinned.

"No." I would not give him the satisfaction.

"See how easy it is?"

"For you, maybe," I pouted.

"Go on, try. See if I can find you."

While Arthur counted, I swam to a farther clump, settled into position and waited to outwit him. Then there he was, finding me right away.

"How did you do that?" Now I was really mad.

"You really want to know?"

"Oh, come on, how?"

"Your nose stuck out," and now he was laughing at me the way I had laughed at him with the strawberry juice running down his face.

"It didn't!"

"No, honest, you weren't far enough under. Let me show you again. Get well under the water." He slid under, choosing a spot deep among the weeds.

"I'll hide again," he said, "so look real carefully."

This time I strained my eyes, checking one reed

21

against another, looking for one that was different in some way. Most of the rushes were swaying slightly; then I spotted one that was jerking back and forth. I swam over and pulled the reed out of his mouth. Arthur came up choking.

"You want to drown me? You wouldn't have found me if a fish hadn't decided to swim close and tickle me. Now, you try again."

I chose my spot carefully and slid well under the water. I was sure I was well hidden. But just like before, Arthur found me almost right away.

"Now what did I do wrong?" I asked, ready to acknowledge defeat.

"Nothing, except that the reeds were blowing in one direction and yours was leaning the opposite way. You have really got to practice if you ever hope to hide from someone who is bent on finding you."

"All right, Smarty, but come on back to the island, and I'll show you something I'll bet you can't do."

We swam back easily, used our outer clothes to dry off, then hung them over some branches while we flopped on the grass.

"Now, what's your trick?" Arthur asked.

"Help me collect some of these slim willow branches, and I'll show you."

While Arthur gathered the twigs, I peeled off the bark and then split and shredded the willow into strips.

"Now," I said, "go get those fish you caught, and I will make a basket for you to carry them in."

In a few minutes I had plaited a small, flat basket with sloping sides and even a slim handle. Then I helped Arthur pack the fish in layers of wet leaves.

"Now that's neat," Arthur said, admiring my handiwork. "You really like to swim, don't you?"

"I love it. I come here as often as I can sneak away."

"You're good. Would you like to learn to swim like a fish?"

"More lessons? You've already beaten me at two. Anyway, I don't have fins or a tail, so I couldn't possibly do it."

22

"Want me to show you how easy it is?"

I nodded.

"All right, look." He held his hand out almost at arm's length, thumb up, palm to the side. He explained that was how most fish were built, the width going up and down or vertical. Then, moving his hand slowly, he showed me how a fish swims, waving from side to side, using its tail to propel it through the water. Even when a fish seems to dart ahead, the tail has given the initial thrust. Then Arthur turned his hand palm down.

"Now watch," he said. He was moving his hand in the same waving motion, but this time up and down rather than from side to side. "See, it's an easy, continuous movement, not push-push-push like a frog."

He motioned me to the water and dove in. Once he began swimming, I could hardly follow him beneath the surface; only a slow-moving cluster of ripples, barely distinguishable from the regular wavelets, revealed that something was moving through the water. In a moment he was back, his head popping up like a jack-in-the-box right at my feet. Tossing his shoulder-length hair from his face, he washed the grass and my legs with a fine, cool spray.

"See how easy it is. Come on and follow me," he called.

After a few awkward flounderings while I tried to accustom my body to the strange movements, I found myself gliding smoothly up and down. All went well as long as I kept my feet close together and used them as a fish uses its tail. It was not long before I had the feeling that I could swim like this without getting tired.

We crawled up on the bank, and I collapsed, letting the sun dry me off, too tired to move.

"I hope," I said in an exhausted voice, "you don't have any more lessons for the day. I might turn into one of your animals."

"None that will take any effort on your part. There is so much you can learn from wild creatures. How an animal escapes from his enemy or defends himself when he cannot escape. Man can study the way animals build their homes for safety and protection and how they stalk their prey. Men would be a lot smarter if they would learn the habits of animals instead of trying to outdo each other."

"Merlin teaches you all this?"

"Yes, and so much more. He says that people look but do not see; they listen but do not hear."

"Or touch and do not feel," I murmured.

"That's it!" he exclaimed. "Be quiet now. What do you hear?"

We sat in muted silence for several minutes. At first there seemed to be no sound at all, as though we were isolated from the world in a fog of silence. Gradually a few sounds pierced the silence, coming nearer, as a torch coming from a distance will first appear as a dusky glow, imperceptibly becoming smaller but brighter as it nears. I heard the faint lapping of water against the beach, then began to distinguish individual waves, as one by one they surged forward, rolled across the pebbles, and then receded. I became aware of a pattern: three waves quickly, one after another, then a hiatus of silence followed by three more waves. The regular melody of the water movement was enhanced by the rough undertone of the pebbles being carried back to the sea with a swishing, grating resistance to this pull of nature.

From above came the calls of birds, again, at first, just a conglomeration of sounds. Gradually they separated themselves into chirping, twittering, short, quick singing notes or long, drawn-out cries. And like echoes of the birds' notes was the whispering of wings as they brushed the leafy branches or an occasional snapping as a small twig was broken. I would have said there was not a breath of air stirring in our warm, sultry glen, but the rustle of leaves and the soughing of wind among the branches said otherwise. Now from the reeds came more sounds, brushing, whispering, the click-click of a beetle, the humming of a bee in the trumpet of a small, blue flower and beneath it all the regular beat-beat of my heart and the soft sighs as I exhaled. The fog of silence had been completely dispelled by the assorted musical sounds of nature. So enraptured was I, I had completely forgotten I was not alone. Arthur's voice, interrupting my reverie, came as the most startling sound of all.

"Well," he said, "what did you hear?"

"Oh," I exclaimed, "so many things—waves, birds, grasses, the bees."

"How many birds?"

"How many? I wasn't counting. But there must have been at least four different kinds."

I blushed under Arthur's praise for having distinguished different bird calls, but my pride was just as quickly wounded when Arthur went on to say that was only the beginning. What I had to do now was learn the unique call of each species so that I could recognize a robin or sparrow just by sound. Then, he said, the next step was to distinguish between two birds of the same species. I argued that all robins, for example, or even all ducks and geese, sounded alike, so that would be impossible. Arthur patiently went on to explain that just as human voices differ, so do bird and animal voices. At first he thought he it was Merlin's magic that enabled him to do it, but Merlin had convinced Arthur he could do it, too, if he would take the time and effort. Day after day he went to the same spot in the forest and lay there for hours, learning to shut out all sounds except those of the birds he was studying. Finally the day came when he found he was hearing not just two doves, but one calling and the other answering.

"So," I said, "you spend hours doing all that. For what reason? It seems to me that if Merlin is your tutor, he would be teaching you more practical things."

As he went on talking, I realized how very little I knew about life beyond the walls of the manor. Arthur explained that knowing what to listen for, knowing what you are hearing, could save your life. At night in the forest, you have to know the difference between normal nocturnal noises and those that warn the forest creatures of a dangerous intruder. Or catching the sound of an animal that normally forages during the day could mean someone was using its call to signal to a confederate.

25

In addition, Merlin had taught Arthur to really see his surroundings; a branch hanging at a certain angle meant a horse had brushed it; at another angle, a man or a group of men. Almost anyone could tell by looking at soft ground if someone or something had crushed down the leaves and undergrowth. But a closer look would reveal if it was a man or horse, even the size and weight of the passer-by. A forest is full of sounds, but a trained ear can immediately recognize if they are the normal snappings and whisperings, or if they are the sounds of someone riding or crawling through the trees.

"So you see," Arthur concluded, "your life may depend on learning to listen and see."

After we left the island and were walking back toward the manor, I saw old Gundrig shambling along the narrow walk that led through the kitchen garden to the stable yard. Misshapen with age, her spine curved into a round hump above her head, and her cheeks were almost lost in the folds of the cape falling from her shoulders.

"Who is that?" Arthur whispered.

"Old Gundrig, said by some to be a witch."

"A witch?"

"Certainly every proper manor has its witch. Didn't you know that?"

"I thought you did not believe in fairies and the supernatural."

"Gundrig is different. I can see her, and she is said to be over a hundred years old. She lives in a deserted hut, once used long ago by a charcoal burner, but she comes here often, and we always feed her. Sometimes she stays and sleeps in the kitchen. She can read the future with her rune stones. Come on, Arthur, let's see if she will tell your fortune." I sped up and pulled him along.

"No need," Arthur said. "I know my future."

"Oh, come on. It will be fun to see if she knows."

"Gundrig," I called, "wait a minute." She turned slowly at my voice. "Do you have your rune stones with you?"

In answer she reached beneath her cape and into the pocket of her long skirt.

"Will you read the future for my friend here?" I asked.

Still without speaking, she motioned for us to sit down, holding the flat stones in her hands. We waited for Gundrig to throw the stones, but she was staring at Arthur as if in a trance, a look of wonder and disbelief frozen on her face. From the depths, as though from a haunted past, she spoke in a monotone.

"Who are you?"

"My name is Arthur. I am the foster son of Sir Ector."

"I know that," she muttered, "but *who* are you?"

"I—I don't know what you mean."

Gundrig lifted her head. "I see a strong, powerful man standing in the shadows behind you. He has his hand on your shoulder. With the other, he is holding something out for you to take."

"Who is he? What is it?" Arthur was vibrating with curiosity.

"The shadows hide a secret for now. It is not yet time for you to know. But I see you holding aloft a mighty sword."

She stopped, staring intently at the configuration of the stones that were still lying in her hand; then quickly she crushed them together in her bony fist.

"Is that all?" I asked.

"That is all."

"You saw more," I insisted, "and just won't tell."

"I tell what I read in the stones, but today they speak a strange language, the language of the old gods, Thor and Woden, and only the gods can read them. Not often do they call on the gods, but when they do, I keep silent." Without another word, she moved away.

"Is she always this mysterious?" Arthur asked. "Or couldn't she think of anything to say?"

"I don't know." I said. "She is always abrupt, but I have never heard her speak of the gods that way."

"Maybe I just have a dull future."

"Or maybe she was cold and hungry. But that part

about the sword was exciting, and the man behind you."

"Oh, sure," Arthur said, "that was probably me carrying a sword to Kay to use in a tournament, with Sir Ector prodding me on to hurry. I told you she wouldn't see anything I did not already know."

It was time to separate. We arranged to meet and go to the island again the next day, then I went to face Marta's scolding for being away so long and getting wet, and Arthur walked to Sir Ector's tent.

However, a runner came during the night to say that Uther Pendragon, high king of Britain, was ill, probably dying, in London. Before dawn the camps were alive with squires preparing the mounts and nobles already departing at a gallop for London, ready to be on the spot when Uther's successor was named. Servants, left behind to strike the tents, would follow within hours. Uther did not die at this time; in fact, he lived for another four years, but the concern over who would succeed him never abated, nor did he ever name an heir.

I saw Arthur briefly as I accompanied my father to bid farewell to our guests. Arthur was tightening the reins on Kay's horse. I sauntered over, pretending to inspect the silver on the bridle.

"I am glad you came to Sanam Manor. I hope you will come back," I said.

"Oh, I will when Sir Ector comes again. Practice breathing with reeds, and maybe I won't catch you next time. And we will work on catching the fish."

"I'll work at it," I said. "I promise."

They rode away, a gay cortege of knights and hunters, but my eyes remained on the young squire riding a few paces behind Kay.

❊ Chapter Three ❊

"Lionors, Lionors!"

I could hear Marta huffing and puffing her huge
bulk up the stairs, her loose felt shoes slapping against
the smooth stone. Only an emergency could move her
that fast. Reaching the top of the stairs, she began
a hurried shuffle along the hall toward my room. I
could picture her reluctant haste—increased age and
weight had combined to create in her a sense of leth-
argy, which she enhanced with deep sighs of exhaustion and frequent self-pitying remarks.

But I loved Marta, who had patiently endured my
childish tantrums and sympathized with my struggle
through adolescence. She had sat by my bed, going
without sleep, when I had the fevers, and she had carefully explained what it meant to be a woman the day
my body sent its sign that I was no longer a child, for I
had been almost hysterical at the thought that I had
sinned or was dying. So now it was my turn to be understanding, to make her feel needed by letting her
dress me when I really would have preferred to con-
duct my own toilette.

"I'm in my room, Marta." It was not fair to make
her search any farther. Red in the face and still holding
up her skirts, she came in gasping and panting.

"Those stairs will be my death yet. I don't know
why you insist on coming up here during the day.
Night's the right time for the bedroom, not the middle
of the afternoon."

"I'm sorry, Marta," I apologized. "I wanted to read

this manuscript, and I thought I would be more comfortable in bed."

"Reading! That's no proper activity for a girl," Marta grumbled. "I thought you were coming to the kitchen with me to check the supplies for the guests."

"The guests!" I had forgotten the hunting party. "Are they here?"

"That's what I came to tell you," Marta answered. "The courier just rode through the gate to say that your father and the guests will be here within the hour. So hurry, get dressed. His lordship will be entertaining some of the men at dinner."

"Oh, bother. I hate those dinners. Can't I eat in my room?"

"No, you can not. Your father wants you by his side. So hurry. Can you dress by yourself? I should be helping in the kitchen."

"Go along, Marta. I'll manage." I tried to sound disappointed, but inwardly I breathed a sigh of relief.

"Your best gown, remember," she added as she went out, still breathing heavily from the exertion.

"Yes, Marta, my best."

I closed the door behind her, took off my wrapper, and resumed what I had been doing before Marta called to me. This room had been my mother's before she died. During the last two years of her life, while she lay an invalid, I had loved coming here, sitting by her bed. Sometimes I sat for hours holding her hand or just looking at her while she slept. When she was awake, she loved to talk about earlier years when I was a baby or even when she was young. I could not know then how much those memories would mean to me after she was gone. Whatever I knew about myself, I had learned from her.

When she died, my father chose to remain in the small room he had used during her illness rather than return to the bed that held the memories of their love and of her pain. I asked if I might move into her room, for although there had been sadness within the four walls, for me my mother was still there, and it was the one place where I could still feel her presence near me.

"You really miss her, don't you, pet?" my father asked softly.

"Oh, yes, sir, I do. Please let me move in. It keeps me close to her, and I feel sometimes as though I can still talk to her."

So he agreed, and though it may seem strange to those who do not believe, she often comes to me in my dreams at night, speaking softly, assuring me of her love.

This day I was trying to recall how she looked before she was ill, to know if I resembled her in any way. Dressing and undressing were such routine matters that I had never really given much thought to my body and how it was developing. Now I could begin to see my mother emerging in me—the same long legs, slim hips, even slimmer waist, and well-developed breasts. I realized now, for the first time, that my mother had been exceedingly proud of her figure. She loved wearing beautiful gowns fashioned from the exquisite materials my father brought her. She had them cut and draped to fit her lovely figure, and I can still see her standing proud as a queen to greet my father's guests. She had a beautiful face, and I wondered if I would be as beautiful as she when I matured.

Inspired by this memory, I was suddenly excited at the prospect of dressing up and being hostess for my father. Could I, too, stand like a queen to greet her guests? The very thought made me stand taller and straighter.

Marta would be proud of me, I thought, as I dressed, smoothing out the wrinkles of a fine, pale-blue gown, carefully fastening my mother's gold filigree necklace around my throat. A wedding gift to her from my father, the necklace had lain in my jewel chest since she had given it to me just before her death. Tonight, I felt, was the proper occasion for me to wear it. Lastly, I brushed my hair the one-hundred strokes Marta always insisted on and that I usually objected to.

Scarcely had I finished when I heard the pounding of horses' hoofs on the cobblestones of the courtyard. As soon as my father had given orders for the stabling

31

of the mounts, he would come rushing in, surrounded by his friends and calling for me. In the past I had always waited for his call, waited for his permission to descend and be introduced. Tonight, however, I thought I would go right down and surprise him by being there to welcome his friends to our home.

Lifting my skirts, I started to run down the stairs. Then I remembered how my mother would have done it, and even though no one was there to watch, I stopped, smiled toward the front hall, and proceeded slowly, one step at a time.

When my father entered, I was standing, poised, by the great fireplace. In spite of my ladylike appearance, he picked me up and swung me around as though I were still a child. But young lady or not, I squealed in his bear hug and kissed his rough beard.

Few introductions were needed, for most of these men were frequent visitors to our home. I greeted each one easily, one after another, and tried to make them feel welcome.

Then I came to one who was standing with a young man, perhaps his son. I did not know them, yet there was something hauntingly familiar about them. My father came to my rescue.

"You remember Sir Ector, Dear," he said. "Ector, this is my daughter, Lionors. I did not expect you to recognize her. She was a little girl the last time you were here."

The stout knight squeezed my hand in friendly acknowledgment.

"And this is his son Kay." My father spoke to the young man next to Ector. "You have grown up, too, young man. I would not have known you if I had not seen you with your father."

While I chatted idly with Sir Ector and Kay, my thoughts returned to the hunt three and a half years earlier when I had met Arthur. Was he with them now? I knew he, too, would have changed during the intervening years, but I saw no one who even slightly resembled him among the guests. Surely he would have been invited to dine with us unless Kay was already as-

suming the prerogatives of a knight and had assigned
Arthur tasks too demeaning for one of Kay's self-as-
sumed stature. If so, maybe he was outside eating a
cold supper in his tent or cooking it over a small fire.
Would I see him while they were here? Would he go on
the hunt? Surely he would be in attendance on Kay. I
was looking forward to riding out with the party, having groomed and ridden my horse every day, preparing
for just such an occasion. My father had given me a
pair of fine peregrine falcons to train and care for.
There would be no way I could stay behind and look
for Arthur unless I pleaded sick. Then I would be put
to bed under Marta's care, with no chance of leaving
the house the whole time the guests were with us. I
could only hope that Arthur would be with them on
the morrow.

I do not know what kind of conversation I carried
on while these thoughts were racing around in my
mind, but everyone was smiling, so I must have been
giving the right answers.

The servants were filling the hall, bringing trays of
food and setting up the benches. Three long tables were
place *U*-shaped in the main hall, the center one
stretching along the length of the huge hearth, the others placed at right angles to it. Flambeaux burned in
sconces on the walls, throwing a sputtering, uneven
light. Between the sconces, the thick stone walls, now
damp with evening moisture, were hung with magnificent tapestries that reached almost from floor to ceiling.
They helped keep the great hall warm, and in the light
of the torches their brilliantly colored scenes seemed to
come alive.

My father was very proud of our home and its furnishings. The long tables were not merely rough boards
placed on trestles, as would be found even in some cas-
tles, but were smoothly planed and polished tables with
heavy, carved legs. Instead of being taken down and
stacked away when there were no guests, two of the tables were pushed against the walls, holding a few pieces
of fine stoneware. When in bloom, fresh flowers filled
the urns, and in the fall I filled these same vases with

armloads of bright red and gold branches. The third table usually stood in the center of the hall, with two or
three chairs nearby, and served to hold platters of fruits
and other delicacies.

Gradually, my father urged everyone to their places,
and he led me to the seat beside him. Kay was on my
right, and I did my best to be gracious, but all I
wanted was for the dinner to end so that I could get to
bed and rush the dawn by sleep. If I could sleep.

Even though three and a half years had passed, and
I had been not much more than a child when I met Arthur, I had never forgotten him and looked forward to
the day I would see him again. For one brief afternoon
he had been my friend.

Through a series of carefully worded questions, by
talking about training falcons and caring for horses, I
managed to learn that Arthur was now Kay's squire
and was at the camp. Even though Kay was not yet a
knight, he prided himself on knowing how to live and
talk like one. In fact, pride was one of his most promi-
nent characteristics. He might have been more charming—and I might have been interested in his
conversation—if the word *I* had not appeared at least
three times in every sentence.

The evening finally ended, highlighted by my father's
quiet approval of my wearing the gold necklace, and I
was able to slip away to my room. In spite of the flut-
ters in my stomach, in spite of worry that I might not
recognize Arthur—or he, me—I fell asleep almost as
soon as I got into bed.

Unfortunately, everything started out wrong the next
morning and got progressively worse as the day continued.

First of all, I overslept. With all the extra people for
breakfast, Marta was busy overseeing preparations in
the kitchen and forgot to wake me. The sun was high
in the eastern sky, its rays flooding my room, when I finally opened my eyes. The horses had been brought
around, and some of the riders were already in the
courtyard. Rushing to dress, I tore the hem of my new
riding dress on a nail in the clothes chest. Not wanting

34

to appear in my old, soiled gown, I had to take time to mend it. Then my fingers fumbled over the fastenings. Finally dressed, I was fortunate enough to be able to tie back my hair and get it under a snood in one try. This was one time I would have welcomed Marta's help. Maybe I would remember to appreciate her from now on.

As late as I was, I could not take time for breakfast. With Marta fussing at me, I did eat a piece of bread while trying to explain that I just did not have time and assuring her that I would not expire if I missed one meal.

Running through the kitchen and scullery, I barely missed bumping into several servants who were removing food and soiled plates from the tables. I skirted around the dogs, hungrily lapping up the scraps tossed out to them, and ran across the yard to the mews, calling to Luk to saddle my horse. That was something I enjoyed doing myself, patting Bonny while I wished her good morning. I liked to check the saddle and reins myself, making sure of the fit and testing the bit to assure myself that it did not irritate her mouth. But that was a pleasure I would have to forego this day. I had forgotten her morning apple, and I hoped she would not repay my negligence by being tempermental. Usually she was very gentle, obeying promptly every command, but she had a stubborn streak that occasionally manifested itself for no apparent reason.

Reaching the mews, I released Peri from her perch, slipping on the hood with impatient fingers. Taking the jesses and creance from the wall, I flew toward the front courtyard, wondering if anyone was left or if I would have to guess which way they had gone and try to catch up.

All this time I was praying Arthur would be one of the party attending Kay and had not been left behind. I went carefully through the field of tents, avoiding dogs and dying bonfires, but as hard as I looked, I saw no sign of the face that had remained in my memory for almost four years. Not knowing Sir Ector's coat of arms, I had no idea which was his location, so I de-

35

cided I had best go on and try to catch up with the hunt, which had quite a head start by now.

Knowing the falconers would stop when they released their birds, I was not too worried about finding them, and after a few minutes I saw them up ahead of me, at the far end of the long meadow. I cantered easily across the low grass, trying to catch my breath and gain some measure of poise. It would never do to come dashing up among them, frightening the birds and at the same time appearing to be flustered. I must be calm and nonchalant, trying to give the impression that my being late was a result of the careful dressing and preparations of a lady rather than the oversleeping of a sluggard. If I sat just right on Bonny and smiled, I could be the gracious lady and make an effective entrance.

After another minute or two, I spotted my father and then saw Sir Ector and Kay, their horses standing side by side. However, I need not have concerned myself about making the right impression, for all eyes were looking skyward, watching a fine gyrfalcon wheel around, finally spot its prey, and swoop down to pierce his talons into a wild hare.

My father noted my arrival with a nod of his head and then returned to watching the action. Was he angry because I was late?

I took advantage of everyone's interest in the birds to study and check carefully each of the guests. Most were on their own horses; a few had dismounted to stretch their legs, check the prey, or walk around inspecting and talking about the distinctive features of the various birds. My father was known for his fine collection of falcons, and he enjoyed showing them off. Most of the men had brought their own, and they spent hours comparing and bragging about how fast or how accurate their favorites were.

Having spoken to Sir Ector and Kay, I glanced casually at the young squires and pages standing or sitting around the edge of the meadow, under the trees, ready to rush to the side of a master when he called. One group of half a dozen were making bets among themselves on the peregrine that had just been sent flying from his owner's wrist. Others were holding second hawks or seeing to pieces of equipment.

As my eyes moved from one group to another, I saw no familiar face. Arthur could not have changed so much that I would not know him, and surely, if he saw me, he would have given some sign of recognition. He must, then, have stayed behind at the manor for some reason. Well, I sighed, I might as well join my father and enter the sport. Peri would begin to get restless if I kept her on my wrist too long and did not let her fly.

Then as I started to ride away, I looked back one more time and saw a slim young man walk out from among the trees, looking carefully around before leaving their shelter entirely. He gave the impression of not wanting to be noticed. Had he seen me coming and disappeared into the woods to avoid meeting me?

I wheeled Bonny around and rode toward him, but he made no move to acknowledge my presence. Even as I got closer, there was no change in his expression; it was as though I did not exist. I stopped and put out my hand, a silent request for him to help me down. He reached up and then dropped me none too gently to the ground, but still no word or change of expression. I saw that I was going to have to make the first move.

"Welcome back to Sanam Manor, Arthur."

"Thank you, my lady."

"My lady!" I sputtered. "What happened to Lionors?"

There was a trace of a smile. "It's good to see you again, Lionors."

"Well," I said, "that's more like it."

There was a shyness about him that I did not dare try to penetrate too soon. Perhaps it was due to his not being included at the dinner the previous night, which on second thought surprised me because he was Sir Ector's foster son, a more important relationship than that of just a squire. So I decided to press on.

"Why aren't you hawking with the others?" I asked. "Where is your horse?"

"He's tethered over there." He pointed to the spot

37

among the trees whence he had emerged a few minutes earlier.

"Go get him," I said, "and come along with me."

"No, I'd rather stay here." No smile now, just a grim frown of determination.

"But why? I remember your saying you loved to hunt."

"I don't want to. Kay took my favorite falcon, a merlin I have been working with for weeks."

"Arthur! Now you're pouting like a child." I was embarrassed for him and furious with myself for nagging him into this confession. His only answer was to turn his back and stalk off into the woods again. So without another word I got back on my horse and rode off. If he did not even want to ride with me, I was not going to let him know it bothered me. I rode straight to Kay, who was standing by his father, and made a point of staying with him the rest of the morning. Kay seemed flattered by my attention, and I was not displeased to have him show an interest in me.

I was not usually vain, but I knew I was looking particularly pretty this day. The deep green of my dress was a flattering color, and a few tendrils of hair, escaping from my snood, curled around my face. The embarrassment over being rebuffed by Arthur had raised a flush in my usually pallid complexion.

If Kay wanted a charming partner during his stay, I would do my utmost to be the most delightful companion he had ever known. I would show Arthur that I did not need him to make the day a pleasant one.

While Kay was watching his bird in flight, I watched him. He was really quite a handsome young man, with strongly chiseled features, clear blue eyes, high forehead. He sat tall on his horse, his broad shoulders and full chest straining against the leather of his jacket. There was no doubt that he could be a very attractive person when he wanted to be, and I laughed and chatted with him for a good part of the morning.

At first it was fun to have a handsome young man, especially one soon to be knighted, attentively treating me as his lady fair, picking up my scarf when I dropped it and tying it around his wrist. I had not long turned sixteen, and this was the first time I experienced having a man look at me as anything but my father's daughter, to be patted on the head and merely tolerated during a hunt.

Then as the morning wore on, the sun got hotter, my wool riding dress began to scratch, and my first flush of embarrassment became a burning red. When a cloud passed over the sun, I was grateful for the relief, but at the same time I felt a cloud pass over my being. The whole thing was false: my laughter, my flirtation with Kay. It was Arthur who should be leaning toward me, explaining the fine points of the bird in flight. I looked at Kay again with clearer eyes, and I realized that his strong features might become harsh if he were crossed. His blue eyes were colder than I first imagined, and with his broad shoulders and full chest he could so easily become grossly fat. He could not hold a candle to Arthur, who was shorter, perhaps, but slimmer, with a fine, gentle face.

When the time came for me to release my peregrine, I discovered that in my haste to get to the hunt, I had tangled the jesses. Now when I tried to straighten them out, I broke one line, and I wasted more time mending them. Poor Peri sat patiently, but then in her eagerness to take off, she faltered, swerved against the wind, and flew erratically up, veering to the right, up and over the low trees. While I was furious at her poor performance, I was more concerned for her safety. She disappeared behind the trees. Although my first instinct was to put spur to horse and follow her, the creance was clear of the trees, and my better sense told me to wait, that she would return to her starting place. In a little while she did return to my wrist, and I gently replaced the hood. But the morning had been ruined, in many ways, and I was grateful when my father signaled our return to the manor.

The servants had set up the tables in the courtyard. Usually I enjoyed dining out of doors, especially on such an unusually warm spring day as this. However, tired and sweaty, I was in no mood for more idle chatter and the men bragging about the exploits of their falcons. My skirt and surcoat were clinging to me, and I felt as though I were burning up. Excusing myself gracefully, I took a flagon of wine and drank it straight down. That was a mistake—on an empty stomach. I forgot that I had not even had any breakfast. The next thing I knew, I was suffering with a raging headache. Afraid I would be sick, I hurried up the stairs to my room.

Fortunately, by pulling off my heavy clothes and dashing cold water on my face, I warded off the nausea and dizziness. Thankful to be back in the security of my own room, I fell across the bed and was soon asleep.

How long I slept I do not know, but the sun had passed below the roof of the stables and no longer filled my room with its glare. Thoroughly rested by the nap, the headache gone, I felt refreshed. There was a tinge of coolness in the air that could only be the aftermath of a quick afternoon shower. Suddenly I felt a new energy pulsing through me, and I knew I wanted to do something exciting: to run, to jump, anything to give vent to this new feeling. The disappointments of the morning were forgotten. I did not care that I was a young lady, a gracious hostess. I wanted to be a little girl again, to ignore such things as flirtations and broken hearts. I wanted to ride out alone on Bonny, with Peri on my wrist, but with no one else. And that is just what I would do.

No heavy wool riding dress and snood this time. I tied my hair back and tucked my chemise into a pair of brown linsey-woolsey *braccae,* or trousers, that I wore when cleaning out the mews and training Bonny. They were torn in places and streaked with mud. My father would be furious if he saw me, but I would make certain he did not. If I knew my father's habits, he would now be in his room, sleeping off a heavy noontime meal, washed down with several flagons of mead. I put on a soiled shirt of the same material as the trousers, laced it carelessly at the throat. Over this I donned a lightweight surcoat split front and back so I could ride astride rather than sidesaddle. Then I jammed my feet into a pair of old boots.

Marta was the one I had to be careful to avoid. For all her age, she could still grab me by the scruff of the neck or the ears and march me straight back to my room, lecturing all the way. I could hear her now—"Shocking, a young lady in trousers! What will your father say? What will he do to me? He'll say it's all my fault. Oh, I've tried to be a mother to you."

No, I must not meet Marta. Looking down the stairs, I saw that the great hall was empty. If my luck held out, Marta would be snoozing in her favorite chair beside the fire in the small eating room. I crossed the hall quickly and headed down the back hall to the scullery. As I neared the kitchen, I could smell something delicious, reminding me that I had had nothing to eat since the night before. On the trestle table were loaves of bread, fresh from the oven. I reached for one that had cooled enough and cut off four thick slices. In the fireplace, a lamb was turning on the spit, while a scullery boy basted it with a highly spiced herb sauce, the juices sputtering on the coals and sending out a rich, pungent aroma. Taking a knife from the table, I cut off several crisp pieces, licking the tasty remains from my fingers. As I went out the back door, I picked two late fall apples from a barrel and put all these things into a small sack I scrounged from the larder.

From there I went through the kitchen garden, the freshly turned earth, ready to be planted with seed, sending up an odor of rich, black dirt. It was a heady, pleasant smell, and I breathed deeply as I crossed to the mews. In no particular hurry this time, I stopped by each of the perches to speak to the falcons, checking this one's talons, adding water to another's cup. They all knew me and returned my greetings with gentle pecks on the hand or impudent ruffling of feathers. Even Peri seemed to sense that my mood was calmer than earlier in the day—or my hand was steadier—for she put up no fuss as I slipped on the hood for the second time in a day. I took down the jesses and creance more carefully, no twisting this time.

41

With Peri settled comfortably on my wrist, I walked across the stable yard, inhaling the strong, powerful odors of horse dung and urine mingled with the dusty aroma of oats and hay. Such farmyard smells never offended me, for they were redolent of life and productive activity. Bonny neighed in response to my call and pawed impatiently as I put on saddle and bridle. She, too, sensed my mood. Leaving by the back gate, we were forced to contain our eagerness to break loose, for we had to cross the pasture where the herdsmen were rounding up some of the sheep.

But when we got to the meadow, I loosened my hold on the reins, touched heel to flank, and Bonny broke into a canter and then a hard, pounding gallop. The wind whipped my surcoat, cooling my hot skin and easing the last remaining tension from the morning. It tore through my hair, loosening the knot of my scarf and finally pulling it off all together. But I did not care. While I rode, my hair streamed behind, out of my way. When I stopped, I could break off a length of Peri's creance to tie it up.

Only after several exhilarating minutes did Bonny slow down, and I, too, was glad just to canter at an easy lope. Ahead was a small grove of beech trees, in the midst of which was a spring that emptied its deliciously cool water into a tiny pond. Its banks were overgrown with wild mint, which seemed to impart its own tangy, sweet taste to the water. I was hungry, and Bonny must have smelled the water, for when I turned the reins in that direction, she picked up speed and headed straight for the trees.

I entered the grove, dismounted, then watered and tethered Bonny. Stretched out, my back against one of the trees, I was contentedly eating when I suddenly had the feeling that I was not alone. I heard a rustle from the other side of a large stump. If my companion were four-footed, I would not be afraid, for the only wild animals that came this close to the manor were foxes and rabbits, or maybe small wild pigs, and they were no danger. If it were a snake, I could only hope it was afraid of me and had already left. If it were human,

42

then I might be in danger, for I had come out un-armed, not even carrying a small knife.

But my shock could have not been greater if the head that appeared above the stump had been the devil himself.

"Arthur! What are you doing here?"

"I might ask you the same," he replied.

"I'm having a picnic. I didn't eat any lunch. Now, how about you?"

"I wanted to think." He was sitting there, legs crossed, looking disconsolate. With his head down, his shoulders drooping, he looked as though he needed cheering up, and I forgot the misery of his having ignored me that morning.

"Are you hungry?" I asked. "Here, I've brought bread and meat, more than I can eat. I don't know why I cut so much. I must have had an intuition I'd meet someone."

"No, I . . ."

"Here, see there is plenty," I urged. "I even brought two apples. Take this, it's delicious."

"Thank you. That meat smells good."

He came around from behind the stump to sit by me, and we ate in silence for a few minutes.

"That was good," Arthur finally said. "I'm glad you came in here. At first I was furious that my hiding place was discovered. I wanted to be alone."

"I wanted to be alone, too," I said. "That's why I rode out by myself."

"You seemed glad enough to have company this morning." Was there a tinge of jealousy in his voice?

"Oh, this morning. I was miserable this morning. Everything went wrong."

"Miserable? You were having a pretty good time with Kay."

"Well, I was not," I insisted. "It wasn't fun at all."

"Why not?"

"Yes, you might well ask. It was your fault."

"My fault?" he said.

"Yes," I said, "so cold, so aloof—no, rude. I rode over to see you, and you hardly stirred yourself to

43

speak to me. I felt like a fool for having asked you to ride when you refused."

"I was mad," he mumbled.

"I know, because Kay had your falcon. But you didn't have to be so aloof with me. I thought we were friends."

"We are," he said, "or I hope we still are."

"I'll always be your friend, Arthur, if you promise not to turn away from me again, to hide in the woods when you see me coming."

"I promise." He smiled. "Are you finished eating? Let's go fly our falcons together—the way I wanted to this morning. Oh, Lionors, I had looked forward to this visit, to see you again, and then Kay spoiled it all."

"But he's not here now," I said. "Do you have your merlin?"

Arthur pointed to a low branch where I could see the handsome bird perched impassively, patiently awaiting his master's signal.

"And your horse?" I looked around.

"Tied just on the other side of the trees. C'mon, let's go."

We rode out, reveling in the joy of being together again, laughing at the crazy antics of a pair of squirrels chasing their tails. The birds whirled and swooped, glorying in their freedom, but returning dutifully to our wrists. Peri was a hunter, but not a killer, so I could usually release the small prey she brought to me. Arthur sent his merlin up only once, after a brown hare, but the rodent slipped down between the roots of an oak tree and escaped.

Tired of hunting, we rode awhile, racing the wind, smiling when we looked at each other, glad to be friends again; then we headed back to the spring to water the horses and ourselves. Getting off Bonny, I caught my foot and fell to the ground. Before I could get my balance, Arthur was lifting me up. Even after I was standing, he kept his arms around me, and I could feel them tighten, pulling my face against his chest— not a really broad chest but very comfortable. As he looked down, his lips brushed my hair, and when I in turn tilted my head back to look at him, I felt them touch mine. Just a touch, but it was enough to set my heart pounding. The next minute he stepped back, and I turned to check my horse. If the kiss were accidental, I had to give myself time to return to normal.

"I'm sorry, Lionors. I should not have taken advantage of you that way."

"Please don't be sorry," I whispered. "I liked it."

Then we both busied ourselves with our horses to bridge the awkward silence until Arthur broke it with a suggestion.

"You know what I would like to do?" he said.

"What?"

"Go to the island, to Ave Lion. Remember the day we spent there? Those were some of the happiest hours I have ever known."

"Let's go then," I said. "We can take a short cut across the meadow and not go near the house."

We galloped across the springy new grass, not saying a word until we got to the river's edge where I kept the skiff hidden. Tethering the horses and finding perches for the birds, we pushed the boat off, clambering in only after it was free of the bank. We did not speak until we got to the landing and pulled the skiff up among the reeds. Arthur helped me out, and we followed the faint path through the trees to our clearing in the middle of the island. Only when I sat down, my back against the old oak, and Arthur was lying on his stomach, his chin propped on his hands, did we begin to talk of all the things on our minds.

"Why did you let Kay get so close to you this morning?" Arthur asked.

"What?" I was puzzled.

"Why did you let him keep touching your knees with his?"

"I didn't *let* him. He kept pushing his horse close to mine. Why bring Kay up? I didn't come here to talk about him."

"Well, I didn't, either, except that he is one of the reasons you found me alone this afternoon."

"Jealous of him again?" I asked meanly.

45

"What do you mean again?" Arthur raised up on his elbow.

"Well, if I remember correctly, the last time we were here, you were unhappy because he would some day be a knight and you couldn't."

"I'm not jealous in the sense of wanting to be him. I'm glad I'm me. I could not stand to be someone else. But I get upset because of the things he can do just because of who he is. I don't know if I really want to be a knight; I do not like killing that much. And yet if it had to be done, if there had to be a battle—say, to protect Sir Ector's lands or your father's—I know I could do it better than Kay. I ride better and shoot farther."

"So?"

"I don't really want that, but I do want to be respected for what I can do. That's it, not for who I am or am not, but for what I can do."

"What do you want to do if not be a knight? What can you do?"

"I will be more than a squire," Arthur asserted. "I promise. I have studied hard and worked right along with Sir Ector, and he has hinted that I will be manager of his estate. I shall be good at it, keeping things running while he is away, checking the accounts. It will be a good life while Sir Ector is alive. But then . . ."

"Then?"

"When he dies, and Kay inherits. I'm really fond of Kay. He has been like an older brother to me, but I do not think I could serve that way under him." He paused a moment. "Really, I am no worse off than if Ector were my real father. I would still be the second son and not inherit anything. If I look at it that way—as his second son—I don't always feel so bad. But it is Kay who is looked up to, Kay whose opinion is asked. Sometimes I think of joining the church. I think I would make a good friar or monk. I wouldn't mind the life of contemplation, but I'm not sure I believe strongly enough."

"What I would really like is to go and live with Merlin, to go to the woods and study the animals and the stars. I have learned such a small amount so far. There

46

is so much more he knows, so much we could search for. From the time he first came to teach me, we have gone to the woods to study; taken a few provisions, learned to live off the land; made snares, found mushrooms, gathered safe berries, found hidden springs. Usually we come back with all the food we take out."

"Ever wonder," I asked, "why Merlin came to be your teacher?"

"Yes, although I thought I knew. I thought he was my father and had left me with Sir Ector to receive a proper upbringing. But when I asked Merlin, he shook his head. I know he would not lie to me. I wish he were my father. I wanted him so much to be my father that I waited years to ask him. I guess I was afraid I knew the real truth. I dreamed up all sorts of reasons why I could not live with him, why he sent me to live with Sir Ector. When I finally faced him with the question, he didn't hedge. He just shook his head; sadly, I think. I was not surprised—disappointed, yes—but not surprised. I think he was so flattered to be wanted for a father that he was speechless. He wiped his eyes on his sleeve—said some dust had gotten in them—then coughed and ahemed a bit. He sat me down as though he were going to tell me the whole story of my life, but all he said was that my father had been a close friend, and he had promised to see me well cared for. I surmised that I was taken to Sir Ector's as a baby because my mother died soon after I was born, but Merlin didn't tell me about either my mother or father, so probably they were not people of importance. But sometimes I think I would like to at least know their names. Am I named after my father? Or a little something about them. But when I mention them, Merlin changes the subject. In fact, I have seen very little of him since we had that talk. He just asks if I am happy, if my foster father is generous. I can't really complain. I am probably better off than if I were with my own parents. Sir Ector has been like a real father, and Kay generally treats me like a younger brother."

"Arthur, all of us have mysteries in our lives, perhaps not as strange as yours, but we learn to accept life as it is. Perhaps you wish you could be a knight like Kay will be, but think how much better off you are than so many. You are living in a castle as Sir Ector's son and learning to become the manager of his estate."

"I know," he said. "I keep telling myself the same thing. But why, then, have I been trained in the arts of jousting, in learning to handle a lance and a bow? Why have I been taught the rules of knighthood, allowed to learn the arts of falconry?"

"Perhaps," I suggested, "because Sir Ector is truly fond of you, because he does think of you as a son. Have you ever thought of that?"

"Yes, sometimes. Most of the time, in fact. I guess it just all came to me yesterday when, riding here, Kay said he was going to hunt with my favorite. He doesn't really care that much which bird he uses. He just said it because he knew I had been looking forward to flying him on his first real hunt."

"Is that why you stayed away from dinner with us?" I asked.

"Partly."

"Something else was bothering you, too?"

"Yes," he said, lowering his head, "but I would rather not talk about it."

"Please," I begged. "You once said you thought you could tell me anything."

"I want to." He hesitated. "But I am not sure I should be the one to tell you," he said finally.

"Tell me what?" I was getting impatient. "You mean I was part of the reason you would not eat with us? Now you will have to tell me."

"When I first learned we were coming here, I began counting the hours until I would see you. Of course, I thought of you as younger, not as a grown-up young woman, but I remembered the fun we had here on the island, and I hoped we could return. Then I heard about you and Kay. Your father and Sir Ector have been friends for many years, and it seems the two of them have been talking about you as a wife for Kay."

"Oh, no!" I was genuinely horrified.

"Yes, they arranged for you to meet each other now, and plan to announce the betrothal after Kay has been invested as a knight later this year."

"But I don't love him. I don't even know him."

"You seemed to like him this morning," Arthur said.

"I told you I couldn't help it if he kept coming so close, and remember, I was mad at you. I wanted to make you jealous."

"And you succeeded," he admitted. "When you rode across the meadow, you were the most beautiful young lady I had ever seen."

"Thank you, Arthur. But you had not seen me yet when you were upset about the betrothal plan."

"No, I just didn't like the idea of your being used, of any girl being used in such a way. I know it is done all the time, but I could not see it for you, Lionors. I remembered your gay, independent nature. You reminded me of a wild bird, free and unfettered. Some birds we can take and train, put on hoods and jesses, and they are happy in confinement. Others never can be trained. They die if kept in fetters, and so we return them to the wild. You are like that."

"Arthur, all this is too much for me. I want to marry sometime, but not yet. I am not even ready to think about it. I know everything there is to run a manor, but I do not know anything about being a wife."

"I've heard you learn that after you are married."

I nodded. "Sort of like learning to ride by getting on a horse and having someone slap him on the flank. All this talk is too serious. Let's go for a swim; there's time before dinner. I need to thrash around and work off some of this restless energy."

I stepped behind a shrub, stripped down to my shift, and plunged in. The water was colder than I thought it would be. Working my arms and legs to restore the circulation, I swam around to where Arthur was waiting. We laughed as we tried to catch fish with our hands, but they were not as cooperative as before. We tried breathing through the reeds, and had a short game of hide-and-seek. But it was not the same, either. We were no longer an adolescent youth and a young girl. On the

49

contrary, Arthur was a stalwart young man, and my wet shift clung to and outlined a woman's body.

I patted myself dry with my shirt and breeches, then slipped them on. There was no way to dry my hair, but I ruffled it a bit in the wind, smoothed it back, and tied it with the lacing from the front of my shirt. When I got to the skiff, Arthur was already there. I walked toward him, and straight into his arms.

This time there was no mere brushing of lips, but a warm, gentle touch that made me want to hold him forever. We stood together a moment, my arms around him, his hands smoothing my wet hair. He tilted my face toward his again, and this time the pressure of his lips forced mine apart, and I was kissed as I had never been kissed before. I responded with a passion that began with a curious, urgent feeling in the pit of my stomach and spread to my breasts until they felt swollen and sore.

Suddenly I felt Arthur's body pressing hard against mine, and his hands were fumbling at the unlaced necklace of my shirt.

"Please, Arthur, stop!" I pushed him away.

"I'm sorry," he said huskily. "I got carried away. But don't ever respond like that unless you want to be made love to."

"I promise." I was feeling half ashamed and half naughty. "Arthur, have you ever made love to anyone?"

"Lionors! You do not ask questions like that."

"Well," I persisted, "have you?"

"Let's just say I am a man and men are exposed to all sorts of temptations."

"That's no answer."

"Well, it's the only one you're getting. Now, hop in the boat. It's definitely time we got back to the house."

We said little on the way back. As usual I was rushing, dreading to be late. I left Bonny in the yard for the stable boy to rub down and went to put Peri on her perch. Bless Marta's heart; she'd found out I had gone riding and had a hot, soapy bath waiting before the fire in my room. Tonight cleanliness was not the main reason for my being grateful for the kettles of hot water she kept adding. Coming home soaking wet, I had gotten chilled to the bone, and the hot water warmed me up quickly. Bless Marta, too, for not commenting on my wet hair or questioning me about it. Instead, she rubbed it vigorously with a rough towel until it was dry. For once I was glad she was there to help me dress, and I managed to run down the stairs to the main hall just as father was leading the guests in to dinner.

Arthur was looking quite splendid in an embroidered tunic. Being the youngest in attendance, Kay, Arthur, and I were seated at the end of the long table. The night before, Father had shown his paternal pride in having me play hostess. But I am sure he was more at ease surrounded by cronies with whom he could exchange wild hunting tales and bawdy stories.

Kay sat to my right, paying more attention to the coarse jokes being told by the man next to him than to me, but every once in a while he tried to slip his hand onto my knee. When shaking it off did not stop him, I finally touched the back of his hand with the tip of my knife, not enough to pierce the skin but enough to let him know I could stab clear through if I had a mind to. He got the message and spent the rest of the meal pointedly ignoring me.

I did not care. Arthur and I had a wonderful time chatting, commenting on the people, laughing like silly children about the way some of them were eating. Arthur tried to imitate one of the men by swallowing a whole chicken wing in one bite, but he had to quit when he nearly choked laughing. I do not know what the other guests thought, but I did not care, for throughout the meal Arthur and I held hands on the bench, hidden by the full skirts of my dress. Undoubtedly part of our hilarity came from Arthur's trying to eat left-handed, casually, as though he did it all the time.

The evening ended with an entertainment hired by my father for the occasion. There were jugglers, acrobats, tightrope walkers, mimes, and a dancing dog.

51

The little black and white mongrel, with a colorful ruff around her neck, was led in on a leather thong by her swarthy-skinned master. Dancing around on her hind legs, balancing on a ball, and jumping through a hoop, the little dog delighted her audience, who clapped and cheered. Then the mountebank asked for two stools, between which he strung a taut rope. With a curt command, the man ordered the dog to jump to the stool and walk across the rope. As the dog put her front paws on the rope, it began to sway. She managed to get all four paws on the rope and started walking across when a slight noise distracted her, and she fell. The trainer hauled her up by the scruff of her neck; cracking his short whip, he directed the dog back to the stool. The little mongrel, whimpering with fear, refused. The montebank, his face now fiery with rage, cracked the whip again, this time across the little dog's back. She continued to cower and whimper. Once more the whip was raised, but before it struck the helpless animal, Arthur pushed back the bench, and springing on the man's back, knocked him to the floor.

Arthur was younger and had attacked unexpectedly, catching the man off guard, but the older man was strong, and the two rolled across the floor, a single mass of furious energy, in equal battle. First one was on top, then the other, attacking and parrying. Only a cry of alarm from one of the servants warned Arthur that the man had pulled a dagger from under his belt.

Arthur jerked aside in time to throw up his arms and fend off the thrust of the sharp point aimed at his throat. The blade slashed across his forearm, opening a long wound that covered both men with blood.

During this last struggle, Arthur had the advantage of being on top, and his sudden movement to avoid the knife threw the man off balance. That brief second of hesitation was all Arthur needed to straddle the man's chest and pin the latter's arms down with his knees, immobilizing him.

During the first of the fray, the guests had held off interfering, enjoying the spectacle of an impetuous young man giving the cruel older man a trouncing he so rightly deserved. A good, evenly matched fight was always a pleasure to watch, and they figured no real harm could come to either. When the dagger flashed, however, they were all on their feet, and by the time Arthur had his burly opponent pinned down, my father had signaled to three of our armed retainers to give Arthur a hand. The surly gypsy was dragged off, scowling and muttering curses, while the guests appeared around Arthur to slap him on the back and praise his courage. Cloths were brought to bind up his arm. The original cause of the commotion, the little mongrel, stood shivering in the center of the room. I picked her up and on the spot claimed her for my own, naming her Tippy in honor of her balancing act.

When order had been restored, my father called in the last entertainer, a minstrel who sang a number of familiar ballads and haunting lays of early Britain, accompanying himself on the lyre. He concluded with an impromptu improvisation about a brave young squire who rescues a helpless dog from the hands of a cruel master. Arthur had become a hero of song and story; the minstrel indicated that he was going to work on the ballad and add it to his repertoire.

It was well past midnight when the festivities ended. There was no way to see Arthur alone, but as he squeezed my hand good night, he asked if we could return to the island in the morning. I nodded and said I would bring a picnic lunch.

Much too excited to fall asleep, I wondered what I could give Arthur to remember me by. Then I thought of my mother's gold medallion. It had a secret spring; when opened, there was space for fragrant salve or a bit of paper, but I had something else in mind to put in it. I cut off a lock of my hair and spent the next two hours braiding it into a fine circle that fit perfectly inside the medallion. Satisfied that it was just the right gift, I curled up and went to sleep.

The sounds of morning awoke me in plenty of time to dress carefully and meet Arthur. I packed a light lunch of bread, dried fruit, and cheese; there was plenty of fresh spring water on the island to drink.

Stopping by the stable yard, I picked up Tippy in the kennels where I had left her until she could be properly housetrained. She had embarrassed herself twice the evening before while the minstrel was singing, but I was pretty sure that was due to nervousness. She would behave herself once she grew accustomed to being in my room. She began dancing and yipping as soon as she saw me. I took one of the rough brushes used to rub down the horses and began to smooth her fur clean of dirt and leaves. She had a beautiful coat, with streaks of reddish brown between the black and white. She had long, silken ears, and her tail was covered with fine, featherlike hair. With her small, rounded nose and slightly underslung jaw, she looked as though she were smiling all the time. As I walked across the meadow, she pranced at my heels, leaving me only to chase a butterfly or investigate an interesting patch of weeds.

Arthur was waiting at the skiff when I arrived. Holding Tippy, I stepped in, and then he handed me the food. After pushing us off, he climbed aboard. Tippy was so excited, she kept running in circles, back and forth between us, nearly tipping the boat over twice. I had named her rightly. Once on the island, we headed for the clearing—Tippy staying right with us—where I put down a blanket and set out our lunch. My new-found pet shared everything, gorging herself on bread crusts and cheese as though she had not eaten in weeks, and with her frail little body, I wondered if the trainer had deliberately kept her hungry. Every time she wanted something, she stood up on her hind feet and danced over to one of us. She especially liked the dried plums that she chewed on the way most dogs worry a bone.

Seeing if she would do other tricks for us, we made a hoop from a supple twig, and sure enough, she jumped through it, then stared at us until we applauded. After that she turned around and leapt through it again. There was no doubt about it; she loved performing. We did not have a ball, but I would find one when we returned home. I would never, however, try to make her walk a rope. I had a feeling her fall the night before was not the first and that the sight of a rope would make her afraid of me.

While we were clearing away the remains of the lunch, Tippy disappeared. In a few minutes she was back, soaking wet, her fine hair now bedraggled and clinging to her body. She carried a stick in her mouth, which she proceeded to present to Arthur, and then immediately ran off again. This time we followed her. Standing on the bank, we watched as she dove into the water, swam to a twig floating on the surface, took it in her mouth, and swam back, depositing her gift at our feet. Over and over she repeated the act, bringing leaves, twigs, and dead reeds until we decided she was trying to clean out the whole river. By a tacit, mutual agreement, we did not disrobe and go swimming ourselves, but waited on the bank for Tippy to tire of her labors. Finally, exhausted by the effort of trying to pull in a large, leafy branch, she climbed up on the shore and trotted back to the clearing. There she collapsed on the blanket and fell asleep.

While she slept, I sat down, resting my back against a tree, and Arthur lay with his head in my lap. There was so much to say to each other, yet we found it hard to begin. He wanted to know what I did every day so he could have a picture anytime he thought of me. I told him I usually helped Marta oversee the needs of the manor in the morning and then spent two or three hours at the loom or tapestry frames. In the afternoon, I worked with my father, riding out over the estates if the weather were good or going over the account books. In the evening, if there were just the two of us, we read or talked, and Father had begun teaching me how to translate the Latin manuscripts.

"You once told me about wanting to command an army," I said. "You should read some of Caesar's writings. Now there was a great tactician. You could learn a lot from him."

"I've given up that dream," Arthur answered. "Even Kay will do no more than follow someone else's orders, and I will follow his."

"Unless you stay on the estate with Sir Ector."

"I guess that is my dream now, to be a good steward for Sir Ector. I like riding out with him, as you do with your father, overseeing the planting and checking on the condition of the crops. I even like pitching in to help with the harvest, working under the hot sun and smelling the toasty odors of the grain. I can't say I am so fond of keeping the accounts. Sir Ector can't do figures, so he has a clerk under whom I work, and he is a shrewish, miserly fellow who reckons down to the last farthing. His hands shake from drinking too much ale, and he has a long nose that drips all the time, but he is honest and sees to it that his master gets everything that is due him."

"It doesn't sound as though you're with Kay much anymore," I said.

"No," he replied, "only when he thinks he needs a squire. Once in a while, though, we still do things together as equals, and I think he really misses the time when we played together and there was less awareness of our difference in station. Its funny; some ways he acts like the younger of us, looking to me for approval or praise whenever he has done something he is proud of."

"Which would you rather do, stay on the estate or ride out to battle with Kay?"

"I don't know. I do know I want to get into at least one skirmish just to see what it is like. At a tournament I would have to stand to one side and watch the others joust, but in battle I would be fighting right alongside." He sighed a long, deep sigh. "It's hard to decide between two things, both of which are only second best."

I bent down to answer him, and as with each time I leaned close to him, some of my hair fell across his face. This time, instead of brushing it aside, he gently pulled on my hair until I was close enough for him to kiss me. Before I realized what was happening, we had reversed positions, and he was sitting up, holding me in his arms. I nestled there, wishing I never had to leave, hearing Arthur whisper over and over how much he loved me, how he had fallen in love with me the minute he saw me again the day before.

56

"You do see now," he said breathlessly, "what I mean by second best. I don't really have the right to say I love you."

"Why not, if I love you, too?"

"Because some day you will have to marry a noble, a lord or duke. And I will never be anything more than a servant."

"Not a servant," I protested, "a trusted steward of Sir Ector's estate."

"But still serving him or Kay."

"Serving, yes, but every man serves someone of higher estate, right up to the king."

"It is not the same thing," he insisted.

"You said Sir Ector loves you like a son. Maybe he will make you a real son. Then you'll be a nobleman."

"Don't dream, Lionors. A foster son is not the same thing as a real one. Even a bastard son of royalty has higher standing than I would have."

"Arthur, I love you, and I can't bear the thought of losing you. From the time you climbed down out of the tree, I knew you were someone special in my life. I will not marry anyone else, I promise."

"No promises. You don't know what your father has in mind."

I was almost crying. "He wouldn't force me into an unhappy marriage. Let's make one promise—we won't marry anyone until we see each other again."

We held each other close, and then I remembered my gift.

"Here, Arthur," I said. I gave him the medallion. "I want you to have this. It was my mother's. And see inside. I braided some of my hair. If you keep this, you cannot forget me."

"Thank you. I will always treasure it, but I won't need it to remember you." He kissed me again. "I did not make a special gift for you, but I want you to have this." He pulled a narrow gold ring from his little finger and slipped it into my hand. "I think this was my mother's, too. No one ever told me, but it was with me when I was taken to Sir Ector's. Keep it close, but

57

don't wear it. Maybe some day I can slip it on your finger."

The warm afternoon sun began to filter through the tiny new green leaves, the rays dancing off Tippy's face and waking her up. She bounced over to us and began licking our faces. Before she could run back to the water and get wet again, we prepared to return to the manor. I held her, wiggling and squirming to get down, while Arthur folded up the blanket. We scattered the few remaining bits of our lunch for the birds, who would come down out of the trees as soon as we left and devour the bread crumbs and cheese rinds.

Because the spring evening was so pleasant, Father had ordered trestle tables to be set up in the courtyard for an informal evening meal. Kay was standing to one side, a quizzical look on his face, dying, I knew, to know where we had been, but too polite to ask. Feeling as though we loved the whole world, we asked him to join us, taking our plates to an isolated corner of the courtyard. Kay seemed genuinely glad to doff his grander-than-thou bearing and sit cross-legged on the ground, his plate in his lap. The day ended on a light, happy note.

In the morning, Arthur and I had an all too brief few minutes together in the mews before we had to part, he to go to the courtyard where the horses waited and I to the window above where I could wave good-by without anyone seeing my tears.

In the privacy of my room, I looked at the well-worn ring Arthur had given me. The inside had been rubbed to a smooth patina, but I thought I could barely make out what looked like the top of the letter *I* engraved there. I wondered if this could be a clue to his parentage. Having put the ring on the chain from which I took the medallion, I slipped it inside my dress. As it lay between my breasts, I wondered when again and how soon I would see Arthur.

⊠ Chapter Four ⊠

The days that followed brought with them a return to the usual routine around the manor: inspecting the fields or studying with my father, learning from Marta how to oversee the women servants in the kitchen and laundry, spending pleasant hours in the weaving room. As the weather grew colder, I spent more time with my father's manuscripts, learning to read Greek as well as Latin under his patient tutelage. One day ran into the next as ceaselessly as one wave follows another toward the shore, with nothing to disturb the calm.

Then just before the beginning of the new year, the pleasant monotony was broken in a way no one had anticipated. At long last the word came that all the people of Britain had been waiting for. They had a new king. When Uther Pendragon died some months earlier, he apparently did so without leaving or naming an heir. There were those who said he had sired a natural son, entrusting him to the care of a close friend who was sworn to secrecy. When the propitious time arrived, the boy would be declared the rightful king. If he were too young, he might be killed in a gratuitous accident or be used as a pawn on the chessboard of politics, and no pawn ever checkmated an opponent. Others believed there was no son, but that the right man would step forward to lead them during some great catastrophe. For the present, all played a waiting game.

We were preparing to celebrate the Christmas holidays. Usually we shared the festivities with neighboring lords, all close friends, either at our manor or one of theirs. When I was growing up, the younger members of the families eagerly looked forward to the annual get together. While the men sat at the tables downing horn after horn of mead and telling stories we were not allowed to hear, the women huddled close to the blazing hearth, knitting, embroidering, and gossiping. They, too, chased us away when they lowered their voices over the choicest tidbits of news. But we really did not care. We were too busy playing hide-and-seek or blindman's bluff until the elders told us to calm down; we were getting too flushed. Then we sat on the floor to toss the knucklebones.

As we grew older, the games gave way to more sedate activities and singing ballads, old familiar ones and the new ones we learned from strolling minstrels who wandered from town to town. In the evening we cleared the floor, and even the adults joined us in the popular folk dances.

This year, however, a huge tournament was being held in London to which all the nobility had been invited. From the time I first heard about it, I anxiously awaited for my father to name the day of our departure. I nagged Marta to freshen up my wardrobe and try to make a few new dresses for my first experience with real court society. Unfortunately, my father was not feeling well, making a slow recovery from a broken shoulder, sustained when he fell from his horse while jumping a hedge. I tried to understand and to hide my disappointment.

Kay was to have been knighted in the fall and would surely attend the tournament, the first since his investiture. If Kay participated, Arthur would certainly assist him in his role as squire. I had not realized how much I looked forward to seeing him until Father said we weren't going.

"I'm sorry, pet," he said, trying to comfort me. "I know how much you would enjoy the excitement of a real tournament for the first time. I remember my own introduction to court society." He digressed, reminiscing about his own days as a fledgling knight among his older peers. Uther was a young king then, and the tour-

naments were wild, ruthless affairs in which partici-
pants ignored more of the rules of chivalry than they
obeyed. More than one knight was mortally wounded
during the mock battles until Uther realized he was losing his best men at play, the very men he would need
when he rode out against his enemies.

"Ah, yes," father said, returning to the present, "this
gathering should be the biggest ever. I have no doubt
that many of the lords will be putting in their bid to be
named king of Britain. It is time that all the diverse
factions were reconciled under a single, strong leader.
No one will have an easy job of it; there are too many
jealousies and no man with a really strong claim to the
throne."

"If there are so many who want to be king," I asked,
"how will they ever decide?"

"By force of power. It will be the man who commands the greatest allegiance who will win the crown.
That is what worries me—our entire land under seige
as each petty king tries to do battle with all of his
rivals. No one will know when his land will suddenly
become a battlefield, and we will be planting bodies instead of crops. No, I think maybe they will show more
sense and line up their forces by having all men swear
allegiance to one or another of the stronger challengers.
There may still be a battle for a final decision, but it
will be contained, and God help us if the outcome isn't
decided quickly. Two especially worry me. King Lot
from the Orkney Islands and King Leodecrance from
the northern border. They are both ambitious men, and
each has his power strategically located, so that with
bribes and promises either one could muster enough
forces to weigh the balance in his favor. In fact, all of
the western and northern factions will have to be won
over or appeased, and that takes a seasoned, powerful
leader." He shook his head. "There is no one in Britain
today with that kind of strength."

I sighed. All this talk of kings and rivalries was too
confusing. Then father veered off in another direction.

"It is time you were introduced into court society.
This would have been a good time for you to meet the

young knights, sons of friends of mine. We need to begin thinking about your marriage."

"Please, Father," I pleaded, "there is plenty of time
for that." Time for Arthur to prove his worth as more
than a squire for Kay.

"Not as much time as you think. I want to see you
happily married and hold grandchildren on my knees.
Your mother, God rest her soul, was expecting you not
much past the age you are now. I could choose for you,
Lionors, but your mother and I shared real happiness
together, and I want the same for you."

"Then let me wait a bit," I urged. "Let me find a
man I can truly love and respect. It won't be long, I
promise."

"We'll see," he answered. "I thought you would be
attracted to Kay; you know, the son of my good friend,
Sir Ector, but I could tell you weren't when he was
here. I was not really too impressed myself. A good
lad, perhaps, but not for you. I promise, we'll go to the
next tournament."

"Thank you, Father, but only if you feel well
enough."

He went on as if I had not spoken. "And we might
even plan to have one here in the spring. Under the old
Roman law, by which this land was deeded to our ancestor, you will inherit my estate, but you will need
someone strong to help you. No task for a woman."

With that the conversation was concluded, and I had
gained the time I needed.

Aunt Helena, Father's widowed sister, had come to
live with us. I was sure brotherly love and charity were
not the prime reasons for bringing her under our roof.
Although Marta had cared for me through the years as
if I were her own—better, really, because I was
the daughter of her beloved mistress—she could not
train me in the arts of being a lady. Aunt Helena saw
to that. She taught me how to drop gracefully to the
floor in a deep bow, how to carry on light but entertaining conversations with courtly acquaintances, and
how to keep smiling and not appear bored when being
regaled with a long-winded hunting story from a pom-

pous, slightly drunk old knight. She took over the running of the household from Marta, much to the latter's chagrin, and saw to everything with a prim mouth and strict hand. I became the recipient of all Marta's grumbling.

"Thinks I'm too old, does she. Doesn't like the way the linens are washed or the food served!"

But we survived even if our old, relaxed ways were replaced by stringent rules and an eye that could spot a speck of dust ten feet away. I escaped indoors with my books or outdoors with my birds and horse whenever I could. Father enjoyed having Aunt Helena to reminisce with about their early years, and he seemed younger and healthier for having her at the manor.

As in all previous years we went to the village church for the celebration of Christmas mass. During the year we worshiped in the manor chapel, but on this one day we joined with all our people in thanksgiving for the birth of our Lord. In the morning, before service, everyone gathered in the manor courtyard, and I helped Father dole out extra measures of grain from our abundant fall harvest. There were also gifts of fruit and sweetmeats for the children and special remembrances for those who had been married or had given birth during the previous year. Then, singing the praises of God, we all walked together to the church. It was a tradition, and one the people of our fiefdom seemed to appreciate.

After service, the family, the village priest, and our servants gathered around the big hearth in our main hall while the great log was brought in and set ablaze. Here father distributed his personal gifts to those who served us in the house, and we exchanged our own presents. I had embroidered a pair of soft woolen slippers for my father, and I was very proud of them, for I had not had to rip out a single wrong stitch. His gift to me was much more sumptuous: a gold necklace set with emeralds and a dress length of emerald green velvet. I wanted to cry because I knew he was trying to make up for my having missed the trip to London.

There was a heavy blizzard during the night, and we

awoke to a world of dazzling white. As far as the eye could see was a broad expanse of sparkling, trackless snow glistening in the icy, sun-frozen world. The snow between the house and the outbuildings was so deep that, molelike, we had to dig tunnels through it to reach the stables and the mews. The men took care of the horses, but I lugged many a kettle of steaming water to keep the birds from freezing and to thaw the water on their perches. During the snowbound days that followed, I often stayed with them, repairing jesses and making new helmets. In the evenings, grateful for a roaring fire, we sat close to the hearth while Father and Aunt Helena told stories of when they were young, each madcap incident reminding them of another. When they ran out of memories, Father might read from one of his precious manuscripts, and I listened with delight, especially now that he thought I was mature enough to be introduced to Ovid and his less-than-respectful anecdotes of the Roman gods and goddesses.

Three days before Twelfth Night, the weather turned warm, and the snow began to thaw into rivers that ran between and around the cobblestones in the courtyard. As soon as they could, the servants swept the place dry, and we had a Twelfth night fete. There were huge bonfires, music, and dancing. Long tables were set up, and the kitchen turned out tray after tray of meat pasties and tarts. Everyone in the village came, and we rejoiced in being out of doors again.

In the midst of the gaiety, a wandering mendicant appeared at the gate. One look was enough to see that he was old; his clothes were ragged, and he had nearly frozen to death. As Father insisted on taking him into the house, Aunt Helena complained loudly, prophesying all sorts of dire results from the diseases he might be carrying. But to no avail. I ran for heavy woolen blankets, and he was soon warm and spooning up hot gruel provided by Marta.

Within a few minutes he looked as though he would live, and he began to tell us a strange tale. Mind you, he had not seen the miracle himself, but he had heard

64

of it from other wanderers who had been present. The heir to Uther Pendragon had been found and declared to be the rightful king. Most of those present at the miracle had immediately knelt down and sworn allegiance to their new ruler.

"What do you mean *discovered*," Father interrupted, "or—or miracle? What sort of nonsense are you mumbling?"

"No, no nonsense, sire. I swear by the holy bones of St. David."

And then unfolded the strangest tale of all. The great tournament had just begun, not the jousting, but the celebration of high mass preceding it. It was a wonder to behold the bishops and priests, as well as the lords and ladies, in their fine robes. Even the holy relics had been taken out of their vaults and, resting in their awe-inspiring caskets of gold and precious jewels, were carried in solemn procession by the older celebrants. It was not until the service was over, and people were renewing old acquaintances, that attention was drawn to a huge gray boulder in the churchyard. It was "like the ones you see on the Cornish coast, sir," and it stood right in the middle of the lawn between the cloisters and the church. But the most amazing thing about the boulder was the sword embedded in it, halfway up the blade to the hilt.

"Yes, sir, I swear, sir, a sword half buried in the stone."

Not just a plain sword, but of flashing, newly burnished metal topped by a hilt solidly encrusted with jewels.

"Diamonds, there was, sir, and rubies, and them green ones like the young lady has around her neck. Begging your pardon, ma'am.

"Then I heard tell that when they examined the sword, they saw writing appear on it like magic. 'Whosoever shall draw this sword from the stone shall be the rightful king of Britain.' I know it's hard to believe, but I made the man who told me repeat it three times."

The old man went on to say that each nobleman

65

there, beginning with the kings, then the dukes, and so on in proper order down the ranks tried to pull out the sword. But no one could. It was then laughingly suggested that even the squires be given a try. No one wanted to leave; the tournament was forgotten. Several squires tried, and then a slim, young man stepped up, and he pulled the sword from the boulder as easily as if it were embedded in a tub of butter instead of solid rock.

The noblemen could not—or would not—recognize a mere squire as their rightful king, so they made the young man put it back, and all tried again. But still the squire was the only one who could remove the sword. At last the archbishop stepped forward and said that the hand of God was in the miracle, and he would be the first to kneel to his new king. To end the confusion, one of the lords said, yes, the young man was the son of Uther Pendragon, reared by him until the boy should come of age. He had not spoken sooner because he, too, was awed by the miracle and felt that God had chosen this way to let the people know beyond all doubt that the young man was the rightful heir to the throne.

It was a marvelous story, but we did not believe a word of it until an official courier came a week later with the same news. A new king had been named, and we were invited to the coronation festivities. No mention of any sword or stone, just the announcement. The actual crowning had taken place immediately, to ensure there would be no change of heart when men reconsidered the emotion-packed day with colder, more calculating minds.

"Well, Father," I asked, "what do you think?"

"I am pleased that Uther's son has been found, and I've no doubt that is who he is. But I do not like the way he is always referred to as a young man. I would be lying if I said I were not concerned about whether he can muster enough strong men to keep him on the throne. The country may be lulled into peace now by the so-called miracle and the excitement of a new king. But he has enemies, and they will not hide behind their seeming loyalty for long. Even an oath of fealty can be broken by men who rate ambition higher than honor."

"Will you go to London for the festivities?"

"Yes, indeed. We will both go," he answered. "Our new king—by the way, what is his name? I can't remember. Something hard to pronounce."

"Arcturus, I think."

"Anyway, he will need all the support he can get, and the more who pledge their allegiance to him as their liege lord, the more the doubters will come over to his side."

When we set out for London, we had several days of hard riding ahead of us. Our entourage included horses carrying servants, armed outriders, a change of personal riding horses for Father and me, and a wagon carrying trunks of clothes as well as blankets and food in case we were unable to find shelter. While we rode, Marta jounced along in the wagon, grateful for the blankets to protect her aging bones. (Aunt Helena had declined to make the trip, for which I was grateful, for I wanted the freedom to seek out Arthur. I could do without her lectures on the proper behavior of a young lady—which did not include intimate conversations with squires.) Secretly, Marta was as excited as I about seeing London, but no one would have thought so the way she grumbled about the work involved in the preparations and the distance we had to travel. I think she had believed all these years that London was just over the farthest hill and not almost the entire width of Britain away from the manor.

We spent but a single night sleeping out of doors, and I found it more exciting than troublesome. After sharing a fragrant stew cooked over a wood fire, the servants built a circle of more small fires for protection. Marta and I made ourselves a comfortable bed in the wagon, while the men wrapped their cloaks about themselves and curled up close to the fires. In the morning I felt as refreshed as if I had spent the night in my own room.

Other nights we stayed at poor inns lacking in even

the most primitive necessities or the homes of friends. The sleeping facilities ranged from a narrow straw pallet that I shared with Marta in a room redolent of mice and stale cabbage to a magnificent, wide bed all to myself with eiderdown coverlets over and beneath me. But the night lodgings made little difference. I slept easily after a long day of hard riding, and I would have been willing to spread a blanket on the hard ground, for every night brought me closer to Arthur. There was no discomfort I would not endure. I was sure I would see him soon. He had to be in London; he had to be there with Kay and Sir Ector.

The problem of convincing him—and my father— that as the future manager of Sir Ector's estate he would be a worthy supplicant for my hand, I would worry about later. He would actually be a wealthy man, and the lack of a noble name or title was of absolutely no concern to me. Father said I would need a strong man to help me run the estate, and Arthur would certainly handle that. But would he be happy in such circumstances, working for his wife? Such thoughts kept me occupied as we rode—much too slowly—over the ice-cracked roads to London.

The royal city was unlike anything I had ever dreamed of: The houses crowded cheek to jowl on narrow alleys, the masses of people milling and pushing their way along, the vendors of flowers and hot pastries calling out their wares. It was like a hundred village fairs all going on at once—the noises, the smells, and the contagious gaiety. From roofs and staffs hung multi-colored pennants, but they were no more colorful than the clothes of the people who strolled beneath them.

We stayed at the home of one of Father's hunting cronies, a distant cousin named Sir Borre, a ruddy-cheeked, placid man who was no more disturbed by the addition of eight people to the already crowded household of his own family of six children and their assorted friends than he would have been if the vicar had merely dropped by for a chat. Dogs and children rolled on the floor together, servants and guests gingerly picking their way around them, as Sir Borre led us up to our rooms.

"We will dine at eight," he said, "if we can clear a way here to set up the tables. I don't know what we will be eating, but there will be plenty of something. Mighty glad you came," he said and for the third time bussed me on both cheeks.

We were not the only guests in the house. It seemed as though everyone in Britain had come to London, and everyone was doubling up, so we were fortunate to have two rooms, which we only had to share with the daughters and sons of the family. At least we were not sleeping four in a bed with strangers in one of the inns.

The daughters of the house held long discussions about whether to wear their blue or yellow dresses and frequently expressed delight over how young—and handsome—the new king was. And he wasn't married! I only half listened after I asked them if they knew where Sir Ector was staying, and they said they had not even heard of him.

Although the actual coronation had taken place the day of the so-called miracle, the king was to go through a more formal ceremony during the current festivities. Tiers of roofed-over seats, like the pavilions around a jousting field, had been set up along the four sides of the lawn between the cloisters and the church, the same churchyard in which the sword had been pulled from the stone. The seats were sectioned off, and over each flew the crested pennants of the king or lord who was assigned that place. The flags seemed alive with the multitude of animals they bore: strange, fabulous griffons, cocodrills, camelopards, unicorns, or lifelike lions, dogs, horses, bears, wolves, falcons, and even a fish or two. Others were more sedately ornamented with flowers and trees. Only one standard carried a flag with a dragon, the flaming red dragon on a gold field, the magnificent guidon of Uther Pendragon. Larger than all the rest, it flew over the throne on which the king would sit.

The road from our cousin's house to the church was lined with people, for this was the route the king would ride to his coronation. Country folk who had walked long distances to share in the event mingled with the common city people. There was a chill in the morning air, and groups huddled around small bonfires that had been built in iron cauldrons. As each warmed their raw hands, they moved back so that others could come forward and share in the comfort of the fire. The gently undulating waves of humanity had come to pledge their allegiance to the throne.

These were the common folk, freemen and serfs alike, on whose strong, broad shoulders rested the real strength of Britain. These were the women who labored in the fields or tended the markets when their men took up long bows or spears in defense of their country against invaders from the north, the east, and even the south. These were the people who would fight to the death for a king they loved, for whom that king, in turn, must be a good and generous ruler. The crowd was noisy and cheered whenever anyone rode by; I wondered if they would have voice left to greet their new ruler when he finally appeared.

We arrived at the church early and found our places quickly, guided by a page attired in red and gold. It was a splendid scene. In the center of the lawn was the throne, on a dais two steps up from the ground and completely covered with a cloth of gold. Behind it, and up another two steps, was an altar centered with a mammoth jeweled cross that reflected both the rays of the sun and the flames of the seven-branched candelabrum on each side. There were velvet-covered seats nearby for the bishops and priests.

Before long I identified the section set aside for Sir Ector, and then I saw him and Kay take their places. But no Arthur. Perhaps squires did not rank high enough to attend coronations even if they were foster sons of a lord. Or maybe I had just missed seeing him. Sir Ector's place was to the right of ours, but I did not dare such an unladylike act as standing up and peering across the people between us.

Suddenly there was a great swelling of sound beginning some distance away, then growing louder and louder, like one tremendous echo reverberating through the crowds. The king was coming! The cheers became deafening as the people in the stands added their voices to those of the crowd in the streets.

Then all fell silent as the king dismounted and began to walk toward the throne. Riding a magnificent white charger caparisoned in red and gold, he had entered the wide gate next to the church surrounded by a retinue of knights and pages. When he came out from under the shadows of the overhanging cloister roof, the sun touched the gold of his helmet, and he seemed suddenly wrapped in a blazing aura of light. Many in the stands saw this as another miracle and hastily crossed themselves. I forgot all my ladylike training and stared as unblinking as the rest. As he walked toward our section, I even forgot to lower myself to one knee in homage. For suddenly he was right in front of us, and I was catching my breath in disbelief and wonderment. My eyes filled with tears as I looked at the slender figure—dressed all in white and gold under the ermine-trimmed robe of scarlet—who moved slowly but self-confidently, looking neither right nor left, along the path to the throne.

"It's Arthur!" I thought I said it to myself, but I must have uttered the name aloud.

"Yes," whispered my father, "that's the English version of Arcturus, that name I said I could not remember."

"But he is my Arthur. He is Kay's squire."

"Hush, Lionors, people are turning to look at you. He is no squire now. He is king of Britain, son of Uther Pendragon."

The rest, hearing Arthur repeat his vows in a quiet, sure tone, was a blur of color and words. Then he was presented to his people, who responded three times, agreeing to accept him as their king. Following this, each noble went forward to kneel before him and pledge in person to accept him as their liege lord. As my father's heir, under the Roman law, I, too, was to pay homage to him.

When our time came, Father and I moved forward,

71

his strong arm steadying my shaking hand. While we walked, I repeated over what I was to say, taking one step at a time, trying to remain calm. I wanted to feast my eyes on him, but was afraid to look for fear everyone there would see how much I loved him. This was my Arthur before whom the nobles were kneeling.

Finally, Father made his pledge, then turned and led me forward to present me to the king. As I stepped up, Arthur rose, fingering the chain of his robe as though to adjust it. Then he sat down again as I knelt before him. According to custom, I placed my hands between his, but before I could speak, I felt the pressure of more than just his palms. He was holding the medallion I had given him which contained my braided hair! He was reassuring me with this token of our promise to each other, and under its calming pressure I was able to repeat my vows of allegiance in a loud, clear voice. When I finished, I looked up, to be reassured a second time by his warm smile. I was almost too shaken to move when Arthur unexpectedly rose again from the throne and helped me to my feet. Somehow I took Father's arm, and he led me back. I dug my nails into my palm to keep from falling.

"Well," Father said when we returned to our place, "I never would have allowed you to go through this if I had thought you would be so nervous."

That night Arthur presided at a banquet. How different it was from the banquet at the manor when we held hands throughout the meal. This time he was the length of the room away. There were musicians and minstrels to entertain, each of the latter trying to outdo the others with new ballads about Arthur and his coronation. As the evening became more relaxed and gayer under the influence of the wine and the friendly smile of their new monarch, the younger guests found it impossible to remain in the seats and urged everyone to find partners and join them in the livelier folk dances. In the midst of this, Arthur excused himself but urged that the dancing and drinking continue, even though etiquette required that everyone leave when he did. I met the younger knights that Father had spoken about and could not help but have a good time amidst all the witty conversations and admiring glances. When Kay joined us, I was not displeased. Taller than I remembered, he bore his knighthood with less pride than I would have thought. Perhaps having Arthur as his king rather than as his squire had humbled him.

"Arthur wants to see you," Kay said as soon as he could speak to me out of earshot of the others. "See if we can move unnoticed over to that door."

Once away from the merrymakers, I followed Kay down a narrow hall to a small room furnished with few chairs but in which a cheerful fire burned. Arthur stood in the middle of the room looking very regal in his white and gold. I wanted to run to him, and I did call out "Arthur" before I regained my dignity and remembered to sink to the floor in a deep bow and address him as "Your Majesty."

"Not between us, Lionors." His smile broadened into a grin. "Or do I have to help you to your feet again?"

"Please! Don't remind me. I have already been chastised enough."

At that we both began laughing.

"I can't believe it, Arthur, I just can't believe it. I was stunned when I saw you this morning."

"I can't really believe it yet, either. Being a king takes getting used to. I am trying, but finding it hard. One minute a squire, the next a king."

"How did you learn—when did you find out? We heard a strange tale of some sword in a stone."

Gradually I was relaxing, and the tension that had built up in me since the morning was easing as I sensed that Arthur was still the same person as when I had seen him last. But was he really the same now that he was king and not the future manager of Sir Ector's estates? I had worried about his being worthy enough to be my husband; now I chilled at the thought that I was not worthy to be his wife. I forced my attention back to what he was saying.

"It's true about the sword. Sometime I will tell you the secret of how I pulled it out. I—and the sword—

73

were given by my father, Uther Pendragon, to his closest friend and confidante because he feared for my life if anything should happen to him before I came of age. He knew that a child as king would be as helpless as a dove among hawks. This friend took me to Sir Ector while I was still a baby to be reared as his foster son. At that time Ector knew only that I was to live with him and be protected. I am sure he must have suspected who I was during the years when there were rumors that Uther had fathered a son. The friend I mentioned was Merlin, who was also with Uther when he was dying, and he pledged not to reveal my identity until the proper time. People fear and distrust Merlin, so if he had just announced who I was, no one would have believed him. People like mystery and the supernatural, so he thought up the sword in the stone to appeal to their imaginations.

"I do not know how the tale came to you, but you might be interested in knowing how it really happened. While everyone was in church before the tournament, Merlin had the stone placed in the middle of the cloister greensward. When the service was over, the people were amazed to find this object in the churchyard, for it had not been there before. The consensus was that it must be a memorial of some kind, perhaps to King Uther himself. With everyone eager to get the joust started, not much more was thought about it at the time. When we arrived at the field, Kay discovered he had forgotten his sword. Actually, Merlin had slipped it from his scabbard while Kay's attention was focused on the stone. Kay sent me back to Sir Ector's house for the sword, but everyone had left and the place was locked. Then I remembered the memorial at the church. At this point I was still ignorant about who I was or the part I was playing in Merlin's charade. I only knew that I had to find a sword for Kay. When the one in the stone wouldn't yield to my first attempts, I remembered a trick Merlin had once taught me, and giving it a particular twist, I pulled it out easily. Hoping I had gotten a sword in time to escape Kay's wrath, I rushed back to the field. When Sir Ector inquired and I told him where I had found the sword, he asked to examine it. Only then were the words visible that said whoever pulled it out would be King of Britain.

"The next few hours were hectic. The tournament forgotten. I must have pulled that sword out over a hundred times, with everyone else trying to do the same but not succeeding. I'll tell you I was grateful when Sir Ector finally said something that convinced them their efforts were in vain. But it was not until the bishop knelt before me that I realized what all the to-do was about. I was the new king. Whew, I'll tell you, that was scary, and I haven't gotten over being scared yet."

Arthur was interrupted in his musings by the entrance of an old man dressed in a plain gray robe.

"Lionors, I want you to meet Merlin."

"How do you do, sir." I turned to Arthur. "He is your teacher that you told me about?"

"Yes, and also my father's very close friend, the one who took me to Sir Ector's."

"That's why he taught you as he did," I said. "Knowing who you were, he prepared you to be king." I reached for the old man's hands. "Merlin, I am glad to know you at last."

"Oh," he answered, "I taught him all I could, but I never brought that glow to his eyes that I see there now. Talk a bit if you must, but do not stay up too late."

With Merlin gone, we became suddenly quiet, clouded by a shyness we had never felt before. We were like two friends who, after being apart for years, greet each other with warm embraces and then find they really have nothing in common anymore. We tried a bit of small talk, but Arthur began yawning, and the silences between grew longer and more oppressive.

"Merlin's right," I said. "You are tired, and I am, too. You go to bed. I'll find Father and have him take me back to our cousin's. I'll see you soon." I said it as a statement, but I knew it was really a question.

"Yes, tomorrow, at the jousting field. I'll look for you there."

He kissed me goodnight, but tender as it was, I felt the kiss was merely an alternative to trying to find something more to say.

I am certain the tournament the next day was a magnificent affair, but I had no heart for it. Arthur, in his special pavilion, was surrounded by many lovely ladies. Even the pageantry and the handsome knights on horseback did not fill the hollow I felt inside. When Kay rode up and asked for a favor to wear on his wrist, I tossed him my scarf without even looking at him. Arthur waved at me once. I was ready to cry until Kay rode up again, and as he lowered his lance in salute, I saw a scrap of paper caught on the point. When Kay nodded in answer to my quizzical expression, I took it off. "Tonight, please, same place."

The sun came out, and I settled back to enjoy the rest of the day.

Later, while I was dressing for dinner, Father came into my room, his face as pale as freshly bleached linen. He had received bad news from home, and it was urgent that we return at once. A disgruntled serf—who said that if there was enough extra grain for Christmas giving, there must be more—had led an uprising against the manor. Two days after we had left, he set fire to the granaries. The fires were out, and most of the grain saved. The uprising was under control, thanks to the competent men left at home, but there was no telling if trouble might start up again.

Knowing we had no choice but to leave, my one thought was to get word to Arthur. Insisting that I needed some time to get my things packed, I set Marta to that task while I was gone. I couldn't hope to see Arthur at the palace, but I could try to reach him through Sir Ector or Kay. Arthur had told me that his foster father had a home in London not far from where we were staying. Ignoring the warnings I had been given about not walking alone through London at night, I grabbed a cloak and hurried out. The streets were darker than ever, and I lost my way several times before I saw the house with Ector's crest over the door.

The man who answered my knock looked me over suspiciously and said, "Sorry, ma'am, Sir Ector has retired. Is there a message for him?"

"Please, tell him Lady Lionors is here."

Before I could say more, I was grateful to hear Kay's familiar voice. "That's all right, Giffon, she is a friend of the family. Please show her up."

The servant led me into a room where Kay sat, but he was not alone, and as I entered, Kay stood up, smiled and left, and I found myself being wrapped close in Arthur's smothering arms. Then just as suddenly he released me, and I thought, one minute a squire, the next a king.

"What brings you here?" Was there a touch of pique in his tone because I had sought him out at a time and place other than the one he had designated?

"I wanted to leave a message for you with Sir Ector."

"Then why not come over here by the fire and give it to me in person."

"Thank you, I will." I could be just as formal as he. "I had no idea how cold it was outside."

While I stood by the fire until I was warm enough to remove my wrap, Arthur remained half way across the room, a strange look on his face.

"There, now," he said, "you look a little less like a frozen waif. Now what was the message that couldn't wait until I saw you later?"

The tone in his voice, the distance he kept between us, forced me to speak in an equally formal manner.

"I wanted to express our regrets, Your Majesty, and to ask your permission to take our leave tomorrow. There has been trouble at the manor—someone tried to attack our granary and then burn it down when he could not get in—and my father feels he must return as soon as possible."

At the words "Your Majesty" I saw Arthur start across the room, then wait until I had finished speaking. He stood before me, defeat and dejection mirrored on his face, but he spoke softly.

"So it's 'Your Majesty' again, not 'Arthur.' Am I—are you—changed so much?"

"I'm sorry, but you suddenly seemed so distant. I was not sure what to say."

"Not distant, preoccupied. Your coming was the answer to an unexpressed wish, but your request is not. I had hoped you would be here for a long time."

"I wish we could," I answered, "but as you see, we must return."

I stayed by the fire, but Arthur moved closer with each word he spoke.

"Lionors, I love you. I have no more right to say it now than I did the last time. I would give up my throne if I could to have you with me from now on, but I cannot."

"I understand, Arthur, really I do."

He was king now. If before he had no right being only a squire, he had less right now when his choice of a wife would not be his alone.

"I need time." He was trying to make sure I would really understand. "I need time to learn to be a king, to govern my people, to unite the kingdom. You said you were stunned to see me. How do you think I felt? One minute I was Kay's squire, going to find a sword for him. The next minute, just by pulling out a sword, I was being proclaimed king. King by birth, maybe, but not by training. I have not spent my life preparing for this role, and I'm frightened. That is why I say I haven't the right to tell you I love you. It means asking you to wait. My work must come first, and I do not feel I should ask you to take second place until I have things well in hand."

"Oh, Arthur, if that's what you mean, I will wait as long as you need me to."

"What I mean? What did you think I meant?" he asked.

"I thought you were trying to tell me you couldn't love me because—well, because you had to have time to find someone else, someone more proper to marry."

"Lionors, I will never love anyone else. There is no one else for me. But if I am to be the king I want to be, there will be months, maybe years of work and some fighting ahead. It will be a lot easier if I know you are waiting for me."

"That is the easiest promise I have ever been asked to make."

Then I tried to lighten the atmosphere a little. "You know, you're not completely untrained. Remember all those lessons Merlin taught you from nature?"

"I've been thinking about them, too, and I think I know what he was trying to tell me. See if you think I have figured some of them out."

Suddenly it was as though we were back again on the island, with Arthur telling me about the fascinating animal habits Merlin had insisted he watch closely. Only this time he was relating them to himself as king. From the spider he learned to beware of webs spun by his enemies. There will be many, and their traps will be just as deadly as the spider's. He must be alert for hidden meanings in what people say. From the ant he could learn to carry a heavier burden than he thought possible or capable of, weights of responsibility and decision. The birds would teach him patience and the foresight not to rush things. Even the best ideas can abort if not brought to full term. Above all, he must try to walk in other people's shoes, to study and know how his people live, to learn how they think. He must never fight for his own glory, but for their safety and peace of mind.

"If I go into battle for them, we will win. If I fight just for myself, we will lose."

"You will be a great king, Arthur. I know you will."

"There will be pressures, I know, for me to marry for political reasons, but I can turn that to our advantage. When I am urged to choose someone from Kingdom A, I will insist that will make an enemy of Kingdom B. Many who swore to accept me did so with their fingers crossed, so I must tread lightly while I

79

work for solidarity. When I have achieved that, I can marry whom I darn well please—and that will be you."

"Just let me know when you want me," I said. "I love you, and I will always be ready when you need me. Learn to be a good king, do what has to be done, and when all is settled, send me word. Will there be many battles?"

"Some, I'm afraid. Will you worry?"

"Yes, and I will pray."

First his arms and then his whole cloak went around me, and I prayed that someday soon I would be as sheltered by his love as I was by his cape. As my mouth responded to the pressure of his, so did my body respond to his body, and I yearned to belong to him wholly and completely.

"Oh, God, Lionors, it will be soon," he whispered. "It will be soon."

When I left him, he was braced against the mantelpiece, head on hand, gazing deep into the fire. Was he already seeing the flames of battle that would face him soon?

We left early the next morning, long before sunup, riding almost day and night to get back to the manor. Yet all was calm when we arrived, those left in charge having gotten things under control, and I regretted our having left so hastily before awaiting further news. The days that I might have spent with Arthur had been wasted by our abrupt departure. Yet I knew the news that my father was returning had forced the dissidents to back off and cause no further trouble. Not being a vindictive man, he did not put the leader to death, but instead dismissed him from our land. Such an act could mean ultimate death if the culprit found no other landowner to take him in. Surly and uttering curses, he left the manor, taking to the woods on foot, though later a horse was missing, and we were sure he had sneaked back to steal it. We had no idea where he went, for none of the neighboring lords had taken him in. But later I learned, much to my regret, what direction he had taken.

Life on the manor returned to normal, and as I went about the daily routine, I awaited the word from Arthur that would take me to him.

⊠ Chapter Five ⊠

But it was to be more than two years before I heard from Arthur again. Messengers brought news of his great battle against the eleven kings who swore to destroy him. Among these were King Brandegoris of Stranggore, King Clarence of Northumberland, King Lot of Orkney, King Urian of Gore, King Idres of Cornwall, King Agwisance of Ireland, and the Kings Cradelman, Nentres, and Carados. Against their massed forces of several thousand men and horses, Arthur and his small army of faithful faced certain defeat. Once again Merlin came to his aid, advising him to send to Brittany for King Ban and King Bors. With their additional strength, the tide turned, and Arthur won the great battle, routing his enemies, but with a tragic loss of men on both sides.

Following this, Arthur turned south and moved against the Saxon invaders; brandishing his famous sword Excalibur, he defeated the Saxons at the Battle of Mount Badon. There were other battles, and the air was filled with the names of many nobles who challenged him in combat, but throughout the land one name sounded above all the others, that of Arthur himself. With each new conquest, he became more admired and loved. He was not only a mightier warrior than his father, the great Uther Pendragon, but he was also adored, whereas his father had been feared.

More news came almost daily, so I was constantly reassured that he was safe, but there was never a personal message for me. I knew truly what he meant when he said being a king had to come first, and I continued to wait.

Meanwhile, word came that Arthur was establishing his court at Camelot, not in London. There on the plains of Salisbury lay an old castle almost in ruins. Some said it had been the fortress of an earlier Celtic king; others said that it was the bastion of an even earlier leader of the Druids. More likely it was the remains of a stronghold built by a Norse or Roman conqueror. But in any event, Camelot was said to be enveloped by the magic aura of a spell cast by a long-forgotten wizard, that only he who would truly unite Britain and seek to establish a perfect kingdom could rebuild the castle. It was true that others had tried to restore it, but always before completion the walls would collapse either by enemy attack or natural causes. Where others had failed, Arthur succeeded, and before long the red dragon flew from the turret of the tallest tower. People felt this augured well for his reign, and again loud were the praises sung for the new king. We were kept apprised of the progress by travelers who passed the manor or stayed to spend a few days. Not only were walls and parapets erected, but lawns and gardens were being laid out and planted. It was to be a place of beauty as well as the center of the kingdom.

On the second anniversary of Arthur's coronation, he was fighting far to the north, but in our village, my father and I presided over a small but gay celebration of thanksgiving. Our serfs and villeins, who had never seen their king and probably never would, were nevertheless proud to live under him and to cheer each time a new victory was announced. To them, Father was Arthur's personal legate, and so he felt it to be his duty as well as a pleasure to join with them in their ritual of offering thanks for the coming of Arthur.

As I promised, I waited. Among visitors to the manor were many young nobles, and while I enjoyed their company, my heart was already taken, and I avoided even mild flirtations. After each such visitor, my father eyed me quizzically, but he never pressed or pressured. As he had once promised me, the choice of a husband would be my own.

The days passed slowly, often tediously, but I tried to keep busy around the manor, taking more and more duties from Marta. Earlier in the year we had lost Aunt Helena, and in spite of our grumblings at her strict ways, we missed her sorely.

Then, in March, my patience was rewarded, if not in quite the manner I had dreamed. A courier from Camelot rode into the courtyard late one afternoon. After being invited in and offered refreshment, he announced the reason for his presence. His Royal Majesty, King Arthur, requested our presence at an Easter celebration of thanksgiving for the victories of the past two years. There would be a mass to begin the festivities, followed by tournaments on the new jousting field as well as hunts on the broad meadows and in the vast forests that surrounded the castle. The prospect of visiting Camelot was exhilarating and eased my disappointment at not having received personal word from Arthur. Perhaps discretion prevented him from singling me out for individual attention. He had bestowed one honor upon us; we were to be his guests in the castle rather than in the tents pitched on the grounds. Whether this was for me or because of my father's age, I could not know.

With Camelot much nearer to us than London, it would take only three days of easy riding for us to cover the miles between. I had two weeks to prepare a wardrobe worthy of a magnificent court. All the most beautiful ladies of the land would be there, many secretly nourishing the hope that Arthur would choose one of them for his queen. I did not worry that I would not be the most beautiful woman there, but I wanted to appear as pleasing as possible in his eyes.

Father allowed Marta and me to rummage through the presses that contained length upon length of beautiful materials he had purchased through the years for my mother, which she had not lived to wear. We selected a sapphire blue velvet for the gown to wear to Easter service. From a lightweight pale-green wool we fashioned a suit for hunting and watching the jousts. It was banded in rich, brown beaver fur. The most beautiful gown of all was made from gold tissue imported from the exotic lands of the East, to be worn at the court banquet. I thought we could not possibly finish in time, but when the day came to leave, everything was packed, and I almost collapsed with relief.

The morning of our departure was overcast, and before we had traveled many miles, we found ourselves in the middle of a downpour. Not far ahead was the Abbey of the Holy Spirit, and Father decided we had better stop there until the worst of the storm was over.

By the time we reached the gates, we were all soaked. The good nuns hurried us in to the fire and brought hot food and drink. Our servants were offered the same courtesies in the kitchen, and space was found in a rude shelter for the horses. The nuns were kindness itself, and we spent a comfortable afternoon, warm and refreshed, while it continued to rain outside. When the weather had not yet cleared by evening, we were invited to spend the night in the guest rooms, which were always kept ready for travelers who sought refuge. The rooms were starkly simple but clean, and we were grateful not to have to try to sleep on the damp ground in makeshift shelters.

Although we had lost several hours by the time we left, for we had joined in the communal morning prayers preceding the simple breakfast, I did not regret the hours spent in the calm presence of these toilers for God. Little did I know that in less than a year I would be seeking sanctuary among them again and not because of inclement weather.

On our way at last, there were no more interruptions. The weather having cleared and turned warm, we enjoyed spending the next nights under the stars sleeping on pallets of straw-filled ticking. By the third night we were in sight of Camelot, its turrets silhouetted against the sunset like ivory chessmen on a pastel-striated alabaster board. Rather than ride on, we chose to stop at a small inn on the edge of an ancient town and to proceed to the castle in the morning.

At dawn, the still winter-brown earth was covered with a thick early mist, not yet dispelled by the sun just rising above the horizon. As we started out, we could see in the distance a single, broad-topped hill, all but its uppermost features still obscured by the mist. Resting on the hill, fog pillowing its base and softening the harsh edges, was Camelot, looking for all the world like a castle in the sky. A single tall tower, a sentinel standing guard over the surrounding countryside, rose from its midst and flew aloft the pennant of the red dragon. The king was in residence.

The courtyard and tremendous main hall were frantically alive with new arrivals and servants bringing in luggage or carrying food and drink to their masters. Bright snatches of conversation filled every corner as old friends greeted one another after long separation. Now and then a hearty laugh and the sounds of back-slapping echoed across the wide expanse of hall.

A young man and woman, assigned to be our personal servants, showed Father and me to our rooms; Marta was too infirm to make the trip this time. We moved up a broad staircase, at the top of which halls led off in both directions. Our quarters were generous in size, and I took a few minutes to become acquainted with mine. The side of the room opposite the door to the hall opened above a low balustrade onto the courtyard below. Slim pillars that ended in curved arches rose from the balustrade to the ceiling, giving the effect of windows through which I could view the busy scene below. The courtyard, more than just a small entryway, was surrounded on all four sides by the castle. In one section of the castle, to the right of my room, a wide double arch led from this inner court to an outer one and to the drawbridge beyond. There were draperies that could be pulled for privacy and that proved heavy enough to shut out sounds as well as light.

Not only was my room large, but everything in it was massive, from the tremendous fireplace that dominated one side wall to the high, huge bed opposite. It struck me at once that it was a particularly masculine room.

During the daytime Arthur was with everyone, riding from one to another of his guests during the hunts and sharing his canopied gallery with various groups at the lists. He had grown a light blond beard and mustache that made him appear mature, but underneath them was still the face of the young man who worried lest he would not be a good king.

The late evenings belonged to us. The second day— after the service in chapel—there was an all-day hunt: for wild boar in the vast forest during the morning, followed by hawking on the plains in the afternoon. Stalking a wild pig was not my idea of a pleasant sport, so I spent the morning alone in my room and then exploring the castle, looking for the library to see if there were any interesting manuscripts I could peruse to wile away my time. One small room had a few volumes, dusty and unread, and I decided that reading was not one of Arthur's loves.

At noon I joined the group of servants who were taking a light lunch out to the hunters. After a morning of no real physical activity, I looked forward to getting on a horse and carrying a well-trained hawk on my wrist. There should be a good supply of small game abounding in and near the woods. When the squires and serfs were sent to harry the quarry from their nests or covies, the small birds and animals would scurry across the meadow, easy prey for the falcons.

By the time we arrived, the hunters had dismounted and were washing in buckets of warm water brought out by the retainers. I joined my father and some of his cronies while we ate the cold repast. Three wild boars had been chased down and stuck with lances, and their captors were walking around extolling the great dangers they had undergone in order to kill the beasts. Now quite dead, the boars appeared harmless until one took a closer look at the great pointed tusks that could completely pierce through a man or horse when the animal was cornered.

Arthur was riding around among his guests, stopping to converse with each group, the figure of a perfect host. He praised the courage of the successful hunters, bragged about the size of the boars, and suggested the order in which the hawking should begin. After he had spoken to my father, he drew me to one side.

"After supper tonight," he said, "I will rise and excuse myself early, saying I have work to do. As soon after as you can, leave and go to your room. I have something I want you to see." Then he rode off before I could do any more than nod.

The rest of the day could not pass quickly enough for me. The hawking was some of the best I had ever seen, but my impatience barely allowed me to join in the cries and congratulations when bird after bird caught its prey. Even when my falcon, a beautifully trained merlin, took off and flew in perfect fashion, circling and diving, I could scarcely take real delight in its performance so eager was I for the afternoon to end. Finally, we began moving back to the castle.

Because the midday meal had been a light lunch, dinner was a mammoth one of many courses: salmon from the cold, clear waters of the river; smaller fish grilled to a crisp, golden brown; haunches of venison; great slabs of mutton and beef; even a few quail, several covies of which had been netted early in the day. To accompany the meats were flagons of ale for those who desired it as well as several varieties of wine.

Most of the guests were tired after the long day in the fields, and following the heavy meal, they were yawning and ready to retire. So no one objected when Arthur rose and asked to be excused to attend to some urgent business of the kingdom. A few men gathered in clusters to continued digesting the dinner along with events of the day. Others grouped around tables to gamble, while the women put their heads together and caught up on the latest gossip. Thus it was not difficult for me to slip away to wait in my room for whatever surprise Arthur had in mind.

I was still in the midst of freshening up when I heard his knock. Saying nothing, he beckoned me to follow him. We went the length of a wide hall to a small staircase that led to an upper level. Here there was a much narrower hall that seemed to be following the inside wall of the castle, going completely around the courtyard. At one point Arthur stopped and opened a narrow door, whispering for me to follow carefully. I could see by the dim light of a single flambeau in the hall that there were more steps. When Arthur closed the door behind me, we were in complete darkness until he struck tinder and lighted a candle. There were stairs all right, rough steps or ledges cut into the stone wall, winding up and out of sight. I guessed we must be at the base of the tower I had seen as we approached Camelot.

With one hand in front holding the candle and the other behind him grasping mine, Arthur led the way slowly up. The steps could have been no wider than the length of a man's foot, so it took all our concentration to keep from falling.

Arthur paused once. "I bet you don't believe I can run up here in the dark, do you?"

"Oh," I said shakily, "I would believe anything right now to avoid an argument that might leave me stranded. But please, just don't show me how you do it."

He laughed and started up again. When next he stopped, we must have reached the top, for he let go of my hand long enough to open a door. I could hear a bolt sliding and a latch being loosened.

"All right, now, here we are. One more step," he assured me, "and you're on solid ground, or at least a solid stone floor."

From the candle in his hand he lit several others, and I was able to catch my breath and look around. We were in a small circular room, obviously near the top of the tower. There was a low table and a couple of benches, but aside from the sconces for the candles, no other furnishings. Yet in spite of the stone walls and plain, rough furniture, it was not a gloomy room. On the contrary, there was an almost cozy, secret-hideaway atmosphere about it.

"Well, how do you like it?" Arthur's question was as eager and as desirous of approval as that of a small boy who has just brought home a new puppy.

"It's—it's very nice." My feeble attempt at sincerity

was completely overlooked by Arthur in his enthusiasm at showing me the place.

"Remember when I told you about the tower room at Sir Ector's?"

I nodded, trying to recall the conversation to which he alluded.

"It was my secret place, the spot to which I fled when I got blue or discouraged because I was left to my own devices while Kay was being trained for knighthood." He paused. "It's hard to believe now that I was ever jealous of Kay. You know, in spite of our change in fortune, in spite of the fact that now he could be jealous of me, he is my closest companion, a stalwart friend. We are more like brothers now than we ever were."

"I'm glad, Arthur. I noticed a change in him, too."

"Anyway, about the room. When I rebuilt this castle, I wanted to include some place where I could get off by myself to work problems out alone, for moments of quiet thought—or just to get away from all the hustle and bustle of court life. There is always something going on or someone wanting to see me. I can't even be alone when I'm dressing."

Arthur finally noticed that during this recital I had been standing in the center of the room.

"Here, Lionors, what am I thinking of." Reaching behind a bench, he pulled out some old pillows. "Put these on the floor and sit down. Those benches are too hard."

Arranging one on the floor and another at my back, I was able to construct a fairly comfortable chair.

"Then," he went on, "I remembered my old tower room, and I wondered if I couldn't have one here. Checking over the ruins before actual restoration beagn, I saw a group of heavy stones laid in a square, much smaller in size than any of the others that seemed to indicate walls separating rooms. When we tried to move them, they were so deeply embedded that I knew they had been in that form originally. The location was perfect for the tower, just inside one of the four corners. That would be my tower. I indicated the size I wanted and even decided on the stone stairs. Even though no one else has a key, if someone should open the door, those stone steps would discourage them from climbing up."

"I certainly agree with that," I nodded. "No one in his right mind would come up here unescorted."

"But you do like my room?"

"Yes, I like it."

"Well," he said as he helped me, or rather pulled me, to my feet, "come see the windows then. There's just these two, but through them I can look out over the whole countryside. It's too dark now, of course, but I'll bring you up here in the daytime."

We left the window, and Arthur found more pillows so he could join me sitting on the floor. He leaned back, exhaling a very long, deep sigh.

"Things are going well now, aren't they?" I asked.

"Quite well, I think. It's taken longer than I hoped to subdue some of the opposition. But then others came over without a fight, so I guess it's balanced out."

"Were the battles very fierce?"

"I don't like battles at all," he frowned. "At first I thought it would be exhilarating to ride into the fray, leading my men in a gallant charge. But when I saw how many had to die—both theirs and ours—in order for me to win, I began to despise, and sicken at, the sight of blood. The men on foot were the worst—no way of escaping, no armor to protect them." He stopped and laid his head on his drawn-up knees. I said nothing.

In a minute he went on. "It's been my dream," he continued, "to unite all of Britain, not with me as conqueror, but simply to bring all the kings and lords together in a unified nation. I don't want to rule over all of them; I just want us to live side by side in peace. Unfortunately, I am forced to fight, to subdue and then take over because some can't see it that way. For them it has to be me or them, not both of us. They can't understand that we can be equal, not one above the other."

Arthur paused only long enough to shift to a more comfortable position.

"I had a dream one night of a tremendous round table, no head, no foot, each man's place as important as every other. I told Merlin about it, and he said I would know when the right time came to build it."

"I've never heard of such a table," I said, "but it certainly would be worth trying. By the way, where is Merlin?"

"I don't know. He comes and goes, and I never know when I'll see him. But he always seems to appear when I need him, so I don't worry about him."

The hour was late, so after a few more minutes Arthur led me back down the stone steps and to my room.

Again the next night, Arthur knocked on my door. This time he led me along the hall to stairs that went up and out onto the parapet encircling the entire roof of the castle. I shivered in the clear, cool air, and he put his wrap around my shoulders.

The black onyx sky above us glittered with a million stars, winking on and off like points of candle flames reflected in a slowly undulating stream. In the distance small bonfires were warming travelers who had stopped for the night or late revelers enjoying a last noggin of ale before going home. The silence was broken only now and then by shouts or challenges from changing sentries. But for me the night was ours alone.

"There's Orion," I said, not really wanting to break the stillness but feeling the need to say something. "And there's the great bear, Ursa Major. There's Arcturus; your name in Latin means 'guardian of the Bear,' you know."

"You astound me," Arthur exclaimed. "When did you learn astronomy? And Latin?"

"Oh, my father and I frequently stroll in the courtyard at night, and he taught me all about the stars. There's the North Star; learn that, and it will always guide you home."

"And I suppose you just happened to pick up Latin during the day?"

"As a matter of fact, I did—every day. Father has a large library of manuscripts. Every day, as long as I can remember, my father and I have read together at least an hour. I've read Virgil and Caesar, but Ovid is my favorite Roman author. Do you know him?"

"No." Arthur frowned impatiently. "Reading did not play a very important role in my early life; Merlin believed in a more practical type of education."

"You must read Ovid someday. He wrote wonderful stories about the Roman gods and goddesses. Some of them are funny, some sad. I always felt sorry for Narcissus who fell in love with his own reflection in a pool and then drowned when he tried to embrace it."

"That's not sad," Arthur laughed. "That's just silly."

"Oh. no." I argued, "Ovid was really saying that it's a kind of death for anyone who loves himself more than he does other people. But I like best the funny ones, like the story of Vulcan who made a golden net so fine he was able to trap Venus and Mars in bed. Then he pulled up the net and invited all the other gods to come and look. I can't imagine most husbands having such a sense of humor."

"Husband?"

"Yes, didn't you know that Venus was married to Vulcan? Mars was her lover."

"You read too much" was all Arthur said.

"More than that. I've been copying some of the old scrolls onto manuscript pages to be bound into books."

"That's a job for monks, not for a young lady."

"What else should I be doing during the two years I didn't hear from you? I thought if I was going to live like a *religieuse,* I might as well be occupied like one. Would you rather I had flirted?"

"Well, I've something better for you to do now." He put his arms around me. "You can tell me how much you love me."

"I will if you stop nibbling my ear."

"It's getting colder," he said. "Let's go up to the tower."

Once there, I settled down among the pillows on the floor, but Arthur remained standing by the window.

"Lionors, I want to marry you as soon as we can."

"I've waited two years, darling, to hear you say that."

"Please don't commit yourself until you hear something I have to tell you."

Gradually, he revealed a dark and deadly secret. He spoke in agonizing tones, like a man pulling out a barbed arrow from his vitals, enduring the pain, knowing he must suffer the agony or die. The pain was intense, but the relief—even with a scar—would be worth it.

As word followed word, I ached to comfort him, but for most of the time I stayed quietly in my seat.

"I intended never to father a bastard. For eighteen years I suffered the limbo of bastardy; worse, I didn't even have the balm of knowing who my parents were. Oh, I was loved, well taken care of. No one could have been a kinder foster father than Sir Ector, and Kay was truly an older brother. But always there, beneath the calm surface, lay the truth. Like an unseen river that flows just below what seems like solid earth, ready to gush forth through the crust at any moment and crumble my steady world . . ."

"But," I interrupted.

"Please, Lionors, let me go on. No, it's true. I'm not a bastard. Although conceived illegitimately, I was born in wedlock. But you see, I did not *know* that. I used to try to imagine what my mother and father looked like, who they were, why they had given me up. Had they died? Were they ashamed of me? Eventually, reason told me that one of them must have been of fairly high estate, or I would not have been given to Ector to raise. But then, I thought, maybe I had been left at his door, and being the kind person he is, he couldn't just let me die. These thoughts didn't torture me too often, and most of the time life was very good.

"Later, learning who my father was made me even more determined to live a continent life. I respect Uther for his greatness as a king, for his ability to unite much of Britain. I know also his fame for sowing his seed at random across the land. How many more of his bastards lie awake at night wondering who they are, enduring a life of shame in far less favorable circumstances than mine? How Uther spent his passions was his affair, but I did not want to emulate him in that way.

"But fate—or my own stupidity—undid all my fine resolves. About eighteen months ago we were having a wild celebration, honoring a decisive victory over one of the Northern factions. It was a double celebration because King Lot of Orkney had finally shown his colors and come over to our side. The strength of the two forces had been in balance until he sent his men and the battle was won, the enemy routed, and the survivors sent scampering over the northern borders. There was toast after toast, and I became drunk. Worse than that, I was violently, disgustingly sick. Talk of continence! I couldn't even hold my liquor. One of the varlets took me to my bed, insisting I drink something that he assured me would settle my stomach and let me sleep it off.

"Hours later I awoke, no more queasy stomach, no headache, feeling only a calm, almost satisfied, lassitude throughout my body. I lay there, eyes closed, grateful for the draught that had restored my sense of well-being. I felt some shame at my behavior, but no real guilt. Then gradually I remembered dreaming, a fantastically realistic dream. The events were clearer and more rational than with most dreams. In it I had awakened to see a small, slim woman—older than I, but still young—with very long, very straight black hair falling over her shoulders and down her back. Wearing a simple white shift, she was gliding out of the shadows and toward my bed. No words were said between us, but I had the feeling she kept whispering my name over and over. In the dream I made love to her. The dream stopped there, or at least I didn't remember her leaving.

"Try to imagine my dismay when I then opened my eyes and saw lying beside me, her dark hair spread out on the pillow next to mine, this same woman. It had not been a dream at all. Gradually, it dawned on me that the sleeping potion must have been drugged. But that did not answer my question of why I should be the victim of such a secretive—and as I knew later, a treacherous—act. She still slept, and I wondered if perhaps she was some maiden who, with a simple weakness, thought she could rise from her lowly station by bearing the king's child. But she was no maiden; of that I was certain. More memories came flooding back, and I knew she was an experienced woman who knew how to lead a young man through his first encounter."

"But, Arthur, you were innocent. Do you think I blame you when you were drugged?"

"Please, Lionors, let me go on to the end. I have to tell you everything, and I don't know whether I can if I hear your voice.

"I might have considered myself an innocent victim, but Merlin taught me that a man is always responsible for his acts no matter where he feels the blame should lie. I had gotten drunk, though I often wonder now if perhaps one of those goblets had been drugged. Nonetheless, I had allowed myself to lose control. No, I was guilty, and not just for that one night. She stayed with me three days; I had broken my vows, so what did three more days matter."

"And there is a child." I didn't need to ask it as a question. It was a statement of fact.

"I have a son, but more than that, he is also my nephew. Yes, you can look in horror. I committed incest with my own sister. Remember I said that Lot had just joined us; also, I was only gradually learning about my parentage. I was vaguely aware that my mother had older children by the Duke of Cornwall. I did not then know that one of her daughters had married King Lot, nor, for that matter, had I met Lot's wife. So the dark-haired beauty I took pleasure with for three days was my own half-sister."

"But she must have known!"

"Oh, she knew. She had known from the moment I was acknowledged as Uther's son."

"Then why?"

"Because she hates and fears me, as she despised my father. She could never seek revenge on him for

96

what he did to her father, so she transferred her loathing for my parentage to me. I know there are many versions of my birth, and maybe you've heard them all, but let me tell you the true story as told to me by Merlin, who was present at all the events. There are many who call Merlin a magician, but as I've told you before, there is no magic in what he does. He is merely more attuned than other men to natural law and how to use it for one's own purpose. But to go on. Gorlois, the Duke of Cornwall, and Igraine, his wife, were at Uther's court for several weeks. During that time Uther found himself more and more attracted to Igraine, and she to him. The duke was much older than she, and her marriage to him had been the usual one of convenience, with no genuine love on either side. They were compatible, and he was kind. But around Uther she felt the first stirrings of real passion for a young, virile man who she knew desired her as she did him. Although they made no attempt to consummate their affair during a busy court season, the duke became suspicious and carried her back to Tintagel. The castle there was known as an impregnable stronghold, and there Igraine could be kept inviolate, or so her husband thought. He himself went to his castle at Terrabil, there to mass his troops and ride against Uther, whom he now considered his enemy.

"Merlin knew of these plans, and when he told Uther, the king invoked Merlin's aid to get him inside Tintagel. He and Igraine had pledged their love, so he knew he would be welcome. There are those who say that Merlin used his magic to transform Uther into Duke Gorlois, or at least to make Uther look like him, and more of his powers to spirit him through the walls since no one saw them. However, there was no need for magic even if Merlin had such power. Igraine had simply received word by a trusted servant of Merlin's that the king was coming. The postern gate, normally bolted shut, was left unlatched; the door to a secret stairway was set ajar, and then very simply amid the darkness of a moonless night, Merlin, the King, and only two other men slipped into Tintagel.

"They did not storm the gates, as others would have it, surrounded by a mighty force who killed helpless varlets, nor did Merlin whip up a cloud of fog to hide them from the guards. It is true that their way was not an easy one, hazarded round by men loyal to the duke who would as soon spear the king as they would a wild boar. Uther wore no insignia, but even so, his stature and features would have betrayed him to anyone who sought his death. The approach to the castle must perforce be made by way of the rocky path that rose almost vertically over a hundred feet up the craggy side of the cliff above the treacherous waters of the cove. Below them the waves dashed against boulders or rushed back in tortuous whirlpools born in subterranean caves. The only steps were the shifting rocks.

"There was a broad, grassy approach across an open lea, normally safe in the sense that there were few bushes or trees that could conceal an ambush. But this way led directly to the main gate and drawbridge, heavily guarded by the duke's men; the very ones, incidentally, who swore that the king must have entered by magic since they did not see him. Obviously, they spread such a rumor both to protect themselves against claims of negligence on their part and to take advantage of the superstitions surrounding Merlin.

"In order to mask his actions of the night, Uther had sent a small force to skirmish outside the walls of Terrabil where the duke had stationed himself, the assumption being that Uther was with these men. There the two forces were joined, and the duke was killed. Before it was known that Uther had actually been at Tintagel that night, it was bruited about that he, himself, had killed the Duke of Cornwall. Later, rumors held that Uther had had the duke murdered. When I was born, Uther called on Merlin to place me with some trusted lord for fear that his enemies would try to kill his only legitimate male heir. And so I lived with Sir Ector, the truth of my birth being hidden from all the world as well as from myself.

"All this, then, is the basis for Morgause's hatred. She saw the night of my conception as a double treachery—against her mother whom, she thought, the king had raped and against her father, murdered by Uther's command if not by the king himself. Her father dead, her mother dishonored, she could only bide her time, the hatred for the king growing ever larger inside her like a malignant cancer that spreads its poison to all parts of the body. The marriage of the king to her mother only helped to make her hatred more deadly, not more benign. I think her only aim at first was to get me in her power, to weave an enchanted web around me, so as to assure a strong position for herself and Lot. But with the knowledge she was pregnant, she knew she had the perfect weapon to dishonor me and bring about my downfall.

"My thoughtless act of passion was more than just fathering an illegitimate child. I had committed adultery with Lot's wife and incest with my own sister."

Through all this last part I listened in abject silence. What was done was done, but loving Arthur as I did, I could forgive all. Inside I still felt that he was innocent, if not of a young man's lust, at least of conscious adultery and incest. He had been betrayed as surely as the Duke of Cornwall had been. If innocence were not enough, if he must suffer the guilt, publicly and in his own conscience, could I not provide some of the strength he would need to rise above the tragedy and be the great king I knew he was capable of being? It was for that reason—to keep from going down under the burden of guilt—that Merlin had taught him so much about life.

More to the point, would he accept my love and recognize it was love and not pity that I felt for him? No experience had prepared me for this; I had no example to follow to guide me to the right words or actions. And my first words *must* be the right ones or I would lose Arthur for good. I doubted that he realized he had been telling all this to a young woman ignorant of much of the world. Would he be chagrined when he realized just what he had revealed to one still young and unmarried? Or perhaps he was trying to show me how much he loved and trusted me—and needed me.

He seemed almost unaware of my presence as he went on talking, as though to himself.

"Adultery, incest, and then murder. Morgause returned home with Lot, and I never saw her again. Even if I could have sought her out, in my ignorance I did not know that there are ways to prevent the birth of a living child. I know now there are drugs, but I doubt I could have gotten to her. In my desperate state I rationalized that the child would be considered Lot's, trying to postpone the inevitable, the realization that she wanted my damnation. At last I knew I must act in haste soon after the child was born. I plotted his murder, a compounding of guilt. One sin, the Greek tragedians believed, as Merlin once told me, begets another and then another. Something went awry, a mix-up of identity, and the wrong baby was killed. Fate would not even allow me that horrible way out of my dilemma. Not only was nothing I wanted accomplished, but worse, an innocent child was dead."

All this time, Arthur had been standing by the window, his hands whitened with pain from gripping the stone sill. During most of the recitation he had kept his eyes fixed on the stars as though seeking guidance, but now he turned his face toward the ground, and from a slight bending of his body toward the casement, I feared that he planned to jump. A plunge from the height of the tower window would mean instant death or, at the least, a mutilated body. Perhaps that would be his atonement for his mutilated soul.

Instinctively, I reached out and touched him—no handclasp, no embrace, just a touch. Unwittingly, I had done exactly the right thing. From his breast came a long, agonizing sigh, and with it he expelled all the pent-up grief and guilt of the past year and a half.

Never again did he mention that past nor did I refer to it. Unlike his dream that became a reality, the occurrences before this moment took on the nature of an illusion. Not that we would ever forget, nor could we erase them from existence. But if they haunted each of us in the dark silences of the night when we were apart, at least they never came between us when we were together.

We were not married during that spring visit, but we were formally betrothed. For one thing, Arthur had two more campaigns to undertake—one to the north and one to the east—before he could return to Camelot and start being, as he said, a ruler and not a warrior, and he didn't want to have to leave me to go into battle right after our wedding. For another, he wanted the court goldsmiths and jewelers to create a crown for me to wear on our wedding day.

At his mention of the word *crown,* a shudder went through me, like a demon dancing on my grave, and from some vast, unsounded depths of memory came the words: "You will be an uncrowned queen." Visions of a child sitting by a fire listening to the voice of an old crone. Did it bode good or ill? Then good sense restored my reason. Even if her words were those of a true seer, they probably merely meant that I wouldn't have a formal coronation.

At my request, we didn't have the betrothal ceremony in the large church with all of the court and guests in attendance. When Arthur suggested we have a private affair, with just the two of us, I was pleased at his thoughtfulness. I didn't know it then, but that decision was to make all the difference in my life. I had come to a fork in the road, and later I often wondered if I had chosen the wrong path.

"Merlin has returned to the court," Arthur said, "and I know he'll be happy to perform the ceremony. As a priest of the ancient religion, his words will be just as binding as those of a priest of the church. In a way, he has really been my father confessor all my life. There's a tiny chapel beneath the main tower, and we can meet Merlin there tomorrow night."

Moved almost to tears by the thought that I would soon belong forever to Arthur, I could only hold him tighter and bury my head in his broad chest.

The chapel was very small, with a low vaulted ceiling, and could have held no more than a dozen people comfortably, but its intimate atmosphere drew us closer together. At one end was a miniature altar covered with a fine linen cloth and lighted with two candles. Merlin, in the ritual robes of his priesthood, stood before it, and as he said the words that joined Arthur and me together for life, he held our hands between his. The ceremony concluded with Arthur putting on my finger the ring that I had worn on a chain around my neck since he had given it to me as a token of his love in return for my medallion.

Our vows of betrothal bound us to a promise of marriage at some later ceremony. Although not yet Arthur's wife, I knew that the promises we made to each other that night were considered as unbreakable as marriage vows. Only death or an act of divorcement could separate us now.

From the chapel we went to the tower room. Instead of just the benches and pillows, the floor was covered with thick skins of rich fur, warm and soft to the touch. New velvet pillows were scattered around, and in the center was a fine table covered with a lace cloth on which rested gold plates and goblets filled with food and wine. Candles in tall silver candlesticks lit the room with a warm glow. A real wedding supper awaited us.

"Arthur!" I was stunned. "Who did all this?"

"I did. I told you no one else ever came up here."

"You brought all this up here? By yourself? How long did it take?"

"At least six or seven trips. But it was worth it to see your face light up when I brought you in."

"When did you find time?" I asked. "You were busy with the court all day."

"Most of it I did last night after you went to bed. Then I brought the food and lit the candles just before I came by your room tonight. I wanted it to be perfect."

"It is, Arthur, absolutely perfect."

"Then come here, little one, so I can hold you and tell you how much I love you."

That night, in the secret tower room, apart from all the world, I became Arthur's wife.

102

We had only four more nights together. As before, Arthur played host to all the guests during the day or spent long hours with my father and other seasoned fighters discussing strategy for the upcoming campaigns. From the little I heard, I gathered that groups north of the border were massing for what might be an invasion. Their forces had increased, their strength grown, and there were additional threats that they would be joined by other forces from across the northern sea.

Each night Arthur excused himself to go to his study to work. Locking the door behind him, he did work briefly and then entered my room, which adjoined his study, through a secret door.

"You mean," I asked, "you knew all the time that door was there?"

"I designed the castle, remember," he said. "Why do you think I put you in this room?"

No woman could be more adored than I was those nights. Arthur was an ardent but gentle lover, a man of great passion and tender caresses. We laughed, we loved, we talked far into the night. Many were the plans we made during those quiet hours. Then we slept until just before dawn when Arthur would awaken and return to his study, to fall asleep again on a narrow cot.

If only those days could have gone on forever, I wouldn't have minded sharing his busy hours with others, but all too soon word came from the north that the uprising had begun. Everyone now concentrated on preparations for moving out at the earliest possible moment. Even my father was caught up in the anticipation of the largest maneuvers ever to be staged at the border. He insisted he was strong enough to go along, and Arthur said he would welcome his attending as an adviser. Then he assured me that he wouldn't let my father get anywhere near the actual fighting, but his advice would be invaluable.

I wanted to stay at the castle, but Arthur insisted I return home.

"Remember," he whispered, "you have something

103

important to do. Prepare yourself to return here as my queen. No arguments now, you promised to obey."

"No arguments, I promise."

There were no tears at parting, but I did a little silent weeping as I rode home, protected by my father's retainers.

⊠ *Chapter Six* ⊠

Three months later, on a warm, sultry morning in July, I walked through the back kitchen garden to the orchard in search of a cool, shady spot where I would not be disturbed. Just beyond the grove of fruit trees was a spring almost hidden by the branches of a large willow that drooped to the edge of the water. Next to the spring was a small stone seat weathered by years and green with moss.

For some reason I was not surprised to see Merlin seated there—not surprised but alarmed, for there had been no word about the fighting at the border. Hot as it was, a sudden chill ran through me.

"Good morning, Lionors." Merlin rose from the seat as I approached.

"Good morning, Merlin. What brings you here? Is there news from the north?"

"There is good news. Arthur's forces have won, and your father will soon be returning home. But I came to see you." He spoke the last words in a quiet tone.

"Then you were on your way to the house," I said. "Shall we walk back, and I can get you something refreshing to drink? We can sit in the garden."

"Thank you," he answered, "but this spring water has quenched my thirst. Since it's cool under this tree, I'd rather stay here where I've been waiting for you to come."

"You knew I was coming this way?"

"Yes, I called you here. You are not surprised, are you?"

"No," I answered, "I guess not. I should never be surprised at anything you do."

"You look pale, Lionors," Merlin said. "Are you well?"

"I'm well," I answered, "but I did have a slight fever and a rash, or breaking out, a few weeks ago."

"Fever? Breaking out?"

"Oh, very mild," I said. "Just two or three days, but it left me easily tired, and this is the first time I've walked this far."

"Well, take care of yourself, child."

I loved Merlin's looks. There was a gentle strength about them that was always reassuring. His face bore witness to the cares of his many years, yet it shone with a serenity a child might envy.

"You've come from Arthur, haven't you?" I asked.

"From his encampment, yes, but not with his knowledge."

"I don't understand."

He put his arms around me and led me to the seat. Quietly but steadily, he told me that I must no longer think about marrying Arthur. "The time is coming when he must enter into a marriage that will help unite Britain."

"But Merlin," I sobbed, "we . . ."

"I know, my dear, you two are betrothed. I was there; I was the one you shared your secret with and was the one who performed the ceremony. But it was secret; no one else knows."

"That makes it no less real," I cried out. "You know the betrothal is as serious and as binding as marriage itself. You know he loves me, Merlin, and I love him. We thought of ourselves as married. No—no, he can't marry someone else!"

"Listen to me, Lionors." Merlin spoke gently, quietly, as though to a child who would not, or could not, understand. "It was in secret, nor am I a priest of the church. I cannot tell anyone of this. It must remain a secret, a simple ceremony that two young people shared because they wanted to seal their love in some way. But it must end there."

106

"But it doesn't end there," and I stopped to let an unbidden moan escape my lips. "It doesn't end with that. I—there is something you must know."

"I do know already." Merlin reached over and took my hands in his. His hands were cool and soothing, and somehow with their very touch my body ceased to tremble, and the words I had ached to cry out were silenced. "I know, Lionors. You are carrying his child, and I'm pleased and happy."

"Happy, how can you be happy with me? You know I'm carrying his child; you say we can't be married, and yet you say you're happy for me. You must be some kind of a fool, Merlin!"

Then I saw the pain on his face, and I was sorry I had spoken so.

"I'm sorry, Merlin. I didn't mean that. I know you're no fool, but I don't understand your words."

"I said I was happy; I didn't say I was happy for you; I meant for the future. You say you love Arthur."

"I love him more than life itself," I answered. "I'm not sure I can go on living now. It would be better that I die than not to marry Arthur and to have to bear his bastard. Don't worry, Merlin. I won't harm him in any way."

"If you love him more than life itself, do you love him enough to give him your life and continue to live?"

"What do you mean?"

"Are you strong enough to love Arthur and all of Britain, too?"

"Your words puzzle me." I frowned.

"If your love is big enough for Arthur, it must also encompass all of Britain. Arthur is Britain, you know. As a king, he is also the country. He must be a strong, good king, and you can help him achieve this goal."

Merlin then grew quiet, as though searching for just the right words, although I had no doubt he knew exactly what he wanted to say. But in that quiet moment those other words returned again from out of the past. "You will be a queen, but you will die uncrowned and unknown." So I spoke first, not waiting for Merlin to continue.

"Go on, Merlin. Tell me what you came to say. I think I am ready."

"Good. I knew you would be." He smiled, "Let me say a few words that I think will comfort you some. Then I'll tell you all I can. First, I think the child you are bearing will be a girl. This will be less hard for you and for the child. A son who is a bastard has a much heavier burden than a daughter. I know. I was one myself. A boy needs to know who his father is and to be acknowledged as his son. My early years were difficult ones, outwardly because I was scoffed at, treated as less than nothing, but inwardly the pain was greater. I longed to know the seed from which I had sprung. I found out, and the pain became less. Enough about me, however; it is about you and your daughter you wish to know."

Merlin then went on to explain what I should do. When the time came that my condition would ordinarily become apparent, long, full robes would hide it. I was to tell no one except Marta, who had been my nurse and was my closest servant. Two months before the child was due, I was to tell my father that I would like to go into the Abbey of the Holy Spirit for a period of quiet and rest.

"He will understand and be eager for you to go because there will be some turmoil in your neighborhood, and it might be necessary for him to go out and fight. He will be glad to have you out of the manor during that time.

"When the child comes," Merlin went on, "I will be with you. All this I will have arranged at the abbey before you come. They will be prepared for your arrival and will have everything ready. Your daughter will stay at the abbey and be cared for there while you return home."

"Am I never, then, to see her or she to know that I'm her mother?"

"That will come in good time," he said. "My plans go far into the future. You will know her, and she will know you. She will be of great comfort to you and to

108

her father in the years to come. You know that Arthur has another child?"

"Yes, a son; he told me about him."

"Mordred, an unfortunate birth. It is to my everlasting shame that I was away and did not prevent it. But your daughter will be everything to him that Mordred is not. And I see no other children for Arthur. Mordred will bring him only sorrow, but your daughter will bring him peace and comfort and in the end will render him great service and aid. So will you, my dear. Marry whom he must, his wife will never give him real peace or happiness. Only you can do that."

"How," I asked, "if I am never to see him again?"

"Ah, be careful. You are reading things into my words that are not there. I did not say you would not see him again. You will see him, although perhaps not often. He will turn to you during moments of greatest pain and strife, and though perhaps real happiness will be denied you both, you will find some comfort when you are together."

"No real happiness," I echoed.

"Arthur was born to be a great king. I trained him for that myself. But no man is promised happiness. However, you will know satisfaction and a sense of peace in the knowledge that you are doing what is right and best. You will achieve a kind of greatness, though your name will be unknown. You will be the one who really holds Britain together, and to you will be granted the care of Arthur when, many years from now, he will no longer be king."

I couldn't understand all that Merlin was saying. My mind was in a whirl, but I was willing to put myself into his hands, to do whatever he said had to be done, and I knew somehow he was trying to tell me that all would be well, that my life would have meaning even if I could not be Arthur's wife and queen. One phase of my life had ended; of that I was sure. The months that had been filled with such great joy and fulfillment were past, and a new life, harder but of more value, was beginning.

"I can promise you this." Merlin was speaking as

though through a mist. "If you believe in me and do as I say, you will not be sorry."

"Oh, Merlin," I said, "you are always so wise. I know what you have meant to Arthur, and I'll try to believe that you can mean the same to me. But I wish you could cast a spell and let me just sleep away the next few years."

He smiled. "I can do better than that. Believe me, you would not want to be asleep during the days ahead and miss some of the greatest experiences of your life. Would you miss having your child or knowing of Arthur's pleasure when he learns he has a daughter? Oh, he will know and be in touch with you. I can do this for you. I can cast a spell, if you wish to call it that, which will remove all traces of the sorrow you now reveal in your face, and I will give you peace of mind and an easy spirit that will be with you from now on. Return to the manor. I'll see you again soon. Whenever you need me, I will be here. I'll know, and I'll come to you."

I started back along the path that led through the orchard and by the river. I turned just once to bid Merlin good-by, but he had already gone. The whirlpool I passed, where the river deepened, tempted me, but I moved on. Merlin said I should live, should give up my life, not to death but to Arthur and Britain, and the least I could do was try. I felt better, as Merlin had promised, and though I had to pause now and then to control the weeping, I was quiet and calm when I reentered the house.

The months went by slowly after I saw Merlin. I filled my days by assuming the responsibilities of a lady of the manor. In August the harvesting began, and since the weather had been good and the land generous, the carts that brought the lord's share to our courtyard were overflowing. Day after day I sat at the table in the center of the court with my father and the steward, later with just the steward when my father was busy elsewhere. We checked as each lot was weighed and measured, then consigned it to the granaries from which the grain would go to the mill to be ground into flour, to storehouses for feed, or to other storehouses for reserve to be used later as needed. One granary would remain locked until the end of the following summer, its contents saved in case of famine or poor crops.

When the orchards began to bear bushel after bushel of fruit I spent time in the kitchen supervising the cooks in selecting those fruits firm enough to be stored, and those that should immediately be put into casks as stewed fruit or sweet jelly. The kitchen, always busy, became the bustling life center of the house as women were hired from the village to help preserve the overflowing mounds of fruit for the winter months. We were anxious this year to store as much food as possible because of the threat of danger from the west. While our workers picked the fruit from the trees, the villagers were allowed to glean the windfalls from the ground, so every woman and child on the manor lands was busy from dawn to dusk.

Because of my family's historical position of neutrality and mediation, we had never been under siege. Nevertheless, my father had taken steps to protect his people. He had built large storehouses in which they could put a portion of their own goods. These storehouses were within the great outer wall of the manor and therefore could be safeguarded along with our provisions if necessary. Although our manor was not as easily defensible as a moated castle, it would take a powerful, long drawn-out siege to capture it because of its position.

So each year the serfs and freemen brought the goods they wished to have stored. Each load was weighed and the amount placed beside the name of the owner. Then, during the year, the owner could request amounts to be doled out. An accurate record was kept of the proceedings. Unlike the few other lords who provided this same service, my father never charged a fee, which often ranged from a low of ten per cent to a high of thirty per cent of the produce stored. This was only one of the reasons my father was truly liked and respected by his people.

111

At least one day a week I went to the kitchen gardens with Marta and collected herbs, which we brought back to sort, dry, and store away for later use. A lady of the manor was often called on to attend the sick and injured. Some of the herbs would be brewed into concoctions to ease pain, to put someone to sleep, or to cure a variety of internal ills. With others we could make poultices to draw out infection, reduce swellings, or clear up a congestion. Marta was famous throughout the manor and the village for the curative powers of her herb brews, and during the fall months she gradually taught me her secrets, which I added to the knowledge of herbs I had learned from Gundrig.

Two days a week Marta and I went into the village where about five hundred of our fiefs and freemen lived. We were accompanied by one or two servants who carried baskets of herbs, clean linens, and perhaps some food and wine. The welfare of our manor lands depended on the health of the people, and so it became my duty to make regular calls on the householders to see to their health and their living conditions.

Most of the cottages, it is true, were small, but my father had always demanded that they be kept as clean as possible. The dirt-packed floors had to be swept out and clean rushes laid once a week. Refuse to be fed to the swine was to be deposited in enclosed, covered bins and used regularly. Wells were spaced throughout the village and checked at frequent intervals to make sure the water was clear and free from scum or dead animals. Instead of each family having a dung heap within their enclosure, certain areas, away from the water supply, were set aside for this, and yards and animal shelters were cleaned out frequently. Heavy fines were levied against those families who broke these sanitary laws. The Roman tradition of cleanliness was still strong within our family. Although some householders grumbled, our people remained healthier than those on many manors. When a member of one family became ill, the sickness did not sweep the village like wildfire as so often was the case.

Marta and I always went first to the cottages where

112

we had been notified there was sickness or a recent birth. Here we left clean linens if there were none or exchanged them for the soiled linen, which we would take back to the laundry to be washed and put up for further use. There were two huge linen rooms in the manor, and it was my job to supervise the washing and mending of the contents and to make certain that the linens we used in the village were kept separate from those used in the manor. I checked each piece to make certain it was clean and had been carefully mended. Then I supervised the folding, sprinkling herbs between the layers to keep them fresh and fragrant. Once the household linens became discolored or too often mended, they were laundered with strong soap and transferred to the shelves holding those for the village.

My father was no rough-and-tumble knight who didn't care whether he slept on a pile of skins or a husk mattress. He demanded clean, fresh-smelling sheets and pillow covers for himself and would brook no less for his guests. Each day clean towels were brought to him with his wash water, and they had better be free from stains. It can be seen that our weaving room was kept busy turning flax into linen thread to be woven into these various products. Even the towels in the kitchen had to be changed every day, and woe to a cook or scullery maid who wiped her hands on a dirty skirt.

There were many who scoffed at my father for his peculiar quirk, but they were the very ones who praised him loudest for his hospitality. They agreed he must have inherited this desire for cleanliness from a Roman ancestor who once walked the land where now our manor stood. It could well be true, for our Celtic forebear had married the daughter of a Roman commander.

After checking the cottages where we were needed, Marta and I always stopped in a few others just to check or to give fruit and sweets to the children while we asked about any complaints or problems. All through the years someone from the manor had done this, but now I felt that the people were particularly pleased to know that their lord's daughter was taking an interest in them. As a result of this tradition, our villagers remained at peace among themselves and content with their situation. Few through the years had petitioned to move to another manor, and even those had been allowed to leave with no penalty or fine levied against them.

One day Marta and I came to the cottage of a woman well advanced in labor. As in most of these homes, there was only one room, a small hearth at one end for cooking and heating. There was a large pallet near the fire on which the whole family slept. A single trestle table and some stools were the only furnishings except for cooking pots and earthenware dishes on a shelf. The woman lay on the pallet, while three children stood around, their eyes wide with wonder and fear.

As I started to place a clean sheet under the woman, I asked her if these were her children.

"No, my lady, their mother sent them to see if I would care for them while she went to the fields."

I told Marta to take the children to some nearby cottage that had a woman at home to keep them.

"I know they see everything that goes on," I said, "but I think we'll be better off with them out of the way. Then come back, because I'll need help. This is my first experience at being a midwife."

I stirred up the fire to get more warmth in the room, then helped the woman out of some of her sweaty clothes and put a second sheet over her. She told me her name was Elspeth.

"Why didn't you send for help?" I asked. "Were you going to do this alone?"

Between gasps she answered, "I did, my lady. I sent my husband, but he hasn't returned."

"I'll see to him later," I said. The pains were obviously coming closer together, and I was anxious for Marta to return.

I projected a few months into the future and tried to see myself lying on a bed in the same condition. Who would be with me then, and would I be able to bite my lip and keep from screaming as this woman was

114

doing? At least I would be on a clean bed in a spotless abbey with nuns, who were kindness themselves, in attendance. But would they reproach me for my sin, not comfort me but remind me that I deserved whatever discomfort I suffered? I hoped Marta could be with me, Marta and her herbs to ease my pain and help me sleep.

Marta returned, and while she sat by the pallet, I took some herbs and brewed a hot tea. It was not strong enough to make Elspeth sleep because we would need her help to bring the baby out, but it would ease the pain. While I spooned it through her lips, she became more relaxed, although it was evident the birth was not far away. Finally, with one long gasp and a powerful contraction of muscles, she gave birth to a son. Marta stayed with Elspeth, finishing up and changing the linens while I bathed the baby in water that had been heating on the hearth.

I examined the healthy, well-formed boy. Sheltered during these past months, he would now try to grow to manhood in this hovel, to spend his life knowing only hard work, beatings, perhaps, and having to compete later with new arrivals for every scrap of food. Even on this well-run manor, life for the serf was a desperate, day-to-day struggle just to keep alive. Could there be something better for him?

Having helped to bring him into the world, I felt that he was partly mine. I was not his mother, but I could be a second mother to him, to watch over him, to bring him to the manor house and raise him, not as my own certainly, but as a ward. But would the mother want that? Would the father approve? The lord's word was final, and I could demand that he be with me, but I could not resort to intimidation. I must have them want it, and their permission would not be easy to obtain. A son was much more welcome in these homes than a daughter. A son could soon help in the fields and ease the father's labor. I must move slowly and cautiously.

Then I thought about the husband. I stepped outside and called to a man passing by.

"Do you know the husband of this household?"

"Yes, my lady. I know who he is."

"Well, would you know where he is?"

The man scuffled his feet in the dirt as though loathe to answer.

"Well, do you?" I demanded.

Then he remembered who was speaking to him, and a new fear crossed his face, the fear of what reprisals might come his way if he refused to answer a member of the lord's family. I didn't often use my position as daughter of the manor to coerce, but I would if I had to. But then he decided for himself, and he answered in the whining, unctuous manner that I so detested in one trying to ingratiate himself with a superior.

"I think, my lady, he's at the alehouse. He was mad this morning when his wife said she had to stay behind and wouldn't go to the fields—the baby coming, you know—so he said if she took a day off, he would, too. He's been there all day, ma'am, and begging your pardon, but in no condition to come home, I'm sure."

"The alehouse," I echoed.

"Yes, my lady."

"Well, go find him," I said, "and tell him to get sober in a hurry. I don't care how he does it. But to get sober and then get home. Do you understand?"

"Yes, my lady. I'm going."

I had an idea my words would be repeated with all the force I wanted. And I was pretty sure he would sober up in a hurry. I would see a very pale young man when he did appear because I knew what even the gentry did when they had had too much to drink and were suddenly called upon to sober up and have all their wits about them. He would force himself to retch until he had regurgitated all of the cheap ale. Then he'd drink plenty of strong herb tea until some of that stayed down. Then, on very weak legs he would start home, and I'd be ready for him.

When I turned back into the room, Marta had just finished settling the new mother comfortably and wiping her face.

"Elspeth," I said, "you have a fine son. He looks as strong and lusty as he sounds."

"Thank you, ma'am, and for all you've done. I was terribly afraid until you came in. I didn't know what I was going to do, my first and all."

"You should not have been alone. Was there no one to send for?"

"I told my husband to get someone, but no one came, only the children to say their mother wasn't home. I was going to send them after someone—then you came."

"Well, you're fine now, and I've sent for your husband. When you're feeling strong enough, I want you to come to the manor and ask for me."

"To the manor, yes, ma'am."

"Don't you want to know why?" I asked.

"To return these fine linens, I expect."

"No, Elspeth, they are yours. I would like you to work at the manor. I have need of another woman in the workrooms to spin and weave. Would you like to do that?"

"Oh, yes, ma'am, but my husband won't like me not working in the fields. He says he can't manage it alone, and he—he—"

"Yes, Elspeth?"

"He wants as big a harvest as possible so he can sell part of it or trade."

I looked around the room. He didn't sell part of his harvest to give them a better living, of that I was sure. I saw no extra clothes or food stored away.

"For what, Elspeth? To spend at the alehouse?"

"Yes, ma'am, every night."

"That settles it," I said. "You come work in the manor house. He can manage the fields alone, and he'll see no part of what you earn. I'll give it to you in goods for yourself and the baby."

"The boy, ma'am, who'll care for the boy?"

"You will," I answered. "Bring him with you, and we'll think of some way to take care of him as he grows."

I had my way to get the boy to the manor. Once Elspeth saw the advantages he would have there, I could bring him up to be my page, and I could assure his future. There would be other children for her, but this one was mine, and if I could save one of them from a life of drudgery, perhaps life would even be a bit easier for the rest that came later.

Within the month Elspeth came to the manor to work. That her husband was furious, I knew, but he did not dare let her refuse my offer, nor would he dare abuse her because of it. He was a cowed man when he appeared back at his cottage the day his son was born, and I was in no mood to be easy on him. My words were few and to the point.

Autumn came early, bringing cold, harsh winds and heavy rains. Marta and I limited our visiting to the few days when the sun shone, and I was perfectly content to stay in, tending to the affairs of the manor house, especially the kitchen and weaving room. I could still remember the first time I had shared the jelly making when I was ten and shut in with a cold. I still loved to sit by the hearth and inhale all the wonderful aromas of bread baking, poultry or meat turning on the spit, their juices running off and sputtering in the hot ashes beneath. Old as I was, I still relished a hunk of hot bread fresh from the oven and dripping with rich meat juices caught as they fell or with the sweet foam skimmed from bubbling jelly.

I almost forgot the unhappiness that lay deep within my being, like a mortal wound that has not quite killed yet cannot ever be healed. Some part of me that was woman, some long-forgotten inheritance from an original earth mother, kept me from complete despair by reminding me that I had a life within me. Though the future I could visualize held no hope for real happiness, it was, like all futures, only a veiled mist whose parting would probably reveal a never-ending stretch of emptiness, yet might—just might—surprise now and then with moments of great joy and fulfillment.

As much as I loved being in the kitchen, I enjoyed even more the hours in the weaving room. There was something soothing about the steady rhythm of the shuttles going back and forth between the threads, of the beater as it pushed against and firmed up each new thread against the already woven cloth. I had always loved the feel of yarn in my hands, of watching raw wool or flax become thread as I spun, and then creating from that thread materials that would eventually be cut and sewn into usable garments. So some days I worked at the loom, some days with the spindle. The women who worked there, young and old, were always cheerful, happy I guess to be indoors in pleasant surroundings. It was considered among them an honor to be selected for this work, so part of their joy, I'm sure, was in feeling superior to those who were not so chosen.

Much of my pleasure, I know, came from having Elspeth and young Will with us. Will was an amazingly beautiful child, and very good, considering how spoiled he was. Strangely, none of the others resented my allowing Elspeth to bring him, a favor never accorded them. Instead, they adored him. As each woman took her few minutes' rest each hour, she would pick Will up and play with him or sing to him if he were sleepy. He spent very little time in the cradle, and I was content to see my future page so well cared for.

If anyone suspected my condition, no one mentioned it. Since the weather had turned bitter cold, we all wore several layers of heavy garments. Only Marta knew, for I had taken her into my confidence when I wasn't feeling well, and I needed her help and advice. Too, I wanted her with me at the abbey. During these days she was my only source of strength and comfort. When I found myself weeping for no reason, she cheered me, and when I didn't want to eat, she grew cross and reminded me that the child I was carrying needed sustenance.

I wanted so much, while working at the loom, to weave soft blankets or fine linen that could be made into baby garments, but I dared not. Instead, I concentrated on replenishing the linen supply except for weaving one piece of wool to be made into a warm cape and hood to wear on the ride to the abbey.

Just as Merlin had predicted, there was trouble in mid-November, and for the first time in many years our manor was threatened. There would probably not be an attack on the manor itself, but there would be fighting all around us, and our house and court would be overflowing with the men who needed to rest or replenish their supplies. I knew my father would agree that it would be best for me not to be around. I also knew some of the lords in the west had resented Arthur's being able to unite so many of the kings and lords in the south and east under his banner, and I couldn't help but wonder if he himself would be among those fighting. Another good reason for me to leave. I could not bear to see him now.

Without hesitation my father granted my request to enter the abbey for a period of rest and contemplation. I'm sure he felt relieved at my being away at this time. He paused only long enough to say, "Yes, you do look a bit pale and tired. You have been doing too much." And to make sure I had everything I needed, he ordered an escort for me, allowed me to take Marta along, and gave me a bag of gold as an offering for the abbey.

How Merlin would have managed everything, I did not know, but I left home with complete faith that all was arranged, that my coming was expected, and that I would be welcomed.

Although suspected by many of being a sorcerer, Merlin had managed to remain in good standing with most of the church fathers. None of his acts had ever been declared heretical, so perhaps they simply considered him wiser than most people. In fact, Merlin himself insisted that when he seemed to be foretelling the future, he was merely basing his deductions on common sense and previous experience. He was a consummate scholar of both nature and human nature, of history and philosophy. He insisted that all aspects of life and the universe were cyclical, and if one knew what a response to a particular action had been in the past, then he could easily foretell a similar response in the future. He had studied the seasons and was convinced that the world went in such cycles that he could easily foresee when drought or heavy storms would appear.

As for his ability to cast spells, he said he merely used a form of hypnotism or persuasion and then could convince a man to be anything he wanted—braver, stronger, calmer, and so on. His explanations seemed simple enough, far too simple, I thought, for I had witnessed the power he could exert, and I was not convinced that he was without supernatural aid.

However, I was sure I knew the real reason Merlin was accepted by the church. He had delivered to the people Arthur, their rightful and long-awaited king. Too long, since even before the death of Uther, had the country been rent by turmoil and vicious rivalries. If the coming of Arthur, as had been prophesied, could unite Britain and bring peace, the church would look with favor upon anyone who aided in the task. Only Merlin, as close friend and adviser to Uther, had known where the sword was hidden that would proclaim the rightful heir, and so he had produced it when the time for testing arrived. In addition, he had been Arthur's mentor through all his years of training and had passed on to him the wisdom and knowledge that Uther would have, had he kept his son by his side.

At any time through those intervening years, Merlin could have produced the sword, but he wisely waited until Arthur was old enough to assume the mantle of authority. Only then, during the feast of Christmas, did he bring it from its hiding place and set it up in the square for all to see. Arthur had told me once why no one else had been able to pull it from the stone. There was no magic connected with the feat, only a trick that Merlin once revealed to him. He said that Merlin could simply have revealed to the people Arthur's true identity, but there was real doubt that they would accept so young and untried a man to rule them. Most people were superstitious and preferred to believe something revealed through the supernatural than something presented as fact. So through the years Merlin had started a whispering campaign, rumors that Uther's true heir would be revealed as the one who someday could pull Excalibur, the great sword of Uther, from a stone where it remained embedded from the day Uther had plunged it in.

Actually, Uther had entrusted the sword to Merlin when he first became ill in London and thought he was dying. He had asked his old friend to keep it until the young Arthur had reached manhood and had the strength to wield it and to assume his father's position. This Merlin had promised the king, hiding the sword away in his cave until the propitious moment. During the ensuing years, after Uther had recovered, Merlin located the rock that he needed for his purpose, a rock that already had in it a cleft, or fissure, several inches deep. Carefully, he drove a wedge in until he had it open to a depth about half the length of the sword blade. With the dexterity of a magician long accustomed to manipulating objects with his hands, he widened the crevice deep in the interior.

Merlin remembered a trick device he had learned of from an itinerant Eastern mystic, the Oriental finger lock. This was a short, narrow tube of fine webbing that was slipped over the victim's finger. The harder he tried to pull it off, the tighter it became. Only if he knew just how to twist the tube could he possibly remove it. Merlin collected a quantity of fine horse hair and thinly drawn wire, then set about constructing the lock along with a spring contraption as he remembered it. He had to make several before he formed one that would not break when pulled hard. The final one he inserted into the cleft of the rock, then pushed the sword point well into it. Over and over he experimented until he was certain that the sword would not come straight out regardless of the strength exerted, but would come out easily with a slight twist. He counted on Arthur's remembering the trick. Everything was ready, and Merlin had the rock and sword set in place in time for the great gathering at Christmas time. The rest was history, but I would never forget the delight with which Arthur had related the story. Arthur had no idea of the significance of his act and was astounded when all the people around him fell on their knees and began hailing him as king.

I set out for the abbey with a small entourage, four mounted guards, two others riding the horses between which my litter was suspended. Marta rode in the cart that carried my supplies and gifts for the abbey. Two guards, followed by the litter and then the cart, rode in front. Two other guards brought up the rear. Even though it was safer than in previous years to ride through the countryside, there was still danger of an attack on two women unless well guarded, and my father had determined to take all precautions.

It took the better part of an afternoon to make the leisurely trip. During most of it my mind was whirling with thoughts, strangely enough not so much wondering about the future, but remembering the past months. I regretted most leaving little Will just as he was becoming aware of his surroundings and beginning to enjoy all the attention he was getting. I would perhaps miss his first attempts at sitting up, his first sucking from the spoon that Elspeth would hold. I thought, too, of the serenity in the weaving room, of how the women had accepted my being there, had gone on with their jokes and gossip as though I were one of them. Would it be the same when I returned? I would have to find some way to stay close to Elspeth, to earn her confidence so that I could gradually remove Will from her care to mine, to keep him with me when she returned to the cottage at night. I would have to wait until he was weened, of course, but I was determined that she would let me raise him and train him to be my page. He would be my only child, for I would not be bringing my own back with me.

Without warning, my reminiscing came to an abrupt end. Litter riding is not the most comfortable way to travel at best, but once you get used to the gentle, rhythmic swaying, and you have horses with a steady, regular pace, it is easy to relax and pretend you're in a cradle or boat. As long as the horses remain in step.

Suddenly, the horse to my right shied at something and reared up. Meanwhile, the one to the left came to an abrupt halt. With one tremendous jolt, my litter was jerked between them, giving a spine-jarring lurch that threatened to topple me off, then settled back down. All in less than a second.

I looked up just in time to see one, then the other, of my front guards fall off their horses, killed instantly with arrows through their throats. While I was trying to comprehend what was happening, a third arrow came winging out, seemingly from nowhere, hitting the man on my right in the shoulder, knocking him to the ground. At that same moment, a group of ruffians emerged from the wooded thicket to our right, a perfect ambush. Then the riderless horse, frightened by the confusion, bolted and ran, tearing apart the straps that secured one end of the little poles. The first jerking pull alerted me to what might happen, and so I was able to brace myself before the final break that dropped the litter to the ground. Feeling the entire weight of the litter tugging at him, the other horse jumped to one side, twisting his straps, overturning the litter, and throwing me to the ground. I looked up to see the frightened horse rearing and pawing the air above me. I tried to crawl away, but my robe was caught in one of the broken poles, and in spite of tugging and ripping, I could not free myself. At any minute I knew that one of those pawing hoofs would come down on me.

The rider, also seeing what was happening, had jumped down and begun calming the horse. Then I felt myself being pulled along the ground and looked up to see Marta and the cart driver dragging me out from under the horse. Limping with a twisted ankle, I let the two half carry, half support me to the cart where I managed to climb in and settle back against one of the piles of clothes. My head was throbbing, and quick, sharp pains darted through my back.

In spite of my discomfort I had enough presence of mind to pull my hood part way over my face. The ambushers would, of course, know that they had stopped someone of importance because of the mounted guard, but I hoped that they wouldn't recognize me as the daughter of the Earl of Sanam.

With two men dead and one wounded, I knew we were outnumbered, but I was sure that the remaining men would soon dismount and engage the outlaws in combat so that the driver of the cart could try to get away during the furor.

I waited, but my men made no move. Then I saw why. Alongside the road were four archers, each with bow raised and arrow nocked in position to shoot. Two were aimed at the guards' throats. The other two were pointed directly at my chest. If anyone even looked as if he were going to move, I would be killed instantly.

Only one of the ruffians was mounted, obviously the leader. He sat his horse off to one side, arms crossed and lying easily over the pommel of his saddle. He was completely at ease, his face reflecting self-confidence and authority. While his features were not ugly, they had been hardened into a visage of coarse brutality. I grew more and more uneasy under his intense stare.

Knowing, finally, that he had my complete attention, he got slowly but deliberately down off the horse and walked toward me. He was tall of stature, taller than any man I had seen so far. (Later I was to meet Sir Gawain, from the same section of the Northland, and only he topped this man, and that by a few inches.) Broad of shoulder and chest, he looked about to burst through his rough jacket. His long, untrimmed hair and beard, a dark roan color, were streaked and matted with dirt.

"Good afternoon, my lady."

Refusing to answer, I merely held my head down.

He reached over, grabbed my chin with one hand to pull my head up sharply. With the other, he slapped me across the cheek. Marta started to interfere, but I stopped her. Resistance could only do more harm at this point.

"When Eldred speaks, you answer." His voice had a rough accent to it, Scots, perhaps, from the northern highlands.

I mumbled a "yes" to him.

"Who are you? Where are you going?" he demanded.

"I'm a serf whose master is allowing me to enter the Abbey of the Holy Spirit. This is my mother, who is taking me there."

"A servant with guards? A likely story."

"My master sent them to protect me, sir."

He reached over and grabbed my cloak. "Servant, bah! This is no servant's robe. And look at your hands. You've never done any rough work, I'll be bound."

"I was my lady's maid. She gave me this robe as a going-away gift."

With a rough gesture, he motioned to a man standing to one side. He was a shrunken, ill-visaged man who fingered the knife at his belt as though eagerly anticipating an order to draw it. A dreadful man. One, I was sure, who would kill on command—or whim. He leered at me as his leader spoke.

"Go back to the camp. Tell them to prepare for guests." He turned toward me. "It's been a long time since I've had anything as young and pretty as you for a bedmate. What do you think of my archers?"

"They look like experts," I said.

"And they are. Very clever, don't you think? One word or signal from me and you'd be dead. You and your guards."

Just then I saw a man I thought I recognized call Eldred aside. The more I looked, the more familiar his face became. I knew him. He was the fief who had set fire to the granary and then been dismissed from the manor. Eldred walked back to the cart.

"A servant, eh! You're the Earl of Sanam's daughter. Did you think your lies would save you?"

I raised my head high. "And what do you intend to do with us?"

"Oh, I've several ideas. I still think I'll take you with me. I might enjoy having some fun with an earl's daughter. I'll wager a fine lady like you has never been tumbled in the leaves under a tree." He laughed raucously. "You might even enjoy it. Maybe I'll let my men have their fun, too. I believe in giving them a special treat now and then."

Turning his head, he gave a high, short whistle.

From out of the woods came a girl no more than twelve or thirteen with an almost emaciated body. Her skirt was torn and dirty, stained with the remains of food. Her blouse only partially covered her and was so ragged it looked decayed rather than just torn. She wore no shoes in spite of the fact the ground was frozen. Her hair was filthy—matted, greasy, and tangled. Dull, vacuous eyes looked out from a flat, white face that bore an absolutely blank expression. Her mouth was open, and her slack lower lip drooled with saliva. All signs of a feeble mentality.

At another signal she raised her skirts above her waist, revealing bony legs, a stomach bloated from starvation, and no undergarments of any kind.

One of the men drooped his bow and struck her across the face with his fist. As she fell to the ground, he dropped on top of her. Throughout the act that followed, she moaned and gouged his back and arms with her fingernails, only increasing the fury with which he took his pleasure on her. They were like two animals rutting in the ditch. I knew there were camp followers. I knew women lived in the forest with the outlaws, but I had never thought I would witness a scene of such gross sexuality.

The gorge rose bitter and burning in my throat. By concentrating on the effort to force it back down, I kept myself from screaming and could partially ignore what was going on in front of me.

The man got up and reached for his bow, resuming his stance. The girl merely brushed off her skirt and disappeared into the forest.

The lewd, sensual expression on Eldred's face made the blood drain from my face; my hands were like ice. He looked at me more closely.

"Bah," he said, "don't be so scared. You might not suit my taste. Too pale and cold. I like my women warm and red-blooded." But he had already unlaced his codpiece, exposing his engorged, erect member, and was climbing into the cart.

As I tried to slide away from him, my robe fell

127

open. The baby chose that moment to kick, and I unconsciously put my hand to my belly.

"Oh, ho, so someone else has been tumbling you, making the beast with two backs," he laughed. "Well, I've heard tell some like them cold and aloof, a challenge, maybe. No, it takes a hot and willing woman to really rouse me."

"You'll let us go, then?"

"Not likely. Your driver will follow me into the woods. I think I'll just hold you there for ransom. The Earl of Sanam should be willing to part with a good bit of gold to get you back safely. And don't worry, I won't touch you." He said he didn't favor putting a head on another man's child, only he used coarse, vulgar words.

He reached out to chuck me under the chin, releasing his grip on the cart. At that moment the driver laid whip to the horses, and we took off in such a burst of speed that the wheels sent showers of dust in all directions. Eldred had his foot on the hub of one wheel. The sudden movement threw him to the ground and sent him rolling across the road into the ditch. Startled by what had happened, the archers dropped their bows momentarily, and my guards put spurs to horses, following as fast as they could. One archer retained his wits and sent an arrow into one guard, but the other stayed with us all the way to the abbey.

The driver had waited for the perfect moment to make his move. Without realizing it, Eldred had stepped between me and the archers, making an unwitting shield to protect me from his men. I was concerned about my men left behind, especially the one trapped by the litter, unable to move. I knew they would be killed.

The horses were not allowed to slow down even for a second until the abbey was in sight. Fortunately, since we were expected, the gates were open, and we drove right through.

I was in such pain that the driver had to carry me to my room, but I remained conscious long enough to tell the nun who accompanied me not to send him back, to

128

find some place for him to stay or he would be killed.

We had escaped Eldred, but I had a strange foreboding that it was not for the last time.

After Marta saw me settled in bed, the nun on duty came into the room.

"Welcome, Lady Lionors, I hope you are feeling more comfortable. I am sure Marta must be exhausted, too, after the ordeal you have been through. We have a room ready for her next to yours."

In spite of the experiences of the day, I was able to sleep through the night. In the morning, I took the opportunity of being alone to look around the room and to examine the view from my window. To my right, sheltered in the corner of two adjoining walls, was a small, very neat and attractive cottage. Just a few feet out and around the other two sides was a low, stone wall encompassing a narrow space that undoubtedly was a garden during the spring and summer months. I could see the neatly spaded plots and borders, and at the corner of the wall was an apricot tree, denuded now of leaves and fruit, but sturdy and probably rich with a succulent harvest in the fall. What a charming place, I thought, and wondered who lived there. I was certain that none of those in the order would live outside the main buildings, and I meant to ask about the cottage the first chance I had. Strangely enough, I did not ask then and only learned more about it years later. I knew, though, that it would be a quiet, pleasant retreat from the cares of the everyday world.

I had been offered the choice of meals brought to my room, but I had decided that I would like to eat with the chapter, although I was advised that they would be quiet meals.

"If you care to," I had been told by a nun on our arrival, "you can join us at nones and then go into the refectory. However, after that service, complete silence is observed, so there will be no one to talk to. After supper we have vespers and then retire to our rooms for the night."

I assured her that peace and quiet was exactly what

I sought, and I would be most happy to follow their rules.

There were fewer than fifty nuns at the abbey, but their gentle voices lifted in nones were as thrilling as any choir I had ever heard. It was even more pleasant than I had anticipated to eat in silence, with no idle chatter to disturb the mood set by the service. Vespers broke the silence only briefly, and then quietly we returned to our rooms. Much later, after I had fallen into a first dreamless sleep, I heard in the distance the soft tinkling of a bell, followed by the muted sounds of slippered feet. Later, I learned that the nuns had arisen for complin, the final service of the canonical day, but completely at peace for the first time in months, I turned over under the quilt and went immediately back to sleep.

I had been given one of the two guest rooms in the main building, and it was a good bit larger than the cells that the nuns occupied. I had wondered, before coming to the abbey, just how well I could adjust to what I thought would be austere surroundings in comparison to my large and colorful room at the manor. But I need not have worried. As plain as the room was, with whitewashed walls and smooth, uncarpeted floors, it was decidedly comfortable. The bed was soft, with plenty of warm covers. In addition there was a wardrobe for my clothes, a chair by the window where I could read or sew, and a second chair so that Marta could join me. There was also a long table that would do double duty as a washstand and to hold my manuscripts.

The days went by more quickly than I could have thought possible. I slipped easily into the routine of the abbey, soon realizing how much peace and security were afforded the inhabitants by the daily, never-changing routine. At first I arose with the first bell, at five in the morning, for matins. This was followed by a light repast at which the nuns were permitted to talk. From then on the rooms were filled with the chatter of the community going about its work very much as we did at the manor. I wanted my days to be as full as possible, so I was given permission to help wherever I could. Marta had found her way to the kitchen and the sickrooms where her knowledge of cooking and healing made her immediately welcome. Since I preferred to sew or read, the abbess suggested that I help embroider the altar cloths that were woven on the abbey loom, or work on the new robes for the bishop. When I tired of this, she encouraged me to take a precious manuscript from their small library and read to one of the older nuns, an invalid slowly going blind.

The busy routine of the day fitted into the pattern dictated by the canonical hours. Before first daylight, the bell rang for matins. At set times during the day, it pealed again for prime, tierce, and sext. The nuns regulated their duties by the time between each service and had learned exactly when to draw their immediate task to a close, but for the first few days I seemed to always be caught with a half-finished bit of embroidery that I couldn't immediately put down, or in the middle of a sentence I was reading. Invariably, I had to pick up my skirts and run, as well as I was able, in order to catch up in chapel. Soon, however, my subconscious adjusted to the rhythm, and I would hear the bells just as I was ready to put down my needle or close the book.

Christmas was celebrated with longer services and more candles in the chapel. But the real recognition that it was a special day came with the appearance of the magnificent roast goose served at midday. Otherwise, the day went by much as any other. I could have wept remembering the way we celebrated at the manor, with great tables heaped with food, a great quantity of presents for everyone, and usually a roomful of guests around the great log burning in the main hall. My father, often so busy away from home, made it a point to be at the manor if he possibly could for the Christmas celebration and to bring as many friends with him as he could persuade to join him. Always there was one special gift for me, something very rare or unusual that he had found during the year. One time it was the beautiful emerald necklace; another time, a magnificent amethyst brooch with earrings to match (for which

Marta had to pierce my ears, and I thought they would never stop hurting).

Nor was I disappointed this year. Late in the afternoon, just as we were assembling for nones, the large bell announcing a visitor at the gate rang. One of the nuns hurried away to see who would be so inconsiderate as to disturb them at this hour. She came back holding out a package for me.

"Here, my lady, this is for you. The courier says it is from your father, but please join us now and be so kind as to open it later after you have retired."

I took the rather large, flat package and hid it as best I could under my heavy robe. The candles in the chapel gave a great deal of light but very little heat, and this December was bitterly cold. Awkward as it was, I managed to keep the package concealed during supper and vespers that followed, but it inflamed my curiosity, just as father used to say that even a copper coin burned a hole in my pocket, so anxious was I to spend it.

I hurried to my room as fast as decorum allowed. Whatever the gift was, he had wrapped it first in a lovely piece of blue velvet. Putting this aside, I saw something made of deep red leather into which had been tooled a design in gold. The design of swirls and curlicues was unfamiliar, but it decorated a charming little case, or box, just right to hold the jewelry he had given me in the past. Opening it, I saw that it was lined with scarlet velvet, and resting on this was a note in my father's hand.

"I am sorry you can not be here for the holidays. Things have quieted down some, but there may still be trouble ahead, so you had best stay for at least another month. The piece of blue velvet is for Marta, and I thought you would like this to hold some of your precious keepsakes. I bought it from a tradesman who had traveled through the south of Europe. He said it was made by the Moors. They may be enemies of Christ, but they certainly do beautiful things with leather. Love," and a scrawled signature that only I could read.

After Christmas, heavy storms and cold weather

kept us all indoors. No more walks along the shaded paths. Instead, we huddled around the one large fireplace in the dining hall, leaving only to tend to the few chores necessary for daily living or to hurry through the cloisters to the chapel for the regular services. Marta was in her element, bustling around, making enough herb tea to float the abbey, but insisting that we drink every drop, a sure prevention for ague, she argued.

In January, while kneeling during matins, I felt the first pains. I was able to stay until the end of service, and then Marta helped me back to my room. She eased me out of my heavy clothes, but insisted that I put a robe over my gown and walk up and down the room in front of the fire.

"The longer you're on your feet, lamb, the easier it will be."

Supported by Marta's strong arms, I felt as though I walked a hundred miles that day—eleven paces across the room, eleven paces back, stopping only now and then for her to rub my back. Then she finally said it.

"All right, now, it's time to get into bed. Here, ease yourself down, and I'll make you comfortable."

Our vigil had been interrupted only a few times by nuns asking if we needed anything or putting more fuel on the fire. Marta had refused to let me have any food, only a sip of tea now and then.

"But Marta, I'm hungry," I wailed.

"No, deary, only a little tea. You'd be sorry when that baby really starts coming if you ate any solid food. I'll have enough to do bringing him into the world without having to take care of a sick mother. You can have a good meal when it's over, I promise."

Sometime late in the afternoon, I heard footsteps louder than the quiet footfalls of the nuns, and soon I heard a man's voice. It was low, but I recognized it immediately. Merlin had come. At first the voices were too low for me to make out the words, but then I heard the very determined voice of Merlin, followed by the equally determined voice of the abbess.

"I've come to see the Lady Lionors."

133

"I'm sorry, sir. No one can go in."

"Then I'll wait here until I can see her, but please give her this."

He must have handed something to her, for I heard her ask: "And what is this for?"

"Give her a spoonful now and then. It will ease her pains and help her sleep a bit."

"Oh, no, sir. I must not do that."

"And why not, pray tell?"

"She must suffer the pain. That is her punishment as a woman for the sins of Eve."

I heard Merlin sputter: "Poppycock. That is ridiculous. No one should be made to suffer if the pain can be alleviated. Now, either you give it to her, or I promise you, I shall enter that room."

In a moment, a stern but shaken abbess came in and handed Marta a vial, repeating the instructions Merlin had given her.

Marta approached the bed, saying, "Here, lamb, take a sip of this. Merlin sent it to you."

After finishing the draft, I drifted in and out of consciousness and came fully awake only when I heard Marta ask, "Don't you want to see your new daughter?"

From that moment on, every waking minute of the day centered on Elise. When she was awake, I bathed and fed her, refusing the offer of a wet-nurse. I scarcely let Marta even hold her. But at night I was more than glad to let my gentle nurse take over her care. For over a month life was one idyllically happy day after another.

Merlin dropped by from time to time; to see how I was doing, he said, but I knew it was to see Elise and play with her. He held her gently on his knees while her tiny fists clung to his fingers or often, to our merriment, grabbed hold of his long, shaggy gray beard.

We never mentioned the idea of my leaving her behind when I returned home, so I was completely unprepared when he asked me, "When are you and Marta going back to the manor?"

"When are the three of us going, you mean. I can't leave Elise behind, Merlin; you know that."

"And you can't take her with you, either—you know that." He spoke each word slowly, pointedly.

"I can say she is a waif who was abandoned at the gate of the abbey."

"That is the very story," he said, "that is being circulated now to explain her presence here."

"Then?"

"And," he went on, "she has already been dedicated to the church."

I let Merlin think I was acceding to his decision. I knew I had a few more weeks at the abbey, for I would remain until we could find a trustworthy wet-nurse who would ask no questions and who could also be trusted with a secret. By that time I hoped to find a way to change his mind.

Suddenly, my new-found happiness came to an abrupt end, a tragic and bitter end. Elise had begun to turn her head at the sound of a voice, a footstep, or a door closing. I laughed and played with her whenever I held her, and it seemed to me she laughed back. Occasionally, I dangled something over her face to see when she would begin to try to reach for it. But she never did. Trying to remember how soon young Will had responded to motion, I asked Marta to try to get Elise's attention. The response was the same. In a panic, I took her to some of the nuns, but they only confirmed my worst suspicions. Elise was blind.

That put an end to all thoughts of my returning home. I would stay in the abbey to help bring her up. I couldn't possibly leave her now, even with the gentle nuns who promised to give her love and protection. No, if I couldn't become a member of the order, I would stay on as a servant if need be, anything to remain with Elise. My father need never know why I stayed.

However, I reckoned without Merlin. He came by, as usual, unannounced. His sorrow was as great as my own when I told him of Elise's misfortune. But he was

135

adamant about my returning home and leaving her behind.

"You cannot stay, but she must. The nuns will take good care of her and train her to live in their world."

"But why can't I stay, too? What is there for me at home? My whole world is here with her."

"No, Lionors, your future is at the manor. Arthur needs to have you there."

"Arthur!" I spat out. "Why should I think of him now? He doesn't need me, and Elise does."

"He will need you. I told you that before. You can not be a real helpmeet to him here."

"Helpmeet!" I shrieked. "Helpmeet! Let his future wife be his helpmeet."

"Do you still love him, Lionors?"

"I don't know."

"Then answer me this. Do you still trust me?"

I hesitated. "I always have."

"Stay here a few more weeks, and—now listen carefully—keep your eyes and your heart open."

Once again I didn't fully understand his words, but I tried to follow his advice. Slowly, I learned what he meant. A young novice had recently entered the abbey. She came from a large family and was obviously lonesome for her younger brothers and sisters, especially a baby sister who had been born a few months earlier. In fact, it was the birth of the last child that had sent her into the novitiate because her family would find life easier with one less mouth to feed.

Shyly, she approached me while Elise and I were enjoying the sun in the courtyard one warm afternoon, and she inquired if she might hold the baby. During the next few days it became more and more natural for us to meet in the afternoon, and while Berthe held Elise, she told me about her life at home with her eight brothers and sisters. She especially yearned to see the youngest, baby Margarete. Because her mother had gone through a long, slow recovery period after the birth of this last child, Berthe had taken complete charge of her, even figuring out how to dilute their cow's milk with water and a bit of sugar when her mother's breasts dried up as a result of fever.

"When she cried," Berthe told me proudly, "I made her little sugar tits, a bit of cloth dipped in sweetened milk. And before I left, she was managing to eat a bit of thin gruel. I'll teach you how to make a sugar tit, my lady, if you like. You'll find it handy when Elise is fretful."

"Thank you, Berthe. Why don't you make one up for her now. I wish, too, that you would try your recipe for cow's milk and see if she will tolerate it. She is beginning to need more milk than I can give her."

Merlin had told me to open my eyes and my heart. When I looked at Berthe with my eyes, I saw a young, sweet-faced woman enjoying a moment every afternoon when she could slip away from the work of the abbey and laugh aloud at the antics of a baby. When I looked with my heart, I saw a girl, scarcely yet a woman, aching with loneliness, the hunger to be with her family assuaged by holding Elise for a few hours each day.

When Merlin suggested the time had come for me to leave, I chose an hour when Elise was sleeping so there would be no sensation of handing her over to someone else. After one last look at her blonde hair, just beginning to curl into tiny ringlets, and the pale lashes fringing her cheeks, I put on my cloak and left the abbey, forcing myself not to think about when I might see her again.

❈ *Chapter Seven* ❈

On his first birthday, some seven months after I left the abbey, little Will came completely under my protection. Another baby had arrived, and Elspeth was more than glad to be relieved of the older child's care. I had a trundle bed made and placed beside my own in spite of Marta's fussing at me for spending all my time with the child of a serf. Marta found it impossible to understand that although he could never take Elise's place, Will gave me a reason to get up every day and kept me from allowing my life to be shattered by self-pity.

When Will became old enough to sleep by himself, I planned to fix up the small room next to mine, the one that I had used as a child. Surprisingly, Father raised no objection when I told him my idea of rearing Will to be my page. Perhaps he was finally getting used to my strange ways and accepting the fact I was not making any plans to marry. He had long since given up broaching the subject to me. Actually, I think he was delighted to have a child in the house, and Will was in grave danger of being spoiled.

Wherever I went in the house or the yards, Will toddled at my heels, hanging onto my skirt until he learned to balance on his chubby legs. He never lisped, and I forbore using baby talk when speaking to him, so his first words to me were *missy* and to my father, *sir*. If I were to bring him up as my page, I had to relinquish any desire to treat him as my own child. He would receive all the love and care he needed to grow up happy and healthy, but it would be tempered with an aware-

ness of the respect due me as his mistress, not his
mother. It would have been grossly unfair to him to
surround his early years with an intimacy that later
would have to be sundered.

From the beginning he knew that Elspeth, not I, was
his mother. When we were all in the weaving room, he
shared his time equally between us. As before, Elspeth
brought the new baby, a girl, with her when she came
to work. Will loved to sit on the floor by his baby sister
and keep her amused while their mother was busy. But
when he grew sleepy or restless, he toddled back to put
his head on my lap or pull on my skirt, his way of
showing he was ready to leave.

I worried lest Elspeth resent his feelings for me, but
my fears were groundless, and I knew why when I saw
her belly swelling with yet a third child. In her own
way, she loved Will; he was her first-born, but her
thoughts were more on earning enough at the manor to
take care of herself and the family at home. It had long
since become apparent that her husband would trade
everything he harvested for ale. I made certain there
was work for her at the manor every day and saw to it
she had a good meal at noon. I remembered Berthe's
saying that she fed her baby sister a thin gruel when
she was only a few months old, and I had the kitchen
prepare some for the baby since now that Elspeth was
pregnant, she could not nurse.

Between the time I left the abbey and Will's birthday, Merlin visited twice to reassure me that Elise was
thriving under Berthe's care. The young nun had been
relieved of other abbey duties so she could devote full
time to her charge. After his second visit, Merlin said
that Elise had begun to crawl, and Berthe was patiently
teaching her to reach out with her hands to avoid
bumping into furniture or other obstacles.

"And soothing her when she does hit something,"
Merlin added. "Berthe is enveloping her with a kind of
love that is better than any form of overprotection. She
has an amazing, inborn sense of how to teach Elise to
live in her world of darkness as though she were normal. She has already made toys for her, and they are

either soft to the touch, or they make a sound of some kind."

"How soon can I see her?" I asked.

"As soon as you can watch her leave again without going all to pieces."

That time came just before her first birthday when I sent two retainers to escort Berthe and Elise to the manor. This was only the first of what were to become regular visits with me. The story that a baby had been left at the abbey during my stay there seemed to be accepted by everyone without question, nor was anyone surprised that I had grown fond of the child and from time to time had her brought to the manor.

While Berthe and I sat in the study sewing or in the garden when spring came, Will and Elise played together like two puppies. Elise was adjusting so well to her blindness that she could do almost anything Will did. Her occasional tumbles once she began walking never seemed to daunt her and were no more frequent than Will's, who was always in such a hurry to get where he was headed that he seemed to trip over his own shadow. At first I had to stifle my inclination to reach out and stop her when she seemed headed for a fall, but Berthe would shake her head as though she were the teacher and I a student who was slow to learn. Berthe used only one method to keep Elise from running into serious danger, and that was a gentle reminder to the child not to wander away from the sound of her nurse's voice.

Another year passed uneventfully; nothing disturbed the calm of our routine. Will, with his warm russet hair, amber-flecked brown eyes, and ruddy complexion, grew more and more to resemble his mother. He not only looked nothing like his father, who had stringy black hair and a sallow complexion, but fortunately he displayed none of the wiry man's mean and surly characteristics. Both Will's stocky form and ready laugh were miniature imitations of his mother's. Elise, who started life as a little butterball, gradually began to slim down as she approached her second birthday. Her tight blonde ringlets lengthened into soft curls that bounced against her shoulders when she ran.

Will and Elise both passed their second birthdays, and I kept alive a small germ of hope that since Arthur had not chosen a wife, we might yet be able to marry. The more time that went by and the more secure the country became, the less I thought he would be called on to contract a political marriage.

From time to time, at irregular intervals, I received messages from him. They all ended the same way: "Kiss our daughter for me and never forget I love you," but contained very little news.

Merlin usually brought these messages, so I was always delighted to see him walking through the gate, sometimes leaning his weight on an ancient gnarled oak rod, as much a part of his attire as his gray robe, or using it to poke the ground and explore under bushes when something unusual caught his attention. A man who felt at home in a castle or a cave, he settled easily and comfortably into the chair in the library that had become his. He always said that once he had the bumps and bulges in the pillows arranged to suit his own contours, he hated to have to start all over again. No matter what I offered him in the way of refreshment, he asked me to make up my special herb brew. He watched me carefully crush and then blend the leaves from three different aromatic plants, including mint. After I poured on them the water that had been boiling over the fire, I let them steep for exactly three minutes. Merlin began sipping it while the cup was still steaming.

"Ah, that was good." Merlin sighed with satisfaction on a day in January right after Elise's second birthday. "I stopped by the convent to see Elise. She's getting to be mighty pretty—just like her mother."

"Thank you, Merlin, but she has her father's coloring. How is Arthur?"

"Fine, just fine."

Something in his tone disturbed me, and I commented. "You are not usually so noncommittal."

"Arthur has been having conflicts with King Leodecrance of Cameliard, who has been vacillating between allying himself with Arthur and joining the factions across the northern border. Arthur has done much to win him over to England's side, even going to his aid when Leodecrance was trapped in his castle, under siege by Ryence, king of Ireland. In many ways, Leodecrance is weak, but he is the leader of a strong force, and his allegiance would strengthen Arthur's position considerably. In fact, with him on Arthur's side, the remainder of the belligerent Scots would probably retire to their highlands and give Arthur no more trouble.

"The two finally came to an agreement, and last week they signed a pact of friendship. In order to make the pact more binding, Arthur married his daughter. Her name is Guinevere."

The word *Guinevere* was the last thing I remember hearing before I awoke in my bed with Marta putting cold cloths on my head and Merlin holding my hands in his. At the mention of Arthur's marriage I had fainted dead away and would have fallen to the floor if Merlin had not seen my face blanch and risen from his chair in time to catch me.

For three days I slipped in and out of consciousness, awake at brief intervals only long enough to swallow the warm broth or sleeping draughts Marta forced between my lips. As far as I could tell, Merlin never left my side, the magnetic power of his strength gradually entering me and dispelling the deadly inertia.

At the end of that time I insisted on no more potions, but asked Marta to prepare and bring up a hearty meal for Merlin and me to share before the fire in my room. I asked Merlin to excuse me while I bathed and put on something more appropriate for a hostess than a nightdress. While he was out of the room, I brushed my hair more than one hundred strokes, an act that had always relieved me of tension and pent-up emotions. When he returned, and Marta brought in the supper, I was calm and ready to talk.

"Marta, this looks delicious. Thank you. I didn't realize how hungry I was."

Marta beamed. "Does my heart good to hear you say that. Dig in, sir, there's plenty more."

"Now, Merlin," I said as we were finishing, "tell me all about Guinevere."

He hesitated. "Are you sure you want to hear?"

"I'm sure," I insisted. "Everything."

"She is an extremely beautiful woman, tall and willowy, with long, deep gold hair and very, very pale blue eyes. Some years younger than Arthur, she is very much aware of her beauty, and I'm afraid Arthur is not going to find life with her easy. She is naturally flirtatious and already has the men at court dancing attendance on her. Oh, I don't mean to imply she has thoughts of being unfaithful to Arthur, but all the knights will be begging to carry her favor into the lists, and she will share her attentions equally among them. There is no man at court now who poses a serious threat to Arthur as a rival for her deeper affections, but he could have his hands full should a younger man appear who might fall in love with her. Arthur is not the vigorous, virile man his father was, and I think Guinevere has the passionate temperament of one who wants life to be full of excitement, with something new happening all the time. The calm, steady existence Arthur seeks at Camelot could well become tedious for her."

Bitterness rose up like gall in my throat. Arthur needed a strong, understanding helpmeet for a queen and wife, not a vain little filly courting the admiration of the knights. It was I who should be at his side listening to his problems, helping him weigh the solutions, giving aid and comfort when his plans aborted. Merlin must have read my mind, for his next statement startled me out of my reverie.

"I want to prepare and caution you about a temptation you will soon face. The queen will be summoning young women of nobility to court to serve as ladies in waiting, something that was not done during Uther's reign or while Arthur was unmarried. The honor will be rotated, each lady staying at court for a year at a time. It will be only natural for you to be invited. You

143

must resist the temptation to be near Arthur at least for the time being. There is no way you can hide your feelings, and the situation would be extremely difficult for him. He is married to Guinevere, and it is vitally important for Britain that the union be a felicitous one, that nothing put it on shaky grounds. Arthur is doing his part to make the marriage succeed."

"Is he happy?"

"He is not unhappy. Remember, Lionors, it is possible for a man to love two women, each in a different way. Guinevere can be a delightful companion, full of wit and vitality, as well as being very sensuous and desirable."

Each word opened a new wound, but I was more hurt by Merlin's brutality than by what he was saying. Never one to be intentionally unkind, his giving such an extravagant description of Guinevere was completely out of character. Unless he had a deeper motive than just telling me why Arthur was, as he put it, "not unhappy."

"If you are trying to ensure that I will not accept an invitation to go to Camelot as a lady in waiting to the queen, you needn't have been quite so explicit in detailing her charms. If Arthur ever needs me, I'll always be waiting here, but I will never put myself in a position inferior to another woman. In my eyes, I am still his wife, but it is not just pride that keeps me here. No, you can be sure, Camelot holds no temptation for me. I couldn't endure the pain of seeing them together."

Merlin remained a few more days, then insisted it was best for me to have him leave.

"It's time now," he said, "for you to stand on your own feet and not become dependent on me. I'm returning to my cave, and I do not know when I will see you again, although I see our paths crossing once more before the end. I have fulfilled my obligations to Arthur and to you, and now the time has come for me to seek peace and quiet."

My world spun around me when I first learned of Arthur's marriage, and without Merlin I would have fallen. Without Elise and Will, I would have fallen spiritually. Priests might speak of a hell they have never seen in terms of fire and brimstone, but I sounded its depths and experienced the pernicious torments. At first I wanted to die and explored all possible methods, but I didn't kill myself, and I knew why. It was neither fear of punishment nor dread of the unknown that kept me alive, but the basic will to live. People might say they want to die or they don't want to live when old and infirm, but I know now they don't mean it. No one wants to die, not really. Life is far too precious even during its most painful moments.

I was sitting in the solarium embroidering a new altar cloth for the abbey in grateful thanksgiving for Elise's third birthday when I heard the sound of horses coming along the road paralleling the river. From the window, high as it was, I could look across the expanse of meadow to the river and see the two horsemen who rode along at a fairly fast canter. As they turned onto the road going past our home toward the village, they disappeared momentarily from sight. I crossed the large room to the windows overlooking the courtyard in time to see my father ride up from the village and hear him greet the strangers with his raucous, jovial voice. Although dusty from the journey, their rich attire and fine horses bespoke nobility. I could see from Father's gestures that he was inviting them into the house, and one of the stable boys was already helping them to dismount.

Remembering my duties as hostess, I went down to the main hall, called to one of the servants to bring wine, and walked out to the courtyard.

"Here she is now," my father said as he beckoned me over. "My daughter, Lady Lionors. Lionors, I have asked these men to stay the night with us. This is Lancelot, son of King Ban of Benwic, and his cousin Perseleus."

"Welcome to the House of Sanam," I bowed. "If you'll come inside, I've ordered wine, and you can rest from your travels."

"Good, good," my father said. "Yes, come inside." As cordial and gregarious as he was, he was also apt to

145

overlook such fine points of hospitality as offering rest or refreshment. Delighted to have guests, he would have kept them standing while he probed for all the latest news.

While the men savored their wine and relaxed muscles cramped from riding, I observed them closely. The younger man, Lancelot, was not unattractive, but not handsome, not nearly so handsome as Arthur. I could say that without prejudice because there were many men who were more comely. Lancelot had a deeply tanned complexion, thick black hair, and strong features. He was not tall, but he carried himself well. His cousin, a few years older, was more physically attractive but less imposing and somewhat less self-assured.

After accepting a refill, the younger man spoke. "I thank you. I had not expected such hospitality. In fact, I was beginning to wonder if we would find any place where we could ask the way."

Now I realized why his words sounded a bit formal and strange; there was just the trace of an accent in his voice, although he spoke our dialect with precision.

"We are on our way to the court of King Arthur," he continued, "where I hope to serve him and prove myself worthy to become one of his knights. We seem to have gotten lost. I'm not sure where we are or where we got off the right road."

My father laughed, "You're not lost. Most people who come across the channel land near here and travel this way."

A cloud crossed Lancelot's face, and I sensed that my father's laughter had hurt his pride. I spoke up quickly.

"Someone misled you if you were not told about this road and our house."

My words seemed to make him feel a little better, so I hastened to add my assurance that they were welcome to stay the night.

"Your rooms are ready, the fires already lit, and water is being heated for your baths."

"But," Lancelot said, "all this will be too much trou-

146

ble for you. We can easily go on and camp out tonight. We have everything we need to make ourselves comfortable. I do not fear spending the night outside."

"Nonsense," my father said, "you will be doing us a favor. We have not had guests in a long time, and I want to hear all the news from your side of the water and what you've heard from Camelot."

"My father's right," I added. "He'll never let you get away until you've brought him up to date on what's been going on in the world beyond this small corner of Britain. But I warn you, be prepared to stay up half the night."

As I excused myself to go and give orders for supper to be served in the library, I heard Father explaining that in the morning he would have one of the grooms accompany them as far as the main road to Camelot and give them introductions to friendly places where they could spend the next night or two. In the kitchen, I ordered more fowl put on the spit, picked out a jar of tart quince jelly to be served with it, and selected fresh fruit and cheese. Then I went to my room to dress for dinner.

I completed my toilette carefully, choosing a red gown banded in gold, one I had not worn since the last brief time with Arthur at Camelot. I redid my hair, tucking a few jewels among the braids. For some reason I felt the need to make myself as attractive as possible for Lancelot, yet not in the way a woman tries to arouse the admiration of a man. It was not a relationship between Lancelot and myself I thought of, but a celebration of the change in my life—and Arthur's— now that he had appeared on the scene. In what way I didn't know, nor would I know for a while, but that sixth sense instilled in me by Merlin was at work, and I only knew I was overjoyed at meeting this young man.

The conversation at dinner was a lively exchange of questions and answers, and the two guests were hard put to enjoy their meal while it was still hot and satisfy my father's insatiable curiosity at the same time. Yes, King Ban was in good health, but there were rumblings of impending war between him and King Claudas.

Lancelot might be required to return home and fight at his father's side. He answered one of my father's questions at greater length.

"I have met King Arthur only once," he said, "during the year he was crowned. I'll never forget seeing him for the first time. Though still young, he was as regal as any king I ever dreamed about. All the others, the knights and lords, were menials compared to him. He spoke about his dream of a round table, of gathering all the knights together so they could work as one to bring peace and unity to the country and end the turmoil. I could only stand to one side and watch, but when my father went down on one knee—one king to another—to acknowledge Arthur as his liege lord, I hungered to be able to do the same, to offer him my arm and my life in his service."

"Tell me," Perseleus broke in, "what think you, Lord Sanam, of King Arthur? Are you as ninny-headed about him as my young cousin here?"

My father answered slowly, but with sincerity. "Arthur has been a good king, a steady leader who has managed to secure the allegiance of many divergent factions and to maintain peace in Britain. He has calmed petty jealousies and resolved a number of problems that Uther Pendragon, for all his widespread popularity, did not even try to settle. Arthur has used the sword when he has had to—he is no coward—but he has also employed diplomatic strategies whenever possible, including a most beneficial marriage."

Afraid they would all hear my heart pounding and see the flush rise to my face, I reached over and poked the fire to give credence to the change in my complexion. All the while my father continued speaking.

"In many ways Arthur is a better king than his father, but not one to be as dearly loved or as long remembered. He is not as volatile nor as flamboyant as Uther, who could spear women all night with as much gusto as he speared his enemies all day. Beg pardon, pet," he added as he noticed my scarlet face, which he mistook for a blush at his crude remark.

In order to recover my poise, I asked Lancelot why

he had not stayed at court, as so many did, to serve as page to an older knight.

"No, I returned home to work and study to become the greatest knight in King Arthur's service. I have devoted all the days and months since then to that one end."

"I trust you will not be disappointed."

"At not being accepted by him?"

"No, at not being the greatest knight." I could not resist the thrust.

My father looked shocked and started to berate me for my rudeness, as well he might, for my remark was entirely uncalled for. However, Lancelot, standing before the fire, drew himself up taller and answered very quickly.

"Victory is reserved for the pure in body and soul. I am not without sin, but I have kept my body pure and therefore strong. I am not a Samson who has had his strength dissipated by the favors of a woman, and I have never failed to confess and do penance for those sins of which I have been guilty."

His sincerity went far to absolve his statement of the ugly aura of inordinate pride, but I longed to warn this young man to watch his step, for the gods delight in watching proud men be destroyed in snares of their own making.

Lancelot and Perseleus rode away the next morning toward Camelot, and I wondered how soon we would hear the young man's name again. We didn't have long to wait, for throughout the ensuing months, tale after tale was brought to us by passing travelers of the wondrous feats performed by King Arthur's newest member of the Round Table. According to them, giants and dragons, as well as those who abjured the rules of chivalry, were slain by the young hero who seemed to wear an invincible armor that neither a sharp spear nor supernatural power could penetrate. If he had feet of clay, they had not yet been exposed.

Then, without warning, some seventeen or eighteen months after Lancelot's visit, word went out from Camelot that King Arthur was calling on all who owed him their allegiance to go with him across the channel to Brittany to fight on the side of King Ban, whose lands were under attack by King Claudas.

A neighboring lord was dining with us when Arthur's courier arrived, and he began muttering complaints about having to cross the water to take up battle when there were more important problems to solve here at home. But my father defended the king's decision to aid a foreign ruler who had been friend and ally when Arthur was sorely in need of both.

"The lad's doing the right thing," he insisted, and I smiled at his referring to Arthur as though he were still a boy. "It's a man's duty to repay tit for tat, and Arthur would not be king today if Ban had not come to his aid at the time of his first great battle against the eleven kings. I'll wager Ban never thought twice about calling on his hundred knights to follow him across the water to fight for a new, young king whose cause seemed hopeless. Ay, and then didn't Ban pledge his allegiance to Arthur as his liege lord? No, no, it is Arthur's duty as feudal lord to give aid and protection to his subjects; it's the law of chivalry."

My father's arguments won the day, and both men prepared to meet Arthur at the rendezvous designated by him for deployment of his troops on the coast. My father was really too old to go into battle; he need only have sent the required number of knights who, by their oath of allegiance, had sworn to fight under the Sanam banner. However, he felt a deep sense of loyalty to Arthur, deeper than just that of vassal to lord.

While caught up in the preparations necessary for going into battle, he seemed to shed ten years, standing taller and appearing stronger than I could ever remember. He wasn't old at all; he had merely felt his prowess as a man diminish through years that offered no more dangerous challenges to his bravery than the charge of a wild boar or the settling of a drunken quarrel between two of his fiefs. He had been a stallion relegated to the duties of a plow horse, and now he was once more smelling hot blood while being freed from harness. He wanted me with him every minute, helping

150

him select the best spears and sword, agreeing with him every time he changed his mind and said "these two" were better than "those two." The assistant armorer, who had also had some training as a battlefield surgeon, was attending Father as his squire, and to him I entrusted a good supply of herbs and salves that my father would have scorned and tossed away at the first opportunity.

Exhausted by my father's energetic demands, I sighed with relief when the two of them rode through the gate. A whiskery kiss, orders to behave myself, and a fatherly pat on the rump kept our farewells from being teary, but once he was out of sight, an icy viper of fear for his safety twisted around my heart, where it would remain until the battle was over.

I was preparing to retire five days after my father's departure when Eric, one of the younger servants, knocked on my bedroom door.

"My lady, there's a stranger in the courtyard, a man asking to see you."

"At this hour! What does he want? Did he give his name?"

"He says, ma'am, to tell you the Strawberry Knight wishes to see you."

After more than five years, Arthur wanted to see me, had come here incognito, obviously wanting no one to know of his visit. I couldn't believe it was really Arthur, who should be on his way to Brittany, but he was the only one who knew that name.

"My lady?" I had forgotten Eric was still there. "What shall I say?"

"I'm sorry. I was unsure for a minute who it could be. Yes, bring him up. But listen carefully, no one must know he is here or learn that anyone has been here at least for the time being. Has anyone else seen him?"

"No, my lady, I don't think so."

"His horse?"

"He had none," the boy answered. "He must have left it outside the courtyard."

I was right to be cautious. Arthur must have teth-

151

ered his mount in the woods and walked to the manor to avoid discovery. I had faith that by taking Eric into my confidence, he would not betray my trust. He was at an age when it is exciting to have secrets, and it is one's sacred duty not to reveal them.

"Show him up," I ordered. "Then go to the kitchen and bring back cold meats and wine. If anyone is about, say I wanted something before retiring. I ate little at supper, worrying about Lord Sanam, so it will seem natural."

"Yes, my lady."

No, I needn't worry about Eric. He would die for me, if necessary, as he had once proved when he stepped in to grab the reins of a rearing horse that threatened to throw me. He would die for his king, too, if he had known it was the king he was serving. I listened for their steps in the main hall and counted each footfall as they came up the stairs.

"Good evening, Sir Ursa." I saw Arthur's eyebrows arch in surprise as I used the Latin term for "bear," a counterpart of his real name, Arcturus. I dared not kneel to him as king nor run to him as lover, so I had been inspired to invent the title to help ease the tension of our first meeting in five years.

"Good evening, Lady Lionors," he answered with a halfhearted attempt to conceal his smile. "I trust I've not inconvenienced you too much by appearing at this late hour."

"Not at all, sir. Will you wish to spend the night?" We were speaking like two puppets, carefully mouthing the words appropriate for the charade we were playing.

"Please," he answered, "if it will be no trouble, and there is room."

There is room enough right within this bedchamber, I thought, but to such a thought I must not put words.

"No trouble at all. Eric, please see that the second guest room is prepared before you bring up supper. Then Sir Ursa can retire when he is ready."

To Eric, the second guest room would imply a less important visitor, and I wanted him—and anyone who might discover Arthur's presence—to have that opinion

152

of my guest. Arthur looked askance, but I would explain to him later about the secret stairway leading from that room to mine.

Eric closed the door as he left. Only then did Arthur remove his outer wraps, and immediately I knelt to do homage to my king. I had not looked upon him long, but in those few moments I saw that much about him had changed. His beard was longer and fuller, widening a face now gaunt from concern for his people and the many battles he had fought to unite them. His hair, once thick and curly around his forehead, had thinned, giving him the brow of a sage. A scar on one cheek was evidence of a wound received since I had last seen him. How I longed to heal it with my touch and to smooth out the fine lines webbing his tanned skin.

Before I could rise, he had his arms around me, pulling me up to him. I heard the release of his breath, like the release of a long-imprisoned sigh, and I felt the pressure of his body against mine, urgent and demanding. Knowing Eric would be returning any minute, I forced myself to pull away from him.

"Lionors?" The hurt tone in his voice echoed his misinterpretation of my action.

"Ssh," I said. "Eric is coming with wine and food. Once he has left, we will not be disturbed."

I busied myself placing a table between two chairs before the fire. When Eric came, he insisted on pouring the wine and wanted to serve us until I insisted that we would need him no more that night.

Although my emotions had been aroused as much as Arthur's, I felt the need to talk, to somehow bridge the years of separation before we resumed an intimate relationship.

"Arthur?" I stopped, unable to find the words to ask how things stood between him and Guinevere. I shifted to a different subject. "How were you able to come here tonight? Aren't you supposed to be organizing your troops along the coast?"

"I've left that task to subalterns who can manage as well as I. It will be at least a week before we're ready to sail, and during that time I'm ostensibly secluding

153

myself in a monastery to meditate and pray for guidance and victory. As soon as I got things lined up, I headed straight for you—just as I planned when I chose that port for embarkation."

"What—" I hesitated. "What about Guinevere?"

"It's you I need now," he answered brusquely, "and you I love."

"I love you, Arthur, but Guinevere is your wife."

"Lionors, you must know ours was a marriage of expediency, not one of love. I'm fond of her, and she has tried to care for me. We have not been completely unhappy, but I have never stopped loving you."

"Yet," I whispered, "you waited five years to come to me."

"I longed to, but I had to wait . . ." His voice trailed off. "I left Lancelot at court to protect her."

"Your best fighter?" I was astounded.

"I have enemies here, too, and—and he has become Guinevere's lover. I would have come sooner, but . . ."

I gave voice to what he was trying to say; "You couldn't be the first to be unfaithful. Only after she gave herself to Lancelot could you come to me." I tried not to sound bitter.

"I think that's it," he nodded disconsolately. "She married me, not loving me but trying to be a good wife. I have not been the husband she wanted. I wasn't able to give her a child, and I wouldn't add having a faithless husband to her other sorrows."

"And," I stiffened, "you never thought you were unfaithful to me, that by our betrothal vows I was your wife, too."

Arthur left his chair and tried to lift me up from mine, but I resisted.

"Please, Lionors, don't turn away now. Have I hurt you that much?"

"Hurt? I've forced myself to be indifferent for so long, I'm numb. I can't remember how deeply I was hurt. But I'll tell you this. I would have died if I could have willed it."

"Are you sorry, then," he asked, "that I'm here now? I'll go if you wish it."

"Sorry?" I took the arms he held stiffly at his sides and put them around me. "No, I'm happier than I've been in a long, long time. You've come to me because you want me. For one day or forever, I'll keep you here as long as I can. I love you, and every moment with you is precious."

"And," he inquired, "are these precious moments to be spent in the second guest room? Is that any way to treat your husband and your king?"

"That's exactly why I did it. You obviously came here in disguise, so who would ever dream I would put the king in a second-best room. It's very drafty and not at all cheerful."

"It doesn't sound as though I'll be very comfortable. Do I have to sleep in there?"

"Oh, but come here. I had a second reason for choosing that room."

I led him to a large tapestry. When held away from the wall, it revealed paneling identical to that in the rest of the room. My father had installed the paneling and hung tapestries as a gift for my mother before her illness. However, when I pressed a secret spring, the panel slid aside, and a short, narrow staircase led to a narrow passage within the deep wall.

"See, from your room to mine. I doubt you'll spend much time in your miserable, drafty room."

Arthur picked me up and swung me around and around. "Lionors, you're a sly one. You try to be aloof and indifferent, and all the time—you're wonderful!"

"I told you, Arthur, I think of you always as my husband. But I had to know if you still truly loved me."

Much later, in that half sleep of dreams, I heard heavy, insistent pounding on the courtyard gate. In the hours before the disturbance Arthur and I had come together hungrily, satisfying the demands of a newly aroused passion, followed by calmer moments suffused with the joy of rediscovering each other. Then soon our very closeness aroused new urgencies and brought us together again until, exhausted and filled with love, we slept. Even as I heard the pounding, I felt his arm around me, his fingers caressing my breast as he, though still asleep, became aroused.

However, when the pounding on the gate was followed by someone knocking on the bedroom door, I sat up wide awake.

"Who's there?" I called.

"It's me, my lady," answered Ian, who had relieved Eric as night guard.

"What do you want at this time of night!" My impatience made me shorter than I meant to be.

"That's what I said, ma'am, when they came pounding at the gate."

"They? Who is they?" I demanded.

"Some men, ma'am, insisting on seeing you. They say . . ."

"Well, what do they say?"

"They say," Ian answered in wonder and bewilderment, "we're hiding the king. They're crazy, ma'am, but that's what they say."

"Are they in the house?" I was reaching for my nightdress and robe while I spoke, trying to gather my wits at the same time.

"No, ma'am, they was so rude I made them stay out in the cold."

In spite of the seriousness of the situation I wanted to laugh at Ian's simple type of vengeance. "Well, bring them in. Take their cloaks and get them hot wine."

"Wine, my lady? For them?" I knew Ian thought my suggestion mad, but I was sparring for time.

"Do as I say," I insisted. "I'll be down in a minute. Awake the retainers."

I turned to the bed where Arthur was holding my pillow, smiling in his sleep. There was no time to wake him gently.

"Arthur!" I rolled him back and forth. "Arthur, there are men here looking for you."

He was instantly awake and alert. "No one knows I'm here."

"Well, someone must think so. They're going to search the house. Right now I'm stalling them while

Ian serves them wine. He won't tell them anything because he doesn't know you're here."

"Where . . ."

"The secret passageway," I said. "Hurry, you can sit on the stairs."

He had just time to grab a light coverlet from the bed to wrap around himself. I could hear voices in the hall below as I slid the panel back across the opening and rearranged the tapestry.

Only then did I see Arthur's clothes. There was no time for panic. A connecting door led to a storage room. I hoped the men would believe they were my father's. I dumped them in a pile as though they had been discarded.

Trying to appear both poised and at the same time outraged for having been disturbed at such an hour, I went down to meet the intruders. I tried to assure them that no guest was in the house, but in surly tones they insisted on searching. A scullery boy, evidently sneaking back from a visit to the village, had told them of seeing a man walk from the woods into our courtyard and then into the house.

For three hours they searched every room, tearing up the linen room by pulling down every piece. All would have to be refolded, some even rewashed. They broke three crocks of our best preserves and turned over barrels of apples and vegetables. They pried through clothes presses, hauling out woolen and velvet gowns as though they were rags. I held my breath when they searched the small storage room, but they merely kicked at the pile of Arthur's clothes, evidently thinking they weren't worth bothering with. Fortunately, Arthur had not even gone into the second guest room, so there wasn't the slightest bit of evidence to betray him. I had tossed the second wine goblet into the passageway with Arthur and pulled the spread up on the bed, so my room passed inspection without arousing suspicions.

From the pain that exploded in my chest when they finally rode away, after leaving muddy footprints in every room, I felt I must have held my breath during the entire three hours. For fear of alerting the servants to the truth, I walked slowly back to my room, bolted the door, and then ran for the secret panel.

Arthur sat huddled on the second step, the small coverlet wrapped awkwardly around him. I couldn't keep from laughing, partly at the sight of his ignominious posture and partly from relief.

"Oh, Arthur, you look so funny!"

"I don't feel funny," he growled.

"I'm sorry, darling. You must be cold."

"Cold! I'm frozen. I'm a living, breathing icicle."

He returned to the room, and I closed the panel behind him.

"Good God!" he exclaimed as he lay in bed while I rubbed his back and shoulders. "I'll never be warm again. You can stop massaging and crawl in here beside me. Maybe that will help." Then he suddenly burst into wild laughter. "Wouldn't my enemies—or my friends—enjoy seeing their king huddled bare-ass naked on the stone steps of a secret stairway!"

I joined him laughing at the picture he painted of himself; then I got serious. "But why must you hide? You are the king."

"Because I *am* king, and my throne is on none too steady ground. There are those who would snatch at any rumor of scandal to dethrone me or even kill me."

"What about the affair between Guinevere and Lancelot? Aren't you afraid the danger lies in that corner?"

"She is as cautious as I must be. No, those who would destroy me would do it by using her."

"How?" I asked.

Arthur rolled over on his back. "By saying they were from Gwen, on her side rather, and setting out to prove me an unfaithful husband. I'd be accused of breaking my own laws and be forced to abdicate in favor of one of them. Then they would desert her after working through her to get the throne. They might even kill me and force her to marry one of them."

158

"But why this great need for fidelity? Your father . . ."

"That's one reason. He could do it. But you know he's remembered for his lust and cruelty. Under our new laws infidelity on the part of the queen is treason, a capital offense. I have made it very clear that a king who makes a law should be required to live by the law. They could turn my own words against me. I was trying to return the court to moral law and order. I was conceived in lust. That's right. Uther lusted after my mother and had her husband ambushed and killed. For what? One night of sport. I wanted to rid the court of that memory. I know, she welcomed him and agreed to it, but it was lust, not love. I may carry my father's blood, but I will not be a duplicate of my father.

"I've tried hard to be a good man; oh, God, how I've tried. Yet look, what are my only two children—bastards! Suffering for my sins."

I put my fingers to his lips. "Ssh, don't say that."

"Yes, they suffer. Mordred is crippled emotionally, hating me with every breath. And Elise, blind."

"No, no," I assured him, "that's not your fault. Merlin said it was the sickness I had when I was carrying her. She's just fine. I'll send for her tomorrow."

"Fine!" he sputtered. "How can she be?"

"Oh, you'll see. She runs around and plays like any normal little girl. She laughs at the birds' singing as if she could see their crazy antics in the sky. She loves to ride on the back of the sheep, gripping the tight curls with complete confidence. She's a beautiful child, Arthur."

"Do you see her often?"

"Oh, yes. Several times a year she comes here for a few days. I'd keep her here with me all the time, but the nuns are doing a beautiful job. She feels safe at the convent and is able to walk all over the place with almost no help. She knows each nun by her voice. I think she even recognizes the way each one walks because she can call her favorites by name as soon as they enter the room."

159

"They're not too strict?" Arthur was all concerned father now.

"Heavens, no. They spoil her with their loving and mothering. She's the child none of them can ever have. They discipline her, and I think the routine is good for her. I notice she gets restless around here, uneasy if we don't have prayers right on time. Oh, I'm very religious when she's here."

"What do they think about Elise here at the manor?" Arthur asked.

"They think what I told them," I answered. "She was abandoned at the abbey while I was resting there. They've never seemed to question that. Even my father. He was away a good bit before she came. Then there was danger of a battle in our area, so he was eager to have me go to the abbey when I said I wanted to spend some time there.

"I almost didn't come home when I learned Elise was blind. I wanted to stay with her, but the good nuns persuaded me it was better for both of us for me to leave her there and return home. When she comes, you'll meet Berthe who's been her nurse and teacher since she was a baby. You'll see how beautifully Berthe handles her."

After the three-hour search and our familiar talk, we slept late in the morning, Arthur going through the secret passage to be reawakened and served by Eric.

None of those on our manor had been more than a few miles from the estate except for Marta, so there was no danger of anyone recognizing Arthur as their king. They might have their own ideas about my entertaining a man during my father's absence, but they kept their opinion of my morals to themselves.

We had nine wonderful days together; picnicking on Ave Lion, riding across the meadows, and hawking with our birds.

On one especially warm afternoon we took the skiff down river, planning to go as far as the bay. Arthur poled while I lay back, watching the sun fleck through the leafy branches and bounce along the surface of the water. The water mirrored the trees so perfectly, we had the sensation of gliding through the top of a rain forest rather than on the river. Two songbirds, larks, vied with each other for our attention; two minstrels entertaining us with their musical ballads of the forest.

When Arthur tired of poling along the shore, we headed for the channel in midstream and let the current sweep us lazily along. The September sun was hot, and Arthur, already sweating from his exertions, pulled off his shirt.

"You're lucky being a man," I said. "I wish I could do the same."

"Why don't you," he grinned. "I won't object."

"Thank you, but no, I'll just pull my skirts up over my knees. That's daring enough."

"Well, at least take off those heavy shoes and hose. You must be sweltering."

"I am." I reached up under my skirts to loosen the hose, rolled them down, and took off my shoes. "Oh, that feels good," I sighed, stretching out my legs and wriggling my toes.

"You know what," Arthur said after a few minutes. "We should go swimming."

"Today!"

"Today, right now. Put your hand in the water. It isn't a bit cold. And there isn't a cloud in the sky. The sun will be hot for another two or three hours. We'll head back for the island and have a swim before supper."

"But I can't!" I insisted.

"Yes, you can. I know you're wearing a shift or chemise, or whatever you call it, because I watched you dress this morning. You used to swim in nothing more than that. I'll take the pole, and you row. We'll get out of this current and be back at the island in no time."

I saw there was no arguing with him, so I took up the oars.

The water was warm on the surface, but the few days of cold weather had already chilled the depths, and even swimming hard didn't warm us up. But the sun was hot, and by rubbing ourselves briskly with our clothes, our skin was soon pink and tingling. While I was fluffing my hair dry, Arthur called to me.

"Come here, beautiful."

He took me in his arms and held me for a long time, smoothing my wet hair, opening my mouth with the pressure of his. This time, when he reached inside the neck of my shift, I didn't resist, but clung to him all the more fiercely as my breasts swelled and my nipples hardened under his touch. The ache in my loins gave way to the ecstasy of relief as he held me so tight I could scarcely breathe. Without a word he picked me up and carried me to the clearing; there, under the sheltering branches of the giant oak, we made love. After, wrapped in the blanket cocoon, we lay on the soft, mossy grass.

"I've wanted to do that for a long time," he whispered.

"I know. So have I," I answered. "How many years since that day we fell in love?"

"I don't count them. I only count the days I'm with you."

He was running his fingers gently up and down my body.

"What a nice, flat belly. So smooth," he cooed.

"I hope it stays flat after this visit of yours."

"Feeling guilty? Like 'as you sow, so shall you reap'?"

"I just don't want to reap a harvest in nine months. It's not fair. The man does the sowing and the woman the reaping."

"But you love Elise?"

"Yes, but no more. Arthur, I'd give you a child every year with love and delight if you were by my side. But I cannot go through it alone."

"I know," he answered quietly.

I had some herbs I had gathered with old Gundrig, and I would make up an abortive potion that night just to be on the safe side.

"You know," I said as we began to dress, "I'll bet Elise would enjoy swimming."

162

"I know she would," Arthur agreed. "We'll bring her here when I return in the spring."

"In the spring? Do you really think you'll be back by then? The battle in Brittany will be over?"

"It should be," he said. "I can't imagine King Claudas continuing to wage a war when our forces join up with Ban's. I imagine he'll put up a fight at first to mollify his pride, but I can't see him courting the danger of a complete rout and loss of all his men. No, he'll retreat into his own territory soon after we arrive, and I doubt that Ban will want to incur more of Claudas's wrath by invading him."

"Arthur, I'm worried about my father. Fired up as he was when he left here, I don't think he'll be content to stay back in his tent and give advice."

"Don't worry," Arthur said as he took my hand. "He'll have all the men watching out for him. He's the grand old man of the troops, and before I left, his tent was already the rallying point. The men all love him and his stories. They're not going to let anything happen to him."

"I hope not."

He kissed me on the forehead. "You just stay here and take care of yourself and Elise. Are you going to tell her about her parents—about us?"

"When she's old enough to understand. Just as soon. I don't want her spending her younger years wondering, as you did, about her heritage. She'll be proud of her father, and I'll try to make her understand why we're separated."

"But not more than we have to be," Arthur said. "I'll try to get here at least once a year so she'll really get to know her father."

One day we awoke to a morning so crisp and sparkling it almost cracked. The trees wore crowns of scarlet and bronze, and each gust of wind loosed a torrent of leaves that flew like a covey of brilliant pheasants to the ground. It was a perfect day for riding.

From the stable we brought a gentle mare. Will was to have his first riding lesson. I had plans for him that included being more than just a page. Already impressed by his quick mind and intelligent curiosity, I saw the possibility of training him to be my personal assistant on the estate. If he were as smart as I thought he was, he could ultimately become steward and assume most of the responsibility.

Will was impatient to get right up on the horse, but Arthur insisted on Will's learning all the rudiments of preparation he had to go through before mounting. Will was fascinated by the attention he was receiving from a handsome knight, and he listened to every word with the rapt attention that would delight any teacher.

"See," Arthur showed him patiently, "you must be careful how you put on the saddle so your horse won't get saddle sores. His mount is the most important property a man owns. A good one can save his life, so you always make sure your horse is in healthy condition. When you're through riding, you rub him down, brush his coat, and feed and water him before you even consider taking care of yourself. I'll show you how to do all that when you've had your ride."

Bless Arthur's heart! He who always had a squire or stable boy waiting to hold the reins and take over as soon as he rode in was having a wonderful time going through all the paces with a starry-eyed little boy. I stood to one side holding Elise by the hand. She was jumping up and down like a puppy on an ant hill.

"What's he doing now, missy?" she squealed.

"Putting on the saddle, honey. It's like a seat that makes it more comfortable to ride."

"Now what? What's he doing now?"

"Sir Ursa has put Will up on the horse and is leading him around."

Elise cocked her head as she did when listening intently. "He's still going slow. Will he get to run?"

"Not today," I said. "That will come later."

"Am I next? Will Sir Ursa teach me to ride?" Elise's words tumbled out, one word on the heels of the other.

"I'm afraid not, honey," I explained patiently. "Too dangerous for you. You couldn't guide the horse."

"But, missy, the horse can see. She knows her way home. Please, please."

164

"Maybe when you're older and stronger. You couldn't hold the reins."

Her eyes flooded with tears. She had always been so good about not pouting or throwing a tantrum when we had to say "no." It made me physically sick to have to disappoint her. She became very quiet and stopped jumping around. Then, as I saw Arthur help Will down, I had an idea.

"Ursa, Elise wants to ride, too. How about a tandem ride around the courtyard with this little lady?"

"A brilliant idea," he responded. "Come on, Elise, we'll show them how to ride."

I thought he would mount and ask me to lift her up, but in one quick, easy movement he swung into the saddle and placed her in front of him where she rested as comfortably as if she were in his lap. Arthur walked the mare around the courtyard while Elise got used to the unfamiliar motion. Her former teary eyes were now sparkling, and her fat curls bobbed around her pink cheeks. Then Arthur headed through the gate and into the meadow, nudging the horse into a gentle canter.

"Missy, missy." Will was tugging at my skirts. "They've gone into the meadow, and they're running. I didn't get to run."

"Hush, Will. Your time will come. Remember, Elise can't see and may never be able to ride alone."

"I'm sorry. Why can't Elise see?"

"It's God's will, honey."

The two riders came back, breathless with exhilaration. Elise was so excited she couldn't stop chattering.

"I rode, Will, I rode," she screamed. "The horse ran. I bounced, but Sir Ursa held me tight."

While Arthur and Will led the horse to the stable for the after-ride training session, I carried a happy little girl into the house to calm her down before lunch. And I was happy, too. I had seen Arthur taking his daughter—our daughter—on her first grand excursion. It was so right that he should be the one to do it.

All too soon Arthur left to rejoin his troops and lead them into battle beside King Ban. Elise returned to the abbey. The war in Brittany raged for almost a year, King Claudas not abandoning the siege as quickly as Arthur was so confident he would. Almost no word reached us from across the water.

The days were long and gray. It seemed as though the sun didn't shine during all of the months the men were away. We awoke to leaden skies that either dripped rain or gusted cold winds. Even spring and summer failed to bring us really warm weather or clear skies. I went through the motions of running the estate, taking what pleasure I could in teaching Will to read and learn a few simple problems in addition. His gleeful pride in being able to print his name brought the first smile to my face in weeks.

Late in August a runner came through the gate with the joyful news that the battle in Brittany was over, Claudas giving up the siege and returning to his lands. The men would be home soon. Within two days my father returned to the manor, carried on a litter slung between two horses and guarded by soldiers. Barely alive, he was paralyzed from the waist down as the result of an arrow wound in his lower back. I prepared a bed in the library, knowing he would prefer being in there than in one of the guest rooms, and with a few minor alterations turned it into a comfortable bedroom for him. I searched through my supply of herbs and studied the recipes I had written down while working with Marta and Gundrig. While Marta brought his strength back with her savory stews, I massaged his back and legs with salves. Whether it was the salves or my hours of rubbing, I was at least able to reduce the intense pain Father was suffering when first brought in, but he never walked again.

Arthur did not come to the manor, but I understood. I knew he would have come with Father if there hadn't been the danger of being recognized, which would have put an end to his ever coming again. However, he sent bad news. Kay had been killed in battle.

⚙ *Chapter Eight* ⚙

Within eight months after his return from Brittany, my father died. He had been a proud, strong, virile, independent man, but the arrow that pierced his spine destroyed all but his pride. Before he left to fight with King Ban, he could ride all day, shoot an arrow from the strongest bow made, and carry home a wild boar across his shoulders. Now he could no longer ride at all, and it was an effort for him even to hold his sword.

A hot-blooded, lusty man, he had shared his bed almost nightly with the most buxom wenches on the estate. I had long since closed my eyes and ears to the furtive hustling of his latest wanton tiptoeing shoeless down the hall to his room for these nocturnal trysts. Fortunately, my awareness of his sexual prowess coincided with the awakening of my own senses to the physical delights and needs of the body. Earlier I might have condemned his apparent faithlessness to the memory of my mother, but the consummation of my love for Arthur as well as the knowledge that I was carrying his child made me more sympathetic. Now my father's lack of interest in the maids who served him, his failure to respond to their presence with a bawdy or suggestive remark, revealed all too clearly his impotence.

Even worse for him, I think, than his lack of strength or virility was his utter dependence on others for even his most personal and intimate needs. Without a word Eric had taken over the bodily care of my father, tending him as gently as one would a baby. It was apparent he considered the task an honor, not a chore,

167

and he assumed the privilege before anyone else could claim it. At night he slept on a pallet by his master's bed, and he must have learned to manage with very little sleep, for my father was never free from pain and required a great deal of attention, especially in the need to change positions frequently. They soon worked out a system of silent signals because every once in a while, with no apparent request from my father, Eric left the room and returned with food or wine. At other times he asked me politely to leave for a few minutes, then opened the door and indicated I could come back in.

My father's pride, however, had not been vanquished by the arrow. With Eric's assistance, he still dressed every morning as meticulously as if he were expecting guests or preparing to ride over our lands. There was never the foul odor of disease or bodily function about him, for at least every other day Eric filled the great wooden tub in the bath with hot water redolent of spicy herbs and carried my father in. While holding his master in the tub, Eric massaged the wasted limbs, easing the pain and trying to restore feeling in them. He even invented a sling of heavy cloth on which my father lay so that he could stay in the water longer than the few minutes before Eric's arm began to tire.

Pride as well as pleasure kept alive his interest in his manuscripts and the affairs of the estate. Many times when we were going over the accounts, I saw that he was exhausted and urged him to put them aside, but he would shake his head and insist he was fine. All of our hours together, however, were not sad ones by any means. For when he felt well, which was often, he delighted in recapturing bright moments of the past by reminiscing about the battles he had fought alongside Uther Pendragon and the hunts in which he had speared the fiercest boar. Best of all were his memories of the years with my mother. How he had wooed and won the fairest maiden in all of Britain. How amazed he was that she, the cynosure of all men's eyes, fell in love with him, a grizzled warrior sixteen years her senior.

"She was barely seventeen when we married, and no

diamonds ever sparkled brighter than her eyes on our wedding day."

He told me about my birth, and how my mother had cried when she found out she had borne a daughter rather than the son she had promised him. "But I was not disappointed, lass, then or since, for I loved you from the minute I first saw you sucking at her breast."

She promised the next would be a son, but there was not a next one, nor did my father ever speak of her long illness.

Yes, for though I watched his spirit atrophy as his limbs became more withered, I remember most our happy hours together and the closeness we shared those last months.

In the spring Arthur sent word that he was coming to visit. My father understood his wish to appear at the manor incognito, recognizing a king's desire to divest himself of all the trappings of royalty whenever possible. Although he could not take charge of the arrangements, he insisted that I keep him apprised of all the details. We went over plans for the meals; I assured him the room for Arthur had been aired and the bed made up with the best linens, neglecting only to tell him which room. Father insisted not only on wearing his most splendid robes, but that Eric fix up a chair for him as well.

"If I can't stand when my—when a visitor comes, I can at least be sitting up, not sprawled out on a bed like a drunken lout."

Oh, lord, I thought, he must not come that close again to saying, "My king."

When Arthur entered the room, the expression in his eyes on first seeing my father confirmed my worst fears. Death had already signaled its approach by signs I had refused to heed. The sunken cheeks, the sallow, parchment skin, the skeleton visible beneath the fleshless body, had gradually become so familiar to me, I was unaware of the startling change in my father since Arthur had seen him last. Although we had only a few hours alone together each night, I wholeheartedly acceded to Arthur's wish to spend as much time as possible with my father. This visit, he acknowledged, was primarily to see his old comrade in arms and seek his advice. They remained closeted together in the library most of their waking hours, Father reluctantly admitting he was more comfortable in bed. I stayed with them when I could, sitting quietly to one side, reading or sewing, for they were seldom aware of my presence.

I remember one conversation, however, for it came back to haunt me years later. Eric remained discreetly out of sight while Arthur was there, so the two were able to speak frankly about affairs of court and country. The discussion this particular day centered around internal dangers rather than threats of attack from the north or the east, and the subject had narrowed down to the question of loyalty among those closest to Arthur.

"Watch out for the Orkney faction," my father warned.

"But, sir," Arthur exclaimed, "Gawain and Gareth are two of my most trusted knights. You can't think I'd be in any danger from them!"

"Aye, lad, but can you say the same for their brothers, Agravaine and Geheris? And—I beg your pardon—how about your son Mordred? He is of their blood and their ilk. Only a child yet, but how is he being reared? To love or to hate? All I say is—be wary. Gawain and Gareth may never do you harm, but if the family is threatened by a challenge to any one of them, watch out. They will stick together like stones in a wall mortared with pitch. And just as impregnable. Have you ever seen the Roman emblem of authority, the fasces?"

Arthur shook his head thoughtfully.

"It was a bundle of sticks or rods tied together around an ax. It signified the unity of the Roman empire. One stick alone could be snapped as easily as a dried twig, but as long as they remained tied together, no one could break them. That is your Orkney clan. The axe is the family pride or name; the sticks are the brothers. And they'll let neither love for you nor concern for country loose that string."

170

There were hours of conversations like this, and I don't know who benefited from them more, Arthur or my father. I watched with delight and increased hope as color came into the latter's cheeks until I realized it was the flush of fever brought on by overexertion. He had called up all his reserves of strength in the effort to be of some use to his king. The determination and energy required to talk with Arthur during those three days were more than he had ever compelled during the fiercest battle, but the rewards were proportionately great. During his last days he had been allowed to serve his king one more time.

For the next two weeks I seldom left my father's side. After Arthur's departure, he let drop the smiling mask of well-being he had worn to ease our anguish. He no longer feigned sleep when his body was tortured with pain, nor an appetite when food was anathema to him. The hardest part was to see him give up the fight, to abdicate his will to live to a wish for death. I was relieved when at last his body succumbed to the need for rest and he remained unconscious most of the time. His muscles lay relaxed, no longer taut with painful spasms, and his breathing was steady and effortless. Occasionally, he woke up, smiled to see me sitting by him, and then went back to sleep. Only once he roused up enough to talk. I urged him not to try to speak, but there was obviously something on his mind that he had to share with me. As it turned out, I was the one to share with him.

It seemed that something during Arthur's stay had alerted him to the fact it was not the king's first visit to the manor. I revealed to him Arthur's appearance as Sir Ursa before they embarked for Brittany. As always, Father came right to the point.

"Lionors, is Arthur your lover?"

"Yes. But it is more than that. We were betrothed many years ago. It was a private ceremony, to be sure, but no less binding." I went on to tell him how we met and when we fell in love.

"Ah, pet, I understand now your reluctance to marry. For certain, I did not want to go until I saw you

171

happily married and hold at least one grandchild on my knee. But you're strong, stronger than most women, and Arthur loves you. I saw that when he was here. He'll protect you, and I do not doubt that he will come as often as he can. It is no sin for a king—even as moral a one as Arthur—to have a mistress."

I did not want to alarm him about the danger to Arthur if our liaison were known, so I made no comment.

"Father, I want you to know something else. You have held a granddaughter on your knee."

"Elise?"

"Yes. Arthur and I were betrothed and would have married if war hadn't broken out in the north. Then, as you know, he had to marry. But I have always thought of Arthur as my husband."

"He is a fine man, Lionors, and I would have been proud to have had him for a son. I'll die happy thinking of him that way. I only wish I'd known Elise was your child when I held her."

"I'll send for her, Father. She can be here within two days and stay as long as you like."

A smile was his only reply as he lapsed into the coma from which he never recovered. I did not send for Elise, but he died thinking he would see her one more time.

The summer brought a warmth to my spirits as well as to the countryside. The sun shone almost every day as if making up for its neglect the year before, and the fields promised a rich harvest. The boughs of the fruit trees bent almost to the ground, so laden were they with succulent apples and pears and apricots. Even the old gnarled and thorny crab-apple trees were prodigal with their abundant offerings. Although my grief was not dispelled by the pleasure I took in watching the fields turn from brown to green as the seeds sprouted, it was eased considerably. The flowering shrubs, the budding fruit trees, awoke in me an awareness of the cycle of life, the rebirth of life after the death of winter.

As busy as the summer had been, autumn was even more hectic, with the harvesting, the storing, and the measuring out of grain to the fiefs on the estate. I was more grateful than ever for the hours I had sat in the courtyard with my father as he delegated what share of the crop was to be stored, what to be meted out, and which families were to get extra shares. In what spare moments I had, I helped Marta oversee the busy kitchen. It was a good year for root vegetables, some of which were carefully packed between layers of straw in the root cellar, while others were tied in bunches and hung from the rafters to dry out in the ever-present smoke that drifted up from the wood fires.

The brilliant scarlet leaves of the sumacs and oaks, the exuberant yellow of the poplars and hickorys, burst forth to celebrate, one last explosion of color, the end of a rich and abundant season.

The winter that followed was particularly bitter. A blizzard ushered in the second week of January, entombing us under a pall of frigid white. It never warmed up enough to melt the snow, but the winds that roared down from the north swept across the meadows like a giant broom, piled up drifts against walls and trees, and then receded.

Marta and I immediately gathered up blankets and warm clothes, filled baskets with food, and set out for the village to visit each house, distributing what goods were needed. It was dusk before we started back, and a bone-chilling wind had begun to blow again. In the morning, Marta was sick with a racking cough and a high fever. She was having difficulty breathing and after much persuasion agreed to stay in bed. I prepared a tisane from one of her own receipts and, ignoring her protestations, covered her chest with a hot poultice. But to no avail. With each hour her breathing became more labored. I substituted steaming mulled wine for the tea, kept replacing the hot stones at her feet, and added more covers to sweat out the fever.

But Marta was old, and her tired body refused to respond to even the most intensive care. The fever was pernicious. It would not abate, but continued to spread through her worn-out body, gradually consuming what little strength she had. I knew the crisis was coming when she could no longer suppress her moaning and

173

her skin was too hot to touch. I had persisted in forcing liquids down her throat, but when she went for twenty-four hours without passing water, I knew something was seriously wrong. I separated her dried, salt-caked lips and prayed for her to swallow the water I poured through them, a trickle at a time. From time to time I felt the blankets beneath her, with more prayers that I would find them soaked. If I could get her through the crisis, there was a chance she would live. Sometime in the early hours of the morning she reached for my hand, and gripping it with the last of her strength, she died.

Scarcely had I seen to the laying out of Marta when one of the men sent to forage for dried faggots found Gundrig dead in her bed. Seeing no smoke coming from her wattle chimney, concern overcame superstition, and he entered the hut to investigate. He returned to the manor carrying her frozen body in his arms. I had not cried for my father, sustaining myself with the knowledge that he was past pain. Exhaustion had dried up the tears I might have shed for Marta, but at the sight of Gundrig's pathetic body, my eyes flooded, and for hours I cried without stopping, allowing all the despair and loneliness and heartache to come pouring out unchecked. My pillow was soaked, but I had no will to raise my head, and I finally slept.

In the morning, still shrouded with sorrow, I oversaw the digging of two graves side by side near the orchard. The ground was frozen, and the servants had to work in shifts. It was all I could do to endure the hours of agony, watching the excavations get deeper and wider, but I could not leave. Because it was getting dark when the work was finished, the priest conducted a brief burial service, and we returned to the house for supper. Even death does not assuage the pangs of hunger, and I had not eaten since the previous day.

Within the span of nine months I had lost three beloved companions. More than that, I had passed a peculiar milestone in my life. There was no one left who remembered me as a child, who could recall with me the foolish things I did when I was three or four. Those who were left knew me only as an adult. To them I had never been a child. Such a moment is a Rubicon that must inexorably be crossed, but one takes that step sadly, knowing there is no one to see the face of the child behind the lineaments of the woman.

I have often heard people say a part of them died when they lost a loved one. They spoke more truly than they realized. A human being grows like a tree, each year adding a layer to the exterior, gradually encircling the person he was the years before. One knows that a long-time friend looks beneath the outer layers and sees the person he first met. One's past lives in the memory of others. The death of a parent brings with it the loss of the child inside; with the death of a husband, the bride dies. And all that remains is a hollow core, a void that no one else can fill, for it has contained the stuff of memory.

The greatest loss comes not from having no one to turn to for advice or comfort. The desire is not to be a child again, but the need is to see in the eyes of the parent the memory of the child that was.

The next few years succeeded each other with very little to distinguish any particular one from those that preceded or followed. As Arthur had promised, he was able to return to the manor at least twice a year. His days with us took on less and less the appearance of a visit and became more like the master's return home after being away in battle. I had as much time with him as many wives whose husbands were occupied at court or fulfilling their obligations of vassel to lord.

The summer that Elise was seven, Arthur taught her to swim. Will had learned the previous summer, and Elise could hardly contain herself when we told her it was her turn. We packed a picnic lunch, rolled up some blankets, and this time I remembered to take towels. The four of us walked across the meadow to the river, Will stopping to pick flowers and watch a caterpillar hump itself along the length of a dead twig, while Elise danced ahead, calling all the while for us to hurry. In the skiff (a much sturdier replacement for the original) I held her in my lap to keep her from jump-

175

ing overboard, and Will insisted on taking one of the oars; to get us there faster, he said.

There was no thinking about lunch until we had all been in the water. Will jumped right in and began showing off how much he remembered until we had to caution him against splashing Elise. But nothing, not even a river monster, could have deterred her in her desire to learn to swim. While I tried to subdue Will and keep him from making waves, Arthur braced Elise in his strong arms. Together they walked to the bank where he taught her to put one foot in front of the other until she felt the edge beneath her toes. Then they sat down while he picked reeds for her to hold until she got used to the feel of them against her skin.

"But, sir," she fussed, "I want to learn to swim."

"In good time," Arthur said with aggravating deliberateness. "First you have to learn all about the river, its banks, and its vegetation. We don't want you to run into something strange and panic. You might drown, and we'd all miss you."

"Yes, sir."

"Good. Now put your hand in the water. How does it feel?"

"Just right for swimming," she annnounced with glee.

"All right," he laughed, "you win. Let's go."

After a few dunkings and the accompanying mouthfuls of water, Elise came up sputtering and gurgling, dangling from Arthur's arm like a fish caught on a line. Undaunted, she begged for more, letting Arthur support her stomach with one hand while showing her how to move her arms and legs. When she least expected it, Arthur lowered his arm, and she kept right on swimming. The day was a complete success. After swimming back and forth between us, guided by our voices, Elise was ready to eat. Will had kept himself occupied diving in among the reeds, chasing a fish that refused to be caught and finally announcing he was hungry.

Between them the two children ate enough to give them both stomachaches, then curled up like contented puppies and fell asleep on the blankets. Arthur lay with

176

his head in my lap, and too sated with contentment and warmth to talk, we dozed off, too.

While we were preparing to leave, Will said, "I like our secret place. It's always fun when we come here. Does it have a name?"

"Indeed it does," Arthur answered. "When she was about your age, Lady Lionors walked along the bank of the river one day and heard something calling to her. She listened very quietly. The sound was coming from the island, and she didn't know whether it was the wind in the trees or the voice of an enchanted wood nymph."

Will's eyes grew as round as an owl's. "It's a magic island?"

"It just might be," Arthur said very seriously. "That's why we always have a good time here. As long as we keep it our secret, whenever we come here it will be a very special day. Anyway, the voice kept calling, *'Ave, Ave,* Lionors.' *Ave* in Latin—which you might learn some day—means 'hail' or 'hello.' The longer she listened, the louder came the voice. There was a magic boat hidden in the reeds, and when she stepped in, it whisked her right over here. Every time she went near the river after that, she heard the voice calling to her, but when the wind died down, the voice became fainter, and it sounded like 'AveLion,' so that's its name."

Will repeated it over and over, saying the two words carefully and distinctly, but when Elise tried to imitate him, all her tongue could manage was "ave Lon," and so from that day forward, the island was known as Ave Lon.

"Sir," Will asked Arthur, "did she ever find the enchanted nymph? Will we ever hear her call to us?"

"No, she never has, but sometime if you listen very, very closely, you can hear her singing among the reeds, and maybe some day she'll even call your name."

"Oh, I hope so." Will was all wonder and innocent belief.

"By the way," Arthur asked him, "has Lady Lionors ever told you about the boy who fell out of a tree at her feet?"

"No, sir. Was he magic, too?"

177

Arthur tossed back his head and laughed. "No, Will, he wasn't magic. Just a lonely boy watching a little girl with her skirts above her knees wading in the river."

"Did he get hurt? Did she ever see him again?" Will was all curiosity.

"Would you believe I was that little boy?"

"You, sir?" And Will laughed, too, trying, I'm sure, to picture Arthur as a boy, but no doubt seeing him as he was now, tumbling out of a tree.

"For shame, Arthur," I said as we walked toward the boat. "Skirts above my knees, the very idea, and falling out of a tree. You climbed down."

"But it made a good story, didn't it? And Will loved it."

When Will was eight, I made him an outfit to wear as my page. He began his training by holding my chair at meals and pouring my wine. Quickly, he progressed to serving guests when they were present, assisting me when I went riding or hawking, working with me in the garden, and running errands around the manor. When he was older, he took messages to the village or helped me when I made my weekly tour to the cottages with food and supplies.

Since my father's death, I had not only assumed all of his responsibilities, but also continued with the tasks I had always done as lady of the manor. Will was of inestimable help to me. In addition to carrying supplies when I made my rounds, he brought information from the village about problems that had arisen or special needs to be answered. Always I had encouraged him to visit his family whenever possible, getting to know his younger brothers and sisters as well as his father who, surprisingly enough, had never voiced an objection to Will's living in the manor. But I made it a point never to cause any estrangement between them. Elspeth became my housekeeper after Marta's death, as faithful a servant as I could wish for. Although she could not live at the manor house because of her family, she did her best to fill Marta's shoes.

By the time Will was in his teens, he was riding with

178

me around the estate, proud of having been given his own horse to take care of and ride whenever he wanted to. When one of the mares foaled, Will was with me at the stables watching with avid interest the miracle of birth. He clapped his hands in pure delight when the colt, still damp from its mother's womb, stood on its spindly legs and began immediately to nurse.

"Oh, ma'am, he's beautiful," Will exclaimed. And indeed he was, a handsome roan with golden mane and fetlocks.

"Would you like to have him, Will?"

"For my own, my very own?"

"Your very own. Sir Ursa has taught you all about caring for a horse, so I shall expect you to do everything for him yourself. He'll feed from the mare until it's time to wean him, but she'll take care of that. I'll tell Luk (now much too old to be called a stable boy) he is to show you where everything is that you'll need."

From that moment on, whenever I wanted Will, I knew where to find him. When the horse was old enough to train as a mount, Will wanted to spend every day riding through the fields. His first errand was to the village, for I knew he was dying to show his family his new possession but wouldn't dream of asking permission. Once he had gotten over the thrill of simply riding his horse, he began to take a genuine interest in the work on the lands, the condition of the crops, and the labor entailed in harvesting. I knew then it had not been a foolish whim of the heart when I took him into the manor. My future steward was developing quickly under my tutelage.

During all the years he was growing up, we continued the lessons in reading, writing, and figures. From the time he was first able to understand about crops and shares, Will sat next to me at the long counting table while I watched the men weigh the various harvests and designated which granary or storehouse each crop was to go to. Soon Will was jotting figures in the account books as I called them out, and by the time he was fifteen I could have turned the whole procedure over to him if the serfs would not have grumbled at

179

taking orders from one so young and a member of a low rank. As it was, I merely sat there while Will made each decision with dispatch, but my presence lent the proper authority to his pronouncements. More and more I leaned on Will as he became the strong-arm my father said I would need to run the estate. When I was tired, he seemed to anticipate my needs and have a glass of wine or a dish of fruit ready when I walked into the library after a hard day.

While Will was developing into a sturdy youth, Elise was maturing in her own way. Gentle but precocious, she had her moments of despair when frustrations due to her handicap seemed more than she could bear. At those times she sought solace by asking Will to take her for a walk or suggesting to me that we ride over to the island. Unable to read or sew, she found release for her tensions in physical activity. Berthe told me that at the abbey they always knew when Elise was feeling depressed because she took on the tasks that required hard, physical labor, such as scrubbing and polishing.

Elise often sat on the floor at my feet while I read to her from the manuscripts as my father had done with me many years earlier. I began with Aesop's *Fables* when she was quite young. Her favorite stories were those that she could visualize, for though her eyes were deprived of sight, her brain was not. She played with Tippy, so she knew what a dog was. When going to the stables with me, she had often helped fill the mangers with hay.

"Tippy would never do that," she said of the dog in the manger, "Tippy's not selfish like that dog."

Some of the other stories were harder for her to understand, but by starting with the animals familiar to her and using them as a basis for description, I helped broaden the picture world she was creating in her mind.

"You know what a falcon is like? You have felt his beak." Here I took her hands and spread them wide apart. "Now that's how long a crane's beak is. So you see why he could stick it down into a jar. A fox is furry, like Tippy, and not much bigger, with a short, pointed nose, maybe a little more pointed than hers."

Elise nodded slowly, and in her busy mind an image was gradually developing.

As she grew, I began to introduce her to the myths in Ovid, selecting the ones I thought would interest her and that she could comprehend. After we read the one about Phaeton's fatal attempt to drive Apollo's chariot of the sun, Elise dismissed the cataclysmic ride as mere fable, but she focused in on the boy's longing to know who his father was and the need for proof that he was truly the son of Apollo. I had known this moment would come, and I was ready for her question.

"Missy, who were my parents? Did you know them?"

"Yes, you are the daughter of a king and a queen."

"Missy, you are teasing me?" The lilt in her voice gave her words the tone of a question in which there was the suggestion that I might not—just might not—be teasing.

"Let me tell you a story, Elise. Once upon a time there was a boy and girl who met and fell in love. They really loved each other very much. But she was the daughter of a nobleman, and he was just a squire who didn't know who his parents were."

"Like me?"

"Like you, honey. Then, all of a sudden he discovered he wasn't just a squire. He was a king."

"He had been enchanted," Elise interrupted excitedly, "by a witch or an ogre!"

"No," I answered, "nothing quite as fabulous as that, although almost as spectacular. For fear that his son would be killed by his enemies, the old king sent him to be reared by a trusted friend, intending to name him as his heir when the boy was old enough to protect himself. Unfortunately, the old king died before he could do this, and the lords began to argue among themselves as to who should be king. There was a great tournament in London that all the nobles attended. The young squire was sent to find a sword for his knight, and not being able to find the one that belonged

181

to his master, he was worried about returning empty handed. He remembered seeing a sword sticking from a stone in the churchyard, and thinking no one would mind—he would return it right after the joust—he pulled it out. He didn't know it was a magic sword that could be pulled out only by the rightful king, but the rest of the nobles did, and they proclaimed him king then and there. Oh, many of them disputed his right, and they tried to pull out the sword, too, but no one else was able to. Only the rightful king."

"That was my father? And he married the girl he loved?"

Now came the difficult part. How to explain to Elise that although in the eyes of the world she would be considered a bastard, I thought of myself as Arthur's true wife. Alert as she was, she would recognize any attempt to evade the issue, and she was old enough to know the truth.

"Times were difficult for the new king because he had many enemies, but finally the day came when the former squire and the nobleman's daughter could be together. They exchanged betrothal vows, which included the promise to be married as soon as possible. But a war intervened before they could fulfill that promise. You were born, and no child has ever been more loved or welcomed."

Here I decided upon a white lie to protect Elise from thinking of herself as a bastard. I knew how this curse had haunted both Arthur and Merlin like a malevolent incubus.

"The war changed many things. For political reasons, the king needed to marry the daughter of a former enemy—the marriage would seal a pact guaranteeing mutual aid in case either was attacked. Although it sorrowed him, the king asked his betrothed to release him from his vows. She agreed, knowing how important the marriage was to the unity of the country, but her heart was broken at the separation. Only her love for her child gave her the strength to keep living."

"Oh, missy, that's a sad story, sadder I think than if they died. But it isn't just a story, is it? You were talk-

182

ing about me—and my mother and father. Are they still alive? Or have they died? Is that why I'm not with them?"

"Elise, your father is—is a great king."

"And my mother?"

"She is no longer a queen, but she was for a few wonderful months, and still is in your father's heart."

"I think I understand why I'm not with them, but I wish I could see them," she murmured.

"You have, often. Your father carried you in front of him the first time you ever rode a horse."

"Sir Ursa! He is my father? He is a king?"

"I'll tell you a very special secret, but you must never tell anyone. Promise?"

"I promise."

"Sir Ursa is King Arthur, king of all Britain, but he can come here safely to see you only if no one knows about it."

Elise had put her head on my knees, and when I reached down to push a loose curl away from her face, I felt the tears on her cheek. Perhaps I was wrong to tell her so many details. At thirteen, she sometimes seemed more mature than many girls several years older.

"Missy."

"Yes, Elise."

"I'm glad Sir Ursa is my father. I love him very much."

No reference to his being king, no special thrill at having King Arthur himself for a father, just a wonderful sense of joy that she belonged to Sir Ursa.

"Missy," she asked wistfully, "where is my mother?"

The tears I had been holding back came out unbidden, falling on her hands, and she looked up.

"I'm right here, honey." I took her onto my lap, holding her close as I had so often held her when she was little and had bruised a knee or scraped an elbow. We were both crying now, and I had to search my pockets for a handkerchief to dry our eyes.

"Mother." How wonderful the word sounded the first time! "Are you a secret, too?"

"Yes, Elise. Someday I'll tell you the whole story, I promise, but just remember that King Arthur—your father—would be in grave danger if anyone knew about us."

"Oh, Mother, I'm the luckiest person alive to have you and Sir Ursa as parents. Let me look at you again."

Elise's "looking" was to run her fingers gently over my face, touching each feature, exploring my eyes, nose, and mouth. She carefully smoothed back my hair and then felt my shoulders and arms.

"Mother, am I as beautiful as you?"

"Oh, honey, I'm not beautiful, but you are going to be."

"Does anyone else know our secret?"

"Most of the nuns do because you were born at the abbey, so you can feel free to talk about us there."

"And I can tell them the story of the magic sword in the stone? How my father became king?"

"Yes, pet, you can tell them that wonderful story."

If falling in love is a mysterious, personal experience, it is only a little less exciting to watch a budding love affair between two handsome, healthy young people.

From the time of their first picnic, when Arthur came back into our lives, Elise and Will considered Ave Lon their own special island. When I was sure he was old enough to handle the skiff and keep Elise out of danger, I allowed Will to row just the two of them over. At first they were brief outings of no more than an hour or two, and I had to exert strong self-control to keep from pacing up and down the near bank until they returned. Each time they went, I extracted a stern promise from Will that neither would go swimming unless there were a third person along. Both were good swimmers, but accidents could happen, and Elise must never be subjected to any real danger or find herself alone and helpless on the island. As far as I know, Will never failed my trust.

Gradually, I extended the length of their stays until

finally, during the summer when they were sixteen, I gave permission for all-day excursions and helped Elise pack the lunches to take along. Tippy, whose demise was mourned by all of us, had been replaced by a less elegant, scruffy mongrel appropriately named Flea. At first the name was short for "Fleabag." When he first came to us, he was a walking hostelry—bed and board—for hundreds of the little insects. After many scrubbings with strong soap, he kept the name because he could get through openings so small we swore only a flea could enter. And he was just as pesky, demanding and getting our immediate attention. But the children loved him, so whenever they set off across the meadow for the island, Flea was right at their heels.

The brightest moment of the day came when Elise and Will ran into the house, plopped down on the floor, and began telling me in detail about their day. Flea would already have fallen exhausted into my father's favorite chair. Since no one else ever seemed to be in it, he claimed it for his own. One day they brought baskets of the tiny, delicious wild strawberries that grew rampant in the glade. They were all for me, they said, and I knew why they were being so generous. Red-stained faces and hands told their own story, and I wondered if I'd be up half the night doctoring sick stomachs.

They told me about listening to the frogs in the reeds and the birds singing as they built nests in the sturdy branches of the oak trees.

"Will climbed up one tree," Elise said excitedly, "and then described exactly how the nest looks. All woven perfectly together like a reed basket."

"You didn't disturb it, Will, did you?" I asked.

"Oh, no, ma'am, I stayed well away, only close enough to see. I got down before the bird came back with more twigs."

Elise reached out for one of the baskets, and Will, seeming to know instinctively what she wanted, guided one within her reach.

"See," she said, "we made these for you, too."

185

"I know you did," I answered. "I knew that the minute I saw them."

"Is this one mine, Will?" Elise asked.

"No, this one over here," and he handed her the second one.

"Look closely, missy; did I do a good job?"

"You did a beautiful job, Elise," I said; "it's perfect. Even the handles are straight and true."

"Will showed me a spider web," Elise went on, "that was so huge it stretched across the path between two of the big trees. And you know what. I touched it so carefully it didn't break at all. Will said if it did break, the spider would just mend it again, but I knew he must have worked terribly hard to build such a big one, and so I was glad I hadn't spoiled it."

On another excursion, Will fished for trout, catching enough for our supper, while Elise sat on the bank and dangled her feet in the water.

"I would have caught more," Will said, trying to act mad, "if Flea hadn't kept jumping in every time I threw out the line."

When he tired of fishing, Will made reed panpipes for himself and Elise. They spent the rest of the afternoon learning to play a few simple tunes on them. They entertained me with one of the popular reels until my feet began to tap out the rhythm, and we ended the evening by my dancing with each in turn while the other played.

Another of their favorite jaunts was to the cool spring hidden in the grove where Arthur and I had once met unexpectedly when each of us had gone there to be alone. From the time her beloved Sir Ursa had taken her up on his horse, Elise was determined she would ride. Once again I had to swallow my fear and allow her to live a normal life. Elise herself had absolutely no fear, nor, on the other hand, was she ever reckless, so I did what I could to assure her safety.

An already gentle mare was trained to keep to a steady, walking gait, or at the most an easy canter. I oversaw the making of a special saddle with a high, slightly curved back that gave her extra support and hugged her buttocks. Over trousers she wore a split skirt so she could ride astride rather than sidesaddle, which allowed her to grip with her knees. She had a sure touch with the reins, but there was always an extra lead rein that never left Will's hand as the two of them rode at a walk or a gentle canter across the broad meadow. It was sheer joy to watch them ride out together, Will approaching strong, sturdy manhood and Elise sitting tall and slim, her silken blonde hair shining like spun gold in the sun.

There were spills, to be sure, but Elise was never seriously hurt, only shaken up a bit. Like any good horsewoman, she climbed back up and rode on. A few times she carried one of my favorite falcons on her wrist, but she never found the same pleasure in hawking that I did, perhaps because she could not see the birds in the full glory of their flight.

I often wondered what Elise and Will talked about on their long afternoons together, but I knew that was one part of their excursions I would never share. How could I have ever told anyone how wonderful it had been to spend lazy hours with Arthur, talking of nothing more important than the right way to catch a fish or how blue the sky was. I was sure that just being together, munching on the tangy wild mint growing along the moist bank of the spring, was enough for Elise and Will.

Until one afternoon in the sewing room, I had thought of Elise and Will as two children who, having played together since they were babies, simply enjoyed being with each other more than with anyone else.

It was late afternoon, and I was alone in the room, the other women having returned to their homes to prepare supper. I had gotten up from the large loom where I was weaving wool for a new coverlet for my bed. After several hours of sitting, I walked to one of the windows to stretch my legs and ease the ache in my back. I looked toward the orchard to see how soon the fruit would be ready for picking.

Will and Elise stood under one of the pear trees. While I watched, he took her into his arms and they clung together in the passionate embrace of two young lovers. I knew I should call out to them, let them know I was watching, but I stood immobile. Even at that distance, I could see how demanding and forceful Will's mouth was as he sought Elise's and how eagerly she responded. This was no first, tentative kiss. When his hand began groping for her breasts, my own ached in memory of that day on the island when my senses were first aroused. How I longed for Arthur's presence beside me. Why could he never be with me at the times I needed him most?

Coming out of my reverie, I saw the two of them walking hand in hand toward the house. Had she denied him as I did that first time, or had she succumbed to love's demands?

Two disturbing thoughts battled in my mind. Disturbing because I should be ashamed of allowing them to enter. At sixteen, the two were old enough to marry, even though it would be some time before Will could assume full stewardship of the manor. The first shameful idea was that I should be grateful someone found Elise attractive enough to make love to. With her handicap, finding a husband for her could be difficult. I never had any thought of her spending the rest of her life in the abbey. But did Will want to marry her or just take advantage of her? Then I mentally castigated myself. How could I think such things of either of them? Elise was attractive and accomplished enough to marry any man she desired, and Will was too honorable a person to seduce her.

The other cruel, nagging thought was whether Will was good enough for her. She was the granddaughter of an earl and the daughter of a king, even if to all the world she was merely an abandoned orphan. When I died, she would inherit the estate and title. By that time her birth would matter little. And if she had a son, there would once again be an Earl of Sanam. Could I allow her to marry the son of a serf who would be her steward and one of her own fiefs? Life is a cycle, Merlin believed, and here I was reliving the concerns of those days when Arthur was destined to be merely the manager of Sir Ector's estates, thinking himself not good enough to ask for my hand.

Shaking myself mentally, I went to my room and freshened up for supper, determined to wait for either Elise or Will to speak to me. I loved them both, and deep inside I knew that what I really wanted for them was whatever would make them happy.

It was obvious as soon as I looked at them with newly awakened eyes that they were deeply in love. I had grown so accustomed to seeing Will take her hand wherever they went, I had not noticed how close to his side he held it or how he reached for her even when they were sitting down. From the day she first toddled after Will, crying out for him to wait for her, Elise had adored him. Now childhood adoration had become a mature affection and need. I was sure they would express their feelings to me very soon and were perhaps just waiting for some hint of approval from me.

Then, with no warning of any kind, a shattering crisis involving all three of us erupted and very nearly destroyed both of them.

At titular head of the manor estates I adjudicated civil offenses, both misdemeanors and felonies, occurring within my demesne. (All ecclesiastical crimes were handled by church authorities.) Usually, it was nothing more serious than a family quarrel or a drunken brawl, in which case a few stern words brought everything under control. Occasionally, there were more major cases such as theft or threatened violence. These offenders were punished by having to reimburse the damaged party by working so many days a month for the latter as well as working on my farms in lieu of a fine. It seemed to me these penalties made more sense and were more practical than putting the offender in stocks on a scaffold for several days of torture in open weather. I had an executioner, but I rarely decreed use of the whip except when husbands brutally mistreated wives or children. And I had never had to sit in judgment for a capital offense.

Until that summer.

Father Hubert, the village priest, came to me first,

saying there was trouble at the inn. That in itself was unusual. Normally, I was notified after the brawlers had been separated and had sobered up. Hot on the priest's heels came Jacob, the innkeeper.

"It's bad, mum, it's terribly bad. Come quick," Jacob urged. "It's murder this time."

"Murder!" I gasped. "Are you sure?"

"Right enough, mum."

"Oh, God," I thought. Bloody noses and broken bones were the usual outcome of the fights, but I'd never known any of my tenants to hit hard enough to kill.

Taking time to get my horse saddled gave me the respite I needed to regain my composure. I could easily have walked to the inn, but sitting high above the crowd would give me a better vantage point and also envelop me with a greater air of authority.

Every vassal on the manor must be jammed into the inn yard, I thought. The crowd made an irregular circle around a bare, open space. They surged forward and then pulled back as though the two figures in its center were infected with a hideous but fascinating disease. One of the two was Will, and the other was Brock, the innkeeper's strong young son. Both were looking down at something on the ground.

The crowd parted like a double gate as I rode up. Then I saw what all had been staring at. Seth, one of the younger tenants, was lying in a darkening pool of blood that gushed from his chest.

I put my hand to my mouth to hold back the bitter gall vomiting into my mouth. If Seth were not already dead, he would be within minutes. While waiting for Jacob to catch up, I looked from Will to his companion. My worst fears were confirmed when I saw Will's hands tied behind his back. I faced an angry mob, and I knew I had to act quickly, especially since Will was an acknowledged favorite of mine.

Jacob answered my questions briefly and to the point. Will had stormed into the ale room of the inn, begun the fight with Seth, and then stabbed him with no seeming provocation. That was all I needed, or

190

wanted, to know for the moment. I announced that court would convene at the manor the next day. There was no need to delay. A speedy trial and swift justice would be better for everyone. While there seemed no doubt of Will's guilt, he would have a fair trial. Although the final verdict would be my decision alone, I requested Jacob and Father Hubert to sit with me. All witnesses were required to be present.

Will was in a state of shock and either could not or would not speak. I decided not to pressure him for any word until the next day. Two of my strongest retainers had accompanied me to the inn. Not living in a castle and having no dungeon, I ordered them to take Will and chain him in one of the smaller storage rooms in the manor house. He was to be allowed enough length to move around, and he was to be given supper from the kitchen.

In the past, trials had been held in the great hall, but this was one case every tenant wanted to observe. Most of the men had been in or near the inn at the time of the killing, so they and their families would not be denied the privilege of their first murder trial. There was an ambivalent feeling about Will in the village. Some admired him for the place he held in my household and for his lack of condescension, and most loved his mother. Others, however, were jealous of him and never made any attempt to hide their feelings. One of these latter was Brock, who had immediately grabbed Will and tied his hands.

Elise had been ailing for two or three days with some vague complaint such as cramps or headache, so I insisted she remain in bed. She had cried all night and was too exhausted to argue. I requested Elspeth to stay with her. An emotional scene with either of them would do Will no good. I did allow them to stand by the window so Will could see them as he came out.

Father Hubert, Jacob, and I sat behind a long table in the courtyard. There were benches for some of the older tenants upon whom I hoped to rely for honest testimony. Dozens more were standing or seated on the ground around us; others had found places atop the wall that commanded a good view of the proceedings. A few urchins had scrambled up into the trees and were hanging by their knees or looping around the branches while waiting for the action to begin. Many had brought lunches in anticipation of a long trial, and while the men argued the case, the women gossiped, nursed babies, and seemed to be thoroughly enjoying the excitement engendered by this break in their usually monotonous routine. I thought of the glee with which people often gathered to watch a public execution, taunting the condemned and making his last moments one of ridicule as well as torture. If I could, I would move through the proceedings with a minimum of delay and try to spare Will as much agony and humiliation as possible.

When Will, still wearing the clothes torn and bloodied by the fight, was brought out, he was chained to one of the trees. He looked up at the window once to see Elise and his mother standing there; from then on he concentrated all his attention on the witnesses. He would be allowed to plead his own cause after all the others had spoken.

Father Hubert required all witnesses to swear on his massive cross—ostensibly containing a splinter of the True Cross—that what they said was the truth. One after another their stories were the same, like the repetitive refrains of an old ballad. Will had entered the inn's ale room in a blinding rage, had picked a fight with Seth, and then stabbed him. No, there was no apparent reason. Seth's young wife cried out anew each time another witness appeared until I threatened to send her away. She held one baby and was expecting another. I knew Seth had married her under threats of violence to his manhood just in time to give the first child a legitimate birth. A vicious young lout, his reputation for being able to tumble any young maiden he desired gave him a certain popularity among the younger male serfs. However, he was dead, and his murderer had to be punished.

No one had offered any defense for Will's actions; no one knew of anything Seth had done to stir up Will's ire to the extent of killing. Although the ale room had been crowded, most of the men were busy drinking and joking among themselves, so they didn't really become involved in what they thought was just another drunken brawl until the force of the fight carried the two combatants outside and onto the hard ground. They only knew that suddenly Brock had screamed, "He's killing him! Will's killing Seth!"

I would soon ask Will to speak in his own defense, but first I wanted to requestion Brock, who had been the first witness. I asked him to stand before the table again.

"You know of no reason why Will should have attacked Seth?"

"No, my lady, none."

"You swore on the cross, you know?"

"Yes, my lady."

I repeated the story I'd been told often enough to have memorized it. "Will started the fight; they knocked each other down, turning over some benches, and this kept up until they rolled outside?"

"Yes, my lady."

"Who was on top? Who seemed to be winning?"

"They was about equal, ma'am, first one and then the other. Didn't seem no way either would win until Seth pulled a dagger—I mean until Will reached for his knife and . . ."

"Wait a minute," I said as calmly as I could, but wanting to explode. "Who did you say drew a knife first? Remember, you swore on the cross."

"Will drew a knife first," was his reply.

"But Seth had already pulled out his dagger! Aren't you the clever one! All this talk of knives, and you knew you wouldn't perjure yourself as long as you kept saying 'knife.' No one ever mentioned a dagger. You must really be eaten up with hate and jealousy to want to see a man die who has killed in self-defense. Now tell the truth. It was self-defense, wasn't it?"

"Yes, my lady, but Will did start the fight."

"That's enough!" I said sternly. "You will be put in the stocks for three days and then banished from this

193

estate forever. Not for perjury, but for failing to tell the whole truth."

I turned to Will. "Will, you are found innocent of the crime of murder, but you are guilty, for whatever reason, of precipitating the fight that ended in Seth's death. He leaves a wife and small children. I hereby decree you shall work five days a month on her fief until such time as she marries again or the children are old enough to help support her."

With that I rose and went into the house. As yet no mention had been made of why Will had sought out Seth, why he was in such a fury. The dagger was later found where Brock had hidden it before raising the alarm.

There was a quiet reunion between Will and Elise at supper, but neither spoke during the meal. I was just as glad. The last twenty-four hours had drained me of all energy. Elise returned immediately to her room, so I was able to talk a moment with Will alone. But he turned aside all my questions, insisting it was something between Seth and himself, of no concern to me. It had been concern enough, I thought, to put me in the position of almost sentencing Will to be hanged. Would he have spoken up if Brock had not trapped himself in his own lie?

After these tortuous events I was not surprised that Will and Elise were more subdued around the manor. Will had killed a man, and Elise had almost lost Will to the executioner. But I was stunned when she told me she was returning almost immediately to the abbey. I was sure that after a few days they would head for the island or go out riding. I was even going to tease a little to see how soon they would admit to being in love.

"But why, Elise? I thought—I mean I . . ."

"You thought what, Mother?"

"I thought you and Will were in love. I was certain you would be asking my permission to marry. Was I wrong?"

"Not completely," she said quietly. "Will has asked me to marry him, but I refused."

"Why, Elise? From what I've seen, you love him."

"Yes, I love him," she answered, "but not enough to marry him."

"Be honest with me. Is it that, or is it because he killed someone? Or because he is of lower birth? If it's the first, give yourself time. If it's the latter, I'm ashamed of you."

Elise began to weep so uncontrollably I had to hold her tight and then apply cold cloths to her face and hands.

"What is it, Elise?" I was almost shaking her now. "You must tell me!"

"Oh, Mother, you're so wrong. I've never thought about Will's birth. If anything, I would think about my own. I'm a bastard, remember? No, don't be miserable. That's not the reason, either. As for Will's killing Seth, there was a good reason."

"Which," I said, "I presume I'm not ever going to learn. Just tell me this. Does it have anything to do with your return to the abbey?"

Elise got up and walked to the window, staring blindly out as though she could see the trees in full fruit and the young birds just daring to try their wings in erratic flight. She turned slowly back to me.

"Mother, I'm going to tell you everything, asking only that you say nothing to Will or ever mention it to me again." In a firm but halting voice she revealed what led up to the fight and her decision to leave the manor.

She and Will had been walking through the orchard and had arrived at the same bench where once I met Merlin. Feeling chilled, it was early evening, she had asked Will to run back to the house for her cape. While he was gone, she had been so wrapped up in her dreams of marrying Will, she had not heard someone approaching stealthily across the soft ground. She was alerted only when Flea began barking and then gave a low canine moan as he was struck on the head. The next thing she knew she was being roughly pulled from the seat, her dress torn off as she was thrown to the ground.

For the first time in her life she knew genuine, heart-stopping fear, a fear coupled with an awareness of what a real handicap her blindness was. Gasping for breath, she began struggling against something heavy on top of her. At the same moment she realized it was a man she was fighting, he grabbed her wrists, twisting her hands under her back. Gagging from the odor of his body and his foul breath, she tried to bite the hand he put over her mouth. She thought she would die of suffocation, but the worst was yet to come. The force with which he raped her had her whole body screaming with pain.

Just leaving the house when he heard Flea barking, Will ran toward where he had left Elise on the bench. He arrived to find her moaning in a semiconscious state and Seth running off toward the woods. Flea was dead. Seth he could take care of later. Elise needed immediate attention. She remembered only his cradling her lovingly in his arms until she became coherent. She didn't need to tell him what had happened. Her torn dress and bloodied skirt were evidence enough. He took off his shirt and, dipping it in the small spring, bathed her face and hands. In spite of her protestations he also cleansed her legs and body of the despicable remains of the rape. Then wrapping her in the cape, he carried her until in sight of the house when she insisted on walking.

Together they decided it was better not to tell me, thinking how the knowledge of what had happened would hurt me. Foolish young children! How much tragedy could have been averted if they had confided in me. Instead, Elise took to her bed, and Will went in search of Seth, who stayed away from the village for two days.

"Oh, Elise." It was all I could do to keep from crying. "What you must have suffered. I hurt all over for you. But why didn't you tell me? You know what the executioner would have done, don't you?"

"Yes, Mother. Will explained it to me. Seth would have been castrated. That's what Will said he was going to do. He hadn't planned to kill him."

196

"But it should have been done legally, by my orders."

"We wanted to spare you the shame."

"I appreciate your concern. But how does this stop you from marrying Will?"

"Please, Mother. I just can't, that's all."

"Because you're no longer a virgin? Certainly Will understands. He hasn't changed his mind, has he?"

"Oh, no, not that. He's asked me over and over since then. I just can't explain, but I can't marry him now."

"You're not afraid of him, are you? As a man, I mean. He'd be gentle, and his love would help you to forget."

"Please, Mother. It's nothing I can explain." Although still sitting beside me on the bed and continuing to hold my hands in hers, Elise was retreating further and further away from me, disappearing into a shell that her emotions had formed to protect her from the physical world. "Something happened to me that day that even I don't understand. It's not exactly a sense of guilt or a feeling of being dirtied; it's not really a fear of Will or a revulsion at being touched by him. It's just a horrible combination of everything that's tearing me apart inside. Let me go to the abbey. Give me time to try to work it all out."

"And Will?" I asked.

"He has agreed to my going. He's trying to understand, but I don't think he'd have the patience if I stayed here."

We decided that if she were going to the abbey, she should leave immediately. The longer she stayed at the manor, the harder it would be for both of them. When she departed the next day, I knew she and Will had said their good-bys in the house. As I kissed her gently on the cheek, I hoped she would return a whole woman again, but I feared the damage to her had been irreparable. I never told Will what I knew.

Elise came less and less often to the manor after that, finding in the calm, steady routine of the abbey the fulfillment of her particular needs. Arthur asked during one of his visits if I thought she would be taking the vows.

"Yes," I said, "she is planning to enter the novitiate in a few months. She told me the other night that it was her wish, and she hoped we would agree."

"They haven't pressured her, have they? She really could come here to live, without any questions asked, just as Will has."

"No," I said, "there's been no pressure. I made certain of that. It is truly her own desire to become a nun. She told me she prayed and thought a long time before deciding. In fact, she herself said one of the alternatives she considered was asking to come here to live. I really thought, as fond as she is of Will, that she would want to be near him. I even thought—well, I was in love with a future steward once, and nothing would make me happier than seeing them married. My romantic heart, I guess, was taking the place of reason. No, she is devoted to the church and to the work of the abbey, especially caring for the older nuns who have become infirm.

"There was one nun in particular she was very fond of. The oldest in the community, she was an invalid for two years, dying from a disease that consumed her vital organs like a smoldering fire. Elise brewed soothing teas for her from some of my herbs, and the old nun told Elise stories from the Bible and about saints and miracles, finding some ease from her pain while she related her favorite religious anecdotes. She even taught Elise how to knit, and your daughter, with her retentive mind, memorized the instructions and now keeps the abbey supplied with woolen hose."

"Do you think our situation," Arthur asked, "has anything to do with her decision?"

"I'm sure it must. But don't be sad for her. She is very happy at the thought of being married to the church. For her, Christ is the only bridegroom she wants. She's learned about life; I've seen to that. She knows what it is to love, and she's chosen spiritual over physical love."

"But is she giving herself time to experience both options? She knows all about spiritual love, as you call it, from the abbey. How about . . ."

"She knows. Oh, nothing serious. Don't be alarmed. But I've seen her spurn Will's advances. Immature ones, to be sure, but with enough ardor to interest her—if she wanted to be interested."

"You saw—and you let them!"

"I was of the same mind as you are now. If she were to make a choice, she at least had to know what she was choosing between. A kiss in the pantry or a hug in the orchard does not constitute an affair, and my seemingly casual appearance on the scene made certain it went no further and let them know I was always close by."

Together we went to the abbey to assure Elise of our love as she took her first vows. Dressed in a gown of sheer white linen that I made for her myself and wearing a crown of fresh flowers, she was as radiant and as confident as a bride going to join her lover as she walked to the altar. There was no denying her happiness or the love enveloping her as the other nuns gathered around to welcome her into their order. For years she had been an important part of their lives, bringing them a special kind of joy, and now she truly belonged to them.

And so several years passed, filled with contentment for me because Arthur came as often as he could. Together we watched our daughter develop into a lovely young woman. The months in between his visits were not lonely ones, filled as they were with the responsibilities of the estate and occasional jaunts to the Abbey of the Holy Spirit to carry in person my tithe of each harvest and to see Elise. Always I left carrying with me the picture of her face glowing with happiness, and my heart was filled with gratitude that she had found her true vocation.

❖ Chapter Nine ❖

With hands on knees, eyes focused steadily on the smoky purple flames, Arthur slouched in his chair at the edge of the hearth. There were fine strands of silver showing now in his blond hair, longer and shaggier than I remembered. He had also let his beard grow so that it was no longer a carefully trimmed, symmetrical frame for his face. His plain leather jerkin and breeches, his simple linen shirt, belied his regal station. With his rough woolen cape and hood, he might have been any weary traveler.

Since he had ridden into the courtyard three hours earlier, no more than a dozen words had passed between us. Silence can be a welcome companion during intimate hours, or it can be an impregnable wall in times of tension. Arthur had never been what one would call a moody person, and during all our years together I was able to understand his need for quiet reflection, and I had been grateful that he sought me out to share such times. Sometimes, sitting in his presence, I sewed or merely relaxed. At other times I slipped quietly out to the garden and worked among my flowers until he sought me out. For almost the first time I sensed—no, I knew—that each moment that passed was adding another stone to the wall. I also knew that Arthur was not going to break the silence, and before I spoke, I had to find the chink in the wall that would allow me to enter into his world.

Arthur was a simple person, not enigmatic, and one could usually believe implicitly in what he said. Unfortunately, not being a natural dissembler, he found it hard to believe that there were people who lied with the same facile grace as he told the truth. Some might call him naïve; others, ingenuous. In matter of fact, he was just a basically honest person. For that reason, his silence was particularly disturbing and perplexing because as soon as he dismounted, he said, in a relaxed, not tense, voice, he had something very important to tell me. An idea that came to him had him excited, and he wanted to share it with me. Then, after we were seated in the library, he lapsed into his unapproachable silence.

"Arthur," I spoke quietly, "do you want your goblet refilled?"

He turned his head slowly as though surprised to see me there or to find himself seated before my fireplace. In his musings he must have traveled many miles through infinity, beyond time and space, to some place where I could not follow. Had his spirit, as some people believed it could, left his body and gone in search of its own private sanctuary? Perhaps back to Camelot, to the secret tower room that Arthur sought when he felt the need for seclusion.

It took a moment for him to return to an awareness of where he was, and then he smiled and handed me his cup in a silent request for more wine.

"Sorry, Lionors," he said, "I must have been more tired than I knew. Have I been asleep?"

"No," I answered, "just lost in thought."

He stood up, walking back and forth, stretching his legs to get the kinks out. In spite of the added years, he stood as tall and straight as when he was first crowned king of Britain. He was heavier by a good two and a half stones, but his stomach showed no sign of a paunch, and his muscles were as taut and firm as ever. If anything, his bearing was even more regal as an older man than when he was in his twenties.

Returning to his place by the hearth, he turned the chair so that he faced me rather than the fire.

"I guess you wonder why I just rode up without letting you know I was coming."

"No," I answered, "just pleased to see you. You should know by now that I don't require advance notice to be ready to receive you. I love you, and waiting for you to come to me is the only thing that gives any real meaning to my life."

"I love you, too, Lionors, and I only wish I could come here more often. It is getting harder and harder to slip away, so when the pressure is more than I can bear, I go up to our tower room, and there at least I can feel your presence and make believe you are there to talk to. But this time that didn't satisfy. I needed you in the flesh. I left, saying I needed a few days of rest and contemplation in the nearby monastery, and as you'll soon see, that was a most acceptable reason for being away."

If he were silent before, words now gushed out from him like a long pent-up river that has finally broken through its dam.

"I want to send my knights on a new quest, a search for the Holy Grail."

I could see he was impatient for my approval.

"I'm not sure I understand," I said, trying to be non-committal rather than discouraging. "If you came here seeking my advice, you'll have to tell me everything that led up to an idea that would take the knights away from Camelot for something other than a good fight."

So began his unusual story. The knights were restless. With most of Britain now united, his early dream had been realized. While he himself would be content to rest from fighting, perhaps leading only an occasional skirmish against the border rebels but testing his skill mainly on the jousting field, the knights were grumbling about the lack of excitement in their lives. He feared that if he didn't find something to occupy their time and release their restless energy, they would turn that frustration against one another and stir up internal strife that must be avoided if the concept of the Round Table were not to be destroyed.

For him, there was a more personal reason—to protect his right to continue his reign as Uther's heir. Although he had been baptized a Christian and had actively followed the rites and tenets of the faith, there were recurring whispers that he secretly worshiped the old gods. The first flames of the rumor were sparked by the fact that during his formative years he was under the tutelage of Merlin. There were many who would never be convinced that the old man was not a sorcerer, but more important, Merlin had never denied that he still believed in the old gods, honoring and protecting their shrines as diligently as he did those of the Christians. In turn, Arthur had respected Merlin's right to worship as he chose; and thus, as king he was condemned for not punishing Merlin or at least banishing him from court as a dangerous pagan influence. Many stories were bruited about: Arthur had a secret pagan shrine in his room before which he and Merlin worshiped; there was a hidden chapel beneath the castle in which black masses were held; or worse, many swore they had witnessed wild, erotic orgies in the woods during which the spirits of Arthur and Merlin, along with other worshipers, left their bodies and entered those of innocent people, making them go mad. It was apparent that the people spreading these tales were abysmally ignorant concerning the true worship of the old gods, and had mingled superstition with what they heard about witchcraft, but this ignorance made them only the more dangerous to Arthur. It did not matter that Merlin had become a recluse, exiling himself from court several years earlier in order to live quietly in a cave and devote his time to reading and practicing the healing arts.

Like a brushfire in a high wind, these rumors spread rapidly in all directions, endangering not only Arthur, but threatening all of Britain as well with a holocaust of rebellion. Time after time, many of those close to him urged that he speak out, denying the rumors and making a public act of confession and penance. But he knew that his words could no more stop the rumors or undo the damage already done than words could halt the progress of a brushfire or replant the fields and forests that had been destroyed. It would take some powerfully dramatic act, not of a moment but of some duration, to capture the people's imagination and keep them enthralled long enough to let the rumors die out from lack of new interest.

The first suggestion was that Arthur obliterate the crest of Uther Pendragon, destroying all the banners, pennons, robes, and so on that bore the design of the scarlet dragon on its gold field. The dragon must be removed from his helmet and shield. He should have a public ceremony during which he melted down his father's famous signet ring, the blood-red stone, carved with the dragon rampant, embedded in its heavy gold band. The idea was to replace the insignia with a Christian symbol. The flag of a Christian king, they said, should bear the cross of Christ, not the dragon of the old gods. Such acts, completely abrogating any belief in the ancient pagan faith and the destruction of its lurid symbol, would secure the position of the throne and Arthur's right to sit there. In addition, there could be masses and galas to celebrate the occasion. These would delight the people and give them something to liven up their otherwise drab lives. Nothing like several days of feasting (especially when the king was providing the food and drink) with a respite from daily toil to ensure a loyal following.

The more Arthur's advisers thought about the idea, the more they liked it. Each one proffered his own suggestions, each better than the last. There would be fairs, complete with acrobats, jugglers, and mimes—following the masses, of course—in every hamlet and village, continuing for several days, maybe even a week, each day ending with a mighty feast, all at the king's expense. There had never been such a celebration in all of Britain, and what better reason for one than the acclamation of Arthur as the mightiest Christian king in the world, with the emphasis on *Christian*.

But Arthur said, "No!" At this he stood up and shook his fist in my face as though I were one of those advisers.

"Can you imagine—can anyone imagine—that I

204

would consent to such a mockery of faith!" he bellowed.

"Please watch your fist, Arthur," I said. "I'm not one of your enemies."

"Sorry." He stopped shouting. "I got carried away. You can see how furious I was at the thought of renouncing the name of Pendragon, which I would be doing if I destroyed the symbol."

He would not dishonor his father's name nor sully his own heritage by replacing the red dragon. With pride the great Uther Pendragon had borne his banner into battle, and Arthur had done the same. Never had it been despoiled by a cowardly act, and the most humiliating act of cowardice on his part would be to renounce what the banner stood for just to prove to a lot of mewling, whimpering dogs that he was a Christian. They could believe in him or not; he did not care.

How clearly could I see him, standing his ground, giving not an inch, while they backed down. However, he did not gloat in this small triumph; he did care, however, and was concerned about his position. Not for his own sake, but because he knew that as his strength ebbed, so did the strength of Britain and all that he had fought for during the years since he had pulled the sword from the stone and been proclaimed Uther's rightful heir.

During the following nights, while Arthur paced his room, he envisioned a new idea, spending hours doing battle with his conscience to assure himself it was the right action. Not only was it a plan that would appeal to the knights, it was truly a Christian course of action, not heretical. The knights would travel out over all the land seeking the Holy Grail. They would be starting a new adventure, one he hoped would pique their curiosity because it would be unlike any quest ever undertaken. There would be glory and rewards, but not the glory that comes from winning bloody battles or the rewards of new lands and submissive maidens. These were the doubts that plagued him: whether the knights would embrace wholeheartedly such a quest or whether they would scorn it as an idealistic whim.

"That's why I came to you, Lionors. I need your help. I'm too close to these problems, and I cannot evaluate them with an objective eye. Am I crazy to think such a quest will appeal to my men? Will it save the kingdom or only postpone the inevitable for a little while longer?"

This was no occasion for a quick, thoughtless answer. I needed time to mull over all he had told me, to weigh the doubts he expressed against the value of such an extraordinary expedition as he had outlined. I sought that time by asking why he had thought of such a quest and why he believed success possible.

He began by talking about the Holy Grail itself, the cup that Christ drank from at the Last Supper. Tradition had it that after Joseph of Arimathea provided a sepulcher in his own gardens for the body of Christ when He was taken down from the cross, the old man left the Holy Land. Some say he had to flee from the wrath of Romans and Jews alike because of his many acts of kindness to the followers of Christ. Others say that he chose to be among the first to leave Jerusalem and travel westward across the face of Europe to preach among the heathens the gospel of Christ. In his last years he came to these islands, and here he died. With him, it is believed, he carried the Holy Grail, or Sangreal, removing it from those who would destroy any object that might become a holy relic and reinforce the faith of the dissident Jews. Whether the grail remained in its original form as a simple clay cup or whether it was embedded in an ornate silver chalice was a dispute that could only be resolved by its discovery. More important to Arthur was the belief that Joseph hid it somewhere on these islands for safekeeping. There were stories handed down from generation to generation that the cup was actually used by the early Christians in Britain whom Joseph had converted from pagan practices, in the faith that its very being would protect it from breakage or loss. Supposedly, at Joseph's death, or more likely with the ever-present danger of rout by Romans or Norsemen, these Christians secreted it away and left no hint of its whereabouts. So, as Arthur explained, it could be anywhere —in a cave, in a cemetery, or even in the hidden recesses of a long-neglected chapel.

"I feel the time has come," he concluded, "when it is destined to be found."

"Will you be among those going?" I asked.

"No, I'll stay at Camelot."

"But," I argued, "if the purpose of the quest is to establish yourself beyond all doubt as a Christian, I should think you'd be the first to take up the challenge."

"No, I'll stay to receive those who return—or turn back. My place is at court."

I wanted to disagree with him, but I sensed that somehow his statement of being needed at court was merely masking the real reason for his not going. Again I must wait for him to speak.

The fire had reduced to embers, and Will came in to put a fresh log on the fire. In spite of the fact that he could have sent a menial to do it, he preferred to serve me himself. The log burned down almost to ashes before Arthur spoke again.

His staying at Camelot was not of his own choosing. Perhaps it was fated that he be denied the privilege of going on the quest as an act of atonement. He was not well. I saw then that the ruddy hue on his skin was merely a reflection of the fire veiling a sickly gray pallor.

"During a joust I took the point of a lance in my leg. The wound was not deep, but it became infected even though the doctors cauterized it immediately with hot irons. For a time there was danger of the infection spreading, and the leg had to be cut open several times to allow the area to drain. It is still painful, and it is not easy for me to ride."

"You should have told me you were in pain," I scolded, "and I would have given you something to alleviate it. When you stayed so quiet, I feared you regretted coming to see me."

"Never think that, Lionors. The soreness from riding eased off while I sat here. It's not the physical injury to my leg causing my illness. The external wound has scarred over, but it left a poison deep inside that eats away at my vitals and for which there is no antidote. I doubt you have any potion among your herbs and salves to counteract the malignant death in life I'm suffering now."

In a tower room many years earlier Arthur had finally found the courage to tell me about his affair with Morgause. Step by painful step he had related all that led up to the birth of Mordred, his incestuously begotten son-nephew. Now once again he forced himself to exorcize the demon of guilt by confiding in me. Like a father confessor, I listened without speaking, and I soon knew that this revelation was the more painful to him of the two. At least the first experience had initiated him into full awareness of his manhood, whereas the second was that a lance, carelessly thrown at a joust, had destroyed that manhood.

Either because of the wound—in the groin, not in his leg—or the cutting and cauterizing that followed, he was impotent. The doctors had tried to assure him that it was a temporary frailty, but months went by and there was no improvement.

For many years he and Guinevere had seldom slept together, but there were times when he needed her.

"With you I have known real love," he said, "and because of this I have been able to understand the bond between Gwen and Lance. I have asked only that they be discreet and not let their—their affair become known. In public she is the perfect queen; within the castle she is a considerate and dutiful wife; when we are alone, she is—kind. In our own way I guess we are fond of each other; at least we share a mutual admiration and respect. In no way does my feeling for her touch the love I have for you. Can you understand?"

I nodded.

"If my moments with you are few," he said, leaning over to touch my hand, "they are also more precious. If only you were close by me. . . ."

So there were times when Arthur turned to Guinevere, who was near, especially when he needed to be reassured that he was still a man. But his attempts to be a husband to her were futile. On those occasions Guinevere remained calm, insisting his inability to perform was due to exhaustion or worry, that at their age it no longer really mattered anyway. Day by day he was more driven by despair. Outwardly recovering physically, he was inwardly dying a slow death.

Then he had a dream. In it Merlin came to him and told him to organize a quest for the Holy Grail. All the knights should take part, but the one that was purest in heart would find the grail and with it the cure for Arthur's wound. Arthur himself must not go, but was to wait for word that the mission had been accomplished. At that moment he would be cured of his ailment.

As Merlin had promised when he left the court, he would return to help Arthur whenever the king needed him. In his cave, many miles from court, he had heard of Arthur's accident on the jousting field, news of any danger to the king traveling fast among the country people. Because he was not unaware of the rumors concerning his influence on Arthur, he did not rush to Camelot to offer his curative powers to ease Arthur's pain. His intuitive sense told him that while Arthur was in no physical danger, the mental anguish was the real travail he would suffer. If he would guide Arthur to a cure for that illness, he must do so from the security of his cave, for his protection as well as that of the king. He could not will himself across space to the king's side, but using all his powers of concentration, he could enter Arthur's mind in a dream. Merlin had once told Arthur that whenever he needed advice, to put all other thoughts aside and think only of the problem at hand and of his old tutor.

In his dream Arthur had been led by Merlin to the door of a small deserted chapel, its walls overgrown with ivy and the path to it slippery with moss. Large oaks stood on either side, their huge branches, heavy with mistletoe, arching overhead like a magnified mirror image of the stones over the narrow door. Vaguely, Arthur became aware that the interior was a replica of the one beneath the castle at Camelot where we had plighted our troth. It was empty except for the altar, more like a table than an altar. The lighted tapers on it and the all-pervading fragrance of incense bespoke the ministrations of a priest or caretaker. As Merlin disappeared from his side, Arthur entered and proceeded down the aisle of the nave to the sanctuary. There was no sound save for the wind outside the walls and the distant hooting of an owl.

Suddenly, the calm was shattered by a roaring that sounded like a thousand waves surging toward the shore. The candles flamed up in the rush of air and then were extinguished. The immediate darkness was like the utter darkness of the grave; the cold walls of the chapel closed in like a tomb. Just as he felt as though he would suffocate, the gloom was dispelled by a soft glow coming from the center of the altar, a pale light that grew until Arthur saw that it came from a brilliant jewel set in the stem of a silver chalice. It could be none other than the Holy Grail. He had been granted the miraculous vision. As he moved toward it, a veiled, shadowless woman in white passed in front of him, and he awoke from his dream.

Somehow, Arthur felt, Merlin had known of his suffering and had, in turn, reached out to him. He was sure that the dream had been his old mentor's way of showing him the path he must take to achieve a cure.

"Yes," I said, "you must follow Merlin's advice, just as you always did in the past. Has he ever been wrong?"

"No," Arthur responded quietly.

If he looked for me to make any comment about his affliction, he would be disappointed. By keeping any reaction to myself, I felt sure I could provide the means to assuage his anguish. But that meant creating the right emotional atmosphere for my ministrations to have the greatest curative effect.

Moving over to where he sat, I put my hands on his shoulders. "You've exhausted yourself telling me all this. What you need now is a good night's sleep, and I've just the potion to ensure that."

Once I had him comfortably settled in bed, I saw to

it that he drank all of the cup I offered him. It contained a brew that would relax him but not put him to sleep.

As he yawned and stretched his body under the warm lamb's wool coverlet, seeking the most comfortable position, I went to the closet that contained my chest of herbs. This was a very old lacquered chest that one of my ancestors on a pilgrimage to Rome had purchased from an itinerant Byzantine merchant. Standing some two feet tall, it had two doors that shut with a small gold lock and key. The entire chest was intricately carved in an elaborate design of trees, fruits, flowers, and vines. Although time had muted most of the colors to a faint grayed semblance of the original, one could easily visualize the once magnificent brilliance of the golden poppies, scarlet apples and pomegranates, purple grapes, and green leaves. The doors opened to reveal two vertical rows of small, identical drawers, eight to a row, each with its own miniature lock and key. My father had given me the chest when I first began collecting and drying herbs for medicinal purposes.

From a shelf above the chest I took down my book of receipts, garnered over the years of study with Marta and Gundrig. The early pages were covered with childish scrawls, detailing the ingredients and methods for simple tisanes. Hurriedly, I passed these by and looked for the one for restoring potency. At the time Gundrig gave me the recipes, she had been reticent about revealing the ailment for which it was intended, only assuring me that I would know when it was needed. The main ingredient was mandrake root, thought to be embued with magic restorative powers. But for my purpose this was not enough. The receipt called for a few drops of liquid crushed from the leaves of three other herbs, two for greater potency and one to act as catalyst to bring out the ultimate power of the root. As soon as I had ground the mandrake to a fine powder with my heavy stone mortar and pestle, I sprinkled the distillation from the herbs over it. Half of the mixture I put aside to be dissolved later in a goblet of wine. Still working with my stone instruments, I patiently blended in more of the liquid until I had a smooth, grainless salve.

All of this had taken almost an hour, and when I turned to look at Arthur, he was lying on his side, his eyes closed. However, with my first movement toward him, he opened them and raised up on one elbow. The brief rest had restored some of his energy and more of his old sense of humor.

"Thought you'd put me to sleep, did you," he grinned, "and escape my evil clutches. I assure you, lady, my intentions are not dishonorable." His ironic laugh tore me apart more than any attempts at self-pity could have.

Although I had some doubts about the efficacy of the mixture I had concocted, I had a second treatment that I hoped would effect the long-hoped-for cure. Just as he said that his real illness lay buried inside him, not in the skin-deep wound, I felt sure his impotency was more emotional than physical. Even as he lay with Guinevere, the vision of her sleeping with Lancelot rose up like a chasm between them, a chasm that his masculine pride would not let him cross. His accident merely gave a final impetus to his feelings that he was less than a man if he could not satisfy Guinevere enough to keep her faithful to him. Without being aware of it, he might have welcomed the accident as an excuse not to have to compete with Lancelot in the one area where he felt unsure of his success. Guinevere could never give herself to him with the consummate love, wholly untarnished by the memory of another lover, that I could. I knew I was hazarding my whole relationship with Arthur, and with his future as a man, but loving him as I did, I had no other choice.

"No," I returned his smile. "I wasn't putting you to sleep. I thought you might like me to rub your back the way I used to." I held up a bottle of lotion tinctured with attar of roses. Hidden within the palm of my left hand was the unguent I had so carefully mixed.

Arthur responded to my suggestion by rolling over onto his stomach. Sitting beside him on the bed, I pulled the covers down to his waist and began at his shoulders, rubbing the lotion into his skin with slow, even strokes. I felt his firm muscles respond by losing their tension and relaxing under my fingers. Gradually, I worked my way down his spine, massaging vigorously with my fingertips. Then switching to the palms and heels of my hands, I worked the broad expanse of his back. When I reached his waist and started easing the blanket down over his buttocks, he voiced no objections.

"Now turn over," I said. "I have a special unguent to soften the skin around your injury where the scar tissue has thickened and pulled it tight."

Rubbing the sensitive area as gently as I could, I began to feel new energy pulsing through his veins. Without a word, Arthur reached up and pulled me down beside him, once again the lover I had ached for every night we were separated. Not the gentle lover of our first youthful embraces, but a man releasing passions kept far too long in thrall to fear.

Later, as we lay sleepily contented in each other's arms, Arthur whispered, "There is no need to look for the grail now."

"Yes, there is," I replied, "not for the cure, but for all those other reasons you spoke of."

"I can find something to amuse the knights."

"No, no, if Merlin sent that message, he had a reason, one you may not even be aware of."

"You think too much. Come here."

As I blew out the candles, I saw the goblet of potion-filled wine standing on the bedside table, a small jewel in the stem reflecting the simmering flames for a brief moment before the room became totally dark.

⌧ *Chapter Ten* ⌧

The beginning of the quests for the Holy Grail, or
Sangreal, put an end for a time to any sense of isola-
tion I had felt through the years. One after another of
the knights found their way to the road that led past
our manor and on to the Abbey of the Holy Spirit.

Beside the door of the chapel at the abbey stood an
ancient, gnarled thorn tree, one of many around the
countryside said to have been planted by Joseph of
Arimathea to remind passers-by of the thorns that
pierced our Lord's brow during His last agony. In the
beginning, crude shrines were built on the sites of the
trees: a rough-hewn cross; a stone urn to hold an offering of wild flowers; a small, patiently carved wooden
statue of the Virgin or favorite saint; or a painted
marker detailing a miracle wrought near the spot.
Some of the thorn trees grew and flourished, nurtured
by both the natural elements and the care of concerned
pilgrims. The same with the shrines. But the years took
their toll of many. Like the seeds in the Biblical para-
ble, those planted on rocky soil withered and died; others were smothered by weeds before their roots were
established, and before long their shrines were allowed
to disintegrate and crumble to the ground.

Long before my time, many of the simple shrines
near the trees that had endured were replaced by village churches, private chapels, monasteries, and ab-
beys, one of which was the Abbey of the Holy Spirit.

It was natural that the knights on the quest for the

Holy Grail would seek out those places where Joseph had supposedly walked. Even though the grail had been hidden centuries before any of the chapels or churches were built, there was a universal belief among the questors that a holy relic would be found in a holy place. Actually two of the chapels, at Glastonbury and at the abbey, vied for the honor of having been built over the grave of Joseph of Arimathea. When the original sanctuaries were being constructed on the sites of the early shrines, a skeleton was found during the excavation at each of these locations, a skeleton that pious followers of the faith venerated as that of the holy man who had spread the word of Christ throughout our islands.

The events of which I speak occurred many years apart, yet the incidents surrounding them and the reactions to them were almost identical. And so two different places claimed to have the remains of the early evangelist.

In each case, the building area was marked off and the digging begun after the land had been blessed by a priest sprinkling holy water and invoking the benevolence of God with the prescribed prayers. Everything went smoothly for several months; the carpenters were raising the scaffolding, and the masons had begun assembling the stones for the foundation. Then the accidents began, almost identical in each case. First a scaffolding toppled, killing three men. After that a block and tackle, moving a heavy slab, broke, and the stone fell on a mason, crushing his back. That night one of the workers was mysteriously killed walking to his home; the body was found the next morning.

All work ceased, the men refusing to go near the place, convinced the devil had cast an evil spell on it. At Glastonbury it was a priest walking around the grounds of the scarcely begun church who turned up the skeleton as he was examining the site for a clue to the accidents. If he found nothing tangible, he had planned to perform the ritual of exorcism in an attempt to destroy the evil spirits and persuade the laborers to return to work. At the abbey chapel, the skeleton was

215

found by one of the stone masons as he was positioning a large granite slab. This latter discovery was made before the accidents occurred, and the superstitious workers said the church was being built over the bones of a believer in the old gods. It, too, was thought to be haunted by evil spirits.

In both situations, the priests were able to turn the discovery of the bones to the church's advantage. They called in other priests; among many possibilities, they considered the legend of Joseph of Arimathea, discussing the details that had passed down by word of mouth through the generations. Once they were convinced beyond all doubt that the remains could be those of the saint and prayed over them for guidance, they announced their decision. The bones were reinterred with the proper solemnity due a saint.

For many it has remained a mystery why two churches could both be so certain they alone had the remains of the first missionary to Britain. For others there was a historical—if not logical—explanation. The bones at Glastonbury were found first, then carefully gathered up and kept in a box while the church hierarchy were busy with their deliberations. Goldsmiths and jewelers were given commissions to design a reliquary splendid enough to encase such a holy relic. It was no larger than a coffin for a small child because the skeleton had not been found intact; rather, the bones were broken and scattered. When the jeweled casket was finished, the villagers and laborers gathered for a solemn mass during which they were allowed to view the relic that would now bring an eternal blessing upon the community. The casket was then closed and buried on the spot over which the high altar would later be raised. At the ceremony, a single large granite block was placed over the casket to ensure that the relic would not be stolen or desecrated. From then on, the construction of the church at Glastonbury went on to completion.

Years later, when similar accidents at the Abbey of the Holy Spirit frightened the carpenters and stone masons into refusing to labor, terrified by fears of evil spirits, the priests remembered how their holy brothers at Glastonbury had battled the demon of superstition. They began their labors by disavowing any thought that satanic powers were at work. Whether the bones were those of a saint or a worshiper of the ancient gods, the simple people were insistent that a spirit was agitated at having been disturbed. While researching the history and legends of the area to see if the remains could be those of an early saint, the priests learned that, according to one of the legends, Joseph of Arimathea had not spent his dying days at Glastonbury, but had later been seen in other areas, among them the site of the abbey. Adding substantial evidence to this possibility was that the second skeleton was not only intact, but the body had been laid to rest with the arms crossed over its breast. Surely this was the way the early Christians would have buried the saintly man, not, as in the former case, in a way so that the skeleton would be broken and scattered. Before the hierarchy at Glastonbury could take their disputed claim to the pope at Rome, those favoring the later miracle moved swiftly to reinter the remains, returning them carefully to the grave where they had lain undisturbed for centuries. By an almost supernatural coincidence, as though directed by the hand of God, the original design for the chapel had located the high altar over the exact spot where the bones were found.

My concern during the period of the quests was not that the finding of the Sangreal might settle these ancient claims, but how all the activity would disturb the placid life of the gentle nuns at the abbey, Elise in particular. The constant stream of knights through the gate threatened to disrupt their quiet routine and leave the abbey itself in shambles.

True, most of the knights were of a gentle mien, dedicated as they were to a holy cause, but their mere presence in a community that had been immune for years to change of any kind would be upsetting. The nuns were accustomed to having prayers according to the canonical hours, and I worried lest the visitors not respect these observances. Would they want to tear up the stone flooring or destroy any of the chapel in their impetuous search?

I worried most about Elise, now a beautiful young lady, who, though blind, would draw admiring glances from any man. Could I be sure that all the questers would honor their vows of chivalry, for as naïve and innocent as she was, I'd no doubt she would not be afraid if she found herself alone with one of them, trusting in God as well as in man's respect for the habit she wore. The presence of other nuns, all females armed only with their faith, would be no deterrent to a man aroused.

My first thought was to send word to her to stay with me at the manor until the quests were over. In my mind there was another danger. Even if the knights were trustworthy and left both chapel and women inviolate, it occurred to me this was an excellent opportunity for any rogue to don the trappings of knighthood in order to plunder the various churches, stealing jeweled crosses and reliquaries as well as the gold and silver they contained. Such felons would have no qualms about any havoc wrought by their lust and greed.

However, I knew Elise well enough to sense that she would not agree. If she were not safe in God's house, then she was not safe anywhere. I started then to instruct Will to take two of our strongest, most trusted retainers and lodge near the abbey, taking turns guarding the religious community. This would station at least one armed man on the premises at all times. Before I could effect the plan, our own placid routine was stirred to new life by the appearance at our gate of a young knight.

Just at dusk one evening, Atholwyn dragged himself into our courtyard, grimacing with pain and bleeding profusely from a knife wound in his side. Set upon by highway outlaws who had jumped him from ambush at the edge of the forest, he had been stripped of his armament. One of the brigands had ripped his side with a knife when he cut Atholwyn's purse loose from his belt. They had stolen his horse and left him lying in the road, unconscious from a blow on the head. After getting through our gate, Atholwyn lost consciousness again and, with night settling in, might have lain there all night unseen by any of us in the manor. Fortunately, I had stepped out into the courtyard to admire and check on a small plum tree planted just that morning. Calling to Will for assistance, we did what we could to stanch the bleeding and then carried the young man into the house and laid him on a bench in the main hall. I gathered clean rags to bind the wound after cleansing it and applying a poultice of herbs to draw out the infection. Will didn't think it was necessary to cauterize the gash with hot irons, but we would watch it carefully for any signs of putrefaction. When we thought it was safe to move Atholwyn without danger of the wound reopening, we put him to bed in one of the first-floor guest rooms.

While Atholwyn recuperated from his wounds and gradually regained his strength, he repaid our hospitality by telling us about the beginnings of the quest for the Holy Grail. Because he was too weak to talk more than a few minutes at a time, he was able to relate only a portion of the experience each day that I sat with him. From his point of view, much that took place was fraught with the supernatural, and he was still in awe of the miracles he had been privileged to witness.

When King Arthur returned to court from his alleged vigil at the monastery, he summoned his knights to gather at the Round Table. (I sensed in the story that followed the hand of Merlin, for I remembered what he had once told Arthur about men being more moved by superstition and the supernatural than by tangible evidence. I also saw that he had passed on to Arthur the ability to create a supernatural phenomena by manipulating what is perfectly ordinary and familiar.)

Arthur wove a story to present his idea of seeking the Holy Grail, a story to arouse the knight's curiosity and recall the early days of chivalry when they went forth to right the wrongs of the kingdom. They must be made to feel that the urgency of the quest touched their personal lives as well as that of Britain itself. Using his own dream as an inspiration, he altered and elaborated it just enough so that each man would feel he was intimately involved.

While he was at the monastery, so Arthur's story went, Merlin came to him in a dream. He was shocked to see the old sorcerer's face, for he had never before seen a countenance so drawn with despair. His hollow cheeks and downcast eyes gave Merlin the appearance of one near death. Without speaking a word, the old man beckoned to Arthur, who rose from the bed and followed his mentor to an open window. Although they appeared never to have left the room, they were now standing on a turreted balustrade at the top of a tall tower instead of in the monk's cell where Arthur had lain down to sleep. The tower rose high enough for Arthur to look toward the west and see the rocky coast of Cornwall. By turning in the opposite direction, he saw the cold northern sea break over the Eastern shore. To the south he espied the wide channel that separated him from Brittany. As he watched, he was horrified to see the Cornish cliffs shatter under the pounding waves and be swallowed up by the sea. One after another, great boulders broke off, to be crushed into small rocks by the ceaseless battering of the powerful breakers. To the east, a mammoth tide moved steadily, inexorably inland, never ebbing, but rising higher and higher until with one vast, cataclysmic rush it swept away land, trees, and towns. Looking now to the right, now to the left, Arthur saw the great masses of water coming closer and closer until he watched all of Britain drawn into the maw of the devouring tidal waves, which no man had the power to stop. All of nature was on such a rampage that even the waters of the channel to the south were heaving and moaning as though giving birth to some giant monster from the depths of hell.

Only then did Merlin speak. The vision Arthur had been allowed to witness was a warning that Britain would be destroyed unless Arthur and his Knights of the Round Table dedicated their lives to saving it. How that could be done would be revealed to him in a later dream, but he was first to fast for twenty-four hours, taking neither meat nor drink save for the bread and wine of Holy Eucharist. After the canonical hour of complin, he was to retire to his cell where he would fall immediately into a deep sleep. As soon as Arthur agreed to follow these instructions, he heard a mighty clap of thunder and saw the flood waters recede to their normal heights; the cliffs rose up again, and all the land was restored.

The next day he followed the regimen as he had been instructed. Once again Merlin appeared, and again he seemed to be looking out the window of the tower. This time, however, there was no flood, but a great calm over all the land. Merlin then directed Arthur's attention toward the heavens, and as he looked, the clouds parted and from out their midst came a rosy glow, which grew until it enveloped the entire night sky, lighting up the countryside as though it were midday. When Merlin waved his hands, the glow vanished, and the night became dark again except for a single star directly above where they stood. Gradually, the star brightened with an intense, brilliant light, and it moved closer until Arthur saw that the blinding rays came not from a star, but from an immense silver cup embellished with precious jewels.

"Look closely," Merlin said, "for that is the Sangreal, or Holy Grail, which your knights must seek in order to save Britain from destruction. It does not matter that most will seek in vain while only a select few will reach their goal. It is the symbol of perfection. Many men seek perfection, and although few attain such a state, their questing after it is what gives meaning to life. Those who undertake the quest but do not find the grail will not have failed, for they will have done as much for the salvation of the land as those who enter the presence of the holy relic."

Just as the grail faded from his sight, Arthur awoke from his dream.

The entire company of the Round Table was so filled with awe and wonder by the story that their immediate response was one of stunned silence. The legend of the Holy Grail was not unknown, but the revelation they might seek and find it was astonishing to them. First they whispered among themselves; then a few began asking questions. Arthur silenced them. He would answer questions and detail the plans he had made before the evening was over, but first they were to relax and enjoy the banquet then being served. The first shock of what the knights had heard began to dissipate as they concentrated on the huge platters of meat and pitchers of mead being served.

When each one was finishing up the last of the food and having his goblet refilled preparatory to easing back in his chair, the hall reverberated with a deafening roll of thunder, and the walls shook as a mighty wind howled through the window slits, snuffing out all but a few flambeaux.

Before the startled eyes of the knights, a brilliant light appeared beneath the vaulted ceiling and began to move across the room, pausing briefly above the head of each knight as it passed. Three times the flaming lamp circled the entire Round Table, and as it was reflected in the men's armor, each knight saw every one of his peers enveloped in a supernatural glow. Then it stopped over the head of Arthur, flickered momentarily, and finally flamed up even more fiery, revealing to the eyes of the now breathless, mute audience a chalice wrought from a single block of pure crystal, carved and faceted like a diamond. Capturing the light from candle flames, it sent back jeweled sparks of red, blue, green, and amber from its fiery, crystalline points to all parts of the room. Almost paralyzed with fear by this last spectacle, the knights fell to their knees, convinced they had witnessed a miracle like that of Moses at the burning bush. Surely God had sent this vision of the Holy Grail to substantiate Arthur's revelation of his dream and to instill in them the belief that the king was one of God's chosen few and an instrument of the Lord's plan for Britain.

Seemingly undaunted by what had just transpired, Arthur called for pages to relight the flambeaux blown out by the wind. When all attention was at last focused on him, he outlined his plan. He had scarcely finished before one by one the knights came forward to pledge their swords and their lives to the quest. The first was Sir Gawain, his own nephew and favorite companion. Swift on his heels came Lancelot, Bors, Percival, and Gareth, followed by all those in attendance.

After Matins the next morning, the knights began a twenty-four-hour fast, staying in the church to observe the order of worship for the remaining canonical hours of prime, tierce, sext, nones, vespers, and complin. They slept a few hours before returning to the church to make their confessions. When the last man had confessed, the bishop granted total absolution, declaring that each was in a penitential state of grace and spiritually worthy to begin the quest. Repeating the ritual every knight must undergo preparatory to investiture, the questers laid their swords, armor, and helmets before the high altar, dedicating them to the work of God. They spent the rest of the night watching over their arms and praying for guidance.

At dawn the next morning Arthur, accompanied by the queen and all the ladies of the court, came to the church. In a service solemn in its tradition but permeated with the excitement of the new adventure, the king led the company through the ritual of investiture, conferring on each man a new title, Knight of the Holy Grail. Bearing on their standards the new banner Arthur had designed in honor of the quest—and which his flag makers had worked day and night to create—the knights marched from the church. It was a triumphant procession, the massed display of the new banners giving added impetus to the united cause. The flag itself was white silk. In its center was a purple shield for the church triumphant, backed by three interlocking gold circles, symbolizing the trinity. The shield bore a white and gold chalice supporting the host. Above this was a single red and gold flame, representing the tongues of flame that appeared to the apostle on Whitsunday as a symbol of Christ's promise to man to send another comforter, the ever-present guidance of the Holy Ghost. Although simple in design, the banners bore a clear message, recognizable to everyone: the knights were on a holy quest.

As the procession proceeded through the church doors, Arthur gave each knight his personal blessing, speaking a few private words to every one of them. From Camelot the knights set out in different directions to begin their quest.

We were as spellbound by Atholwyn's version of the miraculous occurrences at the now-famous banquet as he had been while participating in them. There was no doubt as to the dedication of the men whom Arthur had sent journeying to the far corners of the British Isles. As his wound healed, Atholwyn became restless to continue his own wanderings, which had been halted by his unfortunate encounter with the highwaymen. We were reluctant to let him go, having become genuinely fond of him and entranced by the many stories he told of life at Camelot in addition to the one concerning the quest. He left with the promise that he would return to give us at least the story of his own adventure.

Through the months that followed, many another knight found his way to our door, and each related in detail his own reaction to the appearance of the grail and the experiences he had already undergone. Other than Atholwyn, the visitor I remember best was a handsome young fellow who seemed more like a boy than one who had reached manhood and already been acclaimed a knight. He had a gentle, almost ethereal appearance, the look of one who has been reared among women rather than in the rough and tumble assemblage of men. But he had also a strength and assurance about him that presaged success in any adventure he undertook. Despite completely different coloring and size—he was blond and slender, fine boned with delicate features—he reminded me of someone else who had the same self-confident, almost conceited bearing.

He was polite but reticent. He was grateful for our hospitality and was a considerate guest, but he disdained to answer our queries with anything more than a few brief, almost curt replies. I hesitated to invoke the prerogatives of my age and position as his hostess to chide him for being rude, for I knew that then he would retreat into complete silence, and I would never learn anything about him.

Avoiding any question relating specifically to him, I shifted my conversation to other subjects, asking about some of the people at court to see if I could get a clue as to his identity. He revealed only that his name was Bonric. His response to my inquiries about the court was that he had not been there long, arriving only in time to be knighted by the king just prior to the beginnings of the quest. He knew a few of his peers by name, but was not acquainted with any of them.

He finally opened up enough to reveal that it was his mother's wish that he become a knight and serve the king. It had long been his own desire to enter a monastery and devote his days to the life of a recluse, serving God with prayers and meditation. I was convinced by his hushed, slow way of speaking that he had already spent several years of his short life in a religious community.

Bonric remained at the manor for three days, joining me for meals, but spending most of his time walking through the gardens or along the path by the river, deep in quiet thought. It did not disturb me that he preferred solitude to conversation, for I, too, often sought the sanctuary of withdrawal from people, but I was curious to know if, like many men of a deeply religious bent, he had donned a hair shirt. With his ascetic inclinations, such a garment would appeal to his imagination, the stiff bristles woven into the cloth pricking his skin as his conscience pricked his soul in a constant reminder of his sins. If he did not wear a real garment of wool and hair, had he perhaps woven around himself one created from an awareness of his own mortality and the sins of the flesh man is heir to? How many temptations of the past were now sharp barbs that irritated his soul each time he remembered?

When he first arrived at the manor, he was as tense as a tautly wound spring, but by the evening of the third day he had relaxed enough to join me in the library after supper. I had set some chestnuts to roasting among the ashes and continued turning them with a long stick when he entered, pausing only long enough to look up and smile. When he saw that I was not going to badger him with questions, he allowed himself to succumb to the comfort of the chair and the warmth of the fire.

"I think," I said, more to myself than to him, "that these chestnuts should be just about right. Too much longer and they might char."

I started trying to poke them out onto the hearth without burning my fingers. As I hoped, Bonric left his chair and knelt beside me to help. There is something about working together in close proximity, even with so simple a project as pulling chestnuts from the fire, that engenders intimacy faster than any other way.

"I'll be sorry to see you leave tomorrow," I said after the last of the nuts had been pulled from the fire and placed in a wooden bowl between us. "But I know you are eager to be on your way to the chapel at the abbey. Others have gone before you, but I never learned whether they were successful in finding the grail."

"I'll be successful," was his self-assured reply. Where had I heard that voice before, that same tone that would not acknowledge defeat of any kind?

"You'll return to court?" I asked.

"No, home. My mother is alone; my father is dead."

"You seem very sure about finding the grail."

"I know now that I went through all the preparations for knighthood for just that one purpose—to be allowed to seek the grail. It was my mother's wish—not mine—that I be a knight, and particularly a knight of King Arthur's Round Table. I had been brought up to honor my filial duty of obedience, so after undergoing the months of training, I headed straight for the court for investiture, intending to serve the king for a year and then return home and, if still inclined, to enter a monastery."

He paused, his brow furrowed with indecision, as though searching for the right word.

"I had an experience," he went on, "I have shared

226

with no one up to now. I think I can tell you, and that you will understand."

Beginning in a halting manner for fear perhaps that I would scoff at him, Bonric unfolded another of the eerie, mystical experiences that were becoming so much a part of the quest.

On his way to court he had stopped at a wayside inn for a midday meal and to rest his horse. The landlord warned him that word had come back to the inn of highwaymen some miles up the road he was to take. The route was one frequented by nobles traveling to Camelot, and a band of outlaws had been highly successful in attacking wayfarers without warning and relieving them of their money and valuables. If even large entourages had been unable to escape being robbed, a single knight would be lucky to pass unscathed, if not murdered. Taking Bonric outside and using his sword, the landlord drew a map in the dirt outlining a short cut through the forest. He could circumvent the robbers where they waited at a wide curve in the road and save time as well. Bonric thanked the landlord for his trouble and rode off. It never occurred to the naïve young man that the kindly landlord, probably in the pay of the outlaws, was leading him directly into the spider's web.

Watching the roadside carefully for the landmarks he sought, Bonric turned off the main route where it diverged into two narrow footpaths around a huge oak tree. The detour was well trodden, but if Bonric thought about that at all, it was to assume that the short cut was one used by the local peasantry. He was a naïve young man, but he was not deaf or blind. Being alone, he was not diverted or lulled into complacency by the chatter of companions. He was first alerted to danger ahead when his mare pricked up her ears and began turning her head from side to side. Bringing her to an immediate halt, Bonric listened, sensing more than really hearing the hum of male voices some hundred yards farther on in the very direction he was heading. Now that he was really concentrating, he was aware of more sounds: the pawing of muffled hoofs, the slight

227

rustle of leaves, the crackling of burning green twigs. It was already dusk in the woods, darkening more every minute, but he was able to discern a slim cloud of smoke. Either the robbers were unconcerned about a single rider—for surely they had heard him approaching, as careless as he had been about riding noisily through the underbrush—or they were confident they could capture him with the least exertion on their part.

In that brief moment Bonric had to make his decision. To turn back would be to attract them. Knowing the forest better than he, they could catch up with him in minutes. The same would be true if he tried to circle around them. He chose instead to walk his horse around in a small area, making enough noise to convince the brigands that he was afraid and uncertain and to give the impression that he was retracing his steps to the main road. However, after riding no more than fifteen feet in the reverse direction, he dismounted and led the mare deeper into the forest on his right. After fifty yards of carefully picking his way among the dense mass of primeval woods, he tethered his horse and proceeded several yards farther on foot. He knew he was completely lost, veering as he had around one mammoth tree and then another, ever on the watch to avoid stepping on dead twigs that, with a sharp crack, would echo back to his pursuers. Completely in the dark now, he relied on the careful touch of his soft boots to move him from one soundless patch of moss to another, stepping as cautiously as one fords a rushing stream by means of water-smoothed stones, knowing that a single false step will bring instant disaster.

Finally, exhausted by his efforts, every nerve raw with fear and fatigue, Bonric dropped down on a grassy plot, larger than any other he had traversed. Although only a few feet square, it was large enough to allow him to stretch out in some comfort, easing the cramps in his legs and the pounding of his heart. His hands were bleeding from numerous scratches, his tunic and trousers were torn, and even his soft leather boots were scarred from multiple slashes by rough bark. But he was safe. Sure, at last, that he had not been followed, he fell asleep, putting aside all worry about how he would find his way out the next day.

Some hours later, near midnight by internal reckoning, he awoke to a succession of thunder peals that sounded like a massive waterfall carrying along a flotilla of rocks and dashing them on boulders hidden beneath the spume. Accompanying this titanic explosion of sound were slashes of forked lightning, their barbs aimed directly at the forest. By the first flash, Bonric caught a brief glimpse of where he was. A second and third flash confirmed his suspicions. He had been sleeping on the smooth top of a grave. He was in a cemetery so buried in entangled undergrowth and twisting vines he was appalled to think he had managed to find his way through the maze. Less disturbed by superstitious fear of having slept on a grave than curious about why a cemetery was located in this forlorn and out-of-the-way spot, Bonric took advantage of every lightning flash to explore visually his surroundings while staying put on his grassy bed. One time he spotted a low building not more than twenty feet away, and when a sudden downpour joined the violent battle of the elements, he made a dash for the stone hut, tearing apart vines and brambles as he ran.

He reached the shelter before he was completely soaked, but found to his dismay that the door was latched with a heavy padlock. Shivering under the protection of a shallow portico, he pounded on the stained wooden door panel in an attempt to break the door in. With the first blow, the wood shattered, crumbling to shards at his feet, and the iron lock split in two and dangled from its hasp like the last rusty leaf on a tree. Stunned, but relieved, at the ease with which the barrier was eliminated, Bonric entered the small building. It took a moment for his lungs to adjust to the musty, stale air and the dust he stirred up as he stepped on the flagstone floor. The place was in total darkness, and he remembered that during the brief flashes of lightning it seemed as if there were no windows to help dispel the gloom even if the moon weren't hidden behind storm clouds. He proceeded cautiously farther into the room,

229

feeling his way with each footstep and groping with his hands in front of him to prevent an accident. In spite of moving as warily as a blind man, he struck his shin on the sharp edge of a board, and reaching down to rub the painful area, he touched a low, wooden bench. He sat down, gratefully.

Gradually, his eyes became accustomed to the darkness, and he could distinguish the stone walls, green with moss and spider-webbed with luminescent veins of niter. The walls curved inward and upward to form a rounded ceiling. He saw three other benches paralleling the one he sat on, each no more than six feet long and reaching almost from wall to wall. Having spent the night in a graveyard, he was not surprised to discover that he was in a small chapel and that directly in front of him was a low table, or altar, on which stood a rudely made cross of wood carved or hacked from a single wooden slab rather than constructed of two cross pieces joined at midcenter. Conscious only that he could see more and more clearly, he was unaware that the interior of the chapel was becoming lighter, but with no visible means of illumination. He merely followed his first inclination on finding himself in a church: He knelt and thanked God for delivering him from his enemies and leading him to a place of refuge.

It was then the miraculous vision appeared. Unseen hands lit two candles on the altar, revealing the figure of a knight in full armor lying between them. Hands crossed over his chest, his head pillowed by a flat stone, he lay in state. Bonric's first shock of wonder was increased twofold when a woman shrouded in misty gray materialized inside the walls as though from the very stones themselves and walked toward the dead knight. She carried an object wrapped in white samite laced with gold threads that she placed between the crossed arms of the knight on the altar; then she turned once to look full into Bonric's face and vanished.

Transfigured with awe, Bonric remained on his knees, his eyes focused unblinking on the dead knight, his limbs benumbed with fear. He was now so caught up by the miracle he was witnessing, he was not surprised to see the knight, seemingly restored to life, rise from the altar and walk toward him. In his hands was the object given to him by the veiled woman. Pausing before Bonric, the old knight, gray with the pallor of death, reached out to pass the gift to the younger man. As Bonric watched, the white samite became transparent, and through the gauzy film emerged the shadowy outline of a goblet. When Bonric reached up to receive it, the entire vision—knight, goblet, altar, and candles—dissolved into the shadows, leaving him once more alone in the chilling, mausoleumlike atmosphere of the chapel, with only a memory of the vision to keep him awake the rest of the night. As yet unaware of the quest Arthur would be proposing for his knights, Bonric did not at that time equate the chalice with the Holy Grail.

In the morning he found his horse chomping grass beside the door of the chapel. Bright sun filtered through the trees, and he saw a clear path ahead leading to the road. What he took the evening before to be a vast graveyard was now only a few crumbling stone markers. Gone was any indication that there had been outlaws waiting in ambush the previous day, and Bonric cantered along the path and out onto the highway with only a few forest creatures challenging him for daring to trespass on their domain.

"So," he concluded, "that is why I know I will be successful. Although at the time of the vision I knew I was witnessing a miracle, I did not grasp its special significance. Only after King Arthur expressed his desire that we undertake a quest for the Holy Grail did I know for certain that it had already been revealed to me, surely a sign that I had been chosen to find the holy relic."

I was impressed with Bonric's story and with his sincerity. So many seemingly miraculous events had transpired, beginning with Arthur's own dream, so like Bonric's vision, that I could not help but believe that some power was watching over Britain and had shown both Arthur and his knights the means to prevent the disintegration of the country. Could it then be wrong to encourage this young knight in his belief that he was among the elect who might find the Sangreal? It would surely be a marvelous moment for all of Christendom, as well as for Britain, if the grail were found and then located in a hallowed sanctuary where pilgrims from all over the world could come in pious veneration to worship not it but in its presence.

My thoughts returned from future possibilities to present realities when Bonric asked, "You do believe me, about the vision, I mean?"

"Yes." I answered. "I was merely pondering the number of unusual occurrences already associated with the quest and thinking about all the others who are devoting a year to seek what you are so sure you will be the one to find."

"Some of them may also be as fortunate," he said. "As for the others, they have been given a year off from dancing attendance on the queen and amusing Arthur with mock tournaments."

So even in his few days at Camelot my young knight had become disenchanted with the life. I was particularly struck by his reference to Guinevere.

"And you think you are worthy to find the grail?" I asked. "Aren't there certain conditions required of the man who will be so blessed?"

"There are," he responded quickly, "and I think I meet all of them. I have never broken the commandments nor fallen prey to any of the deadly sins. I eat sparingly, fast on the appointed days, and obey the tenets of the Christian faith. Nor have I ever been tempted to commit a sin."

"How old are you, Bonric? Seventeen?"

"I will be seventeen in two months."

"And you have never had to resist temptation?"

"Never!"

"Most young men your age would not be able to say that with such assurance."

"I know. I have heard them brag about stealing or looking forward to killing without trepidation or ... or ..."

"Or," I finished his sentence, "tumbling in the hay with a compliant serving wench?"

"Yes, ma'am. If a man pure in heart is to find the grail, I have a better chance than most."

I looked at the confident young man and wondered if I should caution him to beware of the sin of pride, the most malignant of the seven deadly sins. He had risen from his chair and was standing in front of the fire. Once again I was haunted by the memory of another standing in the same place in the full glory of youth, as proud as a downy-feathered cockerel of his yet untested manhood. If I could just find a clue.

"Were you at court long before the quests began?"

"Less than a week."

"Did you enter any lists?"

"Only one," he answered, "and I unseated my opponent during the first tilt."

"You must be good, and he was surely embarrassed to be defeated by such a young rival."

"He should have been," he answered. "It was the king's favorite—Sir Lancelot."

Lancelot. Now something really was pricking at my memory.

"You said your mother is alone and your father is dead?" I asked.

"Yes," he responded, "and she, too, is thinking of renouncing her worldly name of Elaine and entering an abbey under the holy name of her patron saint, Elizabeth."

Then I knew—Lancelot and Elaine. Lancelot had had an affair with a young woman named Elaine sometime after he arrived at Camelot. Much of what I had heard was doubtful rumor, but I had learned from Arthur that the basic story was true. And there was no doubt about it; this was Lancelot's son. The air of inscrutability, the proud hauteur, the win-or-die attitude, were all inherited from his father. No wonder he was so young; not yet seventeen. Lancelot had not been in Britain much longer than that.

"I'm sorry your father is dead." Rather than challenge him with the information I knew, I thought it

233

best to agree until I saw if he was dissembling, or if he did not know his father's identity.

"Yes, he died before I was born. I never knew him. Oh, I'm not a bastard, if that is what you are thinking. My father and my mother were married, and he loved her very much."

Elaine had told him something, or he would not have been so quick to defend his birth. A man does not jump to the conclusion that you will immediately think him a bastard when he says his father is dead. But I did not remember that Lancelot's son was named Bonric, nor would my faulty memory help me out. I decided to ignore his remark about his legitimacy and proceed in another direction.

"You know, Bonric, you remind me very much of another young knight who stayed with me many years ago—as well as I remember, about a year or so before you were born. He, too, insisted that he was pure in all ways and had never been tempted by the world, the flesh, or the devil. I longed to warn him to beware the deadliest sin of all, that of pride, but I had not then reached the age where I could speak frankly without caring what my listener thought of me. I often wondered if pride would bring his downfall. He was Lancelot, the very knight you unhorsed. The ancient gods punished men who had inordinate pride; perhaps you were their instrument."

I saw him start at the name, and I knew then that he was aware of his parentage.

"Yes—yes, I bested him. But I did it for myself, not for any ancient gods."

It was time to stop beating around the bush.

"You *are* Lancelot's son, aren't you?" I insisted. "Your father is not dead."

"I do not claim him for a father."

"But he did acknowledge you at Camelot and give you his blessing."

"Yes—no—I mean he recognized me, and I let him welcome me to court, but no kind words of his can ever undo the misery he caused. He seduced my mother and then, knowing he had fathered a child, returned to the arms of the queen. I wish I had never heard his name and would never hear it again."

I tried to reconcile him to an appreciation of his father. "Your father is a great man, the greatest knight, some say, that King Arthur has. I hope the day will come when you will see that and accept him."

"I think not," he answered more quietly. "There is no reason for me ever to see him again once I find the grail."

"Bonric, I admire you and hope you succeed in your quest. Do not let the sins of pride and anger dissuade you from your goal. You can never be pure in heart as long as you hate your father or think yourself better than other men."

He made no response, but asked if he might be excused to go to his room as he wanted to make an early start in the morning. I watched with my heart as a very thoughtful young man retired for the night, whether to sleep or to search his conscience I could not know.

At dawn he rode off, answering my one last question with a serious smile.

"My mother was Elaine of Corbin. I transposed the letters and use Bonric so I will not be recognized as Lancelot's son. My name is Sir Galahad."

⊠ *Chapter Eleven* ⊠

The quests continued for almost a year after Galahad left. One by one the knights returned to Camelot, some stopping by the manor to recount their experiences and share a convivial day or two with me. Atholwyn came bounding in like a long-lost colt. No, he had not found the grail, but he had had a glorious time trying. He was the kind who would find something rewarding in the most tedious, or even dangerous, experience. He had met a young lady, and as soon as he returned to court, he was sending for her, but since his stay with us had meant so much to him, he had come this way to tell me all about her. I was not sure I would have described a close brush with death in quite such endearing terms. After two days he romped off again, promising to return in the near future. I was sure he would, and without any warning.

It was a long time before I heard anything about Galahad, and until I did, I had not realized how very much he had been on my mind. Even then the news was only unsubstantiated rumor sent by word of mouth from some who had been with him at the end. He had not remained in Britain, but had sailed away—in a magic boat some said—to a far-off land. There he found the grail, and there he died. Others were thought to have seen the Sangreal, but if there were hopes it would ever be enshrined in a place where all Christians could venerate it, those hopes were vanquished.

Had the quests strengthened the unity of Britain? I had not seen Arthur for over two years, and my longing

236

for him became almost an obsession. The manor was too quiet now that there were no more wanderers to be entertained—or to entertain me. The household duties that I used to dispatch with alacrity became an endless round of boring tasks, and even the hours in the weaving room were now only lengthening afternoons of tedium. I started translating more of my father's manuscripts, remembering the thrill I used to feel after trying and discarding several versions when I found the exact words I wanted. But even that seemed more like work than relaxation.

I contemplated a retreat at the abbey, but in my present state of mind, the placid routine would probably bore rather than soothe me. In addition, I had no intention of retiring from life yet, and if I found that the work at the manor could go on smoothly without me, under Will's competent charge, I would be even more depressed.

The two years of the quest had been exciting ones; even when we had no company, we waited in anticipation for a traveler to ride up. At first I resented having my well-planned days interrupted at often inconvenient times, but there was no doubt I had thoroughly enjoyed it. When the quests ended, my world became empty and hollow.

I needed a reason to get up in the morning, to wake up to an awareness that something needed doing that would give meaning to my life. Walking in the courtyard one day, I saw what might be the solution. The flower beds were filled with weeds, the espaliered flowering shrubs had been allowed to run riot over the walls, and many of the fruit trees were heavy with dead branches. I had never been an avid gardener, but I had taken delight in our colorful, well-planned courtyard. At least I had always made a point of directing the work, seeing to it that the beds were weeded and the trees pruned. I felt ashamed when I looked around now. My hands actually ached to plunge into the rich earth, to dig and plant, to create new life. Good, hard physical labor was what I needed to work off my frustrations.

Calling to Will, I told him I was leaving the next day for a short visit at the abbey.

"I won't be gone more than three or four days, but I want to see how Elise is getting along now that she has been named assistant to the abbess. While I am gone, I would like you to have these beds spaded up, and check the storehouse for any seeds we saved from last year. Don't let any of the trees or bushes be touched. I'll take care of those when I return, but I do not think I'm strong enough to clean out these beds. The ground has gotten so hard, it may take a plow to turn some of the earth."

I set off at dawn the next morning in a more peaceful state of mind than I had known in a long time. I was looking forward to spending a few days with Elise, but more important, I could look beyond that visit with real anticipation to returning home. The days ahead no longer stretched in a meaningless procession toward no vital achievement.

Through the years I had transported several pieces of furniture and many smaller items to the small cottage within the abbey walls. It had been built originally by the wife of a wealthy lord who had contributed substantially to the church. When he died, she retired there to live out the rest of her days in the peaceful atmosphere of the community, but not as a vow-taking member. After her death, the small house was used occasionally for important guests, but when I was still young, it had been allowed to remain unoccupied and had been unfurnished until I was given permission to use it during my visits. I was attracted to it the first time I saw it, more because of its cozy, compact size than its location. It was a relief after the vast manor house to step inside the small, neat main room with its low ceilings and a fireplace just large enough to heat the three rooms: a small kitchen larder and a bedroom shared the rear half of the house.

The furniture I had brought to the cottage was all much smaller than their massive counterparts at the manor. My bed was the low trundle bed I had slept on as a child, and I did not need a flight of four steps to climb into it. I think the house appealed to me because it was all mine and because there was not a masculine touch in the entire place.

Elise, matured with the responsibilities of her new position, greeted me warmly but more sedately than usual. Once I thought I had lost a daughter when she made it evident she was happier at the abbey than with me. She did not meet me at the gate—I had sent a runner ahead to say I was coming—but waited for me in the cottage so that we could have a few moments alone together before joining the rest of the community. There was a cheery fire in the grate, and she had arranged for a few early daffodils and snowdrops, my favorite colors of yellow and white, to brighten up the room.

No one watching Elise as she walked easily around the room and pointed with pride to the flower arrangement would know she was blind. Never, since she took her first steps under the kind eyes of Berthe, had she let her handicap deter her from anything she wanted to do. Nor had she allowed the nuns to excuse her from duties. She could cook and clean, lead the group in prayers, and even dress and bandage the wounds of wayfarers who sought refuge in the abbey after being attacked by outlaws.

Both of us talking at once, we shared our experiences since last seeing each other until it was time for her to return to the main house. For three days I did just what I wanted to do: joined the nuns for meals and prayers when I felt like it or stayed in my house to read and sew. Elise and I met every evening for a few minutes together before vespers. After that time I was ready to return home, but I knew that if I had not had the work in the garden to look forward to, I would have been tempted to remain.

From then on through the spring months I was scarcely aware of the days passing one into another. I planted, I pruned, I rearranged the climbing shrubs against the walls, and I watched for each slim sprout as it appeared above the rich, black loam. At night, physically tired but content, I returned to the manuscripts and found renewed delight in continuing the translations. The next time I went to the abbey, I would take a few of them and introduce Elise to more of my favorite secular works.

Early one evening, my arms black to the elbow from digging and transplanting bulbs, I looked up from the garden to see a slim young man leaning nonchalantly against the stone wall, eying me with a laughing, almost cynical gaze. It took me no more than a brief glance to know who he was. I had seen his mother only once, but there was no mistaking from whom he had inherited the lustrous, blue-black hair that hung, softly waved, over his shoulders and the huge, deep green, piercing eyes that held a hint of feline mystery. His features, although beardless, were a slimmer, sharper replica of his father's. In a way he was more handsome than his father, but the son's lineaments were cold and cruel compared with the warmth and kindliness of the father's. It was Mordred, bastard son of Arthur and Morgause.

I arose and walked toward the young man.

"Welcome to Sanam Manor, Mordred. I am Lady Lionors."

He was obviously startled to have me recognize him. I wondered if he had intended to visit me incognito. In fact, I wondered why he had come here at all, so far from the home in the north where he lived with his mother.

"Thank you," he answered. "I see I don't have to introduce myself. But how did you know me?"

"I've seen your mother only once, but I always thought she had the most beautiful hair I ever saw."

At that he smiled.

"And," I continued, "you have your father's features. I knew him when he was about your age, and there is no question you are his son."

A shadow crossed his face, wiping out the charming smile and replacing it with a scowl. I was forewarned: his hatred for his father had no doubt been instilled in him by Morgause, and I recalled Arthur's telling me of her desire for revenge on Uther Pendragon through him. Changing the subject, I asked Mordred if he would like to come in for refreshment and to rest.

"I have had my evening meal," I said, "but I can send for some wine and fruit to share before the fire."

"Thank you, my lady. I am tired, and the wine sounds tempting."

His tone was gracious and conciliatory, but I detected beneath it a hint of mockery. I wondered if he ever dropped that facile mask.

"Mordred," I suggested, "why not spend the night here and leave in the morning for wherever you are headed. Unless you have other plans, of course."

"I would like that. No, I have no plans."

"Then come in, and I will have a room readied for you."

I had poured the wine and was arranging the sweetmeats and fruit when Mordred returned from the room a page had led him to. He had arrived at the manor attired in heavy, dust-covered riding clothes. When he entered the library, he had not only washed, but had made a complete change as well. From the small cap on his head to the soft slippers on his feet, he was all in black velvet, as deep a black as his hair, and completely unadorned execpt for a gold chain set with amethysts. He was an impressive if solemn figure.

"Come in, Mordred, and sit by the fire. These evenings seem to be cooler than usual."

"Thank you, my lady. This does look good. I did not realize how hungry I was."

"Good. Now, tell me why you are here and where you're headed."

"I've been to Camelot ..."

"Camelot?" I could not help but interrupt.

He went on to say that Morgause had sent him to be with his father at court, insisting that it was time for King Arthur to acknowledge him as his son and rightful heir. Mordred obeyed, under duress, preferring the wild, lonely expanse of the stark Orkney Islands to the constrained atmosphere of Camelot.

He began to describe the wind-hewn rocks, forever awash with the frigid waves of the northern sea. For days at a time his only companions were the crying sea birds whose melancholy songs were an echo of his own longing to race the wind high above the desolate land, enisled by the surging sea from the great strength of Britain. Or he ran with the shaggy donkeys as they cropped the rough grasses already so stunted by the cold climate; the animals needed to forage over twice as much land each day as their relatives in warmer climes. When tired from his rambles, Mordred lay under one of the sparse trees that bowed to the west, wind bent by the perpetual and mighty breath of Eurus blowing from the east across the cold North Sea.

With his four half-brothers at court, Mordred shared with his mother a tower that stood precipitously close to the edge of a cliff, the only remnant of the once-vast stronghold built by an early pagan ancestor of King Lot. Wind, time, and marauding Norsemen had destroyed all but the tall structure, an immobile sentinel standing guard over a small estuary, the only means of access between the impregnable cliffs.

Built of rocks hewn from the very boulders that capped the surrounding flatlands, the tower looked as though it had been constructed by the same hand that created the islands when they were emerging from chaos. Of all shapes and sizes, the mortarless rocks had been juxtapositioned in such perfect equilibrium that while it swayed like a tall pine before the force of a high wind, the tower never collapsed, only listed a bit to the west like the trees. Each level of the round tower contained a single room, the lower levels joined by well-constructed circular stairways. However, a person ascending to the upper two levels had to climb makeshift ladders made from rough limbs nailed across the trunk of a single tree. The lower rooms, although drafty from the constant wind blowing through the arrow slits, were not uncomfortable. Morgause, as well as predecessors, had furnished them with rich hangings and a variety of chairs and tables. Mordred preferred the topmost level, surrounding himself with only meager necessities, living like a monk in his chaste cell.

Mordred was happy living with his mother, for their

needs and temperaments were similar. Of all the brothers, only Agravaine was closer to his mother, and with him gone, Mordred did not have to share her love. Being the youngest and still a child when the others left, one by one, for court, he had been lavished with Morgause's twisted, almost demoniacal form of mother love, a love made all the more potent by her hatred for Arthur.

"I gather," I said after listening to his description of home, "that you do not like it at court. Surely your father has not been unkind to you, or thoughtless."

"Oh, no, he is kindness itself. He acknowledged me, all right. I am his son and heir, but you know what I really am—a bastard." He spit out the last word.

"I do know," I answered, "but if your father has proclaimed you his heir, surely that means you are accepted as his legal son."

"His natural son, you mean."

"His *only* son," and I put strong emphasis on the word. "Guinevere has given him no children, and I am sure he has often longed to have you with him."

"Oh, no doubt of that," he glowered. "Then why didn't he send for me. Why did mother have to make the first move?"

"I cannot answer that. Perhaps—perhaps he thought you would be ill at ease. Remember he, too, knows what it is to bear the stigma of bastardy."

"But not the fruit of incest! Oh, I've heard the whisperings." He ranted almost like a pouting child exaggerating his hurts. "They look at me as though I were a freak and should sprout horns or a tail. They are amazed that I have human form and wait to see if I will change into something weird when the moon comes out."

"When in fact," I said quietly, "you are really a very handsome young man."

"I look like my father, you mean. And to you he is handsome."

"Yes, you do," I said. "I told you that, but in many ways you are better looking. So you have been at Camelot. How are things up there? I ask many questions because it is the only way I can keep up with the news."

"The knights are restless. There are no real challenges, just make-believe jousts. No one gets killed or goes out to battle."

"The king has always abhorred killing of any kind." Then I realized I had made a mistake saying that. "Where are you going from here?"

"I asked leave of the king to go across to Brittany to visit a knight I met at court. I have been so long in the north, I wanted to see more of the world."

"And he agreed? Good. Did you stop here by accident?"

"No, several at court mentioned your name. They spoke of how hospitable you were to travelers and said I should be sure to stop here."

"Oh," I laughed, "then you were not surprised at my invitation to spend the night. Yes, I often have people stay here on the way to the coast."

"No, ma'am," he said, his temper under control. "I was hoping you would ask."

"And I did not disappoint you. Here, have more wine. You still look tired. Then I will let you leave. I usually retire early."

We sat quietly for a few minutes, neither speaking, both staring into the fire. Or so I thought until I looked up and saw Mordred watching me with an unconcealed look of . . . what? Curiosity? No, more than that.

"What are you thinking, Mordred? You have the look of one who is aching to ask a question but does not for fear of the answer. Speak up. You must learn not to think of everyone as your enemy."

"I lied to you," he said.

"You lied? About what?"

"About traveling to Brittany. I came here to see you."

"I am flattered, but why?" I asked. "Surely not just for my hospitality."

"I want to see my brother or sister."

I was stunned. No one except Arthur, Merlin, a few nuns left at the abbey, and myself knew of Elise's parentage. I hoped my expression of shock, coming before I could control it, would be taken by Mordred as an indication of complete bewilderment at his statement.

"I am afraid I do not know what you mean." My voice was surprisingly calm and controlled.

"Yes, you do. I mean the child you have had by Arthur. Where is he?"

He knew there was a child, but not the sex. Was he afraid of being disinherited, or was there more to it?

"You are out of your mind, Mordred!" I could not keep the fury from my voice. "There is no such child. Do you know what you are accusing me—accusing the king of?"

"Yes, adultery. I am not his only bastard, nor my mother his only mistress. You have been my father's whore—before he married Guinevere and since."

"Mordred, I will not ask you to leave; it is late. And I will forgive your rash outburst because of your youth. But I must ask you to explain your words."

"You are in love with my father, aren't you?" he asked.

"I am fond, very fond of your father. We have been friends since we were children, long before he became king. I have remained his friend, as have many others, for all these years. I am proud, not ashamed, to be his friend."

"But you have never married, have you?"

"I happened to prefer to remain single. Unlike many women, I was fortunate enough to inherit my father's estate. I could because this land was given to my father's ancestors by a Roman emperor, and under the Roman law of the time a woman could inherit. I did not need to marry for either a home or to be taken care of. I never met anyone—" I caught myself before adding the word *else*—"I loved enough to marry."

"But my father has been here frequently," he argued, "often for days or weeks at a time."

"And so have many others. As you said yourself, I am known for my hospitality. I love having guests. When there were campaigns near by or when your father wished to get away from the worries of court, he knew he could rest here undisturbed." I hoped I was not saying too much, but Mordred knew enough of Arthur's movements that I could not lie outright.

"Or to get away from Guinevere!"

"Hush, Mordred. Theirs is an ideal marriage. There has never been a breath of scandal." Or had there been? Had he heard any?

"But she never accompanies him here, does she?" he smirked.

"Guinevere has always preferred to stay at court," I answered. "I do not believe she likes to travel much."

"Yes," he mocked, "I understand the court has many attractions for her." I did not like the implication, but he went on. "You have quick and ready answers, Lady Lionors. But I do have a brother or sister, don't I?"

"Where did you ever get such an idea?" I parried his question with one of my own.

"You spent some months many years ago in the Abbey of the Holy Spirit, didn't you? And when you left, a baby remained behind. I'm right, aren't I?"

"Yes, you are. I was exhausted from overwork here at the manor, and there was trouble in the neighborhood. I spent two or three months there. And yes, there was a waif, a baby girl, left at the gate while I was there. The nuns took her in to raise. She is a member of the order now. Does that answer your question?" Was he a bit relieved that it was a girl?

"Not quite. Does the name Eldred mean anything to you?"

At first the name was completely strange to me, and I started to shake my head. Then I remembered. The leader of the ruffians who had stopped us, threatened to hold me for ransom, and killed some of my men. I thought then I had not heard the last of him. He had seen I was pregnant. While racking my brain to come up with a satisfactory answer, I mumbled the name over and over.

"Eldred . . . Eldred . . ."

"Yes, an outlaw, but also an excellent spy. You made a fool of him, and he did not get ransom money for you, but I have made up for that, He is among the loyal band of Mordred's followers in the north."

"Ransom?" I stalled. "Oh, yes, I remember now. But what did he tell you except that my driver managed to get me away?"

"He said your robe parted, and he saw you were swollen with child."

I had my answer, and it had to be the right one, one that would make sense and end the discussion.

"He thought I was pregnant, and it suited my purpose to have him think so. He would have raped me otherwise. Actually I had my hand on a sack full of jewels and gold hidden under my skirt. If he had taken a good look, he would have known the truth, and I would have been robbed as well as assaulted. And you believed him? You are naïve, Mordred."

"Then or now? If I believe you, Lady Lionors? All right, you seem to have all the answers. But I will find my father's weakness yet; I will see him destroyed."

This was a dangerous, a fanatical young man. Merlin had warned me once that Arthur's marriage must be sacrosanct; no blemish must touch it, or Britain would be ruined, never to remain united. Mordred must never know the truth. How he linked Arthur with Elise and me, I might not ever really know, but I must in no way reveal my part in Arthur's life.

"Your father is a great man, Mordred, a great king of Britain. You must not be his enemy."

"He is not a great king, and he thinks of himself as a god; so do the people. They must be shown he is mortal and that he, too, can fall. I might be wrong about having a sister, though you have not convinced me I am. But I shall find some way to destroy him, to overthrow him, and I will be king."

"So you shall, Mordred, in good time. But vengeance has a way of turning on the avenger. Bring him down, and you just might destroy yourself as well."

"I will not listen. You are full of platitudes, trying to save yourself and your lover. But I warn you, I will find the chink in his armor."

Mordred strode to the door. "Now I suppose you

247

want me to leave. I am sure I am no longer welcome here."

Mordred reminded me again of a pouting child, so much that I wanted to spank him. It was obvious he had never known a genuine, healthy love. But he was no pouting youngster. He was a dangerous young man.

"No, it is late. Stay here for the night, and I will see you in the morning. Perhaps if you admit you were wrong about me, you might be willing to see you have had other misconceptions. Good night, try to rest. I will be here for a little while yet if there is anything you need."

He hated me with all his heart, a heart as black as his suit. He was dismayed at my calmly turning aside each of his arguments, astounded that I did not rave at him or order him out of the house. That he could have dealt with. He had no weapon to fight kindness—either from me or from his father.

When I awoke, early though it was, Mordred had already gone. I was sorry, but even more I was desperately worried. I had not slept much, concerned about the danger to Arthur in having Mordred at court. Had he heard about Guinevere and Lancelot? Was the affair still going on? If so, they must be warned if only for Arthur's sake. I had no sympathy to spare for the two lovers. If they chose not to be discreet, they deserved whatever punishment attended their discovery. But it was not fair to Arthur, who had quietly closed his eyes to their affair all these years so they could be happy and at the same time had used utmost discretion in his relationship with me.

Somehow I had to get word to Arthur.

It was impossible for me to go to Camelot for a number of reasons. It would take several days to prepare for such a journey; I was needed at the manor now that the sowing was well under way; the farms had to be tended carefully with the appearance of the first green shoots. More importantly, one does not arrive at court unbidden, especially a noblewoman who has refused all previous invitations to serve as lady in waiting to the queen. As Merlin had once cautioned, through the years I received a number of such invitations—royal commands really—but managed to sidestep the issue of serving Guinevere with acceptable excuses: my father's age, then his months of infirmity, and finally my own responsibilities to the estate.

Fortunately, there were enough women in the kingdom to fill the positions who really enjoyed the pleasures of court life, or who saw the honor as a means of improving their own standing in life or that of their husbands. I was in no doubt that Arthur had received many carefully worded suggestions that a warm bed and willing arms awaited him whenever he tired of Guinevere or desired some variety in the sport of love-making. Many an earl in the past had suddenly found himself a duke, not knowing—or not caring—that the new crown bore the horns of cuckoldry. That Arthur might have created a number of such dukedoms worried me not at all. I was neither the guardian of his morals nor his father confessor. Such minor lapses from conjugal fidelity would be overlooked where a long-time affair would not.

At any rate, I could not just ride into Camelot and ask to see the king. It was certain, nevertheless, that I had to find some way to warn Arthur of Mordred's malicious suspicions and traitorous threat to usurp the throne. If there were only someone I could trust to make the trip, get into the castle unseen or at least unsuspected, and find Arthur alone. It had to be someone Arthur, in turn, would trust and believe. Better yet would be someone he knew.

For all of his life I had taken Will into my confidence, and he had matured enough to accept such a responsibility. That he loved Arthur, there was no question. He was keen and alert, qualities he would need to get past the guards and into Arthur's presence undetected.

By noon of that day I had worked out all the plans Will would have to learn and memorize: the route to Camelot, the way to get through the gate, and the design of the castle, including which stairs and halls to take to get to the king's room. I had to count on Arthur's still retiring each evening to the small study adjoining the bedroom where I once slept.

"You wanted me, my lady?" Will's response to my call was prompt.

"Will, I have an extremely urgent errand for you to undertake. It could be dangerous and will require a maximum of stealth on your part."

"Yes, ma'am. When do you wish me to leave?"

No heeding, no questions about what was involved or where he was going. Just a loyal acceding to my request, with the thought, I am sure, that he would not be asked to undertake a task that he was not prepared for.

"Oh, Will, I am having trouble putting it into words because I am terribly upset about the situation and a little bit frightened about what I am going to ask you to do."

"Would it help if I asked if this mission had something to do with the man who was here last night and left so rudely this morning?"

"Yes, it does. That was Mordred, King Arthur's illegitimate son, a young man who is very bitter about life and seething with hatred for his father. He is also a very dangerous young man who has made serious threats against the king."

"And my errand?" he asked.

"Will, before I tell you that, I need to explain some things so you will understand. I think maybe you already know, or perhaps have guessed, that Sir Ursa is King Arthur."

"I—yes, ma'am, although I can't tell you at what exact moment I learned his identity. I think maybe it began because I admired him so much and thought of him as a king. Gradually, I associated him with King Arthur."

"Perhaps, then, it will be easier for you to understand what I need to tell you."

In a few minutes I briefly explained my relationship to Arthur, his marriage to Guinevere, and her love for Lancelot.

"Under Arthur's own law, Guinevere and Lancelot

250

will be guilty of treason if they are caught in a compromising situation. I am not concerned for them. If this were only their problem, I would say forget it and leave them to their own consciences. However, if they go down, Arthur and the throne go with them. I can not allow all he has worked for to founder on the rocks of illicit passion. You may think me a hypocrite, knowing as you do now about Arthur and me, but we have never allowed our love to interfere with the affairs of state or endanger them in any way. Our circumspection has brought us much loneliness. My own refusal to insist on our fulfilling our vows prepared the way for him to contract a marriage beneficial to the nation."

"Lady Lionors," Will interrupted, "I could never think of you as a hypocrite, but can only admire you for what you have done."

"Thank you, Will. I did not mean to involve you so deeply in my personal feelings. Now, as to your errand. I want you to go to Camelot, find a way to see the king, and warn him that Mordred either suspects or has proof of Guinevere's affair with Lancelot. If he only suspects, he might be preparing a trap for them."

"That should be no problem for me." Will spoke with assurance.

"It is not as simple as it sounds," I cautioned him. "No one must know you have come from me. To bring my name into this would be to ensure Arthur's downfall from a different direction. Whether you ride during the day or at night, I leave to your own discretion. You will need a cover story for anyone you meet on the road. You are not unhandy with a needle, so I suggest you travel as a journeyman tailor. We will find all the supplies you will need—needles, thread, scissors, some cloth, and so on. And pack them carefully in a satchel. If stopped close to Camelot, you can say you hope to see the king and offer your services."

"I think I can manage that," Will laughed, "even if someone asks me to do some mending. But I hope I won't be called on to tailor a suit of clothes."

"You can always say you are in a hurry to get to

court. I had thought first of having you try to get past the guards unnoticed, but that would be risky. Your cover is ideal, as long as you do not meet Mordred. If you do, he will recognize you, and the game is up. Unless you can think of a plausible reason for being there."

"I will spend my time on the road thinking of one," Will said.

"Good. Let us not worry about that, then. With your cover, you can merely request an audience with the king. As soon as Arthur sees you, he will know something is wrong and find a way to see you alone. Tell him about Mordred's visit and what I suspect."

"I will take care of it, I assure you. You know you can trust me."

"I know I can, Will. Now, how soon can you leave?"

"As soon as I gather all the supplies from the sewing room. Other than that, I will travel light."

"You will need a good, steady mount, but not too fine a one for your assumed status. Meet me at the stables in two hours, and I will give you a purse of money. There is an inn about a day's ride from Camelot, and it will not be unnatural for you to stop there. Between here and there, you will have to rough it, so get food from the kitchen as well."

It was about two in the afternoon when I watched Will ride through the gate. I was confident he could handle the assignment with sureness and dispatch. As long as he did not run into Mordred at the castle. But even then, Will had a quick, inventive mind, and he was sure to come up with something that would explain his presence.

I went to bed that evening with a much lighter heart than the night before. Arthur would be alerted, and he in turn would warn Guinevere. Surely she would see the necessity for caution—or even for the need to break off the affair—in order to save the throne.

Soon after noon the following day, a servant came running in breathlessly. A lone rider had galloped across the meadow, paused only long enough to loose an arrow over the main gate, and then turned and ridden away. He handed me the arrow. Around it was affixed a rough piece of linen. I recognized it as a fragment torn from the sack in which Will had carried some of his supplies. Unwinding it, I saw a few lines written in some sort of crude ink. They were from Will.

"Lady Lionors, I have been captured by a man named Eldred. He said you would know him. He demands a purse of 50 gold pieces, or I will be killed. A messenger will come in twenty-four hours for it."

How well did I know the name Eldred! Was I never to be free from him? I would give almost everything I owned to save Will, but there was much to consider. Fifty pieces of gold were a great deal to give as ransom for a mere steward. This abduction was not just Eldred's idea; he would never have demanded that much for an itinerant tailor. Also, somehow he knew Will belonged to me, and he would not have learned that from Will himself. Not even under torture. No, Mordred was behind this. He might even be with Eldred. One of two reasons lay behind the plot. Either Mordred knew I would try to get word to Arthur and was warning me not to attempt it again, or—and this was a great possibility—he suspected Will was the child I had borne to Arthur.

He had listened with a sneer to my story of a baby girl found at the abbey, and Will was near enough of an age, only a few months' difference, to look as though he had been born at the right time. That was it. Mordred felt threatened by another male child. Come to think of it, he might be under the impression my child was born first. He might not know the exact year I went to the abbey. Eldred's memory could well have been fuzzy on that detail. That would make another son even more of a threat.

If I sent fifty gold pieces to ransom Will, I was practically admitting what Mordred suspected. But I could not let Will be the scapegoat for Mordred's treachery. Not only did I love him as dearly as a son, but he had proved his devotion to me over and over again. I could not let him die even to allay Mordred's suspicions.

I went to the vault in the library where we kept our small treasury. Fifty gold pieces constituted more than half of that treasury, for most of the economy of the estate was based on barter or trade. I found a small leathern purse and counted out the coins carefully, knowing as I added each one that I had no guarantee when I handed over the money that I would ever see Will again. If Eldred were completely without honor, as I suspected him to be, he would take the money and still murder Will. Even now, my foster son might be dead.

There was no sleep for me that night. To keep from pacing the floor, I turned to my ever-present manuscripts, trying—in concentrating on translating Caesar's Latin into English—to make the hours pass quickly. By ten the next morning, I was beginning to count off the minutes before the twenty-four hours would be up. When that moment arrived, I walked to the gate.

With a mixture of relief and horror I gazed on the figure of Will, not fifty yards in front of me. Relief because he was still alive. Horror because of the position he was in. Bound hand and foot with leathern thongs, a gag across his mouth, he sat on his horse. There was a noose around his neck, the other end of the rope thrown over a tree limb and pulled so taut he was already choking for breath. An archer stood to one side, bow ready, an arrow aimed at Will's chest. If I had not had the ransom ready, they would have executed him before my eyes.

There was no sign of Mordred. He would never let me know the part he played in this near tragedy. But Eldred was there, as filthy and as ugly as I remembered him. The huge lips, bulging between his whiskers, were set in a smirk. With a single motion and a remark that started his men laughing, he sent a rider up to the gate. Without a word I handed him the purse. I know I did not take a breath until after Eldred counted out the money slowly, coin by coin, and then commanded his men to set Will free. They cut the rope holding him to the tree and slapped the rump of the horse to start him running toward the gate. Caring nothing about appearances, I ran, too, and led the horse into the courtyard. There, in front of all of them, I helped Will dismount, cut his bonds, removed the gag, and took him into my arms. I had no doubt Eldred would report all this to Mordred, and the latter would think his suspicions confirmed, but I did not care.

When Will had rested, he told me what had happened. He had decided to ride as far as he could the first night. He had tried to remain alert, but in the darkness he did not see the rope stretched across the road, and when his horse tripped over it, two men stationed in the trees above dropped a net over his head. They must have had lookouts stationed along the road to send word back that Will was approaching. There might even have been a spy within half a mile of the manor waiting to see if someone would be leaving and traveling in the direction of Camelot. Mordred must have been certain that I would send a message to King Arthur, and he intended to intercept it.

Yes, Will said, Mordred was there, but he made no mention that Will might be my son. However, there was quite a discussion about the ransom, and although Will could not catch all the conversation, he did gather that Eldred had been startled, then pleased, when Mordred said something to him. They had laughed a lot and slapped each other on the back as though they had caught an unexpected prize of some kind.

Will was closer to me than ever after that; and aware of what I had given to save his life, he vowed to serve me the rest of his days. I asked only that he never refer to the incident again.

When more than three months had gone by with no rumors of trouble at Camelot, I surmised that either Mordred had had second thoughts about destroying his father or that Guinevere and Lancelot were avoiding, by word or action, any intimacy that could be misinter-preted.

Early in September I received a note from Guinevere requesting I attend her as lady in waiting.

⊠ Chapter Twelve ⊠

The invitation was penned in Guinevere's own hand, an informal request for me to attend her at Camelot. Most such invitations were commands written in ornate script and memorized by the messengers who pretended to read them to the recipients so that those noble-women who were not literate did not have to reveal their ignorance. My first reaction would normally have been to send regrets and request permission to remain at the manor. However, there was a short note added in Arthur's writing: "Please come this time. We need you."

The *we* disturbed me. Was Arthur using the royal plural of the throne, or was he referring to Guinevere and himself?

Preparations for the journey went quickly, and I dispatched a courier to apprise Arthur of my coming. Having always enjoyed riding through the countryside, I planned the trip in easy stages, stopping the first night at the abbey. When we were within three miles of the castle, I exchanged the saddle for the palanquin. I could easily have ridden, for in spite of the time we had been on the road, I was not the least bit tired. Nevertheless, I felt my position demanded I arrive in state, even though being this close to Arthur I longed to give free rein to the horse and let him run the last short distance.

Much to my surprise, Guinevere herself was in the hall to receive me. Gracious and lovely, she exuded a natural warmth as I bowed to her.

"Welcome to Camelot, Lady Lionors. I will have someone show you to your room. I think you will recognize it, and I hope you will be comfortable amid the familiar surroundings. I will send word and have you escorted down for supper."

"Thank you, Your Majesty. I am sure I will be comfortable here."

Memories flooded over me as I stood in the room where I had spent some of the happiest hours of my life. Here was the chair on which Arthur had flung his robe. Near it was the door to his small room. The low fire on the hearth looked like the same one before which we sat making plans for our future.

And the bed! How could I sleep in the same bed where Arthur and I had loved, our happiness not yet marred by events that would send us down separate paths? I dropped across it, wondering in my despair how I would have a single peaceful night while I remained in the castle. At the same time, I was overcome with exhaustion. If I rested, perhaps I could recover enough to present a calm face at supper. My thoughts were interrupted by the entrance of the maid assigned to care for me.

"How long before we dine?" I asked.

"Better than two hours, my lady. Would you like me to unpack your things?"

"Thank you, no," I answered. "I am very tired and would like to sleep. Please wake me about half an hour before supper, and I would be grateful to have you help me dress."

I lay down, and though a hundred unbidden thoughts whirled through my mind, I fell asleep within minutes. When the maid awakened me, I was refreshed and more at ease. Along with hot water for bathing, she brought a glass of wine. Strong and sweet, it gave me the courage I needed to see Arthur.

Downstairs, the great hall was filled with people: clusters of men and women standing together, servants scurrying to place food on the long tables. There was a general hum of conversation, sparked now and then by genial shouts from one man to another, and orders being issued to the servers. Then I saw Arthur break away from one of the groups.

"Your Majesty," I said, going down on one knee.

"Welcome to Camelot, my lady. We are very happy to see you," and there was no denying the look of joy and relief on his face.

My assignments as lady in waiting were not difficult ones, many of them the sort of tasks I performed at home. I accompanied the queen when she went riding, and as I still enjoyed the sport of falconry, I took pleasure in my fine horse and well-trained bird. Other days several of us sat with her while we sewed and gossiped. Occasionally, while the others embroidered, I read aloud to relieve the sometimes tedious hours. I had never met anyone who did not enjoy a good story, and the queen was no exception.

When I took my turn in her bedchamber, she liked to have me brush her long hair. As the weeks passed, we drew closer together, and some of our confidences became quite intimate. I gradually became fond of the woman I thought I would hate.

"Are you happy here at Camelot, Lionors?"

"It is an honor to be serving you," I said.

"That is not a real answer. I asked if you were happy."

"Yes, as much as anyone can be who is not in his own home."

"You have never been married, have you?" The question had been asked me many times in mocking, curious, or scornful tones, but never before with simple, genuine interest.

I explained once again that I had been able to inherit my father's estate and had had no need to take a husband.

"But surely," she said, "some time there was someone you loved enough to marry."

"Yes, there was. But he was already married."

Guinevere released a long sigh. Our positions, though in a way reversed, were not very much different.

"Lionors, do you know why Arthur urged that I

259

send for you even though you have always refused my previous requests?"

"I'm not sure," I answered.

Guinevere turned in her chair and motioned to another one.

"Please sit down. We know too much about each other to stand on formality."

I sat where she indicated, not able to conceal my surprise at her statement.

"Don't be alarmed." She smiled. "Arthur has told me all about you." She spoke with no trace of bitterness or hatred in her voice. "In the last few months, Arthur and I have confided more in each other than in all the years we have been married. I am aware of the danger inherent in anyone's using my—my love for Lancelot to destroy Arthur. I also know of your love for each other, and how circumspect you have both been during these years. It has been a trying time for all of us. Lance and I have been forced by recent circumstances to keep apart. Arthur thought it would comfort me to have you here. I know this sounds selfish, but I think he knew, too, that this was the only way he could see you. That is why I asked if you were happy. We would not want you to be miserable just to ease our lives. I know you have a daughter. How is Elise?"

"She is fine. Has Arthur told you much about her?"

"Yes, he is very proud of her. I could not give him a child, you know, so she means a great deal to him. We will probably never be able to speak of all this again, but I did want to thank you for coming."

I saw Lancelot a few times, and he always recognized me with a brief nod. Then he left the castle, going, it was said, on some business for the king that would take him to London and the coast.

Although I saw Arthur at meals, when we were out riding, and at various state functions, our conversations stayed within the bounds of formality and on impersonal subjects. I finally saw him alone when he asked me to walk with him in the gardens.

"You look very well, Lionors."

"Thank you, Arthur." I wished I could say the same to him, but his face was more haggard than I had ever seen it, and his shoulders were stooped with worry.

"Are you happy here at Camelot?" he asked.

"Strange, Guinevere asked me the same thing."

"And your answer?"

"As happy as I could be away from home," I said. "It hasn't been easy seeing you and not being able to touch you or talk with you. I have felt as though I were playing a part, and I am not a very good actress."

"I have not dared try to see you alone," he said. "You realize that. But if you draw your draperies tonight, I think we can be together for a few hours, just as we were when you first came here. Will you listen for my knock at the connecting door?"

When I retired after supper, I drew the heavy draperies as tightly as possible. There was no possibility of anyone's seeing or hearing anything from the courtyard nor of scaling the wall and getting a foothold outside the window. The walls between the rooms were thick, but even so, I was sure Arthur had determined there would be no one in the one next to mine.

For an hour after he came in, we almost forgot that we were in the castle, not in my room at the manor, and that our lives had not become entangled in a maze with no exit. Lying in Arthur's arms, our love renewed, I felt a much-needed sense of belonging enter and fill the empty core of loneliness as his body entered mine. Our desires sated, our personal thoughts revealed, the talk turned to more serious subjects.

"Did Guinevere tell you why we wanted you here?" he asked.

"She said you told her about us and thought my being here would comfort her. That I would be one person who would understand and sympathize with her situation and to whom she could talk freely."

"There is much more to it than that," he said seriously. "I would not have asked you here for such a selfish reason."

"Yes, she said the same thing, even used the word *selfish*."

261

"I wanted us to be together, too; nearly three years is far too long to be separated. If you have missed me as much as I have missed you, then you know why I really asked you to come. It was impossible for me to get away during the time of the quests, and then Mordred's arrival at court really put the quietus on my ever getting away. Maybe I was wrong to ask you to come since, as you say, it is so hard to be in the same place and yet not really be together."

"No, Arthur, I am glad I came. I would rather be here seeing you when I can than alone in the manor knowing it is no longer possible for you to be there."

"I will come here as often as I dare, and we will be together. I must spend some nights in Gwen's rooms to protect us all from suspicion, and I would like you to stay with her occasionally, especially when I am away from the castle. I am afraid of a plot that would force her and Lance into a compromising situation. We are treading among hot coals, and we have to prevent a full-blown conflagration."

I interrupted long enough to tell him about Mordred's visit and my aborted attempt to send a message. His major concern was for Will's safety until I assured him the younger man had not been harmed.

"It is evident," he said, "Mordred will stop at nothing to dethrone me. I will give you the fifty gold pieces. It is the least I can do to repay the enormous debt I owe you."

"No, Arthur. I don't need it, and Will knows why I did it."

"If I had known about Mordred's suspicions of us and his idea about Will, I would never have asked you to come here. One thing is now certain. I do not think that we can ever be alone again. If Mordred fails in a plot involving Gwen, he can shift his attention to us. I love you, and I did not invite you here to endanger your life. If ever you need to see me alone, or if you have word to send me, trust the page who brings your breakfast, but no one else. I have no way of knowing who is in the pay of Mordred to spy on me—or now

262

on you. One more favor. Keep your eyes and ears open."

Knowing this might be the one and only time we dared spend together, Arthur remained far longer than two or three hours. Curled up in his arms, his body warm against mine, I fell asleep content in the knowledge he still loved and needed me.

Without any other warning, a courier brought word that an army of Picts was marching on Camelot from the northeast; the advance scouting party was less than two days' march from the castle. If Arthur moved immediately with a full army, he could wipe them out and send a single survivor to report the rout to the main body.

As Arthur requested, I was sharing the queen's bedroom to thwart all suspicion that she might be seeing Lancelot secretly, even though he was supposed to be in London. On the first night after the army rode out, she urged me to return to my room, knowing I was more comfortable there.

"I know why Arthur asked you to remain here," she said, "but with all the men gone, there cannot possibly be any danger to me. My maid sleeps outside my door, and a guard has been posted there."

I acquiesced, but not without worry. If Lancelot were many miles away, she was safe. But if he had returned unobserved, and they tried to meet secretly, they could be in extreme danger. As Arthur said, Mordred had enough spies in the castle to do his dirty work for him and leave him free of any complicity in the plot.

I slept uneasily the first few hours, listening to every sound of movement within the castle. The guards walked their posts along the turrets, advancing and challenging as they rotated shifts. Sometime after midnight a single horseman rode up, said something I could not hear to the guard at the portcullis, and then rode away.

Suddenly the stillness was shattered, first by heavy footsteps hurrying up the stone staircase and through the halls, then by a clash of steel against steel, screams, and the sound of bodies falling to the floor. To add to the din, from outside came the irregular rhythm of horses pounding toward the castle.

The calm of predawn had turned into a nightmare. From bits and pieces of information, I was able to reconstruct the events of that fatal night. First, Lancelot had sent word to Guinevere that he was returning to the castle. I tried to imagine his unalloyed joy when he learned the castle would be empty of the knights and that he could meet safely with Guinevere one more time.

Second, Mordred and Agravaine had intercepted the message, but sent it on when they realized they could turn it to their advantage. Mordred then dispatched a messenger to one of the groups of men he had ordered bivouacked throughout the woods within a ten-mile perimeter of Camelot, requesting that word be sent about an approaching army. Third, Agravaine and Mordred, with a small detachment, left the main army and doubled back to the castle, ready to spring the trap. It was their footsteps I heard in the hall and they who confronted Guinevere and Lancelot in her room. In the scuffle Agravaine was killed by Lancelot. Fourth, on discovering that the news about an advancing army was a hoax to draw him away from the castle, Arthur turned right around and galloped back. Mordred had perhaps imagined Arthur would rest for the night, giving Agravaine and himself plenty of time to carry out their machinations. As it happened, Arthur's appearance on the scene could not have been better planned if Mordred had choreographed it himself.

In the confusion, Lancelot escaped, but Guinevere was captured. Not even his enemies denied Lancelot's courage, so most felt he thought he could be of more help to her if he escaped than if he remained by her side.

As an adulteress, she was guilty of treason. Having been caught *in flagrante delicto,* she could not enter a plea of innocent when the combined royal and ecclesiastical courts sat to hear her case. Punishment for treason was death by fire, and the date for her execution was announced: at dawn three weeks after the day she had been discovered with her lover. In absentia, Lancelot was also found guilty. As long as he remained in exile on foreign soil, the king would not pursue him. But the minute he set foot on British soil, he was to be bound and delivered to the court for immediate execution.

During those three weeks I never once set eyes on Arthur. He remained closeted in his private suite the entire time. I ate and slept mechanically, trying to fill the empty hours by completing a piece of tapestry. Guinevere had been incarcerated in a small, lower-level room, sparsely furnished with some of her own possessions, rather than in one of the dungeons ordinarily used for felons. I longed to ask Arthur if I could go to her now when she really needed comforting. But I was afraid my request would be misinterpreted if heard by the wrong people.

There was no sleep for anyone the night before the execution, the exact time that Guinevere was to be led to the stake having never been announced. And if the horror of the deed to be performed was not enough to keep one awake, the building of the scaffold was not to be ignored. All night the carpenters worked, pounding together the uprights of the platform, laying the floorboards, fitting the steps into place. Last came the raising of the stake to which Guinevere would be bound. It would not stay up. First the hole bored to take the end hewed to a point was too big. The carpenters had to take up part of the flooring, then replace it. The stake still would not remain upright. The men began murmuring prayers and muttering oaths, declaring that their actions were cursed. The execution should not take place. But finally, after bracing it on all four sides, the stake stayed secure.

Since I was unable to sleep, anyway, I had put on my robe and walked to the arched windows. Pulling back the draperies, I watched the harried action taking place in the courtyard. Was Arthur also sleepless, perhaps pacing the floor in his far-off suite of rooms? Many other curtains were open around the interior wall

265

of the castle. There were other eyes focused on the as yet empty scaffold.

Then I saw a candle flicker in the room around the corner from me, the room that faced the court at a right angle to mine. It was Arthur's study, and no one else ever used it. A second candle was lighted. So that was where he was enduring his vigil through the night. By keeping in the shadows, but shifting my position, I could barely see him sitting there, his head in one hand, his body slumped back against the cushions. Then Gawain came into view, gripping Arthur's shoulders with his two hands. When he said something to the king, Arthur looked at him, nodded, and sat up, placing his arms along the arms of the chair.

I longed to trade places with Gawain, to be the one to give Arthur courage throughout the long ordeal ahead. No word had come from any direction about Lancelot. If he were in the vicinity, he remained well concealed. No attempt had been made to rescue the queen, although Arthur had kept only a minimum guard over her. The penultimate hour had arrived; and once the courtyard was filled with guards and knights, it would be too late—and too dangerous—for Lancelot to attempt it with the few men who fled with him.

Was Arthur suffering the same pangs of conscience as I?

Guinevere was guilty of loving Lancelot, but not of treason. She was no more guilty of that than Arthur and I, who had also loved in secret and in despair. On the very nights she was adjudged to have been lying in the arms of her lover, Arthur and I were also sharing a single bed. There was one vital difference. She had been caught and was being sacrificed for the illicit love of four people who, being forced to put duty before personal desire, had been too weak or too human to keep their pledges inviolate.

Arthur and I had sinned first by rashly consummating our love before we were actually married. He had broken his betrothal pledge to me by marrying Guinevere, and then both of us had willingly sundered his more serious vows to her. Lancelot, within months of

266

swearing allegiance to Arthur and vowing to follow all the rules of chivalry, had recanted his oath by action if not by words. And finally Guinevere had broken her marriage vows to Arthur. Even if I had the order somewhat mixed up, the situation was still the same. Guinevere was to die; Arthur and I would watch her burn, and Lancelot was in exile.

The courtyard began to fill. More guards and knights took their places. The atmosphere of unease was accentuated as the men shuffled from one spot to another, unsure where to stand, and no one spoke above a whisper. Then a single guard moved to the ground-level door opposite me, spoke to the man on duty, and descended the short flight of stairs.

With unfaltering steps, Guinevere walked up from the lower room. She was guarded, but not aided, by four men in full armor. Dressed in a long full shift that fell from a string-gathered neckline, she held her arms in front of her, fingers slightly entwined, her hands almost concealed by the long points of her full sleeves. She wore no jewelry save an unadorned silver cross. Her hair, still blonde and full, fell loosely around her shoulders, bound close to her head with a simple fillet of pearls. In her last act as a queen she would die wearing a crown.

As poised as if she were mounting the dais supporting her throne, she lifted her skirts slightly to climb the three steps of the scaffold centered by the tall, rough-hewn stake. I could not see whether she closed her eyes as she saw the post. Before being bound, she shifted her position slightly and raised her head so that her eyes looked in a direct line to the room where Arthur sat. Her confessor mounted the platform immediately afterward, and there was complete and total silence throughout the courtyard while he bent his head close to her lips, heard her final confession, and gave her absolution. As the executioners began to bind her to the stake, she apparently made one last request that one of the guards denied her by shaking his head and drawing her arms behind her around the post. For the first time, I saw tears in her eyes as she looked at the priest. He reached over, carefully lifting the silver chain, and put the cross between her lips. I surmised that she had requested to be allowed to place her arms over her breast and hold the cross in her hands. Perhaps the priest knew, too, what agony she would endure before the flames burned enough to render her unconscious, and having the cross to bite on would help her keep from crying out.

Her hands were tied behind her first. Then a rope was drawn around her ankles forcing her to stand unnaturally stiff and straight, but instead of degrading her, the position made her appear more regal and prouder than ever. The last rope was crisscrossed around the upper portion of her body. When pulled tight, the fetters accentuated her still firm breasts and slim waist. Even in her despair, her eyes wet with tears, she could never have looked more beautiful.

If I had once hated her, even at times praying for her death so that perhaps I could take her place, I now felt nothing but pity. I did not covet the crown she wore today. In one way we were alike: both of us had loved men we could not marry, and neither of us would ever see these men again. For I felt certain that the death of Guinevere and the exile of Lancelot would weaken Arthur's position—as well as his will to continue ruling—to such an extent that he would probably abdicate in favor of Mordred or retire into seclusion. In either event, I did not doubt that I had lost him forever.

Beneath and next to the platform were placed large logs that would burn with a slow steady flame until all of the queen's body had been consumed. She was not to have the final honor of being cut down immediately upon death and laid to rest with a royal funeral. Around these logs were stacked dry faggots that would catch fire almost immediately after the piles of brush interlaced between them had been lit by torches. To ensure there would not need to be a second or third lighting, the faggots had been smeared with pitch, and the flames from them would blaze up instantly with an intense heat. I remembered some executions where the condemned had smeared oil on their bodies to make sure the flames would ignite them as soon as possible and hasten death. There was no evidence of this on Guinevere, but her frail shift would catch quickly, and her agony would not be prolonged much past the first second of igniting.

Before Guinevere walked in, the courtyard had been crowded with knights in full battle dress, well-armed guards, and a few women of the court. Now the square seemed almost deserted as the people pressed back against the walls in an attempt to get as far away as possible from the stake and the figure that stood there alone. Only one executioner, who was watching Arthur for the command to signal the lighting of the fire, the four guards at the base of the scaffold, and the priest, who continued to pray aloud, were near her.

It was not yet sunrise, too early, even, for the first faint glow along the horizon. The only light in the courtyard came from flaming flambeaux in wrought-iron sconces set at intervals along the walls. The black sky, the red flames, the smoky haze, all conspired to create the illusion that the entire assemblage had been damned and transported to hell. I doubted if there were one among us who would not feel the pain of the flames as they reached her hem, her feet, her hands, and then her face. Never once during all the time Guinevere stood there had she taken her eyes from Arthur's room. Did he have the courage to look at her as she looked at him? Would he grant a last-minute reprieve? After watching her undergo this much of the ordeal, I was sure one vast sigh of relief would go up from the crowd if he did. No one would condemn him for being weak if he withheld the command to burn and replaced it with orders for exile or imprisonment. She was not only their queen; she was a beautiful woman.

Even when the men descended the scaffold and others stood ready with lighted pine knots, Arthur did not give the command. If the waiting was interminable for us, it must have been torture for Guinevere. What was Arthur waiting for? I took another sip from the glass of wine in my hand. One arm was already numb from bracing it against a pillar to keep from fainting when I saw the brush fired.

There must be a storm coming, I thought, as I heard the first faint rumbles of thunder in the distance. If there were rain in those clouds, and it moved rapidly across the sky with the rise of the predawn wind, it might reach Camelot in time to put out the fire before Guinevere died. If she were saved by an act of nature, Arthur might see in it the hand of God and grant her a pardon. I concentrated on listening to the storm, which was approaching from the east; the thunder grew louder, but still no sign of rain. Even a few drops might deter the king from raising his hand to the executioner.

Hardly able to comprehend what I was hearing, I began to distinguish sounds like the thudding of large hail stones on the soft earth. My mind shifted momentarily from the scene in front of me to the farms back home. Unless the storm abated as it moved southwest, the damage to the crops just beginning to sprout and to the fruit trees going from full flower into first fruiting would be extensive. Nearing the castle, the storm seemed to hover over the highway, and the hail grated on the stones of the old Roman road like a barrage of hoof beats.

They were hoof beats! A cavalcade of horses was galloping toward Camelot like an army spearheading an attack. I looked at Guinevere's face, alert with expectation. Was Lancelot leading the horsemen in an attempt to besiege the castle and rescue her? Had Arthur, too, been listening for the sounds heralding the arrival of the man who had always championed the queen's cause?

By this time everyone in the courtyard had heard the horses, but before the men could get the women safely inside behind the iron-studded doors, gather up their arms, and get in position to defend the castle, the invaders had crossed the outer moat. One wondered if the drawbridge had been left down through negligence or intention. Not until the riders entered the outer keep were Arthur's knights and guards ready to fight. In the close quarters of the courtyard many of the men on foot were soon knocked down by even a glancing blow and trampled beneath the horses. Other mounts fell, speared through flanks or neck, adding to the sounds of carnage, their pitiful cries mingling with the moans of the wounded men.

A single flare, dropped by an executioner as he was stabbed, set fire to the brush around the stake. With the arrival of her rescuers, Guinevere had been trying to loose her bonds. Now as the flames began to scorch the scaffold, threatening to carry out the execution even without Arthur's command, the priest hastened up the steps to cut the straps holding her to the stake. At the same time, two of the guards tried to beat out the fire, pulling brush away from the platform and separating the faggots already ignited. Dense, acrid smoke from pitch-soaked wood swirled around the courtyard, beclouding the eyes of the fighters and choking their lungs.

Almost at the same instant that everyone became aware of the fire, a single rider disengaged himself from the melee and turned his horse toward the platform. Although wearing an uncrested helmet and carrying a plain shield, there was no question that it was Lancelot. A single knight stood between him and his approach to the stake via an artificial aisle created by an arch to one side and a line of three dead horses on the other. It was something of a circuitous route, but a more direct approach would involve him with a number of fighters and hinder a speedy rescue.

The footed knight stepped in front of Lancelot's horse, his sword held in front of him as if to parry rather than wield a blow. This struck me as odd. It was as though he meant merely to halt Lancelot rather than harm him.

With the first pass of his sword, Lancelot knocked off the helmet of his adversary. He brought his sword up again, but as he struck a second time, he parried his own thrust, the blade glancing off the edge of his shield. He recognized the knight on foot the same moment I did. It was Gareth, Lancelot's closest friend.

271

They looked steadily at each other for a brief second. Then a strange thing happened. As Lancelot turned his horse to go around Gareth, the latter fell to the ground, blood gushing from his head. Lancelot was unaware of what had happened, intent only on reaching Guinevere. As soon as he had her on his horse, and they rode out through the gate, his men followed. The fighting was over.

Among the first reaching the court to tend the wounded and bear off the dead was Gawain, running down from the second-floor room where he had been keeping vigil with Arthur. He dashed across the pavement to Gareth. With gentle fingers he probed the wound and then felt the pulse. As effortlessly as one would lift a child, he picked Gareth up in his strong arms and carried the body of his youngest, and last remaining, brother into the castle. Tears streamed down the scarred face of the old knight.

The murmurs passing from one survivor to another swelled to a murderous roar: Lancelot had killed Gareth, even after the younger man had removed his helmet, revealing himself to his friend. The knights were calling for Arthur to take up arms and lead them in battle against the man who had willfully killed a defenseless comrade. Within minutes the story making the rounds was that Gareth had approached Lancelot wearing neither helmet nor sword, hoping only to urge him to desist in his effort to rescue Guinevere.

As I thought over what had happened, trying to recall every movement of the two men from the time Lancelot made his move toward the stake until Gareth fell, I made an important discovery. I looked over at the room where Arthur sat partially hidden behind the draperies that could be drawn across the pillared arch. In turn, the same draperies obscured his view of that end of the court, almost right beneath us, where Lancelot and Gareth had met. The same was true for Gawain who was with him. In the melee around the scaffold, those in the courtyard could see little but what was going on right around them, and they were concentrating on their own individual fights. If some witnessed the confrontation between Lancelot and Gareth, from their viewpoint over the shoulders of the men or haunches of the horses, they saw only that Lancelot had raised his sword twice against his friend.

I was the only spectator who observed the clash from a vantage point allowing me to see what really happened. As Lancelot averted his head from the gaze of Gareth, a man dressed in black stepped from the protection of the arch and in one swift movement stabbed Gareth in the temple and re-entered the castle. The next time I saw Mordred, he was crying over the remains of his half brother and urging as adamantly as Gawain that the death must be avenged. I tried to reconstruct what probably had happened. Mordred's love for his half brother, real or feigned, counted as nothing in his monomaniacal desire to destroy Arthur. What better way than to set the king against Lancelot. He might even have had this end in mind when he first plotted with Agravaine to surprise Lancelot and Guinevere in her room. I surmised that Gareth had revealed to Mordred his intention to face Lancelot with the request to leave. It must have been a spur-of-the-moment decision as no one knew that Lancelot was coming. Had they suspected Guinevere's lover might try to rescue her, as I am sure Arthur did, Gareth could have mentioned his plan, giving Mordred the idea of staying near the young knight to await just the chance that fate finally offered him.

I had to get to Arthur.

The urgency of the situation demanded I see him in person, not send a message. Still wearing my nightdress and robe, I went to the clothes press and took out the first dress my hand touched. I hastily slipped on undergarments and was pulling the dress over my head when someone knocked at the door.

"One minute," I called.

When I unbolted the latch, the maid assigned to me entered with a breakfast tray. She was flanked by two burly guards.

"Your breakfast, my lady."

"Thank you. Set it on the table. I will eat when I return from an errand."

"No, my lady," one of the guards spoke up. "You are to remain here until you've eaten and the maid packs your trunks. Then you are to leave the castle. These are the king's orders."

"But I must see the king!" I insisted.

"Sorry, my lady. I have my orders."

The stern look on his face belied any hope I might have of persuading him to let me delay my leave long enough to find Arthur. I found it hard to believe he would send me away so hurriedly without even a personal word even in the face of the tragedy that had just occurred.

"Why the haste?" I asked, trying to decipher the problem of logistics that puzzled me and alerted my intuition.

"The king wishes to clear the castle of guests and begin preparations immediately for setting out after the traitors."

Less than fifteen minutes had passed since Gareth had fallen, yet in that time Arthur had learned of Gareth's death, been told of his approach to Lancelot, and informed that the latter's sword had dealt the fatal blow. It was highly unlikely that there was also time for him to listen to Gawain, decide to ride against Lancelot, and issue the orders repeated by the guard.

The maid had removed all my clothes from the presses and was preparing to pack them in the leathern trunks placed against the wall. Everything was moving too quickly for me to gather my wits and work my way out of this dilemma.

Approaching the guard, I told him, "I must get word to my retainers that I am leaving. I will have them bring my horse around."

"They have already been alerted, and your litter is waiting at the postern gate, guarded by four of the king's men."

It was impossible! It would take time, in all the confusion, to reach my retainers, order the litter, and have them already awaiting me. This was more of Mordred's

274

doing. He must have looked up, seen me at the window, and realized with alarm that I had witnessed his part in the tragedy enacted below me.

My suspicions were confirmed when we reached the litter. It was not my palanquin, nor did I know the men who sat the horses between which it was slung and those riding the four-corner guard positions.

"These are not my retainers," I said.

"Perhaps yours were killed during the fighting."

"Carrying no arms, they were not even in the courtyard. I was told they had been informed of my departure. I refuse to leave until accompanied by my own guards."

The man who brought me down, obviously in a position of command, signaled to a guard who hurried away.

"They will be here shortly," he said. "His Majesty desired you to have extra protection, but I was sure your men had been notified."

Was he being honest with me or just thinking quickly? Perhaps he recognized I could be stubborn and might raise a hue and cry that would attract Arthur's attention, an eventuality that must be avoided at all costs. Outmanned six to four, my retainers would offer no threat, and if acceding to my request would get me speedily out of the way, there could be no harm in humoring me.

When my men arrived, obviously startled at being ordered to leave on immediate notice, we moved off. While the maid was packing my clothes, she overlooked a casket of jewels secured within a small commode beside the bed. I neglected to remind her, thinking it might be just the excuse I needed later to send someone of my choosing back to the castle with a message for Arthur.

About two miles from Camelot, I called to the lead guard and requested that my casket of jewels be removed from the wagon carrying my belongings and brought to me. I am sure he thought we were far enough away to prevent my causing any trouble. In a few minutes he came forward to say there was no such box among my things.

"Have you looked carefully?" I insisted. "It must be there."

"Yes, ma'am, we searched every chest. It's not in the wagon."

"Well, I must have it. May I send one of my retainers back for it?"

"If you wish. But I can't spare any of my men to guard him, nor can we wait here for him. He will have to travel all the way unescorted."

I should have been alerted, when he agreed so quickly, to the possibility of his having a trick of his own up his sleeve. But he allowed me to call one of the men over. I explained aloud what room to go to and where to find the jewels. As I was ostensibly diagramming the location, using my fingers on my lap robe, I whispered a brief message.

"Find the king. Say, 'It was Mordred, not Lancelot.' Say no more, just that."

"Yes, my lady. I'll get the jewels, and I should be able to catch up with you before you've gone many more miles."

I turned in the litter to watch him ride back to Camelot, every nerve in me urging him forward at the fastest speed possible. I tried to figure how much time had elapsed since we left the castle. It did not seem probable that Arthur could have overseen the care of the dead and wounded, rounded up his troops, and prepared them for an extended battle in that period. There was a good chance my message would reach him unless he and Gawain had chosen to ride out immediately in pursuit, leaving the larger contingent to follow as soon as possible.

Less than a hundred yards from me, my rider fell forward off his horse, an arrow in his throat.

I collapsed in the litter. In my eagerness to get word to Arthur—in my stupidity to underestimate my opponent—I had sent one of my most trusted servants to his death. That I had lost all my jewels, save for my mother's gold filigree necklace, which I always wore, concerned me not at all. Mordred must have warned them I might try to send a message back to the castle. A simple denial of my request to get my jewels would not end my attempts, but sudden death was a strong persuader. Only one thing was wrong. None of the guards had left our cortege or drawn a bow. Someone was following us, not on the road but in the woods through which it wound. The clatter of our own horses had covered the sound his made. Mordred was taking no chances that the guards assigned to me would ease up on their vigilance. Or the man who agreed to let me send one of mine back had alerted the hidden rider. I never saw the assassin, but I recognized the gloating laughter ringing through the trees when I fell back onto the pillows as that of my old adversary—Eldred. Once again he had avenged himself for his humiliating defeat at my hands many years earlier.

Perhaps I should have been concerned for my own safety, but I no longer cared. However, there were no more incidents as we progressed steadily toward the manor. From time to time we paused long enough to allow men and horses to rest. Except for excusing myself to attend to personal needs, I remained in the litter, which could be removed from the horses to allow them to graze freely. Fortunately, my captors had the grace to permit me to retire free from their watching eyes.

Will, hearing the approach of horses, was at the gate to meet me. It was his turn, this time, to help me off my mount, which I had finally been allowed to ride. Gathering me in his arms, he supported me into the manor.

⌘ *Chapter Thirteen* ⌘

Britain was paralyzed with crisis.

The lines had been drawn: knight against knight, duke against duke. However, there were no clear boundaries of demarcation between the opposing forces, nothing to indicate who was ally and who, foe. Overnight old friends became enemies as each declared allegiance to either Arthur the king or Lancelot the outlaw.

There were many, once standing loyally beside Arthur, who thought Lancelot had done the honorable thing by rescuing Guinevere. His deed was chivalry at its brightest moment. To them, the death of Gareth was an unfortunate side issue that should never have occurred, but it was not important enough for the king to mount a full-fledged attack against the greatest knight the nation had known. It was better forgotten than allowed to become the first crack in the schism a war would create, tearing Britain apart.

This was the reason many rode out to join Lancelot rather than stay with the forces of Arthur. There were others who went over to Lancelot's side simply because they loved him.

For Arthur, the matter of Gareth's death was the only issue. He might have accepted the abduction of his queen for the chivalric act it was meant to be and tacitly given his approval to the lovers remaining in exile. Certainly such an ending to the weeks of suspense following the court's judgment and verdict against

Guinevere, would have eased his feelings of guilt and removed any necessity on his part for abjuring his own laws. Urged on by Gawain and Mordred, blind to the holocaust that must surely follow when the two forces were joined, he sent notices throughout Britain, summoning to Camelot all who owed allegiance to him. Within two months he led a vast army northeast across plains and hills to *le Joyeuse Garde,* the town and castle belonging to Lancelot. Here Guinevere and her lover were sequestered within its reinforced stronghold.

How long the opposing armies fought, or how many were killed, I did not know, for news reached us only sporadically after Arthur began the siege and then not in any logical order. We might hear of a retreat one day and later learn of the battle that preceded it. None of the details interested me, but the travelers who brought them were warmly welcomed by others in the village and manor who were avid to hear about every battle, every face to face combat, the bloodier the better. Any wanderer who was able to embellish the facts with vivid descriptions found an eager audience in our territory. I listened for only one detail: The king was still alive. If he were killed, the news would spread more rapidly than the fastest hawk could fly. I was only surprised there were no rumors that he was dead. It could mean only one thing: He was not actually fighting. He must have allowed Gawain to lead the vanguard against Lancelot.

During the months since I left Camelot, I had not been idle. Knowing my part in Arthur's life was probably over, I began preparing for a future without him. I had loved and been loved, and even though our times together were few, and often were separated by years, there had always been a surety I would see him again sometime. Now I must live with the knowledge that I might not. The most vital preparation, and the one that took the longest, was learning to be self-sufficient. As independent as I thought I was all those years, running the estate, making decisions involving other people, I had not realized how emotionally dependent I was on Arthur. Either I saw things as I thought he would see them, or I waited until I was with him to get his opinion. Now I must think for myself.

My first act was to make a decision I had long been contemplating. I began taking the steps necessary for moving into my small house at the abbey. Having seen to everything that must be done before I could vacate the estate, I still could remain as long as I liked at the manor house, but I would at least be free to leave when I decided the time was right. As I went around the house from day to day, I began unconsciously sorting things into two groups: those I would take with me and those I would leave behind. When the mental piles got so big they were cluttering up my mind, I began making lists. The "must takes" threatened to be longer than the "leave behinds" until I started a third list, "doubtfuls," that became the catchall for most of my possessions. What I was really doing was humoring myself into putting off the most important step of all.

I set out on a clear, crisp October day for the episcopal seat of the bishop of Glastonbury. I sent word ahead requesting an audience with his holiness about a matter of utmost concern to me and to the church. After a day and a half of easy riding, stopping overnight at a pleasant inn for a good supper and a comfortable night's rest, I arrived at the cathedral town just after noon. Before seeing the bishop, I secured lodgings for the night in the busy town for myself and my retainers, having neither the energy nor the desire to start the return trip immediately. I did not know how long my conference would take.

I was relieved to learn the bishop would see me immediately.

"Welcome, Lady Lionors. Please be seated. I am glad of the opportunity to thank you in person for your generosity to the church and especially the Abbey of the Holy Spirit through the years. I understand you have taken a special interest in one of the nuns there."

I wondered how much he knew about Elise and whether this would have any bearing on my present request.

"Yes, my lord, she was left there during one of my

stays." I was not exactly lying, just side-stepping the truth a little.

"I know, I know," he said. "Pathetic case, the nuns told me, the girl being blind, but I hear she has done well enough to become assistant to the abbess."

"And a very competant one, too." I had to add my word of praise for Elise.

"I hope you had a pleasant trip." His holiness was beginning to fidget in his chair, and if his body were as bony as his face and hands, I knew why he was uncomfortable.

"Yes, thank you, my lord. But I know you are too busy to spend time in petty chatter. I have come to make a request concerning my estate."

"Indeed, so your messenger said," and his rheumy eyes lighted up with anticipation.

"I wish to deed my entire holdings, including the manor house, the lands, and the village, to the church."

"On *your* death, of course, since you have no heirs. I understand you inherited under Roman law, so your land is freehold with no encumbrances or claims by distant male heirs."

"The last part is correct," I said. "However, I wish to deed it to the church now so that I may retire to the small house at the abbey, with no further responsibility for the running of the estate."

I could imagine his mind filling with visions of his own outrider, a monk who supervised church property, managing the estate and lining the pockets of the bishop with generous shares.

"Originally," I went on, "I had planned to deed it to the throne, putting it under the royal protection of the king, but with the country in such turmoil, I am afraid the estate would be neglected. In fact, with the king at war, I would not even know who to approach on the subject."

"Very wise, my child. 'Put not your faith in secular possessions which can be destroyed but in the love of God which is everlasting.' Give them to the church."

If ever a man represented a dichotomy of greed and piety, the bishop was he.

He pressed the tips of his fingers together, tapping them against his chin as he spoke as though to emphasize the irony of every word he spoke and the pleasure he took in having the crown lose a valuable piece of property.

"Have you not heard, Lady Lionors, that the king and Lancelot have ceased fighting? Yes, the bishop of Rochester, having been in Rome, was ordered by the pope to declare a truce between the two factions. The king has returned to Camelot, and Lancelot is on his way to Brittany."

If only I had known! I could have carried out my original plan and perhaps have seen Arthur one more time.

"I'm truly glad," I said sincerely, "that the fighting is over."

"Yes, now shall I have my clerk draw up the necessary documents?"

"Please. However, I have one proviso I wish included in the deed. It concerns my steward Will, who has been like a son to me. I want it stated that he, along with his heirs and assigns for perpetuity, will be allowed to remain on and manage the estate. I believe such a proviso is legally permissible."

I watched with interest as the bishop's eyelids fell, his ferret nose narrowed, and his jowls drooped.

"It is a legal proviso," he said reluctantly, "but are you certain you want it included?"

"Very certain. I would also like documents of adoption drawn up naming Will my legal son and heir. He will never contest the deed of the land to the church, but I want to ensure he will have no problems after I am dead. If your clerk will draw up duplicate copies of each, we can both sign them, and then I will leave. I know you have much to attend to."

While the bishop dictated to his clerk, I relaxed in my chair. I knew now I had done the right thing. I had considered leaving my manuscripts to the church, but as they were secular writings, I did not know what might become of them if some member of the clergy declared them heretical. I would work out some other way to protect them.

When the documents were ready, we both signed them. Cautiously I read each copy over first, and since they were in Latin, the bishop's eyelids opened wide again in his amazement at my command of the language. I thanked him graciously for his time and assured him that a representative from the church would be welcome at the manor any time he cared to send one to inventory the estate.

The evening I returned, I called Will into the library. He had recently married the daughter of a freeman, an innkeeper in a neighboring village. I would see them together shortly, but first I wanted to speak to Will alone. Making it as brief as possible, I explained how I had always planned to retire to the house at the abbey. The one thing preventing me from leaving was my responsibility to my fiefs. I explained my reasons for deeding the estate to the church as well as the proviso that he should continue to live in the manor as steward.

As calm as always, he did not disappoint me with a false declaration of humility or any words to the effect that he was not good enough for the honor. Will knew his own worth, and he had too much respect for me to think I had not considered long and hard before I came to this decision. He did not embarrass either of us by falling to his knees or behaving in any other ridiculous fashion.

"Thank you, Lady Lionors. I will do my best to run things as you have taught me. I hope, though, that you won't be leaving soon."

"Not too soon, Will. There is still much to do. And even after I go to the abbey, I will be back from time to time. I had better warn you, though; be prepared for some unpleasant moments with the representative from the bishop. Be firm, and once he sees how you run things, I think he will leave you alone. Now, go ask Olwyn to step in here with you."

Barely sixteen, Olwyn, plump and pretty, was head over heels in love with Will. No one could ever see his shadow, for standing as close to him as she always did, she completely eclipsed it. She had much to learn before she could be of real help to him in managing the manor house, but Elspeth was still housekeeper, and I was sure she had already begun to put her daughter-in-law through the paces. Will would be more patient with her. He was a doting husband, really still a bridegroom, and Olwyn, with her full breasts and well-rounded hips, looked as though she could be an exciting bed partner for him. No doubt there would be evidence of a child before long.

Olwyn tended to be frightened of me, not yet used to my ways, but eager to please because of Will. I tried to put them at ease.

"Please sit down," I urged. "I want to talk to you both."

Will pulled up two chairs. He relaxed in his, a new confidence already evident; but Olwyn sat on the edge of hers, her hands knotting and unknotting the end of her kerchief. I explained again about the deed and Will's remaining on as manager. More aware of what it meant after hearing it the second time, he had a number of questions. Olwyn said nothing until I happened to mention something about their having my bedroom for their own.

"Oh, lors," she exclaimed. "That big bed is to be ours? We're to sleep in the master's own room?"

"Yes, Olwyn. Will and you are in a sense to be master and mistress of the house. And you will have guests from time to time, so you will have to learn how to entertain them. Will knows; he will teach you."

Will leaned over to whisper something to her, and she beamed.

"Yes, my lady, I'll do my best. You'll not be disappointed."

"I know I won't. I have a wedding gift for you."

I handed her a package containing the gold chain that once held my mother's medallion and then Arthur's ring. It, the filigree necklace, and the ring were the only jewelry I had after leaving the others at Camelot. I debated a long time between the chain and the necklace for her; the former had deep sentimental value

284

for me, but the latter was almost too ornate for her. The chain was associated with young love, and who better to wear it than a new bride.

"Oh, thank you, my lady. This is the most beautiful thing I've ever owned." She was having difficulty with the clasp.

"Help her, Will," I laughed. "Your bride is still nervous. Now I have a gift for you if you will bring me that other scroll on the table."

Untying the ribbon, I opened the scroll to read it, but thought better and simply told him in my own words what it meant.

"When you were born, Will, I was with your mother. You were the first child I ever helped bring into the world, and I knew that for some reason you were meant to belong—at least partially—to me. That is why I brought you to the manor and reared you to be my page and ultimately my steward. You have never disappointed me. Your mother was extremely generous to give up her first-born to my care, and so she has always had a place in my household. I have never regretted that, either, because she is a hard worker. With her permission, I had this document executed. I have long considered you my foster son. You are now legally my son and heir, as will be your children after you. There are reasons, which I think you understand, why I did not deed you the estate, but everything within the manor will belong to you personally. The deed to the church specifically states manor house, lands, and village. All movable property will be yours."

For once I had shattered his calm. Will was not one to remain speechless for long, and between tears and embraces on both our parts, he expressed his wonder and gratitude. Olwyn was simply too dumfounded to take it all in.

"Now," I said, trying to bring us all back down to earth, "there is much to be done. Olwyn, you and I will need to go through all of the linens so you can help me decide which to take and which to leave here. Elspeth will be of real assistance. There are also my clothes. I will take simple things with me. Some can be dis-

285

tributed in the village, and I am sure there are dresses which can be remade for you." Olwyn had a practical side to her, having been brought up in a large family, and it was to this I appealed first.

"Will, you and I will go through other parts of the house, as well as the stables and mews. You will need to decide if you want to keep the falcons or try to sell them. We still have some very fine specimens."

And so the days of selecting and organizing began. With Olwyn and Elspeth assisting, I soon went through the linen rooms, and we began packing boxes. The hours in my room ran longer because Olwyn had to "ooh" and "ah" over every dress, trying some on—they didn't fit—and figuring how to take them apart and recut the pieces to her size. I enjoyed her exclamations of delight, knowing she had never seen, let alone worn, such fabrics as silk and velvet. Elspeth reminded me of Marta as she clucked her tongue over her daughter-in-law's foolishness. But all Elspeth's efforts to tell Olwyn she would never have an opportunity to wear them were wasted breath. I laughed and tried to get Elspeth to accept some of them herself. She shook her head vehemently, but when she thought I was busy in another room, she held some of them up to her and put those in a separate pile.

Will and I spent days making an inventory of the house, stables, and other outbuildings. He reminded me of the first time he learned he was to have his own horse. Now he owned a stableful, but the latest gift could never mean as much as the original one had.

One week, we stayed three days in the library. Will was no Latin scholar, but he knew the value of the manuscripts. He helped me sort them, putting them in separate stacks as I went through them carefully, explaining the contents of each. Occasionally, I took time to tell him about the authors as we rested from our efforts. Those that were to remain at the manor were wrapped individually in oiled paper and packed in boxes lined with well-cured sheepskin. Will marked each box so he would know what it contained. Someday, I hoped, as I worked among them, they would prove valuable to a future scholar. A number I still planned to translate were going with me.

Then, like the reverberations of a death knell, word spread throughout the land that Arthur and Gawain had crossed over to Brittany and were laying siege to Lancelot at Benwic. All my work on the estate stopped. Somehow I knew that the time had not yet come for me to leave the manor. Again we waited while rumor and fact ran hand-in-hand. Word would come that one side had scored an important victory, but we knew all too well that while we were hearing the news, the situation could be reversing itself, the victor now become the vanquished.

Meanwhile, all was not well on this side of the channel. Arthur had named Mordred regent before leaving for Brittany. Always impatient to put the crown on his head, Mordred took advantage of his new authority to claim more power for himself. But he was not yet king. There were still many loyal to Arthur who refused to give in to all of Mordred's demands. To combat this opposition, Mordred resorted to drastic measures. He dispatched couriers to all parts of the kingdom, ostensibly from Brittany, to announce that King Arthur was dead.

The shock waves this news sent across the nation touched every person in some way. The common people, the sturdy roots that held the country together, were desolate with grief. Their king, who shone like the sun on all their lives, had been killed in some far-off land. To some of the more ambitious nobles Arthur's death created the long-wished-for opportunity to challenge Mordred's claim to the throne. While Arthur's son massed his strength in London, his opponents scoured the countryside, garnering what followers they could to support individual claims. If Mordred thought his strategy would place him firmly on the throne, he was quickly disenchanted.

Not since Merlin informed me of Arthur's marriage had I felt so completely lost. It was as though the world around me had suddenly vanished and I was left to wander in a void. There were no tears, no pain, only a feeling of having been deserted. Our manor became his cenotaph.

Two pieces of news brought us to life again. Olwyn announced she was pregnant, and once more we smiled, rejoicing in her happiness. Having never known Arthur, it was hard for her to fathom our deep grief. As she had tried to share our sorrow, we now enveloped her with our concern. Next came word that Gawain had died from a head wound. We might have mourned for him if the same messenger had not also assured us that Arthur was very much alive. Tears and wine flowed together as we celebrated what seemed almost like a resurrection.

Still I did not leave for the abbey. Not until Arthur had returned to Camelot and Mordred was stripped of his newly acquired powers would I feel I was no longer needed.

Before word reached Mordred that his ruse about Arthur's death had been discovered, he had tried to bed Guinevere to further dishonor his father. She fled to the Tower of London, and new reverberations rocked the country when Arthur learned of Mordred's latest infamy. Arthur withdrew his siege on Lancelot and prepared to leave Brittany and return home. Many begged him to seek peace with Lancelot and call on his former knight to join with him in his fight against Mordred. For everyone knew Arthur was facing his greatest challenge, a battle to the death. There could be no truce between father and son. When Arthur landed on the coast, Mordred and his forces were there to meet him.

On a day I will never forget, I received two visitors. The first was a runner with a letter from Arthur:

My Dearest Lionors,
While there is a lull in the fighting, I have time to write you a short note. The situation here is very serious, and I have the feeling I shall not live to see the end of it. I am not afraid to die, but I am saddened by the thought that I will never see you again. I love you so very much.

You have done so much for me, may I make one more request? Regardless of the outcome of this battle, Guinevere wishes to enter an abbey and take the vows. Will you ask Elise to give her sanctuary? She has already left London under guard for Glastonbury where she will await word from you. I know of no other place where she will be safe.

Please tell Elise my last thoughts were of my precious daughter and her mother. If only I could go one last time to Avalon, to rest and find peace.

All my love,
A.

Reading the letter a second time, I mourned inwardly over his words. He sensed impending death. He was not old enough to be so ready to give up life. Lest I forget his request by becoming too wrapped up in my own emotions, I sent for runners, dispatching one to Elise and the second to Glastonbury. The messages I sent were brief. Within three days Guinevere should be safely within the abbey walls.

Soon after the second runner left, I had my next visitor. It had been many years since I saw Merlin, but we greeted each other as though it were only the day before.

"Oh, Merlin, I never thought to see you again. How did you know how glad I would be to hear your voice and see your face? We have all needed you."

"I told you I would return," he smiled, "whenever I heard your call. I have come to be with both you and Arthur. I will be going to him when I leave here."

"To the battlefield?" I asked. "Will you help him?"

"Yes, but not in the way you are thinking. Lionors, Arthur is going to be killed in this battle. And so will Mordred. Father and son will meet alone on the field, and face to face, each will strike a single fatal blow."

"There is no way to stop it?"

"None. Mordred must die, and Arthur is ready to go. He feels there is nothing to live for, and unless a man fights for his life, he is as good as slain."

I showed Merlin the letter from Arthur in which he said much the same thing.

"And Arthur's request?" he asked.

"Guinevere will be welcome at the abbey."

"Your life has not been easy, Lionors, but not without its rewards, I hope?"

"No, Merlin, not easy, but a good life. To know and love Arthur has, I realize now, meant all and everything to me. I would not have traded places with anyone."

"Good-by, my dear. I will see you one more time. After the battle."

And so I began my last long vigil.

⊠ The Promise ⊠

Mourning doves keen in the sheltering oak;
Sturdy the limb where they're building their nest;
Lush, greening clover spreads thick o'er the earth,
                Where Arthur lies at rest.

Bumble bees feed on the nectar-filled blooms;
Cheery the sounds as their numbers increase;
Wild strawberries twine 'mid moss velvet stones,
                Where Arthur lies in peace.

Gentle rains fall on the winter-parched land;
Swollen the river whose waters run deep;
Life-breathing zephyrs stir through Avalon,
                Where Arthur lies asleep.

"In the best tradition of Scarlett O'Hara"
Publisher's Weekly

BARBARA FERRY JOHNSON

DELTA BLOOD

Leah had always known what it was to be a woman, to want as women want. And now, on the night of New Orlean's most dazzling ball, a lifetime of smoldering passions drew her into the deepening twilight, into the bayous that echoed still with drumbeats and Voodoo chants . . .

in an unforgettable saga of the Civil War, as throbbing with life as the splendorous South it portrays.

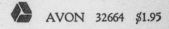 AVON 32664 $1.95

DELTA 4-77